PRAISE FOR SUSAN PETRONE'S FIRST NOVEL, *THROW LIKE A WOMAN*:

"While, on the surface, this is a novel about a woman battling to make her way in the man's world of professional baseball, debut author Petrone presents a stirring and humorous story of a woman doing considerably more than that—trying to rediscover herself, provide for her family, and perhaps find a little love along the way."
– *Booklist*

"*Throw Like a Woman* is that rare baseball novel, both a paean to the game and a deeper exploration of character. Susan Petrone has a fan's heart and a scout's eye. Read it now. Don't wait for the movie."
– Stewart O'Nan, co-author of *Faithful* and *A Face in the Crowd*

"For baseball fans who yearn for a female Jackie Robinson, reading Susan Petrone's fun and absorbing novel *Throw Like a Woman* becomes a kind of prayer. 'Please, Lord! Give talent a chance. Let this dream come true!'"
– Mary Doria Russell, author of *The Sparrow*

"Someday there will be a woman who plays Major League Baseball. And when it happens, I suspect it will be an awful lot like Susan Petrone's fun *Throw Like a Woman*. Susan knows baseball and so the novel – and her hero Brenda Haversham – crackles with authenticity. You can hear the pop of the ball hitting the catcher's mitt."
– Joe Posnanski, author of *The Soul of Baseball*, NBC Sports National Columnist

"Petrone's storytelling is first-rate, and she we~~ ~~ a credible baseball tale with well-d~~efin~~ ~~ characters th~~ ~~ ~~hout."
– *The Wave*

THE SUPER LADIES

SUSAN PETRONE

In memory of Margaret Dolores Adams Petrone,
who was super and most definitely a lady.

The Story Plant
Studio Digital CT, LLC
P.O. Box 4331
Stamford, CT 06907

Story Plant paperback ISBN-13: 978-1-61188-258-2
Fiction Studio Books E-book ISBN: 978-1-945839-24-5

Visit our website at www.TheStoryPlant.com

First Story Plant Printing: August 2018

Printed in the United States of America

0 9 8 7 6 5 4 3 2 1

CHAPTER ONE

IMAGINE THE WOMAN YOU CAN'T SEE.

Imagine the woman who can't be seen.

It sounds like the same thing, doesn't it? In both cases, there's an invisible woman. But the distinction is both grammatical and metaphysical. The first is a failure of the viewer's attention. The second is the woman's choice.

The woman you can't see is actually easy on the eyes, if a bit on the short side. She's thin. Not stick-figure thin but the kind of thin that comes from years of running and countless hours contorting on a yoga mat in an effort to maintain until she dies, to remain as lean and wiry and, let's face it, attractive for the next forty-seven years as she was for the first forty-seven. Her grandmother McQuestion, the one from whom Abra McQuestion inherited a first name and not much else, lived to be ninety-four, and that has always seemed as good an age as any to aspire to. It's the age, forty-seven, that keeps you from seeing her. Forty-seven is not old, not the way Methuselah and dirt and George Burns were old. It is, however, old enough to divert the infamous male gaze to other, younger subjects. It's old enough to be ignored.

For instance, forty-seven is probably double the age of the two young women who couldn't see Abra and walked right in front of her at the grocery store. She stopped by after work to pick up some avocados for the guacamole she was supposed to bring to the office Cinco de Mayo party the next day. She wasn't particularly fond of office parties, but senior staff at Hoffmann Software Solutions were expected to set a good example. It didn't help matters that much of the office still thought Abra was part-Mexican instead of half-Dominican and assumed this was a major holiday for her. Tomorrow Mike Horowitz, the head of Finance, would no doubt give her two thumbs up and chirp, "Viva Mexico!" Every Single Time they passed in the hallway.

So much to look forward to, she thought as she approached the prominent Cinco de Mayo display near the produce section. Bags of tortilla chips and jars of the store's private label salsa were displayed on wooden crates neatly arranged on a round table with a red-, green-, and white-striped tablecloth. Next to the table were two gigantic wooden bowls of avocados, one marked "conventionally grown," the other "organic." Abra took the same attitude toward purchasing organic produce as she did toward food safety while traveling in Third World countries: if you don't eat the peel, you don't have anything to worry about.

She was a step away from the nonorganic bowl when two younger women sidled up to the display and cut directly in front of her. Their shiny blond-highlighted hair was only inches away from Abra's nose.

"Excuse me," Abra said. The young women either didn't hear or didn't care to acknowledge her presence. They just went right on choosily selecting avocados, chatting away about nothing, shifting their ridiculously curvy hips from one shapely leg to another. Abra had been young once. Young and hot. She didn't begrudge these girls their youth or their unblemished skin or their pipe cleaner–like upper arms. Her own arms had better definition, enough to consistently garner compliments whenever she wore a sleeveless shirt. This wasn't a competition of appearance. What troubled her was their complete dismissal of her existence. Abra drew herself up to her full five feet two inches, willing herself to be as large as possible. "Excuse me, but I was here first," she said. "You just cut in front of me."

The toady sidekick turned first. Then the second, the queen bee, turned around. "Oh. Sorry," Queen Bee said. Her voice dropped to a low register on the second syllable, making the apology sound decidedly ironic. "We didn't see you."

Having already gotten what they came for, the two young women walked away. As they passed the oranges, one whispered something to the other, and they both giggled.

"You aren't *invisible*. They were just assholes." This was Katherine's answer the next morning during their run. She and Abra met up most mornings to run through Euclid Creek Park, a narrow metropark that snaked alongside a rare two-and-a-half-mile stretch of suburban creek that wasn't culverted. "Sometimes four miles in the morning is the only thing standing between me and homicide." This was another Katherinism. She was given to declarative statements.

Running was the basis of their friendship. They had met twelve years earlier, during the five-mile Memorial Day race at John Carroll University, whose campus was just a few miles down the road. The race had taken place the day after Katherine's thirty-fifth birthday. Thirty-five felt like a make-or-break year in every aspect of her life—career, marriage, fertility. It was the year she completed her master's in biology; as a teacher that meant a pay raise. And it was the year she and Hal decided they would keep trying to get pregnant for just a little longer—after that, maybe adoption, maybe consider life as a child-free couple.

For the first half mile of the race through twisty, hilly University Heights, Katherine had been aware of the ultra-fit woman with insanely curly hair who seemed to have taken up permanent residence half a step behind her left shoulder. She tried speeding up to drop her, but the woman kept pace easily. In smaller races, Katherine could typically place in her age group if she ran smart—not going out too fast and running negative splits the whole way. The stranger running just behind her with the overly placid expression that made it appear she wasn't even trying looked to be approximately the same age. She'd kick herself if this chick placed ahead of her.

Katherine did the first mile in 7:02. In a 5K, that wouldn't be a problem. For a five-miler, it was too quick. She was already sucking wind from going out too fast. Instead of doing negative splits with a little gas left in the tank to sprint the last eighth of a mile, she'd let the skinny chick behind her get under her skin and make her blow her race strategy.

Easing up her pace made her a little less annoyed at the woman behind her. As she slowed, she faintly but distinctly heard the words "Oh, thank God" coming from somewhere next to her. She looked to her left and saw the skinny chick still running next to her. It took all her self-control not to speed up again. Repeating *Just run your own race*" to herself over and over, she almost didn't hear the skinny chick say, "You set a good pace." She didn't sound out of breath.

Katherine tried not to huff as she replied, "Thanks."

"I haven't raced in ages, so I thought I'd follow some-one with a challenging pace. Hope that's okay."

She was silently pleased that the woman audibly sucked in a gulp of air before saying the words "chal-lenging pace." Well, the skinny chick might have a com-plexion to die for, but she was at least human. Katherine smiled and gave a quick "Sure" in reply.

They ran beside each other in silence for the next two miles. Katherine noticed that the woman had an almost perfect stride—loose but controlled upper body and quick legs that hardly seemed to touch the ground. She was built like a runner too. Not tall, but proportion-ately long-limbed and lean. Katherine wondered when the last time was this chick had eaten a brownie. As they ran, she became aware that her own pace had grown steadier and smoother. And when the timekeeper at mile three called out, "Twenty-two, forty-seven," she realized she was still well on pace to come in under her goal of thirty-eight minutes. Reluctantly, she had to ad-mit she enjoyed running with this stranger.

"You're good," she said finally, aware that this was a fairly hollow statement. There were plenty of good run-ners in this race. It was just that this skinny chick was clearly more than your average recreational runner.

The woman smiled, a broad, genuine grin. "Thank you," she said. Then, almost as if she were admitting a juvenile arrest, added, "I was a sprinter in high school and college." She took a deep breath. "What about you?"

Katherine smiled back and managed to say, "My only organized sport was slam dancing. I was kind of a punk."

"My senior year in high school, I was the only one at Regionals with a Mohawk," the woman offered.

Katherine tried not to slow down her pace as they talked, but this woman was turning out to be kind of cool. "Excellent," she replied.

Somehow this exchange cemented a mutual spark, a feeling of kinship, and they comfortably ran alongside each other to the end of the race. They both began their final sprint at the same moment, and when they hit the chute at the finish, Abra let Katherine go first. They finished a second apart. That feeling of camaraderie, not competition, was still what Katherine got when she ran with Abra. No one else could get her motivated to run four miles at five-thirty in the morning.

Sometimes they talked on their morning runs; mostly they just listened to the *pad-pad-pad* of their own shoes on the pedestrian trail that ran through the park. In the dead of Cleveland winters, they'd hit adjacent treadmills at the Hillcrest YMCA. There was something deliciously hypnotic about the never-ending *whirr* of the treadmill in the gym that sometimes seemed to propel her feet forward involuntarily. The only problem was the scenery never changed. Katherine preferred running outdoors. She loved the infinite variety of the world. No matter how many times they ran the same route, there was always a different bird singing a different song or an unusual cloud formation to catch her eye.

It usually took a mile or so before Katherine started feeling like her body hit equilibrium. In the first few minutes of a run, she could almost feel her cells pulling glucose from her blood and devouring it, could feel her muscles demanding more and more oxygen, and always, always could feel her heart and lungs struggling to keep up with the demand. Time was when she could start running and seemingly within a few steps feel warmed up and ready to go at a race pace. Now that she was a little older, it seemed to take longer and longer to get to that delicious moment of balance when all her muscles were working in sync and she had oxygen to burn. They hadn't changed the route. It was her body that was changing, had changed. As they ran, Katherine felt the slightest little jiggle in her lower belly. That was another recent development, one that seemed to coincide with the cessation of her period. The lack of estrogen had altered the nature of her body fat. *Screw getting older*, she thought and willed herself to pass up Abra.

The park followed the creek downhill. They ran an out-and-back loop. Geography necessitated that the first half of their run was downhill and the second half uphill. They could have driven to the low end of the park so that the uphill portion of the run was first, but driving just to run seemed like a waste of time.

Running uphill is decidedly more difficult than running downhill, especially when it's the second half of the run. It hurts. The hurts part was the crux of Katherine's love-hate relationship with their near-daily route. She disliked the pain but loved the feeling of pushing her body past the point of uncomfortable. It was the closest a middle-aged, suburban female might get to feeling like a warrior on a regular basis.

At their usual turnaround this morning, Abra didn't slow her pace. If anything, she sped up a little. Katherine kept up with her for about half a mile then felt herself starting to fall behind. The pace was just too aggressive. "Geez, give an old lady a break," she huffed, trying to keep pace. They weren't even on the steep part yet. She hated to think a hill she ran every day could break her, but there it was.

Abra jogged back and stopped in front of Katherine, hands on her hips. "I'm four months older than you," she said pointedly but breathing a bit heavy. "You won't be forty-seven until the end of the month." She started back up the hill at the same pace.

Katherine ran up the hill after her. "Did those girls at the grocery store piss you off that much?" she asked. Typically they wouldn't allow themselves to walk until they had at least reached the crest of the last hill at the end of the park. Abra didn't reply but cut her pace down to a slow jog. It was enough of an answer until they were out of the park and on the sidewalk by the war memorial. To the left was East Anderson and Katherine's house; to the right, West Anderson and Abra's house.

They stood on the cracked slate-slab sidewalk for a moment, catching their breath before they went their separate ways. Then Abra said, "Yes, those skanky, pissy little brats at the grocery store annoyed me far more than they should have." She sighed, not a catching-her-breath sigh but a genuine melancholy-infused sigh. "It was like they couldn't even see me."

Katherine wanted to say something wise and comforting, but all she could think of was to ask "Do you want to come over for breakfast? Anna and I will drive you home."

"No, thank you. I need to get to work early. The trade show last week completely screwed up my schedule and now I'm behind." As she was saying this, Abra started walking backward up the street, as though three slow steps now would save her time later.

"But you're still going to the science fair on Monday night, right? Anna really wants you to see her hybrid fish."

"Are you kidding? I wouldn't miss it. I had no idea you could cross a guppy with an endler."

"If you leave a male and a female alone long enough, they will eventually get it on, regardless of species."

Abra rolled her eyes and turned on her heel.

"It's part of the wonder of nature," Katherine called as Abra ran up the block. Then she was gone, and Katherine turned toward home.

CHAPTER TWO

SOMETIMES YOU NEED TO REMIND YOURSELF THAT JUST ABOUT EVERYTHING YOU'RE FEELING IS NORMAL. For instance, periodically reassessing your decision to have children is normal. Margie reconsidered her decision to have children about once week. Sometimes it was because Grant seemed to think eleven-year-old boys didn't need to bathe unless they showed actual dirt. At the opposite end of the spectrum, it might be because Eli had left yet another wet towel on the floor and dumped another pile of once-worn, non-dirty clothes into the hamper, none of which he would actually put into the washing machine. Sometimes it was the general malaise that goes along with the realization that one will never again have anything resembling privacy or a clean house. And sometimes, the worst of times, it was because Joan was being fourteen with a vengeance.

Her daughter was brilliant, athletic, studious, and routinely mortified by her mother's existence. Knowing that such mortification is endemic didn't make it any easier to live with. The current drama revolved around the District Science Fair. To be fair, Margie loved watching Joan develop her complex biochemistry experiment.

It was one of those happy, gooey parenting experiences that made the perpetual lack of privacy, silence, and disposable income completely worthwhile. She had gladly helped negotiate the loan of a CO_2 pump, a pressure cell, and a collecting vessel from Hal, Katherine's chemist husband. She had also volunteered a cheek swab for Joan's analysis (and recruited Katherine, Abra, and a few other women to do the same). She had given opinions on data chart formats (only when asked) and been as supportive yet hands-off as humanly possible. The formal title of Joan's project was "Soy-Derived Phytoestrogens and Breast Cancer: Is There a Link?" However, Margie privately referred to it as "That Fucking Science Project."

Everyone but Eli had been sucked into the science fair vortex. As a senior, he had opted out of the whole affair (and was, Margie thought, perhaps a bit too smugly gleeful about it). Grant had dutifully created a respectable-but-probably-not-prize-winning project on the physics of baseball. His project mainly consisted of close-up photos (with explanations) of his right hand demonstrating how to grip a curveball, slider, and four-seam fastball and a video played on Oh-So-Continuous loop of him demonstrating each pitch and explaining why the grip made the ball move a certain way. Karl just stayed the hell out of the way, leaving his wife to listen to Joan's detailed explanations of the project (which was fun to hear) and her even-more-detailed rants about a girl named Eileen O'Brien, who was the only serious competition in the district at the eighth grade level (which was a drag to hear).

"The state science fair only takes one entrant per grade level from each school district," Joan informed her for the twenty-seventh time the day before the science fair.

"I know," Margie said calmly. They were at the grocery store doing the regular shopping and buying more tofu for Joan's experiment, part of which consisted of extracting the phytoestrogen from the tofu by the impressively named process of supercritical fluid extraction.

"Don't get the *sprouted* kind," Joan said as Margie reached out to grab a package of tofu from the meat substitute section of Heinen's.

"That's the kind we always get."

"That's the kind we always *eat*, but you know I need the Cleveland Tofu Company kind for the experiment. It's crumblier and that gives it a lower reaction point."

Margie took a deep breath. "Look in the cooler. They're out of Cleveland Tofu Company brand. The other kind will work just as well."

Joan tilted her head slightly to one side, a move that she had perfected to visually express her disgust in lieu of rolling her eyes because Karl had once made a comment about eye-rolling teenagers. "How do you know?"

Margie sighed. "You're right. I don't know for sure. I'm speculating." She held up the rectangular package of sprouted tofu. It was marked "Extra Firm" but still felt mushy in her hand. "What I do know is this is the only store I've seen that sells the Cleveland Tofu Company brand, and they're out of it. This is the only kind of tofu they have in stock, the science fair is tomorrow night, and I have to work tomorrow."

"Fine..." Joan said, taking the package out of Margie's hand and tossing it in the grocery cart.

"Look, you have an incredible experiment that is way beyond the level of any other eighth grader—" Margie began only to be interrupted.

"You haven't *seen* Eileen's project. She made her own solar panels that actually *work*, and they power this little *dollhouse*, and I still don't have enough variance in my results to get anything conclusive..."

Joan went on like this through the frozen foods, the deli, the checkout, the ride home, and pretty much the next day and a half. It didn't matter what Margie or Karl said, so Margie didn't say anything, just listened. Karl apparently couldn't help himself and kept trying to use his lawyer brain to pose alternative solutions to Joan's perceived problems when what she really needed was a parent brain to listen and nod and tell her everything would be all right.

The night of the science fair, Margie still believed everything would be all right. There was the standard schlepping of Joan's and Grant's projects up to the high school, but she was used to that. This year was actually easier because there were only two projects to transport, not three. However, Joan's equipment needed to be set up extra early because it would take over an hour to run one final extraction and analysis. Margie elected to do the early run.

The elementary school kids were set up in the gym, while the middle schoolers and high schoolers had their projects scattered in other rooms around the building. Joan was the only middle schooler with an advanced chemistry project, so she was set up in the chemistry lab along with a couple of surly high school boys who looked as annoyed about being at the science fair an hour early as they were to be sharing space with a middle schooler.

Margie watched Joan set up the pump, heat source, pressure cell, and collecting vessel. The CO_2 pump worried her a bit. Joan had used a similar one during a one-week science camp the previous summer (for which Margie and Karl had paid through the nose because Karl was on a girls-need-to-be-encouraged-in-STEM kick, even though their daughter had been a science junkie since toddlerhood). The high school had a CO_2 pump, but Joan was technically still at the middle school and couldn't use it. Plus, as Joan had pointed out far more than once, the school pumps didn't have the pressure capacity of the one she'd borrowed from Hal's lab. She managed to imbue the phrase "It isn't professional grade" with multiple layers of condescension.

In lieu of desks, the chemistry lab featured brown and black wooden counters sticking out from two of the walls. Each counter sported a sink on the wall end, making it look like a row of tiny kitchens. Margie plopped down on one of the tall wood and metal stools at the counter next to Joan's experiment and gave it a little spin, taking in a three hundred and sixty-degree view view of the chemistry lab. She had leaned toward the arts and humanities in high school. That bent continued in college, and she ended up majoring in philosophy. She'd done well in her science courses; there just hadn't been very many of them. The chemistry lab was an undiscovered country. It looked like a place where an enterprising girl could have a good time.

The surly high school boys finished setting up their projects and left the chemistry lab, leaving Joan sorting out her swab samples and Margie twiddling her thumbs. In the open cupboard in the base of the counter lay a stray purple folder. It was empty, so Margie used it as a fan. The low hum of the air conditioning rattled through the metal vents along the bottom of the wall, but she was still sweating. Her hot flashes had a mind of their own.

"What can I do to help?" she asked, giving her stool another spin.

"You're not allowed to help. I have to do this all on my own or it negates the whole point of it being *my* project."

"Okay, then I'll go down to the gym and see if Dad and Grant are here yet."

"No," Joan replied a little too quickly. Margie met her only daughter's eyes. "I want you to stay with me," Joan added, a little quieter now.

"Gladly," Margie said. Being treated like a potted plant can still be a decent-sized parenting win. She watched Joan look through her data sheets. It wasn't as exciting as watching her daughter at a swim meet but definitely elicited the same amount of pride. "Need a fresh cheek swab?" Margie asked brightly.

Joan looked up from her papers. "Actually, yes. I mean, I have to run an extraction now, so the judges know this is all my work and that I'm not just analyzing somebody else's data. But your sample is weird. So are Aunt Abra's and Aunt Katherine's. I should run theirs again too."

"Weird how?"

"Okay, I'm looking for changes in the number of estrogen molecules after I combine the cheek swabs with the phytoestrogen, right? So I ran every sample three times, to make sure the results were correct, and they all showed a consistent level every time, except yours, and Aunt Abra's and Aunt Katherine's. They're all over the place, with way different levels every time I run them."

Margie took an overly dramatic deep breath. "Sweetie, I have to tell you something. Your mother is a mutant."

Joan did the annoyed head tilt. "I know. But would you please give me another cheek swab? And can you get me swabs from Katherine and Abra, like, right now?"

This was the first time Margie had heard Joan call Katherine and Abra by their first names, with no "Aunt" preceding them. There had been a short period where she tried to get the kids to call people "Mr." and "Mrs." But all her fellow laid-back Gen Xer friends were uncomfortable being called "Mr.," half the women preferred "Ms.," and many of them hadn't changed their names when they got married, making the nomenclature even trickier. In the end, it was just easier for everybody to go by their first names, except Katherine and Abra, who received the honorific titles of "Aunt" out of affection rather than obligation. Margie sent them each a quick text, asking if they could come to the science fair extra early to give Joan one last cheek swab so she could run the analysis again.

Abra replied with a quick *"Sure."* After a moment, Katherine texted back, *"I never thought my saliva would be in such demand. Be there in 10."*

"They're on their way," Margie said. Joan nodded and bit her bottom lip, a sure sign she was worried. Margie thought fast. "You know, you're helping to answer a sticky question that no one really knows the answer to. Any doofus with an internet connection and two panes of glass can learn how to make a solar panel on YouTube."

"Solar panels that power a dollhouse."

"They're dolls. They don't need electricity." Joan went from biting her lip to snorting back half a laugh. *Half a laugh is better than none*, Margie thought as she gave Joan a quick hug.

Abra got to the high school first, her sandals clicking their way down the second-floor hallway. Margie could hear more students and parents milling around the halls, but Abra's footsteps had a particular resonance, as though the person to whom they belonged was on a mission. Ever the marketing director, Abra could always be counted on to show up impeccably dressed for any occasion. Even if she was just wearing shorts and a T-shirt to a cookout, the shorts were well tailored, the T-shirt fitted, and nothing had a stain on it from a previous wearing. It was a level of well-put-togetherness that Margie had long ago stopped striving to achieve.

"Hey there, District Science Fair Champion," Abra said as she walked into the chemistry lab.

"I'm not the district champion," Joan said without looking up from the CO_2 pump. "And I won't be if I can't get some conclusive data."

"Apparently our saliva is causing problems," Margie said.

"There's a sentence I never thought I'd hear," Abra replied.

Just then, Katherine appeared at the chem lab door. "I have twelve minutes before I have to go back down to Anna. Where do I swab in?"

"Hi to you too," Margie said, handing each of them what looked like an extra-long, extra-fuzzy Q-tip. "Here."

"You don't need to swab just yet," Joan said. She finished filling the stainless steel pressure cell with chunks of tofu, attached the CO_2 pump, sealed it, and attached the collection vessel.

"Careful with the pressure on the pump," Katherine said. "Hal said it can be temperamental."

"I am."

Every time Margie watched her daughter run the extraction, she felt a surge of pride and wonder that someone who had spent nine months reclining in her abdomen was now capable of such things. At this point, Joan could probably set up the pump, the Bunsen burner, the stainless steel extraction vessel, and the separator in her sleep. She noticed Abra's eyes grow slightly larger as she took in the array of equipment lined up on the counter like an assembly line, all of it connected with rubber piping.

"Is that *tofu*?" Abra asked, pointing at the little pool of water next to an almost-empty plastic tray holding a lonely white cube.

"Yeah," Joan replied, her attention focused on slowly adjusting the CO_2 pump and keeping an eye on the extraction process. "*Sprouted* tofu," she added with no small amount of disdain.

"Why don't you do your spiel for Katherine and Abra? It'll be good practice for the judges," Margie suggested.

"Okay." Joan took a thought-collecting deep breath, straightened up, and went into honor student mode. "Soy and soy products contain phytoestrogens, which are essentially plant-based estrogen. The scientific community is in disagreement over whether there is a link between soy intake and breast cancer. In this experiment, I'm extracting phytoestrogens from tofu by means of supercritical fluid extraction. I'm pumping carbon dioxide and heating it to supercritical conditions, which in this case is approximately eight hundred and seventy degrees." As Joan described each step of the process, she framed that portion of the setup with her hands like the hostess on a game show.

"From there, it'll go into the extraction vessel, where the carbon dioxide will diffuse into the matrix—in this case, the tofu—and dissolve it. At a lower pressure, the dissolved material will then be swept into the separator, and the extracted material will settle out."

"That's impressive," Abra said.

"It is," Katherine added. "But I suspect there's even more to be impressed about."

"Definitely," Margie murmured. It was fun to watch her friends be wowed by her kid.

Joan seemed a little annoyed by the compliments but plowed right on through with her presentation. "The supercritical fluid extraction is the first step."

"I think she just likes saying 'supercritical fluid extraction,'" Katherine quipped.

"Supercalifragilisticexpialidocious," added Abra.

Margie shushed them even though she knew that once Joan was in honor student mode, nothing could stop her. "Once the phytoestrogen has been extracted, I'm combining it with saliva samples from twelve women, five of whom are breast cancer survivors, seven of whom have no history of breast cancer. In analyzing the combined solutions, I looked for an increase or decrease in the number of estrogen molecules."

Katherine puffed herself up like a big guy and said in a deep science fair judge voice, "And what were the results of your analysis, young lady?"

"Stop it, Aunt Katherine," Joan said.

"Sorry."

"The results were..." Joan frowned. "Inconclusive. Your three samples didn't match the other ones. Mom's didn't match the other cancer survivors, and your two didn't resemble the other ones in the control group. That's why I asked you all to give me another swab."

The door to the chemistry lab opened, and a blond-haired girl with perfect skin and a skirt that showed off thighs the circumference of #2 pencils sauntered into the lab. Margie braced herself for the teacher's pet, back-stabbing frenemy that was Eileen O'Brien. "Hey, Joan," the girl said. "How's your data analysis going?"

Joan hardly looked up as she mumbled, "Hi, Eileen."

"Did you get your results straightened out? I mean, they're going to start judging *any minute*."

Margie exchanged a glance with Joan. She couldn't block Eileen, but she could run interference. She quickly walked to the door and used her best gushy mom voice. "Eileen, how nice to see you. I've heard so much about your project. I'll be sure to go down and see it later. Please tell your mom I said hello," she babbled as she ushered Eileen to the door. The look on Eileen's face said she enjoyed Joan's visible annoyance. Margie wondered what went into making a kid who was so full of sour bile. She didn't even seem to mind being kicked out of the chem lab so quickly.

As soon as she had closed the chem lab door, Joan asked her to lock it. "I really don't think that's necessary, sweetie," Margie replied.

"Yes, it is," Joan exclaimed. "Eileen probably has her whole project all set up and she just came up here to sabotage my work."

Margie sighed but locked the door and went back to the counter where Joan's project was set up. "I think you're giving Eileen way too much power. She's not perfect."

"Her experiment works," Joan said, and threw a pencil across the room.

"Joan..." Margie knew that no matter what she said at this moment, it would probably be the wrong thing. "What can I do that won't make things worse?"

"Nothing."

Katherine came to the rescue. She pulled out her phone and typed out a quick text as she spoke. "Okay, I just need to let Hal and Anna know that I'm going to be up here a little longer. Eileen was exaggerating. The judging doesn't start for twenty minutes."

"And you know they always do the little kids first," Margie added, grateful for Katherine's take-charge-and-take-no-prisoners attitude. "You have plenty of time to finish running the extraction and the analysis."

Katherine nodded and held out her cheek swab as though she was presenting Joan with a skinny, fluff-topped flower. "You have all kinds of time. Run the analysis again."

Joan gave a hesitant smile. "Okay."

It sometimes amazed Margie that her daughter could alternately be so in command one moment and utterly reduced to tears the next. *Hormones*, she thought. *Teenage girls are full of them.* Maybe some of Katherine's high school biology teacher vibes were rubbing off on her, because Joan seemed to have a renewed burst of confidence. And if she was running the analysis as the judges came in, so much the better.

"You can show them all the data from the first few analyses, right?" Margie asked. Joan had asked her three different times to take a look at the nifty chart she'd made tracking the results of all the samples with the phytoestrogen. "It's probably more impressive that you aren't satisfied with the preliminary results and are running the problematic ones again."

"Leave it to your mother to be problematic," Katherine deadpanned.

Abra snickered and asked, "What do we do now?"

"Give her some new swabs," Margie answered and put the swab in her mouth. Out of the corner of her eye, she saw steam rising from the container on the Bunsen burner and from the CO_2 pump. Katherine and Abra were joking around, pretending to sword fight with the tiny swab sticks. Joan was actually laughing at them. It was nice to see her stop freaking out over the project for a moment and have a little fun. But the steam was coming more powerfully now, powerfully enough to make Margie stop in midcheek swipe and ask, "Joan, is it supposed to be doing that?" The other three turned to look at the steam rising from the pump and the collection vessel.

"Uh-oh," Joan said at the same time Katherine said, "Oh shit." Before Margie had time to move or even take the swab stick out of her mouth, the entire thing exploded with a tremendous *Boom!* that shook her eardrums and knocked her to the floor.

For a moment, Margie wasn't sure where she was or why she was sitting on a hard linoleum floor. All she could hear was the low hissing of gas issuing out of the CO_2 pump. A cloud of hot, sticky steam enveloped the room. It tasted like sour metal and mingled with the sweat on her arms and legs. The collection vessel was lying on its side on the floor in front of her. Margie blinked a few times, trying to focus. Abra and Katherine were on the floor on the same side of the counter as she was, looking equally stunned. It wasn't until she heard a voice quietly say "Mom?" that Margie remembered exactly where she was and what was happening.

She couldn't stand quickly enough—most of her body parts were sore, and the floor was slippery—so she crawled around the corner of the counter to where Joan was sitting and trembling with tears in her eyes. Margie grabbed hold of Joan and held her tight. "Are you okay?" she asked.

"I don't know," Joan said quietly. She said something else that Margie couldn't understand, and Margie realized she was holding on so tightly the kid could barely breathe, much less talk. Margie eased off on the hug just a bit. Abra poked her head around the corner of the counter, and Katherine's face peered over the top. Joan started full-on crying. "I'm sorry, I messed it all up..."

Margie shushed her, whispering that everything was okay. Abra and Katherine both chimed in that they weren't hurt. "Everybody's fine," Margie soothed through the heavy mist. It seemed like all sound had stopped, or maybe it was just her ears ringing from the blast. "Nobody's hurt, everything's okay."

"But my project..." Joan sobbed. "I'm never going to the state science fair this year. I'm gonna flunk..."

Margie scooted back a bit and took Joan's cheeks in her hands, realizing as she did so just how covered in slimy steam they all were. She looked her daughter directly in the eye, trying to will her to calm down. "Joan, honey, you couldn't go to the state science fair if you were in the hospital either. You're okay. That's the only thing that matters right now."

Margie and Abra stayed on the floor, Margie holding Joan and Abra holding Margie. Katherine stood over them, feeling as though she was guarding them from further harm. There wasn't anything to do. She was confident that the pump wasn't going to explode again, but they all ought to get some fresh air. They should get out of there, if only she could will her legs to move. The world still seemed fuzzy.

The door to the chemistry lab rattled with the insistent shaking of someone trying to get through a locked door. Voices on the other side of the door shouted questions: "What happened? Is anyone hurt? Do you need help?"

"I can get it," Katherine said, less to the others than to herself. She could get the door, she could still move, still think. The shock of the explosion didn't end anyone's life. Still, it seemed to take forever to walk the length of the chemistry lab on legs that felt as though she'd just run a marathon. Once she was there, the door didn't seem to want to open.

Katherine prided herself on being cool in a crisis, but her legs were trembling and hands shaking as she struggled to unlock the door. The sour steam that permeated the room made her feel a little woozy, and her wet, slimy hands slipped every time she tried to turn the deadbolt. All she wanted to do was lie down and rest, but she had to open the door, and it wouldn't open. *Just turn the lock,* she thought, trying to focus. *Turn it.*

She finally managed to get the door unlocked. As soon as it opened, a scrum of teachers, science fair judges, parents, and kids swarmed in. Then there was explaining and explaining and more explaining, as the four of them had to recount what happened, fill out incident forms for the school district, and get checked out by an emergency medical squad. Calling an ambulance seemed like a bit much, and Katherine said so. The superintendent of the school district and a couple members of the board of education who were in the building for the science fair assured her that it was absolutely necessary.

"Why? None of us is going to sue the district."

"Of course not," Margie added. Katherine couldn't help but smile as the assistant principal gushed over Margie with a chorus of "Better to be safe than sorry." He must have known she was married to a lawyer.

The four of them were surrounded by school officials, teachers, and gawking parents and students. It made Katherine feel slightly under siege. Nevertheless, she waited patiently while the medics gave each of them a quick once-over. When it was her turn, she followed a penlight with her eyes, counted backward from one hundred by fives, and told the medics what day it was and who the president of the United States was.

"I don't have a concussion," she told the medic, a slight, wiry African American guy who spoke so quietly she had trouble hearing him over the low rumble of conversation in the room.

"You don't know that for sure. Follow the light with your eyes," he said, moving the penlight up and down and side to side.

"I didn't hit my head. The blast knocked me down. If anything, I may have sprained my coccyx." On a chair next to her, Margie was going through the same routine with the other medic, while Abra gave a blow-by-blow account of the explosion to the assistant principal. Karl had come in and was standing with an arm around Joan. He managed to look protective even though Joan was nearly as tall as he was. Hal had stayed down in the gym with Anna and Grant. There were already too many people in the chemistry lab; why add to the muddle with her worried child and husband?

By the end of the night, Katherine had told the story of the accident so many times it felt like it happened years ago, not hours. Hal kept insisting she go to the emergency room, but she just wanted to go home. She felt a little off but chalked it up to the shock of the explosion. And Anna needed to go to bed. She was already freaked out by the explosion. It had been loud enough to be heard downstairs in the gym, disrupting the entire science fair and, Anna added, making some of the younger kids cry (but not her).

Katherine had every intention of going to work the next morning. It was a school day, and she had students who needed to prepare for final exams. But at 5:20 a.m., when she'd normally be getting up and going out to meet Abra for their morning run, she went right on sleeping. When Hal finally nudged her awake, Katherine opened one heavy eyelid and looked at the clock next to the bed. It read "7:07." She always left for school no later than seven-thirty. She sat up so fast her head conked into Hal's mouth, bruising his lip.

"Sorry, sweetie! Crap, I'm late!" she said. Her head was starting to spin; she had definitely sat up too fast.

Hal was holding one hand up to his lip. "No, yurf staying homph," he mumbled through a swelling lip and a few fingers. A day off sounded heavenly but unnecessary. It hadn't been a *major* lab accident. Hal stopped trying to hold his bruised lip. "I already called the school. They'll find a substitute. The EMTs said you need to take it easy today."

Even as Katherine was saying "I can't take the day off," the top half of her body was gracelessly falling back onto the bed. She could almost hear her pillow whisper, "*Welcome back*" as she sank into it.

CHAPTER THREE

"SURVIVING" A SCIENCE FAIR EXPLOSION SEEMED LIKE A VERB TOO FAR. "It's not like our lives were ever in danger," Margie said over dinner a few days later.

"Of course not. People just like making a fuss," Katherine replied and took another sip of wine.

There had been a fuss, of course. You can't accidentally set off an explosion in a high school chemistry lab without causing a series of aftershocks. Once they'd dealt with the principal and the school superintendent and the paramedics, Margie and Joan had finally been permitted to leave. Then they'd been ambushed in the stairwell by a reporter for the suburban paper who'd been at the high school taking pictures of the science fair. The explosion ended up being one of the lead stories on Cleveland.com the next morning.

"I lost count of how many people sent me the link," Margie said.

Katherine gave a derisive snort, although it might have been a cough. "I've never understood that. Why are you sending me a link to a news item about me? I know what happened."

"Work was the worst" Abra sighed. "Everybody kept stopping by my office and asking about the explosion. I couldn't get anything done." Abra was sort of hunched over her martini, as though trying to shut out the steady din of noise from the crowded bar and live music. Their typical night out meant drinking cheap margaritas at the Mexican restaurant close to home, but surviving a chemistry lab explosion seemed like good excuse to step it up. Plus Katherine's birthday was coming up, so they went to hear her brother, Billy. He was a jazz pianist who played Wednesdays through Saturdays at the Metropolitan, one of the uber-trendy restaurants in the Warehouse District downtown. Dinner at the Metro could run to figures more suitable to car payments, so they opted for drinks and appetizers.

Margie, Katherine, and Abra made a point of getting together for dinner once a month—twice a month if circumstances necessitated. It started out as just Margie and Katherine, who met in their first jobs after college. Margie had been temping in the main office at Wiley Middle School in nearby Cleveland Heights when she met a first-year science teacher named Katherine Sayer. The temp job was, of course, intended to be temporary while she considered "the myriad opportunities available for a philosophy major. Ontologically speaking, I am either qualified for any job in existence or am completely unemployable. While I internally debate this paradox, I'm making copies of permission slips." She and Katherine started eating lunch together, and when the temp job ended, their friendship had continued for twenty-four years.

After that first race together, Katherine introduced Abra and Margie, correctly thinking they would hit it off. They had become each other's extended family of choice. When Katherine's mother was in the middle of a six-month battle with lung cancer that took her from robust to skeletal, the three got together once a week instead once a month. Sometimes it wasn't for a meal, just a beer or cup of coffee and the solace of someone to lean on. When Eli was a spotty, frustrated thirteen-year-old who told his mother he had cut himself "just to see what would happen," Abra and Katherine had been there to tell Margie she wasn't a bad parent and help her decompress during the months when she took Eli to weekly counseling sessions and tried to figure out why her firstborn seemed to hate himself. When Abra's father died, Margie and Katherine were the ones to look after Abra's house and cat and take emergency phone calls in the middle of the night while she was in Florida with her mother, trying to box up a forty-eight-year marriage. And when Abra had her heart and credit rating broken by the same man, Margie and Katherine provided two shoulders to cry on and a suitable nickname for her ex. Four months later, they still referred to him as The Evil Richard Brewster.

"You know, I worry about a lot of things with my kids," Margie said. "Mass shootings and car accidents and date rape…"

"Don't even put that out there," Katherine interrupted.

"And playground injuries and sports accidents. Exploding tofu was never on the list." Joan had been the closest to the source of the explosion. She said her ears were ringing for a few minutes after it happened, but a visit to the pediatrician showed no damage to the eardrum. Joan, at least, was fine. Margie wasn't sure about herself. "Have you guys felt…different since the explosion? Like something is off?"

The question seemed to pull Katherine out of the music and Abra out of whatever she'd been contemplating in the bottom of her martini glass. "Off how?" Katherine asked.

"I've just been feeling sort of weird and tingle-y," Margie replied. Somehow saying this in the middle of the Metro's upscale bar made it sound even more ridiculous than it felt.

Abra and Katherine were silent for a moment, then Abra said, "I felt the same way for about a day after. Kind of the same way you feel after your car skids on ice."

"Or if you've ever been in an accident," Katherine added. "That's how I felt for the whole next day, just kind of shaken up. But it passed."

Margie nodded. If Abra and Katherine were feeling okay, maybe it was just her. Or maybe it was just her imagination.

Billy had been playing an old boogie-woogie-ish tune that she didn't know. Now he ended it with a flourish, said, "I'll be back in fifteen" into the microphone, and came over to their table to say hello. He gave Katherine a bigger hug than usual, then hugged Abra and Margie and asked, "What the hell did you guys do?"

"It isn't that big a deal," Katherine said. "Just a little explosion."

"It was a big enough deal to make the front page of the paper." Billy had the habit of straddling a chair from the back instead of sitting on it normally. Margie wondered if this was to counteract spending so much time on a piano bench hunched over the keys. He was tall, like Katherine, and shared her slightly wavy, dark hair. He kept it very short and, like every night at the Metro, was wearing a jacket and a tie. Even pushing fifty, Billy Sayer was still a hottie.

"Online news—they're always trolling for content," Katherine said.

"I'm just glad you're okay. Margie, your daughter wasn't hurt, was she?"

"Shaken up but unharmed. I think the only thing injured was her pride."

"Hopefully that will heal quickly too. Hey, I only have a few minutes. Do we need to play What's New? I can kind of guess." Billy played music full-time, giving him a schedule opposite that of anyone with a day job. About the only time Katherine or anyone else managed to see him was at a gig. He rarely had time to talk, so years ago they had started playing What's New with him. It was like a conversation that consisted solely of bullet points.

"And you would be correct. I have nothing beyond our minor explosion," Katherine replied.

"Nothing?"

"Umm...I can't believe I'm almost done with my first year of teaching at Beaumont, and if you told me when we were kids that I would grow up to count a few nuns among my friends, I would have thought you were crazy."

"That is crazy," Billy said, "but Mom would be pleased." Margie had two brothers, one older, one younger, both of whom lived out of town and felt more like friends than siblings. The glance that passed between Katherine and Billy at the mention of their late mother gave her a sudden wave of longing. Billy shifted gears quickly. "Okay, my thing is that I met this great woman named Nora." Margie wasn't the only one who saw Katherine's slight roll of the eyes, because Billy added pointedly: "She's a freelance illustrator and likes to draw at night, which means she and I are on the same schedule."

"Then congratulations," Katherine said. "I look forward to meeting her."

"You will. Who's next?" he asked.

Abra gave her a "Go ahead" look. Margie sighed. The one thing lingering at the top of her brain wasn't exactly news. It was more like a deadline: "Eli is graduating from high school in two weeks. Fill in accompanying waves of melancholy and feeling old at your discretion."

"Whoa," Billy said.

"I know."

"I have nothing to follow that," Abra said.

"Nothing?" Billy asked.

"Nope."

After a couple more minutes of the kind of pleasant chitchat that someone in Billy's line of work had to perfect in order to survive, he said good night and went back to the piano. Once it was just the three of them again, Katherine said to Abra, "What didn't you want to tell Billy?"

Abra gave a little resigned chuckle to the table then looked up. "I'm almost too embarrassed to tell the two of you, much less him."

"What?" Katherine asked.

Abra took a breath and seemed to steel herself a bit. "Okay, I'm uh, I'm filing for bankruptcy." This was big but somehow not unexpected given the mess The Evil Richard Brewster had left her. Abra bought her house with him at the tail end of the mortgage loan crisis, ending up with a bad loan for a house that needed more work than the inspection had shown. Using the argument that her card had a lower interest rate than his, Richard also maxed-out Abra's credit cards for everything from lumber, paint, and drywall (which were still sitting in the detached garage) to a vintage Gibson guitar. Then he had decided he didn't want to get married after all, took the guitar, and left, leaving her with an inflated mortgage and a mountain of debt.

Katherine let out a low "Whoa. That sucks."

"What can we do to help?" Margie asked.

"Nothing really, but thank you for asking. There's just no way I'll ever be able to pay down all the debt. About the only good thing is I can keep the house but that's only because I'm underwater on the mortgage."

Katherine's brow furrowed. Margie had always felt bad for any student who ended up on the business end of Katherine Sayer Krenzler's wrath. "You ought to sue Richard," Katherine said.

"I *let* him use my credit cards, Katherine. He didn't steal them. I thought we were a couple and stupidly, *stupidly* let him ruin my credit."

"You've got to stop beating yourself up over him."

"She's right," Margie added. "He isn't worth it." Nothing she could say was going to make Abra feel better or make her less in debt or send any sort of karmic retribution Richard Brewster's way. It made her feel guilty to know she was going home to a dual-income, financially secure household. It would be more accurate to say her income-and-a-half household. Margie's salary as the office secretary at Adrian Elementary School was only a small fraction of what Karl earned. Sometimes the whole idea of being married to a lawyer with a nice house in a suburb with good schools felt like the most ridiculous, overplayed stereotype in the world. She adored Karl, but all the external things that made him a good life partner also made him, and her life, seem overly staid. Boring, even.

"I know," Abra replied. "He's a complete jerk."

Katherine snorted. "That's an understatement."

"Would an interest-free loan help in any way?" Margie asked quietly, even though she knew what the answer would be.

"No," Abra said firmly, then added more gently, "No, thank you. The one sure way to ruin a friendship is to borrow or lend money."

"It wouldn't ruin—"

"I just can't. But I am eternally grateful for the offer." Abra looked pained. "Can we change the subject, please? I wanted you to know about the bankruptcy, but I don't really want to talk about it. Does that make sense?"

They were silent for moment. A woman about their age in a too-tight red dress was standing by the piano singing her heart out while Billy played "Crazy." Billy made probably half his income in tips from tipsy Metro customers who fancied themselves singers.

Margie felt a wave of heat suddenly take hold. She took a sip of water and dabbed each of her cheeks and her forehead with her napkin to quell the rising inferno that stemmed from deep inside her gut.

"Are you okay?" Katherine asked.

"You look flushed," Abra added.

"I'm fine. Just schvitzing."

"You're starting to talk like your mother-in-law," Katherine said.

"Just sweating a little."

Katherine studied Margie's red face for a moment. "You usually only look like this when you've had too much to drink."

"And I haven't. I'm driving tonight, remember? Really, it's nothing."

Abra gasped. "Wait, are you..." She lowered her voice, although it was so noisy in the bar she could have sung the Ohio State fight song and no one would have noticed. "Are you having a hot flash?"

Margie had been looking down at her glass. Why not be honest? She raised her head to meet her friend's gaze. "I could power a small city, yes."

"I don't think I've had one yet," Abra said. She sounded fascinated. "What do they feel like?"

"Like your own personal summer."

"How often do you get them?" Katherine asked.

"Here and there. Not every day. One thing I've noticed is that sugar seems to trigger them for me. Which is okay—maybe I'll finally drop a few pounds."

"Stop it. You're gorgeous," Abra and Katherine said in unison.

"I'm chubby, but thank you anyway." Margie looked at her two best friends, grateful for their presence. She could feel herself beginning to sweat, felt the uncomfortable heat that sometimes made her want to crawl out of her skin. A natural part of aging or not, it was kind of a drag.

"Okay, if we're playing What's *Really* New," Katherine said and took a deliberate pause, "I believe I'm entering my cronehood."

Margie looked at Abra, who shrugged, and then back at Katherine. "How's that?" she asked.

Katherine lowered her voice and took a quick glance around. "I don't want to say it too loudly."

"Honey, we could barely find a server to take our drink order, so I doubt they're listening in on our conversation," Margie said. "Plus, if you're embarrassed to say it too loud, it must be really good."

Katherine leaned forward slightly and said: "It's been eight months since my last period."

"Whoa," Margie said. "That's impressive."

"And early. I mean, not to rain on your bloodless parade, but you're only forty-seven. In a week," Abra added. "I thought it wasn't official until you hadn't had it for twelve months."

"My cycle has run as efficiently as a German train schedule for thirty-four years. Believe me when I tell you that Aunt Flo has left the building."

"In that case, more power to you," Abra said.

"Indeed," Margie said after a moment. She could guess at the tangle of emotions this had to be stirring up in her friend. "Honestly, I kind of wish I were in your shoes. I don't need the eggs anymore."

"I never needed them," Katherine said pointedly. This was true. Margie had seen Katherine's years-long bout with infertility. And Margie and Abra both had been there when she and Hal finally adopted Anna.

"Yes, your eggs have been a great disappointment to all of us."

"To be fair, most higher animals don't breed well in captivity," Abra added.

Katherine gave them a small smile. "Thank you," she said quietly. "I think I've mostly dealt with all that. I mean, we have Anna..."

"The Future Empress of the World," Abra put in.

"So we *are* parents. It just took so long to get there. When Anna came home, we almost jumped right back in with another home study and another application... Then my mom got sick and all these other things happened. I almost got laid off because the school levy didn't pass, then Hal was denied tenure... life happened. A second adoption never did. This just feels like the closing of a door." She paused a moment, looking down at her wineglass, then recovered. "Okay, if there are no objections, let's finish the self-pitying, bad-analogy portion of the evening."

"Gladly," Margie said. "When in doubt, have another drink." Before Abra could object, she added, "I'm buying." It wouldn't make up for Abra's heartbreak, but it was something.

CHAPTER FOUR

On the way home, Katherine called shotgun, so Abra had to sit in the back of Margie's minivan amid soccer shin guards, baseballs, stray sneakers, swim goggles, granola bar wrappers, a rubber-banded stack of Pokemon cards, and a book on playing Minecraft. "How was this shoe not on the seat when we left?" Abra asked.

"I really couldn't tell you," Margie replied over her shoulder. "Things back there just seem to migrate around on their own. Hold it up." Abra did so, and Margie took a quick look at it in the rearview mirror as they pulled out of the parking lot and onto Superior Avenue. "I don't even think that belongs to one of mine."

"Now you know why I called shotgun. The backseat scares me," Katherine said. "I sometimes get overwhelmed with one kid. How do you manage three?"

"I have no life. Duh," Margie replied.

Margie cut south onto East 12th Street and then turned east onto Chester Avenue, which would take them through Midtown, up Cedar Hill, and back home. As they drove by Cleveland State University, she asked

Katherine, "Do we still have to flip the bird to CSU for denying Hal tenure?"

"Nah, the statute of limitations has expired on that one, I think."

"I like the new housing they're building down here," Abra said. "If I ever move downtown, would you two come and visit me?"

"Hell yes," said Katherine.

"Sure," Margie added. "Are you seriously thinking of moving or just toying with it?"

"Toying. If I can unload the house to the bank, I'll have to rent somewhere. And I'd be closer to work."

"If you move, who will I run with every morning?"

"I don't know. Get another dog?"

Chester was a wide, three-lanes-in-each-direction boulevard that took them past the university neighborhood and through the dead zone in between downtown, where most of the office buildings and entertainment areas were, and University Circle, where most of the city's museums and cultural gems were ensconced. Economic development hadn't hit this middle area, and much of it was taken up by vacant buildings, empty lots, and boarded-up houses.

Nine fifteen on a Thursday night in mid-May isn't late and isn't scary. Still, Margie got a bad feeling when she saw a young woman on the sidewalk walking fast, hands folded across her chest, not looking at the man who walked next to her. The girl was a stranger—not her age, not her race, not her neighborhood, but still, the girl was someone, some mother's daughter.

Margie pulled over to the curb, leaving the engine running.

"Why are you stopping?" Katherine asked.

The few other cars on the wide road passed by without slowing. No cars were parked on the street; Margie's van was the only stopped vehicle for blocks. Katherine and Abra followed Margie's gaze to the scene unfolding on the sidewalk. The man was yelling at the woman now. They couldn't make out exactly what he was yelling but heard the words "bitch" and "money" a few times. And they could see his flailing arms, his face leering up against hers. She stopped walking and said something to him, and he hit her. She lost her balance and fell against the chain-link fence that ran along the sidewalk. They were in front of an empty lot, where once there might have been a house but now was only a square of crabgrass and crumbling concrete and stray garbage. For a moment, there were no other cars on the road. There was no one else on the street, no inhabited buildings for a couple blocks either way. If not for them, the woman was on her own.

"Call nine-one-one," Abra said as the man hit the woman again. The woman tried to get away, but he grabbed her shoulders and shoved her hard against the fence.

"There's no time," Katherine said. In a heartbeat, she was out of the car.

"Darn it, come on..." Abra muttered as she fumbled with the sliding side door and jumped out. "Keep the engine running," she said as she followed Katherine.

"I'll go with you..." Margie started to say. No, Abra was right. Someone had to stay with the van, keep the engine running, stay behind the wheel in case they needed to make a quick getaway. Glancing behind her, she backed up alongside the people on the sidewalk. It felt proactive. She could hear Katherine's strong teacher voice saying loudly but calmly, "Leave her alone" and the woman yelling, "Call the police!" It suddenly occurred to Margie that she had a phone. She could call the police. Hands trembling and heart racing, Margie frantically fumbled through her bag for her phone.

She told the 911 dispatcher where she was and what was happening, the whole time watching Katherine and

Abra and the couple on the sidewalk. Suddenly, there was a glint of something shiny in the streetlight as the man rushed toward Katherine. She heard a scream, and then she couldn't see Abra anymore.

Katherine got out of the car purely through instinct. There was someone in trouble—helping is what you were supposed to do, right? It wasn't until she was on the sidewalk, walking toward the man and woman, saying loudly, "Leave her alone" and watching the man turn to face her that she realized she had absolutely no idea what to do next. None. It was then that her heart started pounding and a hot wave of fear tingled through her arms and legs.

Up close, she could see the guy was taller and more muscular than he appeared from the safety of the van. He was maybe white, maybe light-skinned African American with a shaved head. An indecipherable neck tattoo peeked out from under his close-fitting, long-sleeved black T-shirt. She tried to burn a police description into her brain. The woman yelled, "Call the police!" at the same time the guy said, "This is none of your damn business, *lady*" to Katherine. The utter disdain in his voice cleared everything out of her brain except one thought: *This was such a mistake. This was such a stupid mistake.* There was no way this could end well. For a split second, she imagined Hal and Anna without her, wondered if they would think her foolish for getting herself killed in this way. She heard Abra say softly, "Just let her go, man."

Katherine could just see Abra off to her right. Margie had backed up, and the open doors of the van were only a few yards away. She could faintly hear Margie's voice, talking to 911 maybe? Knowing they were both nearby gave her a tiny bit more courage. Katherine took a tentative step toward the woman, who was kneeling by the fence. Her face was bloodied, the sleeve of her shirt ripped. "Miss?" she asked. She looked about nineteen or twenty. Not a woman. A girl. "Why don't you come with us? We'll give you a ride."

"She don't need a ride," the man said.

The rest of the street seemed eerily quiet. Couldn't someone else stop and help? Someone big? Someone male maybe? Katherine wasn't that big, but she was big enough, strong enough. She could help. Slowly she extended her left arm. If the woman wanted to take her hand, she could. Katherine held the woman's gaze, hoping she could silently convince her that leaving with some strangers was preferable to getting beaten up by her boyfriend. Katherine was so focused that she didn't see the knife until it was against her arm, in her arm. The man cut so fast that she hardly saw the blade, only the flash of metal against her pale white skin. It occurred to her that she needed to get out in the sun. *Why am I worried about how pale I am? I just got cut.* She felt the sensation of the blade slicing through flesh, felt a momentary spark of pain, and then the pain was gone. It happened faster than a flu shot—a quick prick, then nothing.

The man only made one swipe, then stopped, triumphant, staring at her arm, expecting blood, expecting her to scream, to fall. There wasn't any blood on her arm or the knife. No blood, just Katherine staring at him wide-eyed and unharmed.

Then the man was on the ground, hit from the side by...something, something Katherine couldn't see. The knife dropped from his hands and landed near her foot. She kicked it away at the same time she heard Abra's voice yell, "Run!" But where the hell *was* Abra? She must be in the van. Katherine couldn't see her.

Katherine said, "Come on" to the woman, who was now up and moving toward her. The woman needed no more convincing and was in the car before Katherine, even before Abra. Where had Abra been? How could she be the last one to pile into the minivan, yelling, "Go! Go!" to Margie, who was slamming on the gas before the door was even closed.

Nobody said anything for a moment. The only sound in the car was that of four women catching their breath, being glad they had breath left in their bodies. Then all of them simultaneously erupted into words of relief and fear, asking each other "Are you all right? Are you all right?"

"Oh sweet mother, I can't believe you all just did that," Margie said. "I thought—Katherine, I honestly thought he was going to kill you."

"So did I," Abra said. "How the hell did he not cut you? How did he miss you?"

"He didn't miss me," Katherine replied quietly. Feeling fine seemed intrinsically wrong, but there it was. Unreal sense of calm? Yes. Pain and blood? No.

Before Margie or Abra could respond, the woman exclaimed, "Oh my God, thank you! Sean would've done me in this time, I know it. Y'all were like superheroes or something. You saved my life."

The three women were quiet for a heartbeat. For the moment, the hyperbole of the phrase "You saved my life" was gone. It was arguably true. This was a new sensation. Frightening and humbling. Then Margie said, "Shoot, I dropped the phone." With one hand on the wheel, she felt around in the great vortex of tissues, empty cups, and scraps of paper in the molded plastic section in between the two front seats.

"I got it," Katherine said, coming up with the phone. The 911 dispatcher was still on the line, wondering what was going on. "Hello?" Katherine said. "We're okay. We got away, the woman is safe. We're going—where are we going?"

"Anywhere away from Sean," the woman in the back said.

"There's a police station right down the street at one hundred and fifth," Abra said.

"Right, I know where that is," Margie said.

A police car with the siren off but lights flashing came roaring down Chester Avenue in the opposite direction.

"Was that for us?" Margie asked.

"I think so," Abra said.

Katherine hardly had time to explain what had happened to the dispatcher before they were at the station. There was a long hour-plus of giving witness statements to a jaded-looking police officer who told them several times how lucky they were to have gotten out of the situation with no harm done. "What you three ladies did was very brave and very stupid," he said in closing.

"We know," Abra replied.

They were told they might be called as witnesses if the woman, Janelle, decided to press charges against her boyfriend. Then they were free to go. The three of them walked out of the police station and to the waiting minivan. It was nearing midnight, and the spring evening had moved from cool to downright chilly. Even so, none of them moved to get into the van. Margie unlocked it and opened the driver's door, then just stood looking at the ground, one hand on the door, the other on the side of the van, breathing slowly. Abra paced in a slow oval near the back of the van, while Katherine leaned against it and gazed up at the few faint stars that could be seen against the city lights. She suddenly wanted to be somewhere quiet, away from the city, away from people. Margie's voice brought her back: "I'm sorry I didn't do anything to help."

What are you talking about?" Katherine said. "If it weren't for you, we never would have gotten out of there."

Abra walked around the van to Margie. "You were the only smart one. I'm sorry I got out of the car. That was stupid." As Abra said this, she shivered, her lips trembled, and she started to shake. "That was so stupid."

"I got out first," Katherine said. "I'm the stupid one."

Katherine almost never saw Margie cry. Even when her eldest child was going through hell, Katherine had been amazed and admiring of her friend's resilience. But now Margie seemed overwhelmed by heaving sobs. "I'm just so glad the two of you are okay," Margie stammered. Crying people generally made her nervous, but Katherine joined Margie and Abra on the other side of the van. When your friends need you, they need you.

Later that night, after she was finally home and in bed with Clinton P. the Cartoon Cat resting on her ankle, Abra replayed the events of the evening over and over in her head. How in the world did the guy not see her coming at him? And how was it that Katherine wasn't hurt? She had been right there, just a few feet away from Katherine. She saw the knife before Katherine did, saw it cut into her friend's arm. Nothing else could have compelled her to take a flying leap at a knife-wielding stranger. And yet it was as though the guy hadn't even seen her. Aside from a small red line on her arm, Katherine hadn't been harmed.

Abra didn't weigh that much—one hundred and fifteen pounds on a fat day. She liked to say it was all muscle, honed by years of running and yoga. Even so, a hundred and fifteen pounds of anything shouldn't have been enough to knock down a six-foot-tall grown man. Unless he didn't expect it, unless he didn't even see her coming. At all.

Her phone beeped. She picked it up off the night-stand and saw a text message from Katherine that read:

"*I feel funky. Can we bag the a.m. run tomorrow?*" She quickly wrote back: "*I feel the same. Sat. a.m.?*"

She held up her other hand and looked at it in the dim light of her phone. Her hand was there all right. Clint obviously saw it, as he took her outstretched hand as an invitation to be petted. Abra obliged, letting his rhythmic purr finally lull her to sleep.

CHAPTER FIVE

WHEN MARGIE WALKED INTO HER DARK, SILENT HOUSE, IT WAS THE FIRST TIME SHE HAD FELT SAFE AND CALM SINCE THEY LEFT THE RESTAURANT. Juno greeted her, tail flapping like a pom-pom. A border collie is a good thing to have if you don't want to be the most neurotic being in the house.

Juno was definitely Mommy's Dog. Somehow they understood each other on the deepest of levels, as though Juno wanted to help shoulder the task of caring for everyone else. Margie sat on the stairs off the living room, just getting lost in Juno's long brown-and-white fur. Hugging the dog was cheaper and quicker than therapy. "I'm glad you're here, baby," she whispered. Juno licked her hand in reply. So what if the dog was really only searching for some stray taste of the last thing Margie had eaten? It made her feel better, as though she belonged to a loving pack.

It never bothered her that Katherine and Abra ran together just about every morning, that they held running in common, apart from her. They weren't in middle school—you didn't have to do everything together to call yourselves best friends. The three of them had saved

Janelle. She could accept that she had played an active role in helping even if she hadn't gotten out of the van.

But Katherine and Abra had done things tonight that she hadn't. Things none of them had even tried to explain. Margie considered the facts as she stroked Juno's silky ears. That guy Sean was strong, of that there was no doubt. She saw Janelle's bruises, and the police had taken her to the emergency room. The swipe at Katherine's arm should have hurt her, yet Katherine hadn't bled a drop. She was fine save for a mark that looked like a scar from a long-ago injury.

Margie was almost willing to accept that perhaps Sean's knife had only grazed Katherine, that maybe they all just thought he had cut her. But what to make of Abra? Margie had watched her friends the entire time she'd been in the van calling 911. The passenger door and the side sliding door were open, giving her a clear view of everything happening on the sidewalk. She had been able to see all four people, except for the few seconds when she only saw three. It was dark out, granted, but not so dark that she would be able to see someone one second and unable to see her the next. There was a moment when Margie would swear on the heads of her children that Abra had disappeared. It was right before Sean fell over. Or was knocked down. Margie saw it happen. No young man just falls over like that. It was clear by how he fell that he had been pushed. The problem was, she hadn't seen anyone push him.

It was too weird to think about when all she really wanted to do was check on her kids and go to sleep. Margie stood up, said, "Come on," to Juno, and went upstairs. Together, she and the dog peeked into each bedroom.

At nearly eighteen, Eli was really too old to be called a "kid," but as she often said to him, "You'll always be my first baby. Deal with it." He was stretched out spread-eagle on his bed, arms and legs everywhere. The past four years had been so difficult for him, but now he seemed comfortable and even content in his ever-growing skin. At six foot one, he already towered over Karl (which wasn't difficult). Being on the tall side seemed to give Eli more confidence. He was pursuing his love of drawing and last year had discovered distance running, both of which seemed to be able to lift him out of the dark places where formerly he tried hurting himself. It was a little overwhelming to think that he'd be starting college in three months.

A little farther down the hall was Joan's room. The only girl and the toughest one in the bunch was how Karl always described her. Joan was still angry with herself about the explosion, not because they could have been injured or because Brush High School's chemistry lab was now covered in phytoestrogen-infused slime, but because it wasn't clear if she'd get another chance to show her experiment or not. The idea of waiting until next year to compete at the state science fair was about as palatable as Margie's suggestion that she use dry ice instead of the CO_2 pump the next time she ran the extraction. Despite her ever-changing teenage moods, Joan was a great kid. Margie hoped she'd continue swimming and playing soccer. Sports and academics seemed to insulate her a bit from the slings and arrows of the Eileen O'Briens of the world.

Last was Grant, who slept in a room that was technically a utility closet but that he insisted on claiming as his own at age seven because he refused to share a bedroom with a teenager. After six months, when they realized Grant would not be moved, they built a loft bed in there to give him a bit more useable space. Now, as an eleven-year-old, Grant had the coolest room in the house. Juno didn't like it because she couldn't climb up the ladder to sleep on his bed. Grant must have smelled okay from a distance, however, because the dog seemed to think her job was done and plopped down on the dirty jeans and T-shirt Grant had left on his floor. Margie was too tired to bother picking them up right now.

Satisfied that all of her children were still breathing, she quickly got ready for bed. Karl was already conked out, sleeping on his back again but, thankfully, not snoring. Once she was in bed, Margie cuddled up next to him. Even asleep, Karl responded, rolling onto his side and spooning with her. In the morning, she'd wake him with a kiss and the start of a hand job, but for now it was enough to feel the security of his body next to hers.

In a family of early risers, Katherine was typically the first one awake. Staying up late and getting up early had always held a certain allure, as though proof her body didn't need the rest or sleep other bodies did, as though her body was special. She awoke at five twenty as she did almost every day—no alarm necessary—and stretched, sorry she'd canceled the morning run with Abra. If you run consistently, run all your life, you will live through weeks and weeks of biding your time while the latest pulled muscle or tendon heals. But if you run consistently, run all your life, you will also live through rarified periods when absolutely nothing hurts. The morning after the incident on the sidewalk was one of the latter; it seemed a shame to waste it.

Next to her, Hal stirred slightly. He was usually awake around six or six thirty, followed shortly by Anna, who greeted each new day with the gusto and enthusiasm only a nine-year-old can muster. Hal liked to get into work early. Manderville Chemical was a great job, especially after the uneasy eighteen months they went through when he was denied tenure at the university.

His new job had actually given Katherine leeway to move from teaching middle school science in a public school to teaching biology at Beaumont, an all-girls Catholic high school a few miles away.

She'd had some doubts about taking the job. To begin with, Katherine wasn't sure if she was still Catholic anymore. Maybe culturally Catholic, but she wasn't sure she still believed. Not in the fervent way she remembered the old ladies of her childhood who seemed to be perpetually bowed in prayer must have believed. Not even in the more pragmatic way her mother had believed, where faith was like a Swiss Army knife you kept in your back pocket for emergencies. But here she was, teaching in a Catholic school and loving it. The all-girl environment turned out to be less touchy-feely and more invigorating than she expected. The girls seemed free, unencumbered. Plus, it was close to home, and Anna could even go there tuition-free if she wanted. Despite the pay cut, she had to admit it was a better life all around.

Carefully, so she wouldn't wake Hal, she got out of bed and crept into the small bathroom off their bedroom. Once the door was closed and the light on, she took a good look at her left arm. There was a fine pink line slicing straight down the middle of her forearm that hadn't been there before last night. The knife had most certainly touched her. Not only had she felt it—here was physical proof.

There was a time, early in their relationship, when she and Hal were driving home from a long weekend of winter hiking. On a back road, shortly after they'd left their rented cabin, a car traveling in the opposite direction spun on a patch of ice and hit them. It was the first time Katherine had ever been in an accident. She'd always heard people talk about time slowing during a crisis, how people could remember every second, every heartbeat of an accident. She'd been amazed to discover it was true, been surprised to realize that she could be surprised by the glacial passage of time and simultaneously acutely conscious of the car spinning toward them, of Hal trying to turn off the road to get out of the way, of the impact as the two cars hit, of snowy woods and sky and road swirling in her vision as their car spun in two complete circles, of the breath she took when both cars had stopped moving, of the silence when she and Hal looked at each other and realized they were both unharmed.

Her mind went back to the confrontation on the sidewalk. She'd felt that same clarity, that same mindfulness when she stepped out of the car. Sean with the knife had cut her. She could remember the moment the blade touched her arm, could remember the feeling of the metal against her skin and the momentary prick of pain as it sliced her flesh. How could she remember the whole thing in such detail if she hadn't actually been cut?

It was too early to text Abra and say she'd changed her mind. Abra was probably sleeping in anyway. And today she wanted to be by herself. Katherine ran her and Abra's regular route, starting off at a fast clip and not letting up, not feeling the need to let up. With the exception of two other runners and a few people walking dogs, the park and the trail were quiet.

The "Why?" of it all knocked around her brain for the entire run. She mentally took a step back and tried to look at the question objectively. An arm—not necessarily *her* arm, just a standard human arm—is sliced by someone who intends to do harm. There is no harm done. Empirical evidence would suggest that something unusual is going on with the arm in question. She needed more data. She didn't have a knife handy, but she could still do some experimentation. If the arm in question could withstand a knife, what else could it and the body to which it was attached withstand?

The far end of the park ended in a parking lot with a picnic pavilion, basketball courts, and a small playground. The playground had a number of ramps and different levels, including two slides of varying heights. *Maybe*, she thought and sprinted to the taller slide. She didn't bother with the ladder but ran right up the sliding board. The platform at the top was about ten or eleven feet off the ground. Not high enough to kill you but enough to hurt if you weren't careful.

Katherine swung a leg over the railing at the top of the slide platform and managed to squeeze herself through the open space between the railing and the low, pointed roof that made the platform look like the turret on a castle. Holding onto the railing, she faced outward and wedged her heels into the tiny space between the railing and the bottom of the platform. She looked down at the wood chips that were supposed to soften the fall when children fell. It was an improvement from the hard-packed dirt at the playground where she grew up, but she was still ten feet up. A wave of vertigo swept over her, a wave that warned: "This is too high to jump." Was the fear instinctual, a holdover of forty-seven years of being told human bodies shouldn't fall off high places? She patted the back pocket of her running shorts and felt her phone. If she injured herself, fine, she'd know everything she'd been thinking about was a load of crap. If she couldn't limp home, she'd swallow her pride, call Hal, and make up an injury story.

But what if the fear wasn't necessary? "It won't hurt," she said aloud and jumped.

You're supposed to roll when you jump from a high surface, but at the last second, she decided not to. Rather, she realized she didn't need to. The instant her running shoes hit the ground, the fear she'd felt at the top of the platform slipped away. It felt as easy as jumping off the bottom step. Nothing hurt. Just for kicks, she ran up the slide again. This time, instead of climbing to the outside of the platform, she decided to go higher. The little pointed roof on top of the slide wasn't so little or so pointed that an enterprising adult couldn't squat on it. She felt like a very small King Kong. She was also considerably higher than she had been before. Looking down, the ground seemed awfully far away. She jumped and hit the ground running. For a moment, she let the "Why?" and "How?" of it all slip away and simply enjoyed the sensation of running fast, of moving like a machine, untiring, indestructible.

Even though she ran full bore all the way, her experimenting made her late getting home. Hal never left for work until Katherine was back from her run because Anna didn't yet feel comfortable being home alone. He was standing in the garage by his car when she reached their driveway.

"Hi," she said, the word coming out like a gasp, not because she was out of breath but because she was exhilarated not to be out of breath. Then the "Why?" came rushing back. She wanted to tell Hal...something. What, she wasn't sure. "I had a really great run and lost track of time. Sorry."

"Thanks for hurrying," Hal said, giving her a quick kiss on the cheek and getting in his car. It was hard to tell if he was being sarcastic or not.

CHAPTER SIX

THE MORNING AFTER THE FIGHT OR THE INCIDENT OR WHATEVER SHE WAS SUPPOSED TO CALL IT, ABRA SPENT A GOOD SEVENTY-FIVE MINUTES ON THE YOGA MAT HOLDING, INVERTING, HOLLOW-BACKING, BREATHING, AND TRYING TO WORK THROUGH WHAT THE HELL HAD HAPPENED THE NIGHT BEFORE.

She could remember very clearly the drive from the Metropolitan and getting out of the van. She could remember the terrified look on Janelle's face and the little trickle of blood on the side of her forehead that reflected in the streetlight. Then there was the knife; the sight of it against Katherine's arm was burned into her memory. She'd felt a wave of sickening anger, or maybe it was fear, when she saw Katherine get cut. It wasn't an emotion she'd ever felt before—a wave of gut-wrenching cramps fueled by blind rage. As she took her flying leap at Sean, the gaping sensation in the pit of her stomach, the cramp, the pain, all of it disappeared in a blink.

That's where her memory got foggy.

One night when she was about ten, Abra had gotten out of bed and walked downstairs to where her father was watching *The Tonight Show* in the living room. Jack

Hanna, the famous zookeeper, was on the show with a tiny monkey. Abra's father let her watch the monkey pee on Johnny Carson's desk then told her it was late and to go back to bed. The next morning she remembered the whole thing as a dream, but her father confirmed it had actually happened. There was the same hint of not quite wakefulness, of consciousness in another realm in the few seconds where she had knocked Sean down then scrambled back into the van. Someone had been yelling, "Go! Go!" to Margie. Maybe it was her. The memory of hearing "Go! Go!" existed; the memory of saying it herself did not.

Abra always drove a few minutes down Green Road to the light rail, where she could park for free and take the train into work. It was cheaper than paying for parking downtown and gave her time to think. The ride was usually uneventful. Abra got on at the top of the line, so she could always find a seat even at rush hour. As the train clicked and clacked its way through wealthy Shaker Heights, past the houses that could only be described as mansions, the cars would start to fill up. For the first third of the journey, her fellow riders were primarily white men and women in business clothes heading to office jobs in downtown Cleveland, with a smattering of students or people of color. As the train got near the beautiful old apartment buildings of the Shaker Square neighborhood, the train would see a broader range of people. The east side of Cleveland had an East Coast/Old New England vibe, with wealthy Shaker playing Massachusetts to the funkier Cleveland Heights' Vermont. South Euclid, where Abra lived, felt like New Jersey. Serviceable but unremarkable.

By the time they reached the cave-like central transit hub underneath the Terminal Tower in the center of downtown, the train cars would be standing room only. Friends in New York or Chicago or Los Angeles would joke that Cleveland didn't have a rush hour. Abra always countered that it did, but it only lasted fifty minutes. By the time the train arrived downtown, she would typically have given her seat to one of the elderly women who always seemed to be riding the train without a set destination.

She had been the marketing director at Hoffmann Software Solutions for nine years. In that time, the company had nearly doubled in size. Sandy in Human Resources was making a big deal about hiring their fiftieth employee. Hoffmann designed and sold inventory management systems for retail and manufacturing clients. When she'd taken the job at age thirty-eight, a director position seemed like an accomplishment. Nine years later, some of the shine of the title had worn off. She was still a one-person department. Being a director just meant she had to go to more meetings and was too tired in the evenings to do much of her own writing.

Abra typically arrived at work around eight fifteen or eight thirty, and it was always blissfully quiet. "Early" for most of the staff was any time before nine. The first sign of anyone else in the office that morning was the echoing laughter of Giles Hoffmann, founder and president, reverberating down the hallway from the kitchen. Giles had the bearing of an athletic Santa Claus. Bearded, burly, and beaming, he was clearly in one of his joke-telling moods. Since he announced his retirement a couple months back, he'd grown ever more jovial. Giles seemed to be doing his best to ensure that everyone at the company remembered him fondly.

A cup of tea sounded good, plus Abra needed to talk to Giles anyway, so she followed the sound of his voice to the kitchen. The company's offices were located in the one-hundred-and-fifteen-year-old Caxton Building in downtown Cleveland. The place was built like a castle, and while one of the two elevators was frequently out of order, Abra loved the building's character and the single fat window in her office that reached from knee height almost to the ceiling. The company's offices had been reconfigured and expanded a number of times, giving the whole place a labyrinthine feel. Hoffmann Software now took up more than half of the seventh floor because Giles had been adamant that the staff not be broken up onto separate floors, but he resisted any thought of moving to another building. What would happen after he retired in August was anyone's guess.

The office kitchen was plopped down in the middle of everything, like the reward piece of cheese in the center of a lab rat's maze. The kitchen was actually just a supporting wall with a sink and a counter. During the ill-fated Suggestion Box Era, someone had suggested enclosing the space with a couple of cubicle panels to make it feel more like a "communal gathering place." (Abra suspected the use of the cheesy phrase "communal gathering place" was why no one ever owned up to making the suggestion.) Some joker occasionally moved the panels in so that the kitchen was reduced to the size of a closet, or moved the panels (and the refrigerator) against the opposite wall so that the kitchen became part of the main hallway. Most of the time it was just large enough to hold the staples of a workplace kitchen: a sink, a refrigerator, a coffee maker, a microwave, and a random assortment of staffers waiting for the coffee to brew.

Giles was holding court with Mike Horowitz, the finance director, and a new intern, an MBA student from Case Western Reserve University named Aletha, who was tall, dark, and intense. The company always had a few interns hanging around. The undergraduates were generally an interchangeable bunch who scurried around from one task to another like eager puppies. Grad students were a bit rarer and far more confident and focused. Aletha was the first MBA student they'd had from Case in years. She'd been kind of a big deal when she arrived a week earlier. Abra liked her because she didn't seem timid when talking to the company president and, more importantly, didn't laugh at any of Horowitz's jokes.

"When I got my first real job out of college, my old Irish grandmother accused me of misspending my money," Giles was saying. Abra had heard this story before. She leaned against the gray fabric-covered panel (trying not to move the kitchen wall in the process) and listened. Giles imitated his grandmother's accent well: "I don't want none of your hard-earned money going to Sinn Fein." Despite having heard Giles tell this story to practically every intern over the past nine years, she still found it kind of funny. "I kept saying, 'No, Granny, I'm not sending money *to* the IRA. I'm putting it *into* an IRA."

Aletha was a polite audience, laughing lightly and smiling in disproportionate relationship to the relative humor of the joke. Horowitz leaned just a tad closer to Aletha. "Are you even *old* enough to know what Sinn Fein is?" he asked.

"The political arm of the Irish Republican Army?" she replied. "Yes, I know what it is."

Abra snickered as she walked over to the counter and picked up the little electric kettle to boil some water for tea. Horowitz was standing almost directly in front of the sink, yet he didn't move out of her way. It was tempting to say something along the lines of "Get your privileged flat ass out of my way," but she simply said, "Excuse me, Mike."

"Huh? Oh, sorry. Didn't see you there, Abra," he said, moving out of the way. Horowitz wasn't necessarily a bad guy. He wasn't exceedingly backstabbing, exceedingly sexist, or exceedingly incompetent. He just seemed to be coasting along through life reaping as many benefits as possible while doing as little as possible to earn them.

"I've been standing here for ten minutes," Abra said. Admittedly, it'd been more like four, but Horowitz never seemed to see her unless it was to say something annoying.

"Morning, Abra," Giles said. "Hey, can we move our meeting to ten? I have an early lunch meeting at eleven thirty."

"We were already scheduled for ten, Giles." She noticed Aletha suppress a little smile. She hadn't meant to make Giles look foolish or forgetful in front of an intern, but apparently she had.

"Was it?"

"Yes."

"Sorry, I'm getting a little cavalier about my schedule now that the retirement clock is ticking." He chuckled in advance over his own joke. "This might be the only time I'm actually shorter than you." Over Horowitz's guffaw and Abra's annoyed sigh, Giles added, "In the military, if someone is going to be discharged before you are, they're shorter than—"

"I know what it means," Abra said, painfully cognizant that none of the other three could ever have been called "short" in their lives.

"Be nice to Abra," Horowitz said. "She's probably just tired because she hasn't recovered from Cinco de Mayo yet." He pronounced "Mayo" like the shortened version of "mayonnaise."

Abra wondered if a watched electric kettle, like a watched pot, will never boil. She didn't turn around. Sometimes if you just ignored Horowitz, he'd go away of his own accord.

"It's actually pronounced 'my-o,' not 'may-o,'" Aletha said.

"Hey, *se hablo Espanol*," Horowitz said, as though he just learned Aletha had won the lottery.

"*Sí, trabajé durante un año en Uruguay.*"

Abra bit her lip and glanced over her shoulder. Free entertainment was, after all, free entertainment. Horowitz seemed to lean his head forward a little, the same way the cat did when Abra politely told him to get out of the sink so she could brush her teeth. "Looks like you aren't the only Spanish speaker in the office anymore, Abra. You are very impressive," he added to Aletha.

Giles patted Aletha lightly on the back. "She is. I'm hoping Aletha can help us make some inroads in the Latin American market while she's here. That's one of my bucket list items before I retire." The whole succession question wasn't a secret. The next company president would be Giles's son, Arthur, who was somewhere in his early thirties and hadn't seemed all that interested in running the company until about a year ago. There would likely be a power vacuum after Giles left. The slightly possessive way Horowitz followed Giles out of the kitchen made Abra wonder if he was angling for a promotion.

Abra frowned as she watched them go and turned her attention to the kettle, which finally had a little steam coming out of it. As she was pouring the boiling water into her work mug, she heard Aletha say, "Nice tea mug. It looks like it could be used as a diving pool."

"You can never get a cup of tea large enough or a book long enough to suit me." Why was she dropping old quotes on the intern? Aletha wasn't her competition. "C.S. Lewis," she added by way of attribution.

"Good quote." Aletha glanced around then lowered her voice slightly. "Um, can I ask you an off-the-record question?"

"Sure."

"I'm not sure how to ask this without sounding paranoid, but that guy Horowitz seems a little too friendly, you know? Do I need to...worry about him?" Her voice trailed off into the netherworld of half-formed statements that imply far more than they say. Abra knew what she meant.

"He's harmless," Abra said. "I know he kind of flirts sometimes, or what passes for flirting, but it isn't what you could call offensive. He won't bother you." Horowitz was harmless, at least in that respect. He kept the company's books well, he awkwardly flirted with the younger women, but Abra had never heard of him actually doing anything untoward. "However, I wouldn't spend more time in Software Development than is absolutely necessary. Sewicki is the biggest offender."

"I'm not sure if I've met him yet."

"Elevator Eyes," Abra said, and gave a fair imitation of Gary Sewicki's standard glance that sidled up and down Aletha's figure before settling somewhere in the region of her chest.

"Oh, that guy. Yeah."

"Still harmless but more creepy. If anyone makes you uncomfortable in any way, let Sandy in HR know."

"Thank you. Please don't mention this conversation to anyone. I don't want anyone to think I'm being difficult."

"I understand. It's always a balancing act."

"So I've learned. There are a few profs at the university who think it's okay to flirt with the female grad students."

"Tenured faculty?"

"Of course."

Abra thought back to her own time in graduate school. The students in her MA program in English had been the standard hodgepodge of lefty feminists of both genders, dewy-eyed Austenites who fantasized about the Lake District, and the intense ones who read deconstructionist literary criticism for fun. There, too, the lit crit professors frequently seemed to favor the male students in the classroom, as though the male brain was better suited to analysis. One of the younger faculty members, Dr. Stanton, taught rhetoric and composition and had a reputation for hooking up with the prettier female students, although no one ever proved anything. Then there had been good old Dr. Alberson, whose idea of social propriety seemed to have lodged at a cocktail party somewhere in 1961. He would always call the female students "honey" and liked to pat them on the knee during a meeting if he thought they didn't understand a point. It was just something you dealt with.

"You're always gonna get those guys," she said. "But you don't need to let them get under your skin. Or your skirt."

CHAPTER SEVEN

Prom had never been big on Katherine's agenda when she was a teenager. Now that she was teaching in a high school, she'd learned that faculty were encouraged to attend prom to "support" the students.

"More like act as unpaid chaperones," Hal muttered as he tied his tie.

Katherine was putting on her new heels—black-and-red sexy, strappy things that went with her dress. She'd never been one to get excited about shoes, but she really dug these. The whole process of getting dressed for prom as an accompanying faculty member was much less fraught than it was when she was a senior in high school. Chaperones weren't on display. "It's my first year teaching there; I kind of need to go," Katherine said. "And I've gotten to know some of these girls. It'll be nice to be there for their last hurrah at the school."

"I liked it when you taught middle school. I never had to go with you to those dances."

"Well, thank you for being my prom date." She stood up just in time to catch Anna, who ran into the room and jumped up into her mother's arms. The sexy, strappy shoes were higher and more precarious than anything she normally wore, but Katherine felt balanced, strong. Despite Anna's best efforts, she didn't knock Katherine over.

"When are you leaving?"

"As soon as Daddy goes to pick up Joan."

"Why do I always have to pick up the babysitter?"

"Because that's the dad's job," Anna said.

Hal looked slightly amused. "Since when?"

"Since always. That's how it's done."

Hal sighed. "Fine. I'll be back in a few."

Anna plopped herself down on the double bed and took a couple small jumps. "It's not a trampoline," Katherine said.

"I know, but it's still bouncier than my bed."

"Stop jumping, please." Katherine sat down on the bed, and Anna snuggled up next to her. For a moment, Katherine didn't think, just enjoyed the coziness of her kid resting on her lap. "Will you be good for Joan tonight?"

"Yeeesss," Anna murmured, drawing out the word so it sounded like it had about twelve syllables. Apparently that was a big thing just now in third grade. The end of third grade. Anna would be in fourth grade in the fall, starting at the upper elementary school. Somehow grades four to six felt like the Wild West compared to K through three. Anna turned upside down, and Katherine was forced to hold onto her legs so the kid wouldn't fall headfirst onto the bedroom floor.

"Can we do wheelbarrow?" Anna asked.

Katherine obliged, holding Anna's legs while her sturdy short arms walked across the bedroom floor. She was a strong little kid, emphasis on the word "little." When they had first decided to adopt from China, a friend of a friend said, "Oh, all those Chinese girls are size one and gorgeous." Katherine still found the comment vaguely sexist and overgeneralizing of an entire ethnicity. But the fact remained that Anna was one of the smallest kids in her class, the smallest of her friends.

Katherine was so glad her daughter was a burgeoning little swimmer. It seemed like those muscles would serve her well later. When other kids wrote, "Eat my bubbles" on their backs with Sharpies before a swim meet, Anna had once asked a friend to write, "Small but mighty." As she held her child's legs and watched her wheelbarrow her way through the bedroom door and down the hall to her own room, she marveled at Anna's strength.

"Aren't you tired yet?" she asked.

"Nope." Anna wouldn't stop until she was next to her own bed. "Okay, lift my legs up. I want to try and do a handstand."

Anna had been trying to learn how to do a handstand for months. She clearly had the strength but couldn't always find her balance point. Katherine raised Anna's legs so that she was streamlined perpendicular to the floor. "Okay, let go," Anna said. She did so. Anna held her legs straight up in the air for about two seconds then let her legs plop onto the bed so that it looked like she was doing an awkward backbend. Then she bent her knees and threw her legs back over herself and onto the floor, ending up in a squat.

"That was impressive," Katherine said.

"Thanks. Marley from swim team can do a backbend and then walk her legs back over. I can only do it off the bed."

"You'll get it."

Anna stood up on her own bed and gave a little bounce. "Will you practice with me more?"

"Sure, tomorrow."

"Thanks. I don't like it when Daddy helps me. He tries to help too much."

"He's just worried you'll get hurt."

"He worries more than you do." She jumped a little higher, as though testing how high she could bounce before her mother told her to stop.

"Should I worry about you more?"

"No, Daddy should worry less. I bet if I was a boy he wouldn't worry so much." As she said the word "boy," Anna gave an extra-big jump for emphasis.

"You're probably right."

"Why do people worry about girls more than boys?"

"Why do you insist on using your bed as a trampoline?"

Anna jumped off the bed and onto the ground. "Because you won't buy me a trampoline."

"I didn't say that."

"Does that mean we can get one?"

"We'll see."

"That means no, right?"

"Usually."

"Boo."

They heard Hal and Joan downstairs and went down to greet them. After the last-minute instructions and goodbyes, they were off to the Renaissance Cleveland Hotel downtown for prom. Even though Hal griped a bit about having to spend the evening with three hundred high school kids, he gave a little smile when they walked into the ballroom.

"Nice," he said, taking in the desert-themed decorations. "I expected Midnight at the Oasis to be tacky, but they did a good job."

"These girls raised a ton of money for this. And they have good taste," Katherine added. The decorations *were* nice. Brightly colored swaths of fabric were draped across the ceiling, making it look as though they had entered a huge tent. The soft amber and gold lights made everything look a little desertlike. Even the strategically placed fake palm trees looked good. They had plenty of room for eating and dancing, but there were still a few quiet, semiprivate spots where she and the other chaperones would no doubt have to break up a make-out session or two.

"Hi, Mrs. Krenzler!" a voice called, and a gaggle of girls who had been in her Biology II class came over, dutiful boyfriends in tuxedos in tow. Katherine was introduced to each boyfriend in turn, then got to show off Hal, who still looked pretty good in a suit. He was taller than most of these boys, yet somehow their youth and energy made them seem more masculine. She often got annoyed with Hal for his reticence to speak his mind, to share what he was thinking and feeling. As she talked to the girls and their dates, she realized these boys seemed to be putting on variations of the strong-but-silent front. Maybe they were just trying too hard to act like men, not boys. Maybe they were nervous or shy around new people, but they did a mediocre job at polite small talk. Meanwhile the girls talked a mile a minute, answering questions about their summer plans, talking about the after-prom, and complimenting the sexy, strappy shoes.

One girl, Taylor, held back a little, holding her boyfriend's hand and occasionally whispering something to him and giggling. Katherine remembered Taylor as a reasonably good student but the type who always had an excuse that blamed someone or something else if she did poorly on a test or didn't complete an assignment. She hadn't said much to Katherine beyond "Hello," but now she spoke up, just loudly enough to be heard. "Oh look, here comes Zee," she said. It was an innocent enough statement, but Taylor's tone was infested with unmistakable disdain. Katherine turned her head to see Zee Garver, a student she hadn't had but knew by reputation.

Zee had been the subject of a number of conversations in the faculty lounge because of her gender nonconformity. One or two faculty members and a handful of parents had apparently made a stink a year earlier when Zee wore a suit and tie to the junior prom. Katherine hadn't taught at the school then, hadn't had Zee in class, but knew she was an excellent student. She was also one of the stars of the cross-country and swim teams, all of which made her inclined to like the girl. Tonight, Zee was wearing a perfectly tailored tuxedo with a rainbow cummerbund and bow tie. She wore her blond hair super short, a boy cut. If the tux pants weren't so well tailored to show off an unmistakably female hip and rear, she could easily be mistaken for a boy. Her date wore a straight-cut dress reminiscent of a 1920s flapper, right down to a pageboy haircut. Taylor's date snickered as they walked by.

"Bye, Mrs. Krenzler," Taylor said. "Have a nice night." Every word she said was, on the surface, polite, but Katherine could hear an abrasive, sarcastic edge underneath.

"We'd better go too!" the other girls said brightly and followed Taylor over to a table on the far side of the ballroom. She noticed a few of the boys glanced over their shoulders at Zee and her date, not necessarily dirty looks, just looking. Examining.

Hal seemed unfazed by most of this. "Where are we supposed to sit?" he asked. He sounded bored and annoyed already.

"Anywhere. With some of the other teachers, I guess. Don't you think that was kind of weird?" Katherine asked as she scanned the tables for other faculty.

"What? The girl in the tux? Who cares?"

"I don't care. I'm just kind of disappointed that some of my students seem to have a problem with it."

They moved among the tables, Hal hanging back and looking as though he'd rather be anywhere else. Katherine tried to be sympathetic. He hated crowds to begin with and had only met a handful of her colleagues in the short time she'd been at the school. He was polite and friendly whenever she introduced him to someone, but when they finally sat down at a table and had a moment alone, he was silent, dour even. For a moment she almost wished she'd come alone.

"Thanks for being here," Katherine said, and nudged her shoulder to his.

"You're welcome," he sighed. She nudged him again, a little gentler this time. "What are you doing?"

"Um, being playfully romantic?"

"No offense, but being in a roomful of high school kids is the exact opposite of romantic."

She moved one hand onto his thigh under the table. "Come on, doesn't prom night make you feel like a horny teenager?"

"No." He scanned the crowd of kids. "Why are all these girls dressed like prostitutes? I thought prom dresses were supposed to be long and formal."

"Most of them are," Katherine replied, taking her hand off his thigh. She rested her chin on her hands and looked at all the young women in their prom dresses, half of which were cut a couple inches above the knee. The ones that were long and semiformal had slits that showed off firm teenage thighs or necklines that plunged halfway to the basement. They didn't look like the prom dresses she remembered. These girls were dressed like women, deliberately sexy women.

"Dear, you're being too generous," Hal said in his mansplaining voice. "And just for the record, Anna will never, ever be allowed to wear something like that." With a slight nod of his head, he indicated a girl and her date walking past. The girl's dress was tight enough that Katherine truly wondered how she managed to go to the bathroom but short enough that it probably didn't matter. "You can practically see her underwear."

"Why are you looking at teenage girls' butts?"

"Isn't that why they're wearing them? So the boys will look at their butts?"

"You're not a *boy*," she replied. The conversation was heading into argument territory. She wasn't even sure what was at stake here. She didn't necessarily think Hal was wrong, just too judgmental. These were her students, her girls. She knew many of them, knew them as clever, funny, silly human beings. Why should she care that their dresses were short? Wasn't "too short" just a matter of opinion? Yet it still troubled her. Much as she wanted to tell Hal he was being old-fashioned, perhaps even a little sexist, part of her agreed with him.

One of the things she had discovered she loved about teaching at an all-girls school was how free the girls were. Without the daily distraction of boys, most of the girls seemed focused, happy. There was still plenty of drama—teenaged girls seemed to be brimful of drama, but there was also plenty of silliness, of girls being themselves and not caring how they looked. Wearing a super-sexy dress changed that dynamic, as though the first thing you were supposed to notice about any of these girls was a breast, a leg, a well-shaped rear end, not her creativity, her talent for science, an ability to calculate complex numbers in her head. They should be allowed to wear what they wanted, but Hal's words still rang true. She couldn't imagine letting Anna wear a short-short, skintight dress to prom or anywhere else.

Katherine stayed away from any possibly incendiary conversation the rest of the night. Hal being Hal didn't say much, but he went through the motions and even danced a couple slow dances with her. It wasn't exactly a date night, but it was okay. Katherine thought they could have had more fun if Hal would just stop acting as though everything on earth was beneath him.

At the end of the night, after she had made a point of saying goodbye to a few of the other teachers and the principal ("Get the brownie points, babe," Hal encouraged), they stood in the arched entrance to the ballroom and took a last look around. Prom was definitely starting to wind down. A good number of kids had already left for the after-prom.

"Do you have to go to this after-prom thing?" Hal asked.

"I don't *have* to, but it's at Electric Avenue, that retro arcade on the west side? You wanna play pinball and video games all night?"

"Sure, then we'll pay the babysitter half our mortgage this month."

"I'll take that as a no."

"Yes. Can we go?"

Katherine didn't answer. Hal was getting into one of his single-minded moods. He wanted to leave. Period. When he was like this, nothing she or anyone else in the world could say or do would change his mind. Katherine appreciated decisiveness, but a little flexibility once in a while would be nice.

As they turned to go, Taylor came leading her much-slower boyfriend by the hand, talking enough for both of them. "Mel and Gretchen and Ashley are already at Electric Avenue and Caitlyn and her guy are leaving now. I don't want to be the last ones to get there."

Katherine couldn't help but smile watching Taylor's enthusiasm and her spiky-haired boyfriend's lack thereof. Maybe it wasn't just her and Hal.

"I just gotta take a pee break. Meet me right there," she said, pointing to the bank of brass-doored elevators. Taylor gave her boyfriend a kiss and scampered off down the hall in heels, Katherine noticed, that were higher than her own.

They ended up standing in front of the elevators with the boyfriend, who gave a dull "Hey" in response to Katherine's greeting. She was a little surprised when the kid got on the elevator and rode down to the lobby with them. *Maybe he got confused,* she thought. He looked like the type who didn't pay attention.

When they got to the lobby, Katherine asked Hal to wait a moment while she adjusted one of the straps on the sexy, strappy shoes. They were starting to hurt. For a second she felt foolish for having worn them. As she was fixing the shoe, she watched the spiky-haired boyfriend walk over to the registration desk and announce he was checking in for the night.

"That's weird," she whispered to Hal, who was checking his wallet for the parking garage ticket.

"What?"

"Taylor's boyfriend is getting a room."

"So?"

"So that means he isn't taking her to after-prom."

"None of our business," Hal said. "Your shoe okay?" He didn't wait for a response, but as Katherine was now standing upright, took her hand and started walking across the lobby to the door marked "Parking Garage."

"But I'm her teacher. I mean I was last semester." She stopped walking, forcing Hal to momentarily stop as well.

"Katherine, she's past the age of consent, and you aren't her mother."

"We should do something."

"What?"

"I don't know...something."

"It's none of our business," Hal repeated, a little more gently this time. "Let's go." He started walking across the lobby, not waiting, just expecting Katherine to follow. She hesitated, worried that maybe one of her students was getting into something she wasn't expecting and didn't want, wondering if she was overreacting, and mostly feeling a growing sense of anger at Hal for not giving a shit either way.

Hal was holding open the door leading to the parking garage, waiting for her with an annoyed look on his face. Single-minded Hal wanted to go home. Period. That was always what he wanted. He never seemed enthused about going out or anything else for that matter. Katherine took a last look over her shoulder at the spikey-haired boyfriend as she reluctantly followed her husband.

Hal was silent on the ride home. That was pretty typical for him too. Katherine liked to debrief a bit in the car after a big event, while he processed everything internally. The differences in their personalities had always been there. In the past, Hal's quiet ways had been endearing. She could think of a lot of words to describe the way he dealt with—or didn't deal with—the world and the people in it. "Endearing" wasn't one of them.

All through the silent ride home, Katherine kept thinking about the fact that one of her students might need some help. It *was* her business. And Hal had kept her from it.

CHAPTER EIGHT

BETWEEN SOME END-OF-THE-SCHOOL-YEAR EVENTS AND WORK COMMITMENTS, KATHERINE DIDN'T REALLY TALK TO ABRA OR MARGIE FOR MORE THAN A WEEK. When they found a spot at the starting line for the annual five-mile Memorial Day race at John Carroll University, Katherine realized she and Abra hadn't run together since before The Incident With The Knife.

She and Abra always ran the Memorial Day five-miler together. Last year, Eli had run it with them while Margie, the husbands, and the younger kids did the one-mile Fun Run. This year, Joan was doing the five-miler for the first time, and she queued up at the starting line in the middle of the pack in between Katherine and Abra. Eli and his long legs politely said, "See you all at the finish" and headed toward the front of the three hundred or so assembled runners.

Katherine watched the top of his head and its shaggy brown hair move through the crowd. "I remember when I used to smoke that kid in races."

"You always let us win," Joan said.

"That was when you were really little. Once you hit middle school, all bets are off."

"How old do you need to be before I have to start letting *you* win?" Joan asked.

"Gads, you are *so* your mother's daughter," Katherine said.

Joan gave a tickled little grin and drifted a bit closer to the front, maybe so she could start with Eli.

Abra looked over and said, "Sorry I've been MIA for our runs. I've had to get into work early the past week, so I've just been running in the evening."

"No worries. My schedule has been weird too." She checked to see where Joan had gone. There were other runners around them, some chatting, some stretching, some with ear buds firmly planted, all of them waiting for the starting buzzer. In a crowd like that, no one is actually listening to each other. Still, Katherine felt the need to lower her voice. "This may sound strange, but have you noticed any, I don't know, unusual changes to your body lately? Since the last time we all went out?"

Abra's expression made it clear she wasn't holding back information. "No. Why? What's going on?"

"I've had some...changes." This was really an instance where it might be easier to show rather than to tell. "Okay, you know how you've always been faster than I am?"

"No, I'm not," Abra said politely, grabbing each of her feet in turn for a quick quad stretch.

"You are." The announcer had started giving a general outline of the course, telling everyone to pay attention to the volunteers and the arrow signs. The race was going to start any moment. "I feel...faster lately. Stronger."

"That's good, right?"

"Yeah, I'm just not sure why or how." She wasn't exactly sure what she wanted to say. "Do you mind if we don't run together this year?"

"Of course not. You going for a personal record?"

"Yeah, I am." This was true. She felt like she could get a personal record without trying. Hell, she was feeling so strong lately, it felt like she could set a course record if she wanted to, if they even had such things for recreational races. This was just another recreational race among thousands across the country. It wasn't anything special. Maybe she wasn't anything special either—just another middle-aged body running for its life. But maybe she was.

Even after years of running, the moment right before a race started was still nerve-wracking. She'd always start thinking too much about the actual distance she was about to run. The distance would somehow become mammoth, insurmountable in her mind. Today, she was thinking that five miles wasn't nearly long enough.

The hum of conversation quieted down, then there was a heartbeat of absolute silence before the sound of the starting buzzer propelled the crowd forward.

The first hundred yards or so of any race is a process of runners finding their pace and their place. Fast runners pass slower runners and everyone settles in. Katherine used this time to steadily move her way toward the front. She saw Joan and fell into pace next to her. There had been several years where she and Hal thought they'd never be parents. Married and divorced twice, Billy didn't have any kids. For a while, Margie's kids seemed like the closest thing she'd ever get to being an aunt, much less a mom.

"How are you feeling?" Katherine asked.

"Ask me in a couple of miles," Joan replied.

"Abra's right behind you. Do you want to run with her? I'm feeling extra good today and want to go for a personal record. Do you mind?"

"Of course not, go. Beat Eli for me!"

"I'll do my best," Katherine said and sped up again, side-stepping around and easily passing a barrel-chested guy running alongside a trim woman with a serious runner's build. In a recreational race, if you pass someone, you won't see them again. Katherine passed just about everybody, running at a pace that would normally have done her in after about four minutes, a sprint pace, somebody else's pace. Not only did nothing hurt, she never hit the threshold where her heart and lungs couldn't keep up with her body's need for oxygen. She was breathing as easily as if she were walking.

She ran quickly, easily, and very soon was trailing behind the lead pack of a twentysomething white hipster guy with a handlebar moustache and a tattoo sleeve on his left arm; two shirtless guys, one white, one black, wearing John Carroll University shorts; and Eli. That was it. The view from the front of the pack was a lot different than from the middle. For one thing, you had to pay attention to the route instead of merely following the people in front of you. More than that, running with the lead pack felt like freedom.

As she ran, she pondered what the hell was happening to her body. Muscles have a limit. Every time the muscles in her legs strained and worked, they should have developed microscopic tears, tears that would then heal and build stronger muscle. It was the same principle as weight lifting. This was Physiology 101. Only her legs didn't feel sore or fatigued, hadn't felt sore or fatigued in a couple of weeks. Not since the whole Incident With The Knife.

Okay, let's work backward, she thought as she ran. What had happened before The Incident With The Knife? The explosion in which she, Abra, and Margie had been sprayed with liquefied tofu. Before that? Nothing, except the loss of her period. The idea of linking some sort of crazy strength to the loss of her period seemed so ridiculous that she snorted back a laugh right around the second mile marker.

Eli looked over his shoulder to where she was running, just behind him. "Hey, Aunt Katherine. Wow, you're flying."

"So are you," she replied. An almost-eighteen-year-old boy running in front of a forty-seven-year-old woman is logical. He's younger and stronger. It only gets weird if the boy is running in front because the woman is letting him, because she is choosing to run behind for a few miles.

A *knife, an explosion, strength*, she thought. *How does a blast of tofu—no, it was a blast of phytoestrogens*. Could that make a difference? Could that somehow have reacted with her hormonal and physical shift? Somewhere around mile three she thought, *You don't bleed anymore*. This simple statement to herself made something in her brain click into place. *What if you don't bleed at all? What if you can't be hurt?* Maybe she was exponentially faster and stronger because strain didn't harm her muscles. Nothing seemed to harm her. To be sure, she wanted to do one more experiment, but that would have to wait until after she kicked this race's butt.

After the race, everyone congregated at Margie and Karl's house for a cookout. This had been their Memorial Day ritual for years. Even though it sometimes seemed like a lot of work, and Karl would occasionally gripe about having to host half the world, they both enjoyed having their friends over.

Margie loved their hidden three-street neighborhood that was one suburb over from Katherine and Abra. Most of the backyards on their block were open, with kids running back and forth among yards, sprinklers, sandboxes, and swing sets. Joan and Grant liked having Anna around as a temporary little sister. Eli was always nice with the younger kids, although this year he hung around the house, helping Karl and Hal with the grill and Margie in the kitchen because he wanted to learn how to cook before he went to college.

"Better late than never," Margie said.

"That's very admirable," said Katherine as she unloaded the dishwasher. Margie loved that her friends knew her kitchen as well as they knew their own. "Everyone should know how to cook. And not just boxed macaroni and cheese."

"It's hard to learn how to cook when you're the child of a control freak."

Katherine and Abra looked from Margie to each other and started to laugh. "Your mother is not a control freak," Abra said. "Now Katherine: *there's* a control freak."

"It's true. I am. Ask Anna."

"I keep trying to tell you, Eli, you hit the mommy lottery." Margie sighed. She knew she had trained her kids well because Eli completely ignored their teasing. He stood in front of the island in the middle of the kitchen. On the giant wooden cutting board in front of him were a cantaloupe, half a watermelon, a colander of washed purple grapes, and a pint of strawberries. He picked up the large French knife in one hand and balanced the cantaloupe on its stem with the other. "Oh honey, no," Margie said. "Always cut a melon this way," she said, drawing an imaginary line around the equator of the cantaloupe with her finger.

"Oh," Eli said and turned the melon slightly.

"Do you know how to tell if it's ripe?" Katherine asked.

"Yeah. If Mom bought it, it's ripe," Eli said with a smile.

Ignoring him, Margie picked up the melon. "You want it to be soft but not mushy. If it's a rock, it'll take ages to ripen. Here, sniff it."

"Sniff it?" Eli took the cantaloupe gingerly and held it up to his nose. "It smells like cantaloupe."

"That means it's ripe. But not as ripe as that T-shirt—when was the last time you washed it?"

"It was clean this morning."

"Is that the shirt you wore for the race?"

"Yeah. You always tell me not to put clean clothes in the wash."

"If you wore it for the race, it's not clean."

Eli lifted an upper arm to his nose and took a little sniff. "Maybe I'll change."

"It might be a good idea."

"Be right back. Leave the fruit. I'll do it."

Eli loped out of the kitchen and up the stairs. Margie watched her oldest go, feeling a strange mixture of parental pride and relief that she actually needed to tell her teenage son to put on a clean shirt. Some of Eli's OCD tendencies seemed to have lessened as his depression lifted. And she realized she couldn't remember the last time she really had to worry about what he might do to himself later. "He's turned out okay, hasn't he?" she said.

Abra looked up from where she was happily filling deviled eggs. "More than okay, sweetie," she said.

"He's fine," Katherine added.

Margie watched both of her friends for a moment, feeling a wave of love for everyone around her. She waited until Katherine paused in unloading the dishwasher and Abra put down a half-filled deviled egg, and they both looked at her.

"What?" Abra asked.

It seemed like one of those situations where the best course of action is just to dive in. "So," she said brightly, "anybody turn invisible lately or, I don't know, get cut and not bleed?"

"No," Abra said at the same time that Katherine said, "Yeah."

She and Abra both stared at Katherine, who gave a little shrug. The open window above the kitchen sink looked out onto the backyard. Hal and Karl were on the deck, drinking beer and watching the grill. Anna, Grant, and Joan had moved from the creek to playing soccer in the yard with Juno. No time like the present. "Okay, beer, living room, now."

Katherine and Abra didn't protest, and soon they were seated in Margie's living room, where there was some semblance of privacy. "Talk to me," Margie said.

Katherine took a deep breath. "I think there's a connection between the explosion and the whole thing with the knife and what's happening to my body."

"What *is* happening to your body? I mean, you ran an incredible race this morning. Is that what you mean?"

"Yes, but there's more than that." Katherine took a breath and paused as though what she had to say was monumental. "I could have finished the race faster today."

Margie wasn't a runner, but she knew Katherine's final race time was astonishingly fast. She'd finished third overall, even beating Eli, who lost a bit of steam in the final mile. How much faster did she mean?

"You were running, like, five-minute miles the entire way," Abra said.

"Five-twelves actually," Katherine said. It was just like her to have to correct someone.

"Regardless, you were faster than I've ever seen any woman our age run. Not to be rude, but you were faster than I ever thought you were capable of running."

"I wasn't capable of it until the explosion."

Margie thought about that for a moment. The explosion had felt like some kind of turning point, but she couldn't put her finger on why. Joan didn't seem affected—she was still pissed off that it had happened, but she remained the same fourteen-year-old bundle of contradictions she'd always been. Margie herself had had a strange tingly sensation for a few days after it happened, but that was all. That still didn't mean Katherine couldn't have been affected in some way. "What do you think happened?" she asked.

"This is a crude theory—I'd need to see Joan's data to really understand it, but my working hypothesis is that the explosion caused a hormonal shift."

Abra half snorted. "You're kidding, right? How does getting hit with a blast of wet tofu equate to a hormonal shift?"

"Joan had already run the extraction. It was a blast of concentrated phytoestrogens." Katherine paused for a moment, as though looking for the right words. "You know how I told you my period stopped eight months ago? Crazy as it may sound, I think there's a connection between my not bleeding and my *not bleeding*."

If it were anyone but straightforward, meticulous Katherine, if she hadn't seen for herself the knife cutting into Katherine's arm, Margie would have dismissed the whole thing as a joke, as impossible. Still, she couldn't help but say "That sounds nuts."

"I know. But it explains a lot."

"What's the connection with you getting so fast all of a sudden?" Abra asked. She looked unconvinced.

"I have another theory," Katherine said. "Your body has thresholds, points after which you can't go any faster, can't lift any more weight. It's where you've used up all the glycogen stored in your muscles and your heart can't pump blood fast enough to meet your oxygen demands. Essentially your body is so exhausted that it can't do any more work. But if your body can't be hurt, if it *can't hurt*, then it doesn't reach those thresholds. It can go on indefinitely and do anything."

"Like run five-minute miles," Abra said.

"Five-*twelves*," Katherine corrected.

This was all a bit much to take in, but it explained more than just Katherine. "Abra," Margie said, but then wasn't sure what to say. "Has...has anything else unusual happened to you since the..."

Katherine finished the question: "Since The Incident With The Knife?"

"What? Oh, no. I mean, I was there. You both saw me."

"Actually, I didn't see you," Margie replied. "At least for a few seconds I *couldn't* see you."

"So you think the explosion did something to me too? It couldn't have; my period hasn't stopped."

This seemed to make sense, then Katherine said, "Didn't you say you felt like people couldn't see you lately?"

Abra burst out laughing. "Are you saying you think I can turn invisible?"

"Don't look at me," Margie said. "I didn't say it." *I thought it, didn't say it.*

"If people don't notice me lately, it's because I'm middle-aged and flat-chested in a world that likes young and curvy, not because I can turn *inVISible*." Abra waved her arms around as she said "invisible" and added an overwrought, ghostly "Woooo!" before plopping down in the recliner.

"I know it sounds ridiculous," Katherine said.

"It sounds impossible. And from a science teacher, no less."

"It's implausible, but it's not impossible," Katherine said. "And remember, this is coming from a science teacher. You *can* make something invisible—you just have to bend light around an object so that it doesn't cast a shadow and it can't cast a reflection."

"No reflection? So now I'm a vampire. Thanks." Abra leaned the recliner back all the way so that she was almost lying down. "You. Are. Out. Of. Your. Gourd."

Katherine stood up and leaned over the recliner so she could look Abra in the eye and say to her face: "No, I'm not."

Margie heard Eli's heavy footsteps running down the stairs and couldn't help but grin at the sound. "Sometimes I think my children don't actually go down the stairs so much as they succumb to gravity. Could we maybe table this conversation for a moment? Kids," she added with a nod in the general direction of the stairs.

Katherine sat down next to Margie on the sofa and put her beer bottle on the coffee table. "Actually, Eli could help me. I've been doing some experimenting," she said. "But there are things I don't know about bleeding and...cutting."

For a split second, Margie felt her heart stop. She knew what Katherine was asking. Eli hadn't cut for three years, of that she was sure. He was doing great, although sometimes it seemed like she and her eldest were walking through a minefield called emotional stability. She still worried one poorly placed step would blow up their lives again. She looked at Katherine's open, pleading face. "I wouldn't ask under normal circumstances," Katherine said.

"I know you wouldn't," Margie replied.

Margie had always believed that she'd know if one of her children were in trouble, that her gut would instinctively tell her if one of them were in danger. That Maternal SuperSense wasn't going off. Trusting her gut, she called Eli into the living room and asked him to sit down next to her. He looked a little puzzled. "Am I in trouble?" he asked.

"No, no, not at all," Margie said.

"Does somebody have an ugly niece they want me to go out with or something, because you know that won't turn out well."

"No, sweetie. I, um—"

"I" Katherine interjected, "I wanted to ask you—"

"About cutting," Margie said. She could see Eli visibly retreat and suddenly felt horrible for asking him. "Forget it."

She looked at Katherine, who nodded and emphatically said, "Forget it. Wrong question."

Eli looked from his mother to Abra to Katherine. "Why ask me and then say 'forget it'? It isn't something I do anymore," he said with enough conviction that Margie's heart felt a little better.

"I thought you wouldn't want to talk about it."

"No, that's okay. I can talk about it." Eli took a deep breath. "So what do you want to know?"

Katherine took the stammering lead. "We...I wanted to know if you ever knew of anybody who found a way to cut themselves without bleeding."

Eli looked down at the coffee table for a moment. Margie watched his deep brown eyes, tried to follow him into his most painful memories, found that she couldn't. "So, uh...I remember a couple of times in group somebody would talk about how they tried to cut themselves without bleeding so there wouldn't be anything to clean up or they'd try to cut themselves and not leave a mark because they didn't want anybody to know they were cutting. You can't do that, so people would just cut themselves in weird places. I met this one girl who used to cut her pits."

"Her armpits?" Abra asked.

"Yeah. She wanted to feel something, to feel the pain."

"I'll bet she did," Abra said.

"But everybody bleeds," Eli said. "You get cut, you bleed."

"What if you don't feel anything?" Katherine asked suddenly. "I mean, were there any kids who cut themselves or hurt themselves and didn't feel anything? No pain?"

"I can't speak for anyone but myself, but I don't think so. Feeling something, pain or whatever, is kind of the point. There were times when I just felt like this big lump of nothing. So feeling pain was at least feeling, you know, *something*. It kind of gets you high—it makes you feel like you're in control of something. So yeah, it hurt but it made me feel other things too. Sometimes it felt like all the bad things I was feeling were pouring out of the cut with the blood." He paused and looked at the three of them, puzzled. "Why are you asking me this?"

Margie looked from Katherine to Abra then said, "It's a long story. There is nothing wrong and nothing to worry about. Thank you so much for talking to us, honey."

Eli was incredulous. "That's it? Pick my brain about cutting and then tell me to move along? Geez, Mom, I'm not a little kid. You can tell me."

"I can't..." Margie looked helplessly at Katherine. It was her secret to tell.

Katherine stood up. "You know what? Yes, you can. It's time for an experiment. Come on." Without another word, Katherine walked out of the living room and down the short hallway to the kitchen.

"Wow, she must be serious. She didn't even pick up her beer," Eli said.

Margie "tsked" him.

"What?" he protested.

They walked into the kitchen to find Katherine standing by the sink, the long, sharp French knife in her hand, poised over her left arm.

"Whoa, whoa!" Eli said. "Mom, what the hell?" He rushed over and grabbed the knife out of Katherine's hands. "Aunt Katherine, what are you doing?"

"I think I know what she's doing. But why not use this knife?" Margie said and handed Katherine a paring knife.

"Wait, you're *letting* your friend cut herself? Mom, this is messed up."

Margie grabbed Eli and gave him a big hug. "Sweetie, I know this looks strange."

"It's an experiment, Eli," Katherine said. "That's all. I have a hypothesis. It's been tested once. I'm going to replicate it under more controlled circumstances."

"My hypothesis is that you're going to bleed all over the freaking kitchen."

Abra spoke up. "No, she won't, Eli. That's the thing. We're pretty sure she won't." Margie noticed Abra had picked up a dish towel and was holding it at the ready. Abra caught her looking. "Just in case," she added.

Katherine had the knife against her arm. "I'm more than pretty sure," she said. "Here goes nothing." She put the edge of the paring knife up to her right arm and ran the blade across her forearm. Nothing happened.

"That knife probably isn't that sharp," Margie said. "Sorry, I've been meaning to get it sharpened and keep forgetting."

"Mom."

"Sorry."

Katherine placed the knife against her arm and looked completely out of her element. "Eli," she said. "Eli, I know this has to be the weirdest thing your mom and I have ever done, but I have to ask you: how do you cut yourself?"

Eli looked at Margie. "It's okay," she said. "I know it's seems crazy, but it's okay." Eli looked at the knife poised next to Katherine's arm. For a moment, he looked lost and vulnerable. Margie felt a million miles of guilt. She put a hand on his arm. "I'm sorry, sweetie," she said. "Forget it. This isn't fair."

"No, I'm good, Mom. You wouldn't be doing this if you didn't have a good reason. I have no idea what it is, but I trust you."

Margie's eyes welled with tears as she looked up at her son. "Thank you."

Eli took a deep breath. "Okay, put the blade right against your arm, so it's pushing against your skin. Then you push a little harder and turn the blade down just a bit so it can...cut. It's kind of like going off the high dive for the first time. You just have to do it. Press down hard and swipe."

It's a leap of faith, Katherine," Margie said. "It may not hurt at all."

"Of course it's gonna hurt," Eli said.

"No, it won't," Katherine said and sliced her arm.

CHAPTER NINE

ABRA HADN'T BEEN EXACTLY SURE WHAT TO EXPECT, BUT WHEN SHE LOOKED AT KATHERINE'S ARM AND SAW A NARROW CUT AND NO BLOOD, SHE WAS UNABLE TO SPEAK FOR A FEW SECONDS. The first time it had happened, there had been nothing but a lone streetlight and the headlights of the minivan illuminating the scene. Margie's big, sunny kitchen had no shadows, nothing to make you think what you're seeing is a trick of the light. In natural light, what you see is what you get.

Eli's jaw dropped as he stared at Katherine's arm. "You aren't bleeding," he stammered. "Nothing."

"Oh my gosh, you really aren't!" Margie said and started to laugh. Katherine looked up from her arm, her face a combination of shock and relief. "I'm sorry," Margie said. "I know it isn't funny but it's—wow."

Katherine's face broke into a huge smile. "Yeah," she said. "I kind of can't believe that worked. It didn't even hurt. I mean, I felt it, but it was like running your fingernail against your arm or something." She took the knife and made a second slash on her arm. Still no blood.

"Don't get too into the cutting thing, Aunt Katherine."

"I promise, this is the last time I will ever, ever cut myself on purpose," Katherine said and dropped the knife into the sink. Katherine and Margie just stood and laughed for a second, then even Eli joined in. Abra understood their relief, but there was more going on here. She walked around the kitchen island to where the others were standing and reached for Katherine's arm, stopping the laughter.

"Look," she said.

All four of them stared at the two thin red lines on Katherine's arm, the only indication that there had ever been any cuts there.

"The scar from the other night is completely gone," Katherine admitted.

"You've done this before?" Eli said.

"No! Lord no, Eli. Please just, keep this to yourself, okay?' Katherine stammered.

"Aunt Katherine had an accident the other night, that's all," Margie added. "There's nothing to worry about." At that moment, Grant, Joan, and Anna came bursting into the kitchen through the deck door.

"Dad says everything is ready," Grant announced. "They sent us in to get the sides."

Joan took in the pile of uncut fruit, the half-filled deviled eggs, and lack of other food and said disdainfully, "Which aren't even ready."

Margie exchanged a look with Abra that said *Teenage girls are supposed to have an attitude, right?*

"Mom?" Anna asked, walking over to examine Katherine's arm where the two thin pink lines were still visible. "Are you okay? What happened?"

"Nothing. I think I scratched myself too hard or something." Katherine reassured Anna that she was fine as they all made a quick effort to finish the side dishes and get everything outside and onto the picnic table.

Later in the afternoon, after they had eaten, the younger kids and most of the adults were outside playing an enthusiastic game of Sardines. Abra came out of the downstairs bathroom to find Eli in the kitchen eating what was either his second or third hamburger of the day.

"Beware," he said, "Anna's looking for you."

"Thanks for the warning. Are you ready for graduation?"

Eli had just taken a huge mouthful of hamburger but gave a muffled "Uh-huh" and a thumbs-up.

"See you out there," Abra said as she walked around Eli and headed for the deck door. The second she stepped outside, Anna bounded up the deck steps and grabbed her hand. "Aunt Abra! It's your turn! Come and hide with me."

"Hide where? What are we playing?" she asked as Anna pulled her along to the oak tree in the center of the yard, where everyone but Eli was standing. Juno was there too, but she was mingling around the humans, making sure no one had gone missing. An aging tire swing that Karl had put up when the kids were much smaller hung from one of the tree's lower branches, and Joan was standing on it, swinging away in all her fourteen-year-old glory.

"We're playing Sardines, even the grown-ups," she announced. "It's like reverse Hide and Seek—one person hides and then everyone else has to go and look for her."

"Or him," Grant said.

"And when you find the hider, you join her—or him"—she managed to make a quick face at Grant without losing a beat—"in the hiding place. And it's over when everybody has found the hiding place."

"How do you win?" Abra asked.

"You don't," Margie said. "It's cooperative instead of competitive."

"Hippie," Abra said gently, to which Margie only smiled.

"Are you ladies gonna gab all day, or are we going to play?" Hal said.

"Play!" Anna squealed. She grabbed Abra's hand and whispered, "I have the best hiding place." Everyone else closed their eyes and started counting. ("To forty this time," Anna commanded.) "Come on," she said and started running across the lawn.

Abra good-naturedly followed right behind Anna, who was making a beeline toward a stand of trees and bushes that connected Margie's and the neighbor's yards. She guessed there must be a little spot in the middle of all that greenery where Anna wanted to hide. Abra was wearing an old pair of cotton shorts and the new race T-shirt from this morning—a little mud and a few grass stains wouldn't hurt that outfit. She was happy to go anywhere her surrogate niece wanted to hide. Juno ran alongside them. As they ran, Abra kept one eye on Anna and one ear on everybody else, who were gleefully counting up a storm. With her mind momentarily focused on other things, she didn't notice when Juno cut right in front of her. Abra saw the dog at the last second and tried to pivot to avoid a collision.

She didn't succeed. As her right ankle twisted and she hit the grass, she felt an intense pain in her gut. The only time she could remember feeling something similar was right before she took a flying leap at Sean and his knife. "Crap!" she hissed, not loud enough to get Anna's attention or to drown out the drone of "Twenty-eight, twenty-nine..." coming from the tire swing. Nobody but Juno heard her. And nobody but Juno could see her either.

CHAPTER TEN

ABRA SAT ON THE GRASS, ANGRY, FRUSTRATED, AND IN SERIOUS PAIN. JUNO WAS LICKING HER FACE AS IF TRYING TO APOLOGIZE FOR KNOCKING HER OVER. Her right ankle was throbbing and already swollen. *Dammit, dammit, dammit,* she thought. She looked up at the deck and saw Eli staring at her in shock. Why didn't the boy come down and help her up? She looked over at Anna and saw an equally surprised expression on the little girl's face. Anna was only a few feet away, yet she wasn't making any move to help either.

Abra made a half-hearted attempt to get up on her own, but it hurt. Sure, it was only a twisted ankle—it'd probably be okay in a week or two—still, why the hell wasn't anyone helping her?

She felt...different. She had experienced this feeling just once before, a sensation of being lighter than air, of floating. She looked again at her puffy ankle. She could see it. Juno was still licking and sniffing her, so clearly she was visible to the dog. It wasn't like Eli or Anna to just stand and stare and not come over to help. They weren't staring at her, exactly. Their eyes weren't focused on *her.* It was more like they were staring at where she had been.

For a moment, she just sat, trying to be fully conscious of how light her body felt. It felt downright ethereal. Then she looked at her quickly swelling right ankle, and the pain and her body came rushing back.

From over by the tire swing came the shout of "Forty! Ready or not, here we come!" and then a general chorus of "Why aren't you hiding?" and "What happened to Abra?" Katherine reached her first.

"Can you get up?" she asked as she gently helped Abra to her feet. She leaned on Katherine during the brief controlled mayhem as everyone tried to give advice. Those few seconds of pain and solitude on the grass didn't seem so bad anymore. Finally Hal and Eli locked arms and picked her up chair-style.

"Get her inside," Margie said. "I'll get some ice."

"Mom, I need to talk to you," Anna said.

"Hold on a second, sweetie," Katherine replied. "Let's get Aunt Abra fixed up first."

"But it's *about* Aunt Abra," Anna said in a stage whisper.

"Don't worry, sweetie. She's going to be fine."

In the jumble of people surrounding her, Abra realized no one was actually paying attention to her—they were all focused on her ankle and offering their opinions on how badly she was hurt. Abra caught Anna's eye and got a broad smile in return. Anna held her skinny little kid arms out at her sides, glanced left and right as though she was looking for something that wasn't there, then put her hands to the side of her head and gave Abra a crazy, shocked look. Anna had obviously seen something surprising, something about Abra. But she hadn't done anything except fall and hurt herself.

Hal's vantage point gave him a good look at Abra's ankle. "Do you have an Ace bandage at home? 'Cause you're gonna need it."

"You can borrow my crutches from when I hurt my ankle last year," Grant offered.

"Do you want to go to the ER?" Margie asked.

"No, I don't think it's that bad."

Eli and Hal carried her inside to the family room, where Karl propped up her ankle on the mess of throw pillows that were older than Grant ("But not quite as dirty," he quipped) while Margie went to the kitchen for some ice. She returned holding a family-size bag of mixed vegetables wrapped in a dish towel.

"It's cold and it conforms to the shape of your ankle better than ice," she explained as she placed it on Abra's ankle.

After a few moments fussing, Abra found herself surrounded by a circle of adults and children. They were all friendly faces, but having everyone staring at her felt a little awkward. "You know, I don't think this is going to heal in the next five minutes," she joked.

"You're right," Margie said. "Shall we take you home?"

Karl offered to drive Abra back to her house, but Margie nixed it. "I'll take her. You have to be at work early tomorrow," she said. "Everyone here under the age of eighteen has to go to school tomorrow. Even people graduating in eight days and turning eighteen in thirty-seven days." Eli rolled his eyes. "And you have to teach in the morning," she said to Katherine.

"To be fair, you have to go to work too," Katherine said.

"Yes, but I just have to answer the phone; I don't have to *think*."

"It's finals week. I don't have to think either, just proctor exams."

Margie ended up driving Abra home, and Katherine promised to drive Abra's car back to her house in the morning.

Once she was settled in the passenger seat of Margie's minivan, Abra let herself sink back and be still. Being around her family of choice was always equal parts lovely and tiring. Karl had put some ice in a plastic bag for her. After it slipped off her ankle the third time, Abra just put the bag on the seat next to her.

"Does it hurt?" Margie asked with a glance in Abra's direction.

"Not so much now. Thanks for driving me home," Abra said.

"Are you kidding? Everybody else is cleaning up my house. I feel like I'm getting away with something."

They made a quick pit stop at the drugstore so Margie could run in and buy an Ace bandage and some ibuprofen. As she waited in the car, Abra replayed her tumble on the lawn over and over. There was something odd, something she couldn't explain about it. "Something happened when I hurt my ankle," she said as Margie got back in the car.

"What?"

"I don't know..."

Margie shifted the van into reverse and backed out of the parking spot. "You brought it up. You obviously want to talk about it."

Abra tried to clear her thoughts and just speak the truth, the facts. "The only other time I felt like this was the night I knocked over Sean with the knife." Margie didn't say anything, but a raise of her eyebrow said enough. "Right before I knocked him over, I had this intense pain all through my abdomen, like my body was turning inside out. I had that same feeling tonight, right when I tripped."

"Was it from the pain of hurting your ankle?"

"No, it was just before that—that split second when I was going down. My ankle didn't really start to hurt until I was sitting on the grass. But both times, I had this strange sensation after the gut pain. Like I was floating."

The word "floating" hung in the middle of the minivan. Abra could almost see the word "floating" hovering—well, floating—right there underneath the interior light. *What a silly thought.*

"Maybe you were disassociating," Margie offered.

"Maybe."

They had pulled into her driveway. Abra was immediately grateful for having bought such a tiny house. She'd told Grant not to bother with the old crutches, but Karl had put them in the car anyway. They were almost too short—almost.

"Good thing Grant's so tall," Margie said.

"Good thing I'm so short."

"You're perfect just as you are."

The idea of using crutches had at first seemed like an admission that the ankle was worse than she cared to admit, but it did make getting around much easier. Abra managed the three steps from the side door to the kitchen on crutches without too much of a problem. Her bedroom was on the second floor, but the small guest room and bathroom on the first floor would do just fine for a few days. Margie went upstairs to bring down a week's worth of clothes and Abra's toiletries from the second floor while Abra plopped down on the sofa in the living room and put a few pillows under her leg. Clint jumped up and gave her ankle delicate little cat sniffs.

"Hey buddy," she said, and managed to pull him close for a cuddle until the cat jumped down and meowed loudly. "Oh, you didn't get fed tonight. No wonder you're ticked off."

She picked up her crutches and hobbled into the kitchen and over to the corner where Clint's food and water bowls were. She leaned one crutch against the counter and, using the other one for balance, bent over on her good leg and picked up the food bowl. It was kind of like doing the triangle pose in yoga. "No problem," she said, proud of her flexibility and balance. The large plastic container where she stored the dry cat food was at the opposite end of the L-shaped kitchen. Carrying the cat bowl over there while each hand was already holding a crutch was problematic. She put it back on the floor and slid the empty bowl along the floor with a crutch until it was next to the shelf where the cat food container was. "Guess what, Clint?" she said brightly. "Your bowl is getting moved over here until further notice."

Margie came downstairs, hands full of clothes, and called Abra into the guest room. Then she apologized for getting Abra up, even though Abra was already up. She let Margie fuss over her a little bit. Abra went down to Florida to visit her mother once a year at Christmas and let her mom make a fuss over her, but that was it. She wasn't in the habit of being nurtured like this.

Margie set up Abra on the sofa with her ankle elevated and got her a glass of water, a fresh bag of ice ("With a bowl to put it in later so it won't melt all over the place in case you fall asleep"), the television remote, the book she'd been reading, and her reading glasses and set them all within easy reach. "Is there anything else you need? Do you want me to stay?"

"I'm fine. Thank you," Abra said. She sighed. Maybe being nurtured once in a while wasn't such a bad thing. "You're a good mom."

"No, I'm not. But I play one on TV," Margie replied and leaned over to give her a hug. "I'm going to go downstairs and clean Clint's litter box for you. Then I'm leaving. Good night. I'll talk to you tomorrow."

"Thanks for everything," Abra said. She leaned back against the pillows and realized just how tired she was.

"My pleasure," Margie said as she walked out of the living room. She heard Margie's footsteps go down to the basement, and, a few minutes later, Abra heard the click of the lock in the side door just as she fell asleep.

CHAPTER ELEVEN

KATHERINE HELPED CLEAN UP AT MARGIE AND KARL'S HOUSE, THEN SHE AND HAL GOT A RELUCTANT ANNA TO GO HOME. Anna never liked leaving the Josephs' house because it was the closest she ever got to having siblings.

Katherine often talked to Anna about her own mother, who died when Anna was a baby. She always said the one thing that made her sad was that Anna never got to know her grandmother. But late at night, when it was just her and Hal, she would admit a second regret—how much she wished that Anna had a sibling. Hal was ten years older than she. When they met, he was just a smart, sexy guy in his late thirties. It hadn't seemed like much of a stretch to tie her future to his. It was only after they struggled with infertility then started the adoption process, after they had wasted time and energy with a public system that wanted them to foster when they only wanted to adopt and then switched to international adoption that their age difference became an issue. Hal didn't want to be fifty years older than his child and didn't want to retire with a child in high school. Over the years, Katherine had secretly hoped for a gift from the universe in the form of a surprise pregnancy. Hal wouldn't say no to that—he just didn't think it was responsible to pursue another adoption.

Now that she had crossed over the hormonal bridge, the decision seemed final. No more periods, no more opportunities to get pregnant. They were destined for one child. *But what a kid*, she thought as she tucked Anna into bed. Anna was one of those people who attracts other people, the kind of kid teachers love to have in class because they're smart and kind and funny and other kids like to play with for the same reason.

Anna always preferred to have her mother tuck her in, while Hal had become the preferred morning parent so Katherine could run. Katherine loved bedtime, loved the honesty and candor that came out as her daughter lingered between wakefulness and sleep. It was the time of day when Katherine learned things like the name of the first boy Anna ever really liked (*In third grade?*) and that a kid at school had asked if she knew her "real" parents. (Anna had said, "Yes, I live with them," which made Katherine's heart soar.) Tonight, she learned something she already suspected.

Anna was cuddled under her comforter, along with a fleece Cleveland Indians blanket she had taken a liking to, her pink crocheted baby blanket on which the entire mojo of the house seemed to rest, and fourteen stuffed animals of varying sizes and species.

"How is that comfortable?" Katherine asked. "It looks lumpy."

"It's not. It's cozy," Anna replied plainly.

"And you aren't too warm with all those blankets?"

"No, I'm fine."

"Okay then. Lights out—it's an hour past your bedtime and you still have school tomorrow. And so do I." Katherine turned out the light and was about to leave Anna's room when her daughter's voice stopped her.

"Mommy, wait. I have to tell you something. It's important." Something in Anna's voice told Katherine that this truly was important, more so than the time, for instance, she had woken Katherine up at 2:33 a.m. because she absolutely had to tell her mother that if they ever got another dog, "Crumpet" would be a great name for it.

She kept the light off but went back into the bedroom and sat down on the edge of Anna's bed. With just the light from the hallway, Anna's little round face was mostly in shadow, but Katherine could still see the expression in her eyes. Whatever she had to say, it was gonna be a doozy. *Dear God, please don't let her have kissed a boy at school. It's way too early for that*, she thought. "What it is it, sweetie?"

"Okay, you know when we were playing Sardines and you were all counting and Aunt Abra and I went to go hide and then Aunt Abra fell? When she fell..." Anna paused, as though she wasn't sure if she should say what she wanted to say. "Okay, when she fell, Aunt Abra disappeared. She can turn *invisible!*" Anna whispered the last word, as though it was too amazing even to be spoken out loud. "Eli saw it too."

Katherine was speechless. To have Anna and Eli see the same thing she and Margie saw the night of The Incident With The Knife seemed like confirmation of something that was too strange and unbelievable to get her head around. There was no reason for Anna to lie. And at nine years old, she knew the difference between reality and fantasy. "Did you talk to Eli about this?"

"No...but he was right there on the deck, he was looking around for her too. She disappeared. And then we both saw her just pop right back up. Like this *pop!*" She flipped a finger in her cheek to make the sound.

"Are you sure she wasn't hiding somewhere and then just jumped from behind a tree or something?"

"It was *after* she hurt her ankle. She couldn't jump out from behind anything; she was just rolling around on the ground like, 'Owie! Owie! Owie!' *She wasn't there,* and then she was."

Hal poked his head into the bedroom. "Excuse me, but wasn't it lights-out about ten minutes ago?"

If the situation were reversed, Hal would say she should lighten up and stop being a stickler for rules. She tried not to let her annoyance show. "Just a minute," she said. Katherine stood up and then bent down to kiss Anna on the forehead. "You need to go to sleep now, sweetie. But I'm going to ask you not to talk about this to anybody else, okay?"

"Why not?"

"It's kind of a big thing, isn't it? Some people might not believe you."

Anna's big, almost-black eyes looked directly into hers. "It's true."

"I know," Katherine replied, and somehow she knew that it was.

⊛ ⊛ ⊛

Katherine woke up at her usual time the next morning and put on her running clothes. But instead of her regular run, she grabbed Abra's car keys and drove Abra's car to her house. She opened the side door by the kitchen and poked her head inside. "Abra?" she called tentatively. Maybe it was too early, but this was the time Abra woke up every day, the time they met to run most mornings.

Clint greeted her at the top of the three little steps leading from the side door to the kitchen. "Meow to you too," Katherine said as she scooped the cat into her arms. "Abra? Are you awake?" she called. This time she heard a groggy voice coming from the living room. Katherine walked through the skinny "L" of a kitchen and dining area and hung a left into the living room. Abra was there, still in her clothes from the day before. "Oh honey..." Katherine said when she saw her disheveled friend. "How do you feel?"

"Crappy."

"Can I get you anything?"

"A bedpan. Or not." Abra gathered up her crutches and hobbled off to the bathroom while Katherine cleaned up the bag of melted ice and her glass from the night before. It seemed proactive. She had originally planned to just return the car, see how Abra was, and then go for her run. Instead she started making breakfast. By the time Abra emerged from the spare bedroom in some clean clothes, Katherine had scrambled eggs, toast, and orange slices on the kitchen table.

Abra entered the kitchen, a little surprised at the effort. "You didn't have to do that," she said, leaning on the crutches and staring at the breakfast on the table.

"Sure I did," Katherine replied. "You're my friend and I love you."

"Shouldn't you be running?"

"I'd rather have breakfast with you," Katherine said as she sat down opposite Abra. "But I have to eat fast so I won't be late for work."

They ate in silence for a moment, then Katherine said what had been on her mind all night. "You wanna hear the cute thing Anna said to me before she went to bed last night?"

Abra smiled. "Of course."

"She said you can turn invisible and that she and Eli both saw you when you reappeared."

Abra calmly bit a mouthful of toast, chewed, swallowed, and slowly washed it down with a sip of tea. Only then did she look at Katherine. "Do you know how ridiculous that sounds?"

"Yes. I also know that my kid doesn't tell lies. And neither do I and neither does Margie." This was the crux of the issue. It was the most ridiculous thing she'd ever heard. She would have said it was impossible except that she herself had run five-minute twelve-second miles in a race the day before and then sliced her arm open and was completely unaffected by both events. "There are now at least four people who've seen you turn invisible and then reappear. We all can't be seeing things."

"I have no idea what to say to this," Abra murmured.

"Me either. Maybe we don't say anything right now." Katherine was used to having answers, to being able to find the answer to any question. To have this question, situation—what would you even call it? To have this dangling in front of her with no discernible explanation was both infuriating and enticing.

"Trust me, I'm not about to go around telling people I can suddenly turn invisible or that you've become somehow indestructible." Abra looked at her tea mug for a moment. "This is nuts," she said without looking up.

"I know," Katherine sighed. She leaned back and took a bracing gulp of tea. It had cooled to the perfect drinking temperature.

The two of them sat at Abra's kitchen table, Katherine staring at her toast and absentmindedly petting Clint, who was purring around her ankles, Abra looking intently at the eggplant-purple kitchen wall. "You know I was going to paint my kitchen this summer. That's going to need to wait awhile," she mused.

Katherine smiled at this feeble attempt to change the subject. She wasn't any more comfortable talking about it than Abra was. "These are like, um, superpowers," she said quietly. Saying that with a straight face took a lot of effort.

"Yeah," Abra replied. Their eyes met and they both half snorted a giggle. "That is the most ridiculous thing I've ever heard."

"I know, but Anna saw you. Margie and I saw you. Eli saw you."

The intensity in Abra's voice matched her own. "And we all saw *you*."

Katherine wasn't sure how to respond. She had growing empirical evidence that her body was at the very least becoming less susceptible to injury and growing stronger and faster out of proportion to her current workout schedule. Using words like "indestructible" felt beyond premature. "I'm gonna need a little time to wrap my head around this."

"Me too," Abra said. "Hey, you should get going or you'll be late for school."

Katherine glanced up at Abra's silver Art Deco–style kitchen clock. "Holy crap, yes," she said, jumping up.

"Do you want me to drive you home?"

Katherine was hurriedly picking up the breakfast dishes and loading the dishwasher, but Abra's question made her stop. "Darling Abra, I appreciate the offer, but you shouldn't be driving anywhere. In fact, you should probably think about taking the day off from work."

"For one brief, shining moment, I forgot about the ankle," Abra said.

"That's good; it means you're healing or something."

"Thank you for everything," Abra said. "You've been awesome."

"If the situation were reversed, you'd do the same for me, right?" Katherine finished putting everything in the dishwasher. "Okay, gotta go. Call if you need anything."

Katherine sprinted the entire way home, feeling as though she could conquer the world should it need conquering.

CHAPTER TWELVE

Margie and Juno had an understanding. She took the dog for a walk twice a day; in return Juno offered undying love and loyalty and never asked to be driven to a friend's house or to a practice. Most of the time, Margie felt that she spent her life behind the wheel of the minivan, driving somebody somewhere. Even though Eli had his driver's license, more often than not she couldn't give him the car because Joan or Grant needed to be at swimming or baseball or soccer practice or piano or cello lessons or a friend's house or *somewhere*. Her rear end might as well be permanently attached to the driver's seat.

"I'm going to teach you how to drive, Juno," she told the dog on their morning walk. "You're a smart dog. You could do it." She had considered taking up running so she could go out with Katherine and Abra in the mornings, but they were longtime runners. She'd only slow them down. And she had to admit that she loved the solitude of walking with the dog in the early morning. It was perhaps the only time of the day when no one asked her for anything.

Back when Karl was working seventy-hour weeks as an associate in a big firm, they had taken the plunge and bought the worst house in the best neighborhood they could afford. It had friendly neighbors, big yards, and old trees. The only bad thing was the lack of sidewalks. When they were childless, it didn't seem like such a big deal. Once her kids started riding bikes, Margie had pangs of anxiety whenever they wanted to ride around the block. Sometimes she envied Katherine's cozy older neighborhood filled with smaller houses and busy sidewalks, but Margie loved their house, loved the way the backyard met up with all the other backyards and led down to a little creek. The only thing she didn't love was the guy in the black SUV who used the neighborhood as a shortcut and sped down her street every morning going twenty miles over the speed limit. The driver's schedule must have matched hers, because he invariably came zooming by when she was walking Juno. She couldn't change her work schedule, and the dog needed a morning walk. An early-morning sidestep out of the way of a speeding car was a small price to pay for a job that let her live the way she wanted.

At that first temp job after college, Margie decided she enjoyed working in schools. The hours were great even if the pay wasn't—her workday hours generally matched the kids' school hours and she had summers off to be with them, which saved a fortune in childcare and summer camps when they were little. Granted, she probably couldn't have done it if she hadn't married a lawyer, but her life worked. Working as the office secretary at Adrian Elementary School wasn't the career path she had dreamt of years ago, but it made her happy. Aristotle said happiness was the one goal that was an end in itself, and he was pretty much the *New York Times* of philosophers. She was happy she never had to think about work when she wasn't at work. There were enough people in her house; she didn't need to bring her job home too.

Eli going to college in the fall had started her thinking about her job in a new way. In seven years, Grant would be graduating from high school. Once all her kids were grown, what would be the point in having the summer off if they weren't there?

The week after Memorial Day was packed with the last few days of school. Margie was too busy to brood, which was just as well. She had never found brooding or worrying to do much good. Saturday brought a rare evening to herself. Karl and Grant had a guys' night out at the movies and the arcade, Joan slept over at a friend's house, and Eli went to a graduation party. Margie had settled in with the dog, a book, and a large glass of wine when Eli texted: "*Party a bust. Can u pick me up?*"

While Eli was old enough to drive himself, if he took the van, half a dozen kids were guaranteed to ask him for a ride. It just seemed like an invitation to an accident. Dropping him off and picking him up felt safer, and Eli didn't have to say no to a bunch of kids asking for a ride.

She brought Juno along for company. The dog loved to ride in the car. So much of an animal's life is dependent on where and with whom it lives; Margie always felt responsible for the dog having a good time.

The party was on a street called Edenhurst, a ten-minute drive away. Eli just said it was being thrown by "this kid named Christopher," who had a brother in Joan's grade. Eli's text said that the house was set far back from the street. If it weren't for the cars parked up and down the block, she never would have spotted it. The heavily wooded yard stretched a good two hundred feet from the street to the house.

Margie texted Eli to let him know where she was. He texted back, "*Talking to Jamis. Party just got better. 10 min. Plz?*" Jamis was one of two boys who were openly out in the graduating class. Eli was not the other one. Although Margie kept wanting to ask why Eli would be interested in a boy named after a brand of bicycle, she was happy he was talking to somebody who might actually like him back. She could wait ten minutes.

Margie scratched Juno's head for a bit, scruffing up the dog's fur so she looked like an Ewok. For some reason, the dog loved this. Out of boredom, Margie ate one of the mini Snickers bars stashed in the glove compartment. She hadn't had dessert after dinner, so she ate another one.

"Okay, Juno. I'm going to stretch my legs. Sorry I forgot your leash. You stay here and guard the car." She opened all the windows a few inches so the dog would be okay. The evening air was cool but not cold. After a wave of hot flashes earlier, it felt refreshing. Juno whimpered as Margie got out of the car. "I'll be back. I just have to go get Eli." The dog wagged her tail at the mention of Eli's name. Margie suspected Juno's vocabulary had expanded to include the names of her fellow pack members.

There were so many cars on the street that Margie had ended up parking a full block away from the house. As she started down the sidewalk in the direction of the party house, she saw a group of three girls and one guy walking toward her. In the glow of the streetlight, she recognized the boy as a sometime friend/acquaintance of Eli. She was pretty sure his name was Derek. The four kids had been talking and laughing but quieted down as soon as they got close to Margie. "Hey, Mrs. Joseph," the boy said.

Rather than get his name wrong, she just said, "Hi and congratulations!" The kids gave a chorus of "Thanks." As they passed by each other, Margie saw them off with a "Drive safely, kiddos."

"We will!" one of the girls said, and then they all erupted into giggles. As she neared the house, she could hear a low hum of music and voices. Were this kid's parents even home? Lucky for them the house was so far from the street. If it were right alongside the neighbors' houses, somebody would start complaining. It was the perfect party house. No wonder half the kids in the graduating class seemed to have shown up here.

She knew better than to go anywhere near the house, but it was nice to take a little evening walk. Margie walked past two more houses and crossed a side street. Knowing that Eli's ten minutes was more likely to be twenty, she kept going. When she reached Richmond Road, one of the main north–south arteries through the area, she turned around and started to walk back. As she neared the party house again, she spotted a car coming slowly down the street toward her. The windows had writing in soap on the sides that read "Class of 2018 Rules!" The car was full of teenage boys. So full, in fact, that one of them was sitting on the hood.

"Speed up!" one of the boys inside yelled. The driver obliged.

The kid on the hood whooped then screamed, "Okay, okay! Stop!" to a chorus of "Loser!" and "Wuss!" The car jerked to a stop, and the boy on the hood slid forward and toppled off onto the street.

"Holy shit, man! You almost killed me," he exclaimed and took probably more time than was necessary to get up, just to show how big a hit he had taken.

One of the boys said, "You just need more liquid courage, dude." There was a bustle of trash talk and movement as the first boy climbed into the passenger seat and two other boys got out of the car and scrambled onto the hood. They were all so engrossed in their thrill riding that they didn't notice the woman standing on the sidewalk until she pulled the Mom Card.

Margie hadn't planned on saying anything at first, but she could see this escalating. *There's a reason it's ille-*

gal for teenagers to get drunk, she thought. *They do stupid things*. Where the hell was Eli? He could help, but he was still in the party talking to the funky and fabulous Jamis Barberton. It was up to her. She yelled, "What the hell are you boys doing?" in the same overly deep voice Karl used to yell at the dog when Juno tried to steal food off the coffee table. It worked. The boys froze.

She walked up to the car, a big four-door sedan that seemed about to explode with teenage testosterone, and laid one hand on the edge of the hood. The two boys now perched on the hood shrank into the smallest balls two teenagers can make, as though this crazy lady might not notice them if they could just melt into the car hood.

Margie's heart was pounding. She kept trying to tell herself that she had nothing to be afraid of. After all, she was the grown-up in this situation. She looked at the kid driving, a ruddy-faced boy with thick black hair that hung across his forehead like the raccoon tail on Davy Crockett's hat. He sat behind the wheel of the car, looking out the open window at her, mouth slightly agape. Margie kept her left hand on the car, figuring the kid wouldn't try to make a quick getaway if she was still touching the car. The hood felt cool—they obviously hadn't been at this very long. "Do you really think this is a good idea?" she asked the driver.

"Is what a good idea?" he said blankly. Margie didn't say anything, just tilted her head slightly to the side as though she was trying to get a better look at him. Kids would always cave if you waited long enough. "We're just playing around," he added mildly.

"You're playing around with your lives," Margie said. The hood was starting to feel hot, very hot, but Margie kept her hand there just in case. "You're supposed to ride inside the car, not on the hood."

"It's a free country," the kid said, and a few of the other boys snorted back laughs.

Margie was starting to feel foolish. Why had she thought a bunch of drunk teenage boys would listen to her? Now her hand was starting to feel very hot—not her hand exactly; the metal of the car hood around her hand felt like it was burning up. She realized she had started to sweat; either she was nervous or this was the most epic hot flash she'd ever had.

"You can't tell us what to do," one of the boys in the backseat said. The streetlight cast deep shadows on the car. She couldn't see the kid's face, only that he was sitting in the middle. "Fat old lady can't tell us what to do," he muttered just loud enough for everyone to hear.

Margie felt the area around her hand get hotter as she said, "If you're acting like idiots, I can."

The two boys sitting on the hood jumped off with a lot of unnecessary noise. "Get back on. She can't stop us," the loudmouthed kid in the backseat said.

"No man, it's too hot," one of them said.

There was a sizzling sound, and slowly steam began to rise from one side of the hood. Margie still had her hand on the car, feeling the heat grow, and suddenly she realized that she felt the heat because it was coming from her. She turned her eye from the driver of the car to the hand that still rested on the car. She was causing the car to overheat.

"What are you doing to my car, lady?" the driver said. He turned off the engine, but the steam from under the hood only increased.

The first time she gave blood, back when she was seventeen, Margie had been fascinated by watching the blood flow from the needle, through the clear rubber tubing, and into the bag. The fact that the needle was stuck in her arm, that it was *her* blood, didn't bother her. The process was more compelling than the small prick of pain from the needle. She had that same feeling of removed fascination now as she kept her hand on the car hood, feeling the heat flow from her body to the car. When she replayed the words "fat old lady" in her head, she could feel the heat intensify, and there was a satisfying rise in steam coming from the car. The horrified looks of the driver and his friends were even more satisfying.

The two boys who'd been on the hood had backed away from the car, and those inside were slowly getting out, as though Margie might turn her hot hand on them. She only removed her hand from the car when the mouthy kid in the backseat got out. Ironically, he was kind of pudgy himself, with a soft, round middle that would be a potbelly before he was thirty. She turned to face the kid head-on. "Guess what?" she said to his bewildered, chunky face. "I *can* stop you."

Margie took a dozen steps across the tree lawn to the sidewalk and came face-to-face with her eldest child. Eli stared at the boys and the steaming car and then looked at his mother in amazement.

"Come on," she said.

Eli wisely didn't say a word, just followed his mother back to the minivan, where Juno greeted them as though they had been gone three days instead of twenty minutes. They drove in silence for two blocks before Eli asked, "Mom?"

Margie's nerves were still on edge and her head too filled with what had just transpired, too full of questions to talk. "Not now," she replied. When she didn't say anything else, Eli took the hint, although Margie could tell by the way he was playing this complicated little game with his fingers that he was doing everything in his power to stay calm. The finger game was something Eli had done ever since he was a little boy and had to be patient. Eli's fingers danced in his lap during the ten-minute car ride home. Margie pulled the van into the garage, killed the engine, got out, and let Juno into the yard. She still hadn't said anything else to Eli. What do you say to your child when you just caused a car to overheat purely by touch? Instead she wandered out into the backyard, watching the dog sniff this way and that, hot on the trail of something.

Eli gingerly walked up and stood next to her. She could hear him shuffling back and forth on the balls of his size-thirteen shoes. "Um, Mom?" he said finally.

"Whatever you're going to say, Eli, I don't know the answer," Margie said. "I don't know how or why that happened."

"I was just going to say that that was totally amazing."

"Thank you."

"And you really need to call Aunt Katherine and Aunt Abra."

CHAPTER THIRTEEN

On Sunday morning, when the rest of the family was still in bed and Joan at her sleepover, Margie sat at the wooden, oval-shaped table that took up half the kitchen. The kitchen table always seemed be populated by stacks of stuff. There were bills, or an article that Margie thought Karl would like, or offers on a less expensive natural gas choice, or notes from Grant's school, or a letter about graduation, or Joan's summer swim team schedule, or a stray overdue library book, or whatever magazine Karl happened to be reading before he went to bed—all these things migrated to the same place. The kitchen table was Ground Zero of family communications.

Margie made a bigger stack out of a few smaller stacks of papers and cleared enough space for a paper towel, a glass of cold water, and a meat thermometer. She put the thermometer in the glass, held the glass with her left hand, and thought about heat. She thought about deserts and saunas and rain forests and the best sex she and Karl ever had (in a refrigerator-sized motel room in Carson City, South Dakota, during the hour Karl's parents took all three kids out for ice cream). After three minutes of clutching the glass so hard she felt like it might shatter in her hand, the water temperature didn't appear to have changed. She took a sip. It seemed only nominally warmer purely by sitting in a warm kitchen in early June. She tried it again, thinking *hot, hot, hot* and willing her inner body temperature to rise. Still nothing.

"How did you feel last night...?" she murmured. Then she remembered. Why not try it? Even though it wasn't even eight in the morning, she got up and went to the snack cupboard, which was abundant in the salty realm and painfully low in the sugar area. She managed to find a miniature bag of plain M&Ms likely left over from the previous Halloween and getting a bit waxy-looking. Nonetheless, in the interest of science, Margie ate them. She waited a minute then went back to the kitchen table.

Sugar really did seem to be a trigger for the hot flashes, as she almost immediately began feeling flushed and warm. She was holding the glass, but the temperature didn't rise much. Margie thought back to the night before and the rude kid in the back of the car (she was almost certain he was the same kid back in Eli's second grade class who stole half the classroom's Valentine's Day candy and then blamed it on the class hamster). The memory of him saying, "fat old lady" was enough to make her blood boil. It was either her blood or her skin. As she thought about the undeserved insult, Margie felt herself perspiring, just as she did whenever a hot flash washed over her. Only this time, it didn't just heat her up; it warmed up the water in the glass too. The temperature on the meat thermometer started to rise. Still Margie continued clutching the glass of water, thinking *heat,* thinking *rotten, horrid little git.* Then the water in the glass started to bubble and boil.

That's when she called Abra and Katherine.

She didn't bother saying hello, just: "I need to show you something."

"Hi to you too," Abra replied. She sounded groggy. "You do realize that Sunday is the one day when I sleep in?"

"Sorry. But I can do something unusual."

"I don't want to know about what you and Karl get up to in private."

Margie paused, feeling the need to show rather than tell. "Something unusual in the same way that you and Katherine can do something unusual."

There was dead silence on the other end of the line, then a quiet "What?"

"I kind of need to show you."

"Well, you're obviously more awake than I am. You might as well come over here."

Katherine and her family had plans with Hal's family later that day. "I can meet you two for breakfast if it's that important," she said when Margie called her.

"Abra's house. Half an hour. Bring food."

"Got it."

If Katherine were in a war movie, Margie always figured she'd be the character who manages to find a generator, twenty-seven blankets, and a case of penicillin in the middle of a disaster area. Margie arrived at Abra's with a bowl of fruit salad. Katherine brought something she called a Brazilian quiche. "It needs to cook for thirty to thirty-five minutes," she said, "but I figure we can talk while it's in the oven."

"Doesn't the oven need to warm up first?" Margie asked.

"I called and told Abra to preheat it," Katherine said, getting three plates out of the cupboard.

"Geez, you *are* efficient." It would be easy to dislike Katherine. She was taller and thinner and somehow managed to maintain a family and a fulfilling, responsible grown-up job at the same time. Plus she had just won the breakfast war. Long ago Margie had learned the key to Katherine: she was only in competition with herself, no one else. So Margie didn't resent her, didn't feel bad that the Brazilian quiche smelled amazing. What did bother her was, once Abra and Katherine were seated at the table waiting for her to do something, the ability to boil water through her own body heat started feeling like a silly party trick. It certainly wasn't as cool as invisibility or being impervious to injury.

"What's wrong?" Abra asked.

"Nothing." Margie had been standing in the middle of the kitchen, a glass of cold water held in front of her as though it was a bouquet of flowers. She lowered the glass a bit. "This is stupid."

"We'll be the judge of that," Katherine said. "Oh come on," she said in response to Margie's hurt expression. "I was just joking. If you called us, it must be good."

"Please show us," Abra added.

"Okay." Margie had eaten a double-stuff Oreo on the way over just to prime the hot-flash pump. She held the glass out in front of her again and started to think *heat*. "You know how I've been getting these hot flashes? Well, last night, when I picked up Eli from a party, I discovered that they can be pretty epic."

"How epic?" Katherine asked.

"Watch." All three of them stared at the glass in Margie's hands, watching as it went from clear, motionless liquid to slightly clouded with tiny bubbles to big rolling, boiling bubbles. Abra's gaze went from the glass to Margie's pink face.

"I never would have believed it if I didn't see it," she said.

"Last night I made a car overheat."

"What?" Katherine said. "And now you just made that boil. You heated water to two hundred and twelve degrees Fahrenheit *with your body*. It's unbelievable."

"No more unbelievable than you two," Margie said. She didn't know what else to say. Apparently, neither did Abra or Katherine. Thinking about any one of their new abilities too closely was mind-boggling. Margie put the glass of hot water on the table in between Katherine and Abra. Katherine immediately reached out and picked it up.

"That's one hell of a hot flash," she murmured, feeling just how hot the glass had become. "Everything I've ever learned about the human body has been completely shattered in the last few weeks."

Margie leaned against the smooth butcher-block kitchen counter. She had always secretly envied Abra's clean, nicely decorated little house. Margie was pretty sure her own house wouldn't be clean until all three kids lived somewhere else. "Abra, have you, you know..." she stammered, "turned invisible lately? Eli told me what he saw when you hurt your ankle."

"It hasn't happened since then," Abra admitted. "Maybe it was just a... Oh God, I don't know what it was."

"Remember what I said about the explosion?" Katherine asked quietly. "Maybe it affected all of us, just in different ways."

"Maybe." Margie paced around Abra's kitchen and headed for the living room, where she knew Clint would be looking out the front window. She picked the cat up and carried him back into the kitchen. Holding a purring, cuddling animal made talking about all this a little more palatable. "He's comforting," she said in reply to Katherine's quizzical look. She thought back to what she knew of Joan's experiment. "You might be right," she said.

"How so?" Abra asked.

"Joan needed us to give her another sample because our results were messed up. Only ours. I was thinking about the other women she got samples from. There were a few other moms from her swim team and from school, but they're younger parents. Those women are in their thirties. And the other cancer survivors were ones I knew from my support group, and they're all older."

Katherine leaned forward in her kitchen chair, focused. "I'm not exactly following you."

"I think we were the only samples from women who are, you know, actively going through The Change." She said this not knowing if it made sense or not. She wasn't a scientist, but the distinction seemed important.

"Joan was hit by the explosion too. Is anything going on with her?" Abra asked.

"No."

"But that makes sense. She's a kid," Katherine added.

"It's just the three of us."

The kitchen timer rang, and Margie handed Katherine a pot holder. After all, it was her quiche. Nobody said anything until they were seated, eating, thinking. "So what do we do now?" Katherine asked.

Abra chuckled. "I don't know, maybe I should try sneaking into a movie for free."

Katherine was aghast. "Are you kidding? You can turn invisible and you want to resort to petty thievery?"

"I thought it'd be fun."

"But we could *do* something with these abilities. Something good," Katherine said, her eyes shining with the same light they had when she was in front of a classroom explaining the miracle of cellular reproduction. "This is going to sound really stupid, but we could, we could fight bad guys or something."

"Fight bad guys," Margie repeated. "Have you been talking to Grant lately?"

"I know it sounds like something an eleven-year-old would dream up, but if we can do these unusual things, then together we could maybe make a small difference here or there. Like Janelle. We helped her."

Abra broke the silence. "We did," she said. "If we hadn't stopped, there's no telling what might have happened. He could have killed her."

"You two saved her. I just drove the car," Margie said.

"It was all three of us."

"And what am I going to do with this...skill?" Margie said as she picked the glass of water up off the table. It had cooled slightly. "Make the room uncomfortably warm for the bad guys?"

Katherine stood up and took the glass from her. "I don't know. But what you can do is pretty stinking incredible. We have the ability to make a difference. We should use it."

Margie thought for a moment. Growing up, she had never been the kind of girl who played with dolls or knew how many kids she wanted when she was twelve or had her wedding planned before she even met her future husband. Yet she had to admit, she'd become that woman, the one who creates life accomplishments through her kids and her spouse instead of on her own. Time for something different. "Okay," she said quietly. Katherine was already standing, so she stood up too. It seemed appropriate.

Abra struggled to her feet and leaned against her chair. "I'm in. I've got nothing else going on in my life. I'm not even doing the crazy cat lady thing right."

"Our neighbor's cat had kittens," Margie said. "I can get you a starter kit."

"No," Abra said. "I'd rather give this superhero thing a try."

CHAPTER FOURTEEN

THE PROBLEM WITH DECIDING TO BE A CRIME-FIGHT-ING SUPERHERO IS THAT BAD THINGS DON'T HAPPEN AT YOUR CONVENIENCE. They certainly don't happen right on your street when you're sitting on your front porch on a Sunday afternoon with your laptop and an el-evated ankle. After Katherine and Margie left, Abra had most of a Sunday to herself. She had managed to hobble out to the front porch, laptop clutched in one hand. Her ankle was still tender, but she could walk on it provided she was wearing the Ace bandage. It seemed like a small victory. Still, she was hobbled, dependent. It was that de-pendency, that realization that she didn't have anyone in her corner full-time that sent Abra to Leap.com, a dating website.

For most of her life, Abra hadn't had a problem meet-ing men. She'd been with Evil Richard for most of her forties. Now that that relationship was over, it seemed she'd apparently passed from "ripe" to "expired" without knowing it. To be fair, she didn't have many opportuni-ties to meet people. Most of the single men she encoun-tered through work were very young techie types who truly seemed way too young for her. And most of her favorite activities were solitary pursuits. All she wanted was a decent guy around her age. It didn't seem like an outrageous request.

Abra had a skeletal profile on Leap—three recent photos, the basic questions answered, a few sentences about her interests (running, hiking, books, good food) and what she was looking for in a relationship. Of the guys who messaged her after seeing her profile, a few had been interesting enough in their emails to warrant a face-to-face meeting (she felt compelled to rule out major grammatical errors, such as guys who didn't seem to know the difference between "they're" and "their" or who used apostrophes with wild abandon). None of the dates amounted to much. There hadn't been any real connection. She hadn't yet tried messaging anyone directly. Now it seemed time to take a more proactive approach to finding someone. With her ankle still in recovery, she had some time on her hands. Why not spend it cruising dating sites?

Abra set what felt like pretty broad parameters for her search: single male of any race between the ages of forty-two and fifty-two within fifteen miles. She wasn't averse to crossing the Cuyahoga River to the west side for the right guy. Age-wise, that gave her five years on either side of her own age, which seemed just right. The search turned up nearly six hundred results. There had to be a few decent, like-minded men in there.

The first thing that struck her was how many guys had grainy, unflattering profile pictures. Two had selfies that bore an uncomfortable resemblance to mug shots. The good-looking ones wrote the least; the dorky-looking ones wrote the most. Abra tried to click equally on the profiles of the good-looking ones and the ones who perhaps weren't conventionally handsome but had a kind smile or a playful expression.

"Okay, SlimDaddy, let's see what else you like to do," she murmured as she clicked on SlimDaddy's name. His profile photo showed him after a race—he was wearing a bib number. They obviously had running in common. SlimDaddy also liked sailing, farmers' markets, and nature. He was forty-four to Abra's forty-seven. He had one child (a teenager). *Not a problem*, Abra thought. She was seriously considering messaging him, when she got to the end of his profile and saw that he was only interested in women aged thirty to forty-three.

"Fine," she said out loud.

She cruised around her search results a bit more, clicking on a profile here and there. One profile showed a heart-stoppingly handsome guy with thick salt-and-pepper hair, light olive skin, and a jaw that could be used to chisel marble. "Hello, Monty1226..." Abra said. She knew it was shallow, but she clicked on his profile. There were six other photos there, and he looked equally as good in all of them. The great profile pic wasn't a fluke; he was just a fine-looking human being. He listed his profession as *"business owner,"* which could be anything. Abra scrolled down to the rest of his profile. *"I'm a self-made man who knows what he likes. In no particular order, I'm a fan of fine wine, fine women, classic cars, the 2nd Amendment, and AC/DC,"* she read. Could you base a relationship on wine and AC/DC? Monty1226 was fifty, but his profile said he was interested in women twenty-five to forty-five. "You're older than I am, but I'm too old for you?" she said to her laptop.

She clicked back to her search results and scrolled down. That's when she saw the photograph for Foodie815. "Richard..." she muttered.

The picture was unmistakably The Evil Richard Brewster. She had taken it herself two years ago while they were hiking at Punderson State Park. Richard was standing by the edge of Punderson Lake in autumn, the sun was bright to his left, and behind him you could see a forest at the peak of fall colors. The light and trees made Richard look better than usual. Now the bastard was using it as a dating profile picture. Against her better judgement, Abra clicked on Richard's profile. The least she could say for him was that he didn't misrepresent himself. He really was forty-nine and really was a restaurant manager who enjoyed camping and hiking, food, and Cleveland Browns football. *At least I don't have to see the Browns lose anymore*, Abra thought. Richard was a season ticket holder, and Abra had frozen her tail off far too many times watching a sport she didn't even like. She looked further into Richard's profile. Under *"longest relationship"* he had put *"six years."* That was her. Those six years had been part of her life too. This sidelong mention of their relationship seemed to nullify the whole thing. She was just a footnote in his life. *Bastard.* "Next time I'll find someone who loves basketball," she muttered.

"Hey, Miss Abra, why are you talking to your computer?"

Abra looked up to see two of her next-door neighbors, sixteen-year-old Ariel and her six-year-old brother, Darnell, who was staring at her with huge brown eyes. Between the eyes and the still-chubby cheeks, Darnell knew he was damned adorable. "Good morning," Abra replied. "Actually, I wasn't talking *to* the computer. I was talking to somebody *on* the computer."

"Oohh! Video chat! Lemme see!" Darnell squealed and ran up the short driveway to the porch at the same time that Ariel said, "Darnell, leave Miss Abra alone."

Abra quickly closed out her web browser. The neighborhood kids certainly didn't need to know she was cruising dating sites. "Sorry, Darnell. All done."

"Awww. Can I see your computer? Please?"

Abra was pretty sure the family didn't have a computer at home. "How can I resist that face? Five minutes, but don't touch any of my open documents," she said as she put the laptop on the porch.

"I won't!" Darnell said, reverently taking the computer and settling in on the concrete steps of the narrow porch.

Abra looked up from Darnell to meet Ariel's eye. "You know you're just making him more spoiled, Miss Abra."

"Sorry."

Darnell was the youngest of five kids. He knew how to get attention. Ariel was the one whom Abra thought needed a little spoiling. The eldest, her life seemed to revolve around sports and taking care of her younger siblings. Ariel was the kid taking shot after shot on the beat-up basketball hoop in her front yard at all hours. The *bounce-bounce-bounce* of the basketball used to get on Abra's nerves until she realized that Ariel would use any excuse to get out of the house.

"How's your ankle, Miss Abra?"

"Much better, thank you. What are you doing with yourself this summer, Ariel?"

"Not much. Babysitting, practicing my basketball, maybe running. I'm thinking of doing soccer next year."

"Read any good books lately?"

"I read a couple of the mysteries you told me about, the ones with the lady detective in Chicago? Those were good."

"Glad you liked them."

Abra always felt she was walking a fine line with Ariel and her family. She wanted to help, but she didn't want to play the crusading do-gooder neighbor either. "Ariel, do you have any time to do some yardwork for me? Maybe mow the lawn and do some weeding? Between my ankle and work, I'm not sure how much I'll be able to do. I'll pay you, of course."

Ariel's eyes shone behind her square-framed glasses. "Sure. Thank you."

Abra had never paid anyone to do yard work before and, frankly, knew she couldn't afford it. But she was pretty sure Ariel could use a few extra dollars in her pocket. Frankly, half the people in the neighborhood could. South Euclid had developed as a bedroom community during the fifties and sixties. It had a few neighborhoods with spacious homes on big lots, but probably half the housing stock consisted of small bungalows like hers. And just like most other older suburbs, the city was now falling prey to the same crumbling infrastructure and fleeing middle class that had emptied out the big cities. Between age, the mortgage loan crisis, and the recession, their neighborhood probably had more in common with neighborhoods in the city than those in suburbs farther east. Their block alone had two foreclosed houses.

She and Ariel watched Darnell as he played a game at an online site called Math Maniacs.

"We used this site in school last year," he said knowledgeably, navigating it like a pro.

"Wow, when I was in kindergarten, we spent most of our time coloring and playing Farmer in the Dell," Abra said.

Darnell looked up at her in wonder. "Dell like a computer?"

"No, dell like out in a field. There were no computers. No internet. It was the Dark Ages."

Ariel snickered. "I'll come over later to do the lawn," she said to Abra. "Although I might only be able to do it for part of the summer." Ariel looked at the sidewalk and then at her house. She lowered her voice a little: "We might be moving."

"You're kidding. Where to?"

"I don't know yet."

"We're gonna live somewhere else," Darnell said in a sing-songy voice that didn't seem nearly as concerned as his older sister's.

"Come on, Darnell. Miss Abra has stuff to do," she said, and took Darnell's hand. "See you later!"

She watched as they walked down the street, maybe toward the playground at Bexley Park, although that was a pretty long walk for a kid Darnell's age. Maybe just somewhere out of the house.

She'd had enough of the internet. Abra shut down the laptop and brought it inside. There was plenty of Sunday left. She stepped back out onto the porch and made her way down the steps to the driveway. A little fresh air was the best medicine. She tentatively walked down the driveway to the sidewalk. It was tempting to do a short run, but she knew her ankle wasn't strong enough for that. Just walking for now. She walked up and down the drive a couple times, focusing on maintaining a proper walking gait, no limping, seeing if the ankle would withstand a longer walk. The second time she turned around in her snug little backyard, she heard loud voices coming from next door.

Ramon and Latrice, Ariel and Darnell's parents, were good neighbors. Ramon worked graveyard shift at the UPS facility out near the county airport, while Latrice worked a series of retail jobs. Ramon was one of those guys who always appeared to be in a good mood. He seemed to like Abra because they were both part Hispanic, as though that gave them common ground. Between working jobs that kept her on her feet all day and taking care of five kids, Latrice always seemed friendly but tired.

With a lot of kids in the house, there was typically some noise coming from next door, but not angry yelling. Not like this. There wasn't much of a divider between her yard and theirs, just a quartet of forsythia bushes that had already lost most of their yellow blossoms. The forsythia had been planted long before Abra bought the house. They were large enough that sometimes she saw Darnell and his friends climbing in them as though they were trees.

Ramon and Latrice were in their kitchen, near the open window. Instinctively she knew this had something to do with the family moving. It wasn't any of her business. It wasn't. *Not your monkey...not your circus*, she thought in a vain attempt to squelch her curiosity.

Abra had never tried to turn invisible. Each time it had happened, it just happened—more more like a daydream than reality. *What if? What if I really can?* She concentrated for a moment on nothing, on everything. How do you turn invisible on a beautiful Sunday in early June? It felt like an actor looking for an emotional memory. It felt fake. Her body knew the difference. Even if she did manage to turn invisible, how would she know? Each time it had happened, she'd been too preoccupied with what was going on around her to notice if she could see herself. The thing she did remember was how it felt—a quick sensation of having her body turn inside out then the glorious feeling of being something that light didn't need to bend around, as though she *was* light, made of light.

Abra stood in her driveway, feeling the early-afternoon sun pulse down on her. Katherine's voice kept running through her head, saying, "You can make something invisible; you just have to bend light around an object so that it doesn't cast a shadow."

How do I make you bend around me? she murmured softly. *I'm not here. I can't be seen*, she thought. It was like trying to find the magic word to a charm or a spell. Growing up with a name like "Abra," every third person she met thought it was clever to call her "Abracadabra." Would that it were so easy. She whispered, "Abracadabra" then, "Now I'm invisible," "You can't see me," and "Disappear." None of those worked. This was a stupid idea. *You can't turn invisible*, she thought. *You can't bend light around you.*

Then she thought perhaps the light didn't need to bend.

"Pass through me," she murmured to the light. And it did.

Abra looked down and didn't see herself. She saw the wavy tendrils of the old baggy shorts she was wearing, small waves of her T-shirt, and on the ground, she could see half of her sandal—just the part that covered the Ace bandage on her ankle. It took a moment for her to realize that everything directly touching her skin was invisible; everything that wasn't touching her skin was visible. She slipped off her sandals. Now the only thing visible was the loose fabric of her shorts and shirt. Well, if no one could see her, no one could see her, right? She took them off.

A pair of stray shorts and a T-shirt lying in the middle of the driveway looked odd, so she walked a few steps to the corner of the house and stashed the clothes on one of the faded chairs that sat on her uneven brick patio. As she walked, she noticed something else: her ankle felt great. It didn't hurt, and she could walk normally, smoothly.

The low rumble of Ramon's and Latrice's voices was still audible. Feeling as nosy as she ever had, Abra walked across the driveway and through a narrow opening in between two of the forsythia bushes. Her bare left foot hit a rock.

"Dammit," she hissed. There wasn't much point in being invisible if she was making noise. No more talking. Instead, she focused on keeping her mind open, allowing the light to pass through her. She wasn't sure if that's what was actually happening. The thought that she was standing in her bra and underwear in the neighbor's backyard made her stifle a laugh. She held her hand in front of her face. Nope, couldn't see it. *Crazy or invisible*, she thought.

Latrice's voice through the window brought her back. "I am not letting them throw us out of our own house," she said. "We are out of here before that."

"Baby, I know, I know..." Ramon kept saying.

"Why didn't you make them change the rate?"

"You know I tried, but they had a million different fees. I told them we haven't got enough for the house payment now."

"You fix it. You're the one who said we could afford it. You're the one who said you'd be making more money in a few years so it didn't matter if the payment went up."

"I didn't realize it was gonna go up that much! North-Coast Home Mortgage are bunch of crooks."

Their conversation went around and around. Abra gathered that they'd been snookered into an adjustable rate mortgage a few years earlier when mortgage companies were handing out mortgages to anybody with a pulse, regardless of whether they could afford it. Now it was ballooning. She stood in Ramon and Latrice's backyard for a moment, listening to them fight and worry, wondering how she could possibly help them, when she heard new voices. Ariel and Darnell were back, walking up the sidewalk toward their house, with Darnell singing a made-up song about being hungry. Ariel had said she'd come over to do the lawn. This seemed like a good time to make her exit.

Abra started picking her barefoot way back into her own yard when she realized she could see her own feet. *Darn, darn, darn*, she thought. *Light, light. I don't bend light.* "Pass through me, pass though me," she breathed. Again she felt as though her weight had lifted. Stepping on a couple of acorns in bare feet just sort of tickled, and her ankle again felt strong and sure. Looking down, she couldn't see her own feet, couldn't see her shadow. Darnell's loud, off-key singing covered any noise Abra might have made rushing back to her yard.

She grabbed her shorts off the patio chair and held them close to her stomach, hoping no one would see a pair of khaki shorts and a T-shirt flying through the air on their own. She could wait until she was safely inside the house before putting them back on. For a moment, she merely stood on the patio, marveling at what had just happened.

She had turned invisible, of that she was sure. And she had done it on command. She was standing outside in her underwear and nobody could see her. Abra had to run inside before half the neighborhood started hearing disembodied laughter.

CHAPTER FIFTEEN

MARGIE KNEW ELI KEPT A BLOG. A few years back his therapist had suggested he keep a journal to work through his struggles with cutting and self-acceptance. Somewhere along the line, the handwritten journal had become a blog. Why Eli would choose to write about his problems and deepest feelings in a blog that anyone with internet access and a working knowledge of English could read, Margie wasn't sure. To that end, she and Karl had made him promise not to use any real names or locations and no photographs of people's faces. Margie used to check the blog on a regular basis just to keep an eye on things, like a park ranger taking a walk through the territory to scan for smoke. She never left a comment, but a surprising number of kids and parents had. The blog seemed to have served its purpose. It helped Eli through the toughest period their family had yet experienced, and it even seemed to have touched a few other families in a positive way.

He didn't do the blog anymore, said he didn't need it. And that was a relief. It seemed a signal he genuinely had put that phase of his life in the past. Margie hadn't visited A Cutting Tale in months, so she was a little concerned when Eli sent her an email one evening. Not a text, a proper email. For him, this was the equivalent of sending a handwritten letter in cursive. The email was short and cryptic. It just read, *"Mom, I wasn't sure how to share this with you, but I know I have to. Hope you don't mind too much. Love, Eli."*

Margie had to take a couple of deep breaths and remind herself that just because Eli was updating his blog didn't mean that he was cutting again. It didn't. She was so focused on trying not to worry that she didn't read the URL in the link he sent; she just clicked.

Instead of taking her to A Cutting Tale, the link took her to an online comic called The Super Ladies. The front page featured a red-and-yellow banner with the title and cartoon drawings of three women. The tallest figure had long, wavy hair and stood with her arms folded, looking muscular and somewhat indestructible. The smallest figure was wiry, with short curly hair and a darker skin tone. Her hands were at her sides, but she looked ready for anything with an expression that said she had a secret she wasn't telling you. The third figure was a little rounder but drawn to be voluptuous and curvy. Her hands were outstretched and looked as though heat waves were coming from them. Unless Margie's brain had completely backfired, these figures were supposed to be Katherine, Abra, and her.

There weren't many strips yet—the first comic had only been posted about a week before. But there was Margie making a carful of rowdy teenage boys overheat with just the touch of her hand. There was Katherine, cutting her arm at the kitchen sink and triumphantly showing that she was unharmed. And there was Abra, tripping over the dog (Margie figured she could forgive Eli for using Juno's real name) and turning invisible. Eli had done some editorializing, developing these events as the beginning of a running story about three middle-aged suburban women with superpowers. It was well done.

Margie hated typing anything longer than a sentence on her phone; she preferred her old laptop with its real keyboard for emails. She usually spent half an hour or so before bed reading *The New York Times* online or checking email. Eli had gone to bed unusually early. Now she knew why: he didn't want to be around when she saw the comic. For a long minute, she wasn't sure if she was angry or elated. On one hand, he was sharing something personal without consulting her or Abra or Katherine. Wasn't it their story to tell, not his? But he hadn't used their names, and the cartoons weren't necessarily caricatures. They were obviously based on the three of them, but the Super Ladies in the comics weren't supposed to *be* them. If you didn't know the three of them and hadn't seen firsthand examples of their powers, you would think it was entirely fiction.

Eli had also given the characters nicknames. The one based on Katherine was "Indestructo." Abra's character was "Shadow." Margie's was "The Schvitz." *You are so my child, Eli*, she murmured. That's when Margie decided she was elated.

She sent the link to Katherine and Abra. Then, because she didn't want to wait, she texted each of them too. It was after ten. Abra still had to work in the morning and was an early riser to boot. She was probably in bed. But Katherine was on summer break. She was probably still awake.

Modern technology gives the illusion that everyone you know is sitting around just waiting to return your call or text. The idea that you should be able to make instant contact with anyone you wish makes waiting even three minutes for a response an anxiety-inducing experience. Instead of waiting, she went upstairs to see if Eli was still awake. His door was mostly closed and the light was off. She poked her head into his room for a moment and listened to him breathe. He didn't sound asleep, but he didn't seem to want to talk either. It could wait until morning.

She went back downstairs to the living room, where she'd left her laptop. The house had a living room, which stayed relatively clean because the furniture wasn't as comfortable and no one sat in there unless Karl's mother was over, and a family room/rec room/God-awful-mess that was much more conducive to actual "living" than the living room. Margie didn't dare leave her laptop in the family room. The chances of someone borrowing, sitting on, or spilling something on it were astronomical. She'd left her phone in the living room too, and it rang almost as soon as she walked in the room. It was Katherine.

"Tell your child that the character should be Indestructa, not Indestructo. Feminine ending," was the first thing she said.

"So I take it you like the Super Ladies comic?" Margie asked.

"Yeah, I think I do. And not just because I'm a closet narcissist."

"I wouldn't say *closet* narcissist..."

"Stop. I like it because he's taking our story and re-telling it in his own way."

"That's how mythologies start."

"Exactly."

After she hung up with Katherine, she got a two-word text from Abra: *"Love it."*

The last thing Margie did before bed was send a quick reply to Eli: *"Please use the feminine ending—it's Indestructa, not Indestructo. How is it I never made you take Latin?"*

✹ ✹ ✹

Katherine enjoyed the solitude of running alone in the mornings. She missed Abra, but solo runs for the past couple weeks had given her ample opportunity to experiment with the limits of what her body could do. The limits kept expanding.

She was starting to feel responsible for doing something—anything—with her powers. It seemed logical that she needed to go out and find some wrongs to right. Their neighborhood was filled with three-bedroom, one-bathroom bungalows that had been built in the fifties and early sixties, when the area was booming. She liked the cozy feel, loved that they lived in a diverse area with neighbors of different races and backgrounds. But after a few hundred predatory loans, house flippings, and foreclosures, a whole swath of the city was hanging onto its middle- to lower-middle-class status by two paychecks and a few thin strands of freshly mown grass. Still, the police blotter in the local paper only showed small crimes, most of which were centered in one of the two nearby commercial districts. The ones that weren't seemed to be pretty benign—a stolen bicycle here, an unlocked car broken into there, a domestic disturbance that involved a lot of yelling but no violence. She felt secure in her neighborhood, felt secure letting Anna walk down the block to a friend's house—usually with Hal surreptitiously keeping an eye on her from the front porch because he was overly protective, not because Anna was in any sort of danger. It wasn't a wealthy neighborhood, but it was a safe one.

When she told Hal the next evening that she was going out, she didn't say she was going out looking for trouble, although she had to admit that was the intended purpose. Hal assumed she was going out with Margie or Abra and simply said, "Make sure Anna knows you won't be home before she goes to bed." That was one of the benefits of having a disinterested husband: the evening was completely hers.

Actively seeking out crime in the making is a delicate situation. The full reality of this hit Katherine as she drove out of South Euclid and into neighboring Candlewick Heights. Seventy years ago, Candlewick had been a strong, desirable suburb. Bordering the city of Cleveland, it had some gorgeous architecture, including a number of houses built by John D. Rockefeller, and a massive city park. Then pretty much every bad thing that could happen to a city happened to it over the decades—closing of the streetcar lines, unemployment, a fleeing middle class, corrupt city politicians, poverty. Now it had half the population it formerly did and an unemployment rate above twenty percent. If you were going to find bad guys doing bad things, Candlewick might be a likely place to start.

It was only seven thirty on a Wednesday evening in the summer. There were a few people out on the streets, walking or waiting for a bus, even a couple of kids on bikes zooming around simply because they could. She saw a few pairs and groups of teenage boys walking down Euclid Avenue, Candlewick's main thoroughfare. If you went far enough down Euclid you'd end up in downtown Cleveland. This section of Euclid Avenue mainly consisted of boarded-up buildings and chain fast-food restaurants. The teenage boys could be up to no good, or they could just be walking because they didn't have transportation or bus passes. Either scenario was equally likely. Then she felt like an ass for assuming she'd find something bad happening simply because she was in a low-income neighborhood. Time to regroup.

Candlewick bordered the University Circle neighborhood of Cleveland, a two-square-mile area of museums, universities, and other cultural assets. There was a great little bar called the Barking Spider tucked away in what used to be a carriage house. They always had live music and in nice weather opened the wide carriage-house doors so patrons could sit out at picnic tables with their drinks and listen. It was a bar where a woman alone could feel comfortable.

Before she got out of the car, Katherine grabbed a pair of cheater reading glasses that Anna insisted she buy when they were at the Shaker Square farmers' market a few weeks earlier. Katherine had mentioned that she sometimes had trouble reading small print. Anna immediately picked up on this and dragged her to the vendor who sold one-of-a-kind, hand-painted everything. There among the whimsically painted light-switch plates, garbage cans with unicorn-horn handles, and handmade cell phone covers was a selection of reading glasses in different colors, each one with tiny flowers or insects painted along the edges. Anna had insisted her mother get a pair of red cat-eye frames with little daisies painted along the sides. Katherine kept them in the car for emergencies and to humor the kid. If nothing else, they'd come in handy if she just hung out reading the free entertainment magazines stacked by the door.

Katherine bought a beer and sat at one of the picnic tables in the back, just enjoying the cool evening air and the old-time stride piano of the musician playing inside. Try as she might, she couldn't get the image of Taylor's arrogant, spikey-haired boyfriend checking into the hotel out of her mind. She should have done something just to make sure Taylor wasn't getting into something she didn't want. *What could I have done?* She had blown that moment. Worse, she had let Hal make the choice not to get involved for her.

What can I do? There was documented evidence she could withstand cutting and high falls. Her runs were getting faster and her workouts tougher, but, if anything, her fatigue level afterward or even during was nil. Nothing hurt. Ever. *Maybe I really am indestructible.*

What would that actually mean? Katherine had always felt the standard female sense of caution when going out alone. In college, it meant the buddy system at a party. As an adult, it meant parking near a light or a security guard after dark or keeping an eye on her surroundings and a key in her hand, just in case she needed a makeshift weapon. Such precautions had become second nature. They were simply little things you did as a female navigating the world. Hal never understood her habit of leaving a light on if she and Anna were going to be coming home alone after dark, or her insistence on having the car interior light go on when the door opened.

What if she didn't need to do those things anymore? What if she could do absolutely whatever she wanted whenever and wherever she wanted, without fear?

It was time for another experiment. She didn't necessarily want to get into a fight—she didn't like violence—but she needed a gauge, a way of measuring her growing strength against the opposite sex. The back area of the bar held three picnic tables. One was empty, she sat alone at the second, and at the last were three guys who appeared to be in their midtwenties. They looked like they might be graduate students from the university. Not big guys, but not the typical Case Western Reserve University engineering nerds either.

No fear, Katherine thought. "Excuse me," she said. "I'm doing an experiment on leverage versus muscle mass as it relates to gender inequity and was wondering if I could arm wrestle each of you." Regardless of whether what she said made sense, saying it somewhat quickly and matter-of-factly made it sound legit. If they were grad students, they were probably so used to studies with long titles that her request wouldn't seem odd. If they weren't, they'd never admit to not understanding.

The three of them looked at her and then one another. There was some uncomfortable chuckling. Then the thinnest of the three, a pale-skinned guy who probably only had to shave seven facial hairs a day, said, "Sure. You said this is for a study?"

"Kind of, yes," Katherine said as she sat down opposite him.

"Do you work at Case?" asked the beefiest of the three. He looked like he might play a competitive sport.

"No, but I'm a science teacher." She realized it would be polite to find out something about them. "Are you students?"

"We all just graduated," the thin guy said. "I'm starting my MBA in the fall."

"Me too," the beefy one said.

"I'm the odd man out," the third guy said. He was dark-skinned with a slight accent. Maybe from the Caribbean? "I study computer science."

"Well, nice to meet you all," Katherine said. "Thanks for helping me with my experiment," she added. She didn't really feel like making new friends and merely placed her elbow on the picnic table, hand up, ready to arm wrestle. For a moment she felt foolish. *What are you trying to prove?* she thought. It wasn't so much having to prove something as having proof, some sort of empirical evidence of her female strength against male strength.

The thin guy grinned sheepishly. "I'm not very good at arm wrestling," he said.

"That's okay. It's for science," Katherine replied.

She had forgotten how intimate arm wrestling could be until they clasped hands. She was touching a stranger. The guy with the slight accent put both his hands on top of theirs. Now she was touching two strange men. Katherine tried not to focus on the absurdity, only on the task at hand. With a lilting "One, two, three, wrestle," he removed his hands from theirs. Now it was an arm-wrestling match.

Katherine knew the techniques to help win at arm wrestling—she had learned them years ago while trying to beat Billy. She had never managed to beat her big brother, but she dispatched the skinny business major in 1.4 seconds (according to the beefy one, who recorded the whole thing on his phone).

"Could we try that again?" the skinny guy asked. "I wasn't quite ready." Katherine let his friends be the ones to say, "Sure you weren't." She merely raised her arm and beat him again. "Let Josh try," the skinny guy said.

Josh was the beefy one. As they clasped hands, Katherine noted that he wasn't chubby; there was muscle on that future MBA arm. Nonetheless, she beat him twice in a row. After she slammed his hand down the second time, Katherine had a moment of doubt, of wondering if she had just pissed off a stranger, if that was foolish or safe. *No fear*, she thought.

"You're really strong," Josh said. "Are you a weight lifter?"

She wanted to say, "No, I'm a superhero" or "No, I'm a scientist," but that sounded too cocky. "Just strong, I guess," she said. She looked over at the guy with the Caribbean accent. He looked to be in decent shape and was kind of tall with long arms. He would have a definite advantage as far as leverage.

He smiled. "Sorry, but I'm left-handed. It wouldn't be fair."

"But I need some left-handed opponents for this study. Would you, please?"

"All right then." With a shrug, the guy sat down opposite Katherine and placed the elbow of a long left arm on the picnic table. She noticed that beefy Josh had his cell phone out again and tilted her head down so that her face would be obscured by her hair. The extra leverage didn't help the guy with the lovely accent. She beat him twice, left-handed. Her muscles felt fine, not at all like they'd been straining or working.

By this time, some of the people who'd been inside listening to the music had wandered outside, intrigued by the sight of a grown woman defeating three young men in arm wrestling. A guy about her age only with far more gray hair asked if he could go up against her.

"Sure, why not?" was Katherine's reply. She didn't mean to slam the guy's hand down, but it almost felt too easy to beat him or the four other men (including one guy with biceps the size of telephone poles) and one woman who tried arm wrestling her. She lost count of how many times she was challenged, but she won every time. Far from making anyone angry, her success bred more challenges and more success. At a certain point, it became comical. There was a lot of laughter. She had three beers lined up in front of her, each one bought by a different person she had beaten arm wrestling. It was starting to feel like a party.

The guy with gray hair sat down next to her. "Your arm wrestling skills are quite impressive, Ms...?"

Something about the evening made Katherine want to stay anonymous, so she said the first name that came to mind: "Jones."

"Ms. Jones," Gray Hair said with a nod. "I love your glasses."

The reading glasses were of such a light prescription that Katherine had momentarily forgotten she'd put them on, but now she was glad she had. Better people remember the glasses than her face. "Oh, thank you."

"Someone said you're a science teacher. Is there some sort of Archimedean secret behind all this?"

Men who reference Archimedes in a bar are either showing off their intellect or trying out a pick-up line. Or both. Katherine suspected it was the latter, although it had been ages since anybody had hit on her. Whether that was a result of circumstance or decreasing attractiveness was open to speculation. As a teacher, the vast majority of her colleagues were female and she was surrounded by children. Almost everywhere else she went it was with Anna or Hal or Abra and Margie or other parents. It was a rare occasion to be out and not immediately tagged as part of a couple or as a mother. The idea of being someone else for a little while was intriguing. "No secret," Katherine said. "Just strong, I guess."

She and Gray Hair made small talk for a few minutes. More people joined them at the picnic table. Katherine beat a few more people at arm wrestling. As the bench on their side grew more crowded, Gray Hair moved a bit closer to her.

"What's your first name?" he asked. The tone of his voice and the proximity of his leg to hers felt oddly exciting. He wasn't bad-looking, maybe a little older than Hal, but where Hal was tall and angular, this guy seemed slightly rounded with more substantial shoulders. Cuddly. For some reason, she focused on his mouth. Gray Hair had a nice smile, with beautifully formed, full lips. For a moment, she considered what it would be like to kiss him, considered throwing all caution to the wind and just kissing a stranger because she wanted to.

One of the biggest problems with long-term relationships is that it's impossible to experience the exhilaration of a first kiss more than once. After nearly two decades of kissing the same man exclusively—a man who rarely seemed enthused about the whole kissing thing—the prospect of one last first kiss was tempting. But not yet, not now, not while she was still married. She might be having doubts about her marriage, but this wouldn't clarify anything.

"Excuse me," she said, trying to extricate herself from the picnic table without shoving either her crotch or rear end into Gray Hair's face. No more beer, no more flirting, time to go.

"Do you have a first name, Ms. Jones?" he repeated, a bit too coyly.

Katherine said the first name that came to her head, "Indestructa," as she walked away.

CHAPTER SIXTEEN

THE SUMMER INTERNS AT HOFFMANN SOFTWARE
TYPICALLY CONGREGATED IN THE CONFERENCE ROOM
AT LUNCH. To be fair, they were scattered all over cre-
ation, with desks and computers shoved into cramped
nooks and corners to give them some semblance of a
work space. They needed a little room to spread out, but
the conference room was across the hall from Abra's office. It made for loud lunchtimes. It was always a relief
after lunch when they all went back to whatever space
they called home.

Aletha was working with Abra, who was a department of one, and the sales force, which was a department of eight. At first it had felt as though her territory
was being invaded, but after a few meetings with Aletha,
Abra realized that her earlier assessment was correct:
she was very sharp and a good egg to boot.

The conference room was the largest open area in
the office. The chairs didn't exactly match, and the long
wooden table was old enough to have burn marks on it
from the days when people smoked in offices, but Abra
loved the space. It was perhaps the only room in the entire office that had never been partitioned and thus still

had the original polished wood molding along the base-board and intricate plasterwork on the ceiling. It always felt like she was stepping back in time when she entered the conference room, even if it was currently filled with the anomalous sight of millennials staring at their phones. She never could figure out why all the interns bothered to eat lunch together if they weren't actually going to interact.

Abra waited until she heard the interns begin packing up their cutesy bento boxes and brightly colored insulated lunch bags that took up all the extra space in the refrigerator even though, as Abra had reminded people more than once, they were insulated and didn't really need to be refrigerated. She took a step backward, away from the conference room door, and looked down the hall. No one was around. The interns seemed awfully far removed her experience. She was curious as to what these kids were thinking. *Pass through me*, she thought.

Each time she became invisible, there was that familiar tug on her gut, as though she was turning herself inside out, then came the feeling of being lighter than air, of being light. She looked down and realized that she was now a loose blouse and an A-line skirt standing in the hallway. She went across the hallway to her office, glad that being invisible seemed to take all pressure off her still-a-little-sore ankle. Staying invisible, she quickly took off her blouse, skirt, and shoes and laid them on her desk chair where they couldn't be seen from the door. Then she crossed back to the conference room. Most of the interns were still in there. Abra couldn't remember all their names. They had a new crop of undergraduate interns every summer. Although she'd never admit it, half the interns looked alike to her. They always seemed to get some mix of computer science and business majors. Maybe it was her imagination, but the girls all seemed to be white with long, straight hair. They were typically the sales, marketing, and finance interns. The programming and tech interns all seemed to be male of varying races and in need of exercise and quality time outdoors. Abra was one of the few minorities in the office. She had to admit that was another reason she liked Aletha—sometimes it was hard being one of a handful of women of color in the office.

This year's crop of interns had a Matt, an Arjun, a Diwas, two Ryans, two Rachels, and a Miranda. The Miranda was the only one she was sure about because the name reminded her of *The Tempest*. They were all still in the conference room along with Aletha.

Abra had never found the marketing interns to be all that helpful to her. Their writing was generally atrocious. And while some of them were clever, their ideas always seemed to revolve around social media. They didn't appear to understand that the decision makers who purchased Hoffmann's inventory programs weren't the same people running their company's social media feeds. It was difficult to get them to see the bigger picture. Aletha seemed to get it, but judging from the conversation in the conference room, she wasn't getting much support from her fellow interns. When Aletha brought up the marketing research the other interns were supposed to be doing, only half of them seemed to pay nominal attention. All three of the young women and two of the young men still had their phones on the conference table in front of them or on their laps and were surreptitiously typing away as Aletha talked.

Invisible, Abra crept up behind one of the Rachels and looked over her shoulder. *"So sick of this,"* the girl texted. The other Rachel, sitting two chairs away, typed something and her response immediately showed up: *"Me 2."* Miranda was sitting immediately to Rachel #1's right. She was typing away on her lap, looking up once in a while as though she was paying attention. Abra read the words "Kind of sick of A" and then "Acts like she's in charge." Aletha was the only other person in the office whose first name began with the letter "A." Abra tried not to breathe on Rachel #1's neck as she read the on-going text conversation over her shoulder. They were going to town on Aletha, most of the other interns, as well as a few of the staff. While she could mostly agree on their assessment that Gary Sewicki in Software Development was "kind of creepy," the rest of it was just mean-spirited.

Miranda didn't text anything for a minute or two. Then she texted, "LOLZ, check this out" with a link. Rachel #1 clicked on it, and Abra was shocked to see the Super Ladies online comic. It was the one where The Schvitz shuts down the car full of teenage boys. Eli had done a nice job evoking the image of a clown car as the boys bailed out of the overheating vehicle. The tagline had a curvaceous Schvitz saying, "I'm taking the whole 'hot' thing to another level." Rachel #1's snort masked Abra's stifled giggle. It was an odd sensation to think about random strangers reading the Super Ladies comic. It wasn't necessarily about her, but she was part of the inspiration. It made her feel as virtually naked as she was literally half-naked in the conference room.

As Aletha wrapped up the impromptu meeting, Abra realized she had to get back to her office and put her clothes back on. She had been so focused on reading the interns' text messages and staying invisible that she hadn't thought about the absurdity of standing in the office in her underwear—even if no one could see her.

As the interns shuffled out of the conference room, she slipped around them and back to her own office. Mike Horowitz was lingering by her door. Crap, she thought. Abra pressed herself up against the hallway wall so none of the interns would accidentally bump into her. Then it was just her and Mike standing in the hallway. Why didn't he leave? Who just stands around in the hallway outside someone's office? *Go away*, she thought. *Shoo!*

Horowitz wandered into her office and stood by the window, no doubt glancing out at the family of pigeons that had made a nest on the ledge across the way. It had proven to be a popular attraction among her office mates. Even the people who claimed to hate pigeons enjoyed looking at the chicks. *Don't look on the chair. Don't look on the chair*...Abra thought. Horowitz turned around, and the small, neatly folded pile of clothes on her office chair caught his eye. For a second, the light-filled feeling left her, and she suspected she was becoming visible. After Gary Sewicki, Horowitz was the last person she'd want to have see her in her skivvies.

Pass through me, she thought. *For the love of God, pass through me*. Abra felt the now-familiar gut-wrenching tug as her body moved from visible to invisible. Horowitz gave the clothes a quick look, lifting them up a bit with one hand as though to confirm that they really were women's clothing. He gave a little shrug and walked out of her office. Abra breathed a sigh of relief, went into her office, and closed the door. She redressed in record time.

Breathe; everything's fine, she thought. It was only then she realized she'd broken out in a cold sweat when she saw Horowitz looking at her clothes. "I'll tell him I went for a run at lunch," she said aloud, testing the lie to see if it held water. It sounded legit, and she made a mental note to leave some running clothes in the office. Reading the interns' text messages had satisfied her curiosity but didn't tell her anything important. It was the equivalent of sneaking into a movie while invisible. But it did give her an idea.

Later that night, as she was making dinner, she called for backup.

"Hey," Abra said as soon as Margie answered the phone. "What's up?"

"Making dinner. What about you?"

"The same." Abra had her phone lodged between her shoulder and her ear as she tore up lettuce for her salad. "Ugh, hold on a second." She switched the phone to the other shoulder. "You know what I miss about having a landline? Having a phone large enough to rest on my shoulder so I can talk and still do things with my hands. I'm getting a crick in my neck."

"The bane of the multitasking woman," Margie said. "If you want my landline, you'll have to pry it out of my cold, dead hands."

"Why pay the extra money?"

"Because I like knowing who's calling my kids."

"They have their own phones."

"Grant doesn't. And I like having one central number where people can still communicate with us as a family. I think I need to write an essay on this."

"'In Praise of the Family Landline'?"

"Yes. I'm going to steal that title too."

"Go right ahead. Hold on again." Abra shifted the phone back to the other shoulder.

"Why don't you just put it on speaker?" Margie asked.

"Ummm...because I like to do things the hard way?" Abra replied as she lay the phone on an uncluttered portion of the counter and hit the "speaker" button. "There, much better."

Margie's voice sounded slightly warped through the cell phone speaker. "Did you call just to gripe about phones?"

Abra gave a tomato a samurai chop. "No, I need to ask a favor." Now there were tomato guts all over the cutting board. "But I'm playing with sharp knives, so maybe I shouldn't have called now," she said.

"You know I will grant you any wish that's within my powers."

"Thank you. Can we get together one afternoon next week?"

"Sure. You're still coming over on July Fourth, right?"

"Absolutely. This is for something different. Can we do a week from Thursday?"

"Yeah, but what exactly are we doing?"

"Superhero stuff."

A genuine cackle came out of the phone. "I'm there."

CHAPTER SEVENTEEN

SUMMER MORNINGS AT THE JOSEPH HOUSE USUAL-
LY RESEMBLED THE AFTERMATH OF A REALLY GREAT
PARTY: THE KIDS SLEPT LATE AND THERE WAS TYPI-
CALLY SOME KIND OF A MESS INVOLVING FOOD TO BE
CLEANED UP. Karl was always up and out of the house
first. Working in a small firm doing contract law beat
the seventy-hour work weeks back when he did corpo-
rate, but he still had to be in early.

Margie went through her usual morning rituals:

1) Walk Juno, making sure to avoid the guy in the
black SUV who sped through their neighborhood every morning. As usual, she jumped out of the way and
yelled, "Slow down!" to no avail.

2) Do five Sun Salutations on the deck off the kitchen
to pretend that she was still "doing yoga," to rid herself
of insane revenge fantasies against the guy in the black
SUV, and to purge the lingering resentment and doubt
about whether her chosen life path was slowly corrod-
ing her sense of well-being.

3) See what type of destruction her family had
wrought. Even if the counters were clean and all the

dishes in the dishwasher before she went to bed, things seemed to spontaneously multiply overnight.

When she walked into the family room and saw Eli sprawled on the dark brown sofa that took up most of one wall, it took her a moment to remember that she had, in fact, not added any more children to the household. The sofa was a thrift store find that dated back to her and Karl's first apartment. Every time they thought about replacing it, some major appliance would fail or a car would break and they put off getting another sofa. After years of supporting countless rear ends and lower backs, the cushions had become concave, each one resembling a great misshapen lump of fudge with a bite taken out of it. One had to be close to exhaustion to fall asleep on the family-room sofa.

The small notebook and pencil stub Eli carried just about everywhere lay on the floor. A larger drawing pad was on his lap. Margie glanced down and saw that he'd been working on a new Super Ladies cartoon, this one depicting Indestructra in feats of superhuman strength, starting out arm wrestling a bunch of people at a bar and ending up with her pushing a little old lady's stalled car up a steep hill to a gas station. At the end of the strip, the little old lady says, "Thank you, Indestructa Jones!" to which Indestructra replies, "Don't thank me. Thank my DNA!" The last panel showed the little old lady saying, "DNA? Darn, that's not covered by Medicare." This last line had a big "X" through it, so it looked like the punchline might not make the cut, although Margie thought it was kind of funny.

She put a gentle hand on Eli's shaggy head. His hair still felt as soft as baby hair to her. "Hey sweetie, good morning," she said softly.

Eli slowly opened his eyes. "Hi, Mom," he said groggily.

"Maybe you ought to go up to your room. You'll be more comfortable in your own bed."

"Ohhkay...except there's some stuff I need to finish."

"Finish it after you get a little more sleep. You aren't in school yet. You don't have any deadlines," Margie said as Eli sat up and swung his long, spindly legs off the sofa.

He picked up the drawing and started looking around for his pencil. "Yeah, but I need to get a new comic up on the site."

"Why? What's the rush?" Margie said as she picked the pencil stub up off the floor.

"Page views, Mom. I'm building a readership. I put a new comic up every Monday and Thursday."

Up until this point, Margie had thought the Super Ladies comic was just a fun sideline, something Eli was doing as a sentimental joke and maybe, if he stuck with it, an undergraduate thesis project. It just seemed somewhat theoretical, a hobby. The idea of the Super Ladies comic having a readership just seemed, well, kind of silly. When Eli told her that each installment was getting more page views and comments and shares than the installment before, she was momentarily floored. "Wait a minute," she said. "You can say that you've doubled the readership with each installment, but you're talking twenty people instead of ten people, right?"

"Well, at first, yeah," Eli admitted. "But it keeps growing. The last strip had more than fifteen hundred page views the first day. Pretty cool, huh?" Fifteen hundred was more than twenty, but in internet terms, it was a tiny little fingerling potato. Then Eli added that he'd only been doing the strip for two weeks. "My goal is to get up to ten thousand page views per strip by the end of the month. I want to keep it going once I get to school too."

"Do you think you're taking this a bit far...?" It was difficult for Margie to find the words when she wasn't even sure how she felt about all this.

"And I have a really good plan to increase page views. I've started a Super Ladies feed on IcyU."

"That means nothing to me."

Eli rooted around for his phone. "Oh, it's a social media site where you can share pictures and video clips and let people know where you are and stuff."

"It sounds like a one-stop shop for stalkers."

Eli looked up from his phone and gave an exasperated little sigh. "You can change the privacy settings if you want. It's just another way for people to connect. And it's cooler than Twitter and Tumblr."

"What about Facebook?" Margie asked. She still had a Facebook page out there in the ether, although she didn't check it too often.

"Uh, yeah. Facebook is kind of...for older people," Eli said delicately. He held up his phone. "Here. Look at this. I sent the link with the login information to you, Aunt Abra and Aunt Katherine a few days ago."

"You did?"

"Yeah. Aunt Katherine is the only one who responded. She knew what it was because all her students are on IcyU."

"Sorry, I thought it was spam or something."

Eli gave her a my-mother-is-hopelessly-out-of-it look then showed her how to log on to the account and talked her through the IcyU interface. It was kind of fun. You pronounced it "I See You," but the site was structured a bit like a college campus. The IcyU logo was a cartoon polar bear cub that was, by any standard, freaking adorable. "Because who doesn't love polar bear cubs?" Eli said.

"Climate change deniers?"

"True. Okay, so we're new and don't have a lot of followers yet. We're freshmen. As we get more followers—except they call them classmates—and more seniority, we move up. You start only being able to post a hundred and fifty characters at a time. Then you move up to two hundred, then two fifty, then three hundred when you're a senior."

"So the people who've been there the longest have more to say?"

"It's just that they've been sort of vetted by the community."

"What happens when you get to three hundred characters?"

"Graduate school. Then you get like five hundred characters." He went back to the phone, clicking on one of the icons. "One of the cool features is that you can major in different subjects. For instance, the Super Ladies feed links to the online comic, so one of our majors is art. Get it? So people looking for art-themed Icers can find us under 'art.'"

"Icers? I know I'm not what most people would define as 'cool,' but that's a really lame name."

"Yeah, I know. That's the only dorky thing about the site. Other than that, it's pretty hip. And everybody's using it. It's growing faster than any other social media site."

Eli's enthusiasm was so rare that she hated to say anything that might squelch it, but this also affected her life. "The strip and the IcyU feed—isn't it all a bit much?"

Eli looked genuinely surprised. "Mom, what you and Aunt Katherine and Aunt Abra can do is pretty amazing. I understand wanting some privacy—that's why I made up those names for you—but, you know, this makes a really great comic. Nobody knows that it's real." Eli must have read something in Margie's face because he asked, "Are you, I don't know, embarrassed or something?"

"No, not at all," Margie said. It wasn't the first time she had ever lied to one of her children. She tried not to feel too guilty about it. "So where did you get the idea for the arm wrestling bit?" she asked.

Eli's grin made him look like a giant, mischievous imp. "You haven't see it?" He grabbed his tablet off the floor and called up a video. "Last night, I was Googling the word 'indestructa.'"

"Because you don't trust your mother to give you the correct feminine Latin ending."

"Come on," Eli said with mock exasperation. "I was playing around. And this came up. Here," he said, putting the tablet into her hands. As soon as Margie saw the video on the screen, she knew she and Katherine would have a lot to talk about.

✹ ✹ ✹

Anna, Joan, and Grant were all on the Sea Monkeys Summer Swim Team together. Joan was on it because she liked swimming outside and winning her heats, which she usually did. Grant swam because baseball practice wasn't until the afternoon, and he was starting to realize that being one of only a handful of eleven- and twelve-year-old boys on a team with a plethora of eleven- and twelve-year-old girls was an asset rather than a liability. Anna swam because she worshipped Joan as the big sister she didn't have and wanted to be just like her. With their mornings occupied by swim team, none of the three ever complained about being bored during the summer, and they all slept soundly at night, so Katherine and Margie kept signing them up.

Katherine had been late for practice, so the few good chairs were already snagged by the other swim team parents. She'd settled in next to Margie on a recliner that was missing a couple vinyl straps, so she had to keep shifting her weight to make sure one of her butt cheeks didn't fall through the gaps. They were quiet for a few moments, and Katherine leaned back and closed her eyes, just soaking up the morning sun and listening to the rhythmic *splish-splash* of thirty-two kids swimming laps outdoors at the same time. There was a distinct but indeterminate *hmm* from Margie.

"What?" Katherine asked.

Margie looked up from her phone and coyly asked: "So what have you been up to this week?"

"The usual."

"Out fighting crime or perhaps performing unusual feats of strength?" As she said this, Margie held up her phone so Katherine could see it.

"*What*?" She scooted over to Margie's recliner and squished in on the end so she could get a better look. There was the Super Ladies online comic with the Indestructa character arm wrestling a series of people. Eli had drawn each of her opponents progressively larger, which made the final frame of a yawning Indestructa looking at the nails on her left hand while slamming down a Hulk-like arm with her right even funnier. "I didn't even tell him about this. How did Eli find out?"

"He found an unusual video online," Margie said. "I suspect that the backstory to this whole thing is fascinating, *Indestructa Jones*."

"I didn't want to use my real name," Katherine replied, trying not to sound too defensive. Watching the video in the light of day was disconcerting. The whole thing had been an experiment, not something to share with the world. The comic was one thing—that was an interpretation. The comic was great. A video was much more immediate. And it wasn't an interpretation—it was a documentation of real life. Her life. She was glad she had worn the loud reading glasses. She hadn't done that great a job hiding behind her hair, but half the comments focused on the glasses, not her. If she was going to do something like this again, she'd need the glasses. She had posted one or two things to the IcyU account for fun, not thinking that Eli probably checked it frequently. "He even got the pushing-the-car part."

Margie slid her star-shaped sunglasses to the top of her head. "That actually happened?"

"Kind of. I helped this older couple whose car was stalled. I pushed it up Cedar Hill to a gas station."

"How did Eli find out about it?"

"The Super Ladies posted it on IcyU." Katherine called up the site on her phone and handed it to Margie so she could read: "*IC_SuperLadies posted: One stalled car pushed up a hill. One more random act of kindness.*"

"Aw, that's sweet," Margie said. "That is kind of what we're doing, isn't it? Using our..."

"Superpowers?"

"That sounds freaking ridiculous, but yes. You're helping people. That's pretty cool."

"Thanks," Katherine said. It was all pretty damn cool. Even if it felt like she wasn't doing enough, she was at least doing *something*.

Katherine liked to be doing something. The start of summer vacation always made her feel a bit restless. Once the school year was over, there was so much she wanted to do, so much to accomplish. People often said, "Oh, you're a teacher? You only work nine months a year," which really got her goat. They didn't know that she was at school cleaning and planning lessons and holding meetings for a few weeks before school started and after it let out. Then there were the continuing-education and professional-development workshops during the summer, and the sixty-hour workweeks during the school year. Yes, her job did allow her to be here, right now, watching her kid swim at ten thirty on a Thursday morning in late June, but she had invested a whole lot of time and energy in order to make mornings like this possible. And watching swim practice still didn't help her accomplish any of the personal goals she'd set for herself. She had a stack of books she wanted to read, the Natural History Museum had a lecture series she'd promised herself she'd attend, she had to complete at least one continuing ed workshop this summer, and she had vowed to finally strip the ugly striped wallpaper out of the small foyer by the front door and paint it. That last project had been on her list almost every summer since she and Hal bought the house twelve years earlier but had never risen high enough on the priority list to get done.

The biggest thing was the garden. She'd done some simple cross-pollinating of a few different bean plants last year and saved the seeds. She and Anna started some of the seeds inside and planted everything else outside back in May, but her plans to track the plants' growth wasn't happening. She wasn't much of a scientist if she couldn't even keep track of her own experiments. Sometimes calling herself a scientist felt stupid. She wasn't a scientist; she was just some high school biology teacher.

She tried to keep her frustration at bay the rest of the day, even though Anna only worked in the vegetable garden with her for twenty minutes before growing bored. She managed to do some laundry and minimal cleaning while Anna played with a friend. At least the house didn't look like a complete pigsty.

Hal called and said a few people were going out for a drink after work and would she mind if he went with them? It wasn't a real question, just his passive-aggressive way of saying he'd be home late. She and Anna had a fun dinner on their own then settled down for a cutthroat game of Uno. When Hal got home, Anna jumped up from the living room floor and practically knocked him over. It was getting near Anna's bedtime by then, but instead of starting to wind down, she wound right back up because she hadn't seen her dad all day. Somehow it felt like Hal was intruding on their evening, like a guest who had overstayed his welcome rather than a member of the family. She knew that wasn't entirely fair, but knowing didn't change her feelings.

Anna was happy to crawl into Hal's lap and tell him about swim practice and playing with her friend Crystal afterward. "We did a lemonade stand and made seven dollars each."

"Wow, that's great," Hal said. He glanced over at Katherine. "Is that pure profit or gross sales?"

"When you're nine, you don't have any overhead," she replied.

"We gave Mom free lemonade because she made it," Anna offered.

"That was very kind of you," Hal said, giving her an extra hug.

Hal truly was a good dad, listening to Anna's circuitous telling of her day, adding in questions and exclamations at the right time. It was easy to see how much he valued Anna and her opinions. If nothing else, he was a great dad. Anna got to bed late because she wanted to stay up and talk to Hal, and Katherine knew the kid would be tired and cranky the next day.

Eventually it was just the two of them in the living room, Hal watching the Cleveland Indians play the Texas Rangers on television, and Katherine reading a book on the Higgs boson. For every set of parents, it will eventually be just the two of them.

"Do you realize that we are now closer to Anna's going to college than we are to her coming home after the adoption?" Katherine asked. "That just boggles my mind."

Hal didn't look up and didn't respond, so she repeated the question.

"I heard you the first time," he said.

"You didn't say anything."

"There's nothing to say. She's getting big. I'll worry about her going to college when she goes. Which will be around the same time I'm supposed to retire," he added quietly as he turned his attention back to the game.

"The world is not going to end when you retire," she said.

Hal paused the television. "Katherine, I'm sorry, but I've been listening to people all day. I'm tired, and I don't have the luxury of staying home all day. I don't get a summer vacation."

Katherine wasn't quite sure how to respond to this. She took a deep breath and said, "This is one of those conversations where I'm not sure which one of us is being a jerk. Maybe we should change the subject."

"Gladly."

Katherine decided that Hal's tone answered the question as to which of them was being a jerk. Even so, later, as they were getting ready for bed, she walked up behind him as he was undressing and finished pulling off his T-shirt for him. She wrapped her arms around his bare chest, gave the back of his neck a little lick, and then rested her cheek in the slight curve between his shoulder blades. "Hi," she whispered.

"Hi."

She moved her hands to his chest, he turned around. After a moment, Hal kissed her back. Maybe not with the full-on passion she might have wanted, but he was at least kissing back. This was good. They needed this. Not the sex so much as the connection, the intimacy. She unzipped his pants. "You don't have to do anything. I'll drive," she said.

Things were moving along for a moment then Hal jumped backward. "Ow, easy there!" he cried. "You aren't starting a lawn mower."

"Sorry," she said. "I got a little carried away."

"That's okay. Look, honestly I'm really tired and I'm just not in the mood."

She put her hand back to work, more gently this time. "It seemed like you were getting in the mood."

Hal sighed. Truly, he looked pained, as though he knew he wasn't giving his wife what she wanted but just didn't have it in him. "No." There was a finality in his voice that made Katherine realize that even her best moves weren't going to have any effect.

"It just seems like you're always tired," she said quietly.

Hal gave her a quick kiss and said, "When you're fifty-seven, you'll understand." Then he got into bed. *I'll never be as old as you act*, Katherine thought, but managed to keep from saying it out loud.

IC_SuperLadies posted: *Sometimes you fight crime. Sometimes you go to bed early.*

CHAPTER EIGHTEEN

EVEN WHEN MARGIE WASN'T WORKING, IT WAS TOO EASY FOR THE DAYS TO GET AWAY FROM HER. There was a never-ending parade of children and appointments and errands and tasks that it seemed no one but she could do. For instance, she was the only one who realized it didn't make sense to leave Eli's dentist and eye appointments until the week before he left for college. The dental insurance only paid for cleanings at six month intervals; going now meant he could schedule his next cleaning for winter break. She was the one who marked the calendar for mundane things like giving Juno her anti-flea treatment because the one time the dog had gotten fleas, they practically had to fumigate the entire house. It was just a little pill that the dog seemed to think was a treat, but if she asked Karl or one of the kids to do it, they invariably forgot or didn't put a check mark on the calendar to note they had done so, leaving Margie to go into the drawer and count the remaining pills. She kept trying to remind herself that her life was a blessing, that she was incredibly fortunate to be able to give her time to her family. But being held responsible for every last shitty little detail was driving her nuts.

There was something more. There is always something more. She knew all about the problem that has no name and smart women sidetracking their own careers to take care of husbands and families. This wasn't anything new. This annoyance and dissatisfaction and occasionally feeling that she was leading a life of quiet female desperation wasn't anything new, but it was *her* annoyance and dissatisfaction and quiet desperation.

She wasn't getting hot flashes the way she used to. They still cropped up unannounced. She'd be going about her day when it suddenly felt like she was sitting and sweating in the sunshine on a ninety-degree day. Every older woman she had ever talked to about it said they came and went. Since she made the glass of water boil at Abra's, she'd only tried to muster up a hot flash on her own once, and that was to open a jar of pickles. It was easier than holding the jar under hot water. That was about the only thing the epic hot flashes seemed to be good for. Stupid stuff. Not big things like righting wrongs and fighting crime. Plus she was still responsible for eight million other shitty little details.

Grant's twelve-and-under baseball league had games every Monday and Friday evening, which had raised some questions about whether or not he should stay with it, because Karl worried it would interfere with Friday night Shabbat. Growing up on the east side of Cleveland, Margie had had plenty of Jewish friends and exposure to the religion. But as an Italian Catholic, she had never really partaken in any Jewish rituals except for a few weddings and funerals and a Seder or two. It was only after she met Karl and started to see how his family melded ancient traditions with modern life that religion became real for her. That was why she converted.

She and Karl were middle-of-the-road reformed. They went to synagogue on the High Holy Days but not every week. One thing they always did was celebrate

Shabbat on Friday evening. That was nonnegotiable. It reminded Margie of the big Sunday dinners she had grown up with, when the entire family would get together. She loved the ritual of gathering her family around her, lighting the candles, praying, and sharing a meal. It was the one thing she insisted on. Except you were supposed to light the candles before sunset and weren't supposed to do any sort of work from sundown on Friday to sundown on Saturday. It was a day of rest. She and Karl took a more modern approach to the Sabbath than many of their friends, but they tried to keep to the work prohibition—no cooking, no cleaning, no homework. And in their house, no electronics on Friday night. Despite occasional pushback from one kid or another, having the entire family put away all their electronic devices one night a week was a blessing. Without the distractions of phones or tablets or televisions, her kids were reminded of their own humanity, of the joy and pleasure that comes with face-to-face communication.

Grant didn't want to give up baseball. He had launched an impressive argument that revolved around game time (six o'clock) and sundown during the summer months (anywhere from eight thirty to nine o'clock). "They still limit us to seven innings or two hours. I believe we can make this work," he announced. Eli and, in a startling show of solidarity, Joan had backed him up. So did Margie. She had voluntarily converted when she married Karl but still maintained a somewhat loose interpretation of religious dogma. When Karl realized he was outvoted, he relented. Thus far, the family experiment in Friday evening baseball had gone smoothly.

The Friday before July Fourth was rainy and cold. Margie hoped the game would be canceled and spent the day doing the semiannual Going Through Old Clothes, Sports Equipment, and Games For Goodwill. With Eli getting ready for college, it seemed like a good time to go through everything the kids had outgrown. When Grant told her the game was on, she hustled him out of the house to get to Forest Hill Park in time.

Eli had taken to doing the five miles from their house to Forest Hill as a long run and then riding home with her after Grant's games. Joan was at a friend's house but texted and said she'd get dropped off at the park. As she ended up doing at most of her children's sporting events, Margie sat alone, trying not to feel too resentful that it was her time, her life that was passing by while everyone else was leading theirs. Karl texted that he was running late because of an accident on the Shoreway but thought he would get to the park in time to see at least part of the game.

It was still cool and damp out, and Margie was glad she'd remembered a jacket. Summer or not, it would be a good night to eat the chicken and veggies she'd put into the crock pot before they left the house. She might be lenient about religion in some ways, but she did her best to observe Shabbat reverently, including the prohibition about work—even turning on a stove—after sundown.

The infield looked okay, but she saw a spray of water splash up in left field as Grant went after a fly ball during the first inning. And when his team was up in the bottom of the second, he took a slide into third base that covered his pants and front with mud. Getting his uniform clean was going to be fun.

She'd been sitting at the top of the small aluminum bleachers but in between innings stood up and walked behind the dugout to stretch her legs. She knew better than to try and talk to Grant through the fence. Some things were simply forbidden. The grandfather of one of Grant's teammate was sitting alone in a collapsible canvas chair on the edge of the paved walkway that ran behind the field. He was a tall, lanky African American man who unfailingly wore a Cleveland Indians baseball cap. Margie wasn't sure of his name, but when he learned that she and Grant had Indians season tickets, he talked baseball with her every game.

She was pretty sure the grandfather didn't know her name either, because he greeted her, as he always did, with a hearty "Well, hello there, young lady!"

"Hi. Why are you sitting way over here?"

"The grass is too damp, and the bleachers are too cold. It hurts my arthritis." As if to emphasize the point, he rubbed his right knee.

Margie stood next to his chair so she could still watch the game while they talked. "I'm sorry to hear that. It is kind of nasty out here tonight."

"Were you at the ballpark last night? The Indians had a rain delay."

"Watched it on TV. We split a twenty-game package with some friends. We're generally there on Wednesdays or Sundays."

"Looks good for this weekend against the Royals though." The grandfather always knew who the Indians were playing. He was as devoted a fan as Grant.

They talked baseball for a while. His grandson, Al, played first base and was one of the tallest kids on the field. "He takes after me."

"Because he's tall or are you a good hitter too?"

The grandfather smiled. "Both. I used to smack the hell out of that ball. Excuse my language."

"Not a problem."

"And I could run like a gazelle too. Played outfield like your boy." He rubbed his right knee again. "I just hope Al didn't inherit my knees. When it's cold and damp like this, it hurts."

Cold, Margie thought. *What's the antidote for cold? Heat.*

"This is going to sound a little strange," she said, squatting down next to his chair. She tried to think up a plausible explanation. "I've been doing some reading on healing touch. Could I try to help your knee?"

"Healing touch? What is that?" He didn't sound convinced.

"I think I can make your knee feel better. At least for the moment. May I put my hands on your knee?"

"Are you coming on to me, sweetie?" the grandfather asked with a mischievous grin. "Go ahead if you think you can help."

Margie had never tried harnessing a hot flash without a little sugar first, but this was important. This was another person in pain, and she had the ability to do something about it. She placed both hands on his bony knee, felt the stick-figure legs beneath his well-worn old-man khakis. She didn't know where to focus her gaze, so she closed her eyes and hoped no one was watching them. *I don't need a lot of heat*, she thought. *Just a little. Just enough to warm his knee and ease his pain.* She thought warm; she thought heat. She thought dog days of summer when your clothing sticks to you and the driveway is too hot for bare feet. She thought arid deserts and blazing bonfires and steaming pots of soup and eye-watering hot chili, and slowly she felt a gentle ripple of heat flowing through her body and into her hands, into the grandfather's knee.

"Hey there," he said. She felt his knee bend slowly under her hands and opened her eyes. "That feels better. What did you just do?"

Margie had been so focused on the doing, on the helping, that she hadn't thought about what might happen after the helping. What she had just done was, to put it lightly, unusual. Now she had to explain it. The things we do don't happen in a vacuum; they are seen by other people, done to or for other people, and sometimes those other people are going to ask awkward questions. She stammered through her made-up explanation again.

Al's grandfather looked skeptical. "I'm not sure I understand," he said, "but my knee feels much better. You have magic hands, young lady. I thank you."

Margie murmured a hasty "You're welcome" and retreated back to the bleachers. This whole using-her-powers-to-help thing was going to take some thinking and planning. A disguise maybe? She didn't have time to think about it right then. When she got back to the bleachers, she found Joan and Eli sitting side-by-side on the top row. Joan was texting away on her phone. Eli was wearing his running shoes and shorts and had on a retro Ramones T-shirt that probably cost more than the tickets Margie had paid to see the Ramones when she was in college.

"Hey, Mom!" Eli said as she sat down in between him and Joan. Joan gave a distracted "Hi" without looking up from her phone.

Even though Eli was sweaty from his run and Joan was in TextWorld, Margie gave them each a quick hug. She was pretty sure Joan didn't notice.

Eli had the little notebook and pencil he always carried, even in the pocket of his running shorts. Margie always marveled at how the notebook—that one or a larger one—went everywhere with him. You'd think after his run it would be damp, but it didn't seem to bother Eli. She surreptitiously glanced over his shoulder to see if he was sketching out a new Super Ladies comic, but he was just doodling some little cartoons based on the ballplayers.

"Eli, do you want me to get the car blanket?"

"No, thanks, I'm fine," he said with a small smile.

"Are you sure? It's kind of cold out here."

"I'm not cold. And it's already the top of the seventh. They'll be done soon."

Grant's team, the Chargers, were the visitors and down 6–5. The first out of the inning came on the first batter, and it looked like they'd coast out of there in a few minutes, giving them plenty of time to get home and put the finishing touches on dinner well before sundown.

Margie was glad she'd had the foresight to put something in the crock pot before she left the house, because Grant walked and ended up scoring a run, which made Margie ready to burst with pride. However, it also tied the score and meant the game wouldn't be over as quickly as she thought it would.

Karl showed up in the middle of the inning. "I should have just told you to go home," she said to him.

"Nice to see you too," Karl said, giving her a kiss on the cheek.

Grant's team ended up losing by a run in extra innings. By the time they all got home, it was eight forty-five and everyone was ravenous. Joan took Juno out, Karl grabbed the candles, and Margie shooed Eli and Grant to the bathroom to at least wash their hands before dinner. Margie had walked into the kitchen barking orders at her family and feeling like Super Mom. Then she saw the unplugged crock pot.

"Oh crap."

"What?" Karl asked, following her gaze. "Oh."

The kids wandered back into the kitchen.

"Uh-oh," Joan said. "Way to go, Mom."

Margie had noticed her daughter's latest growth spurt seemed to include the addition of a bad attitude where her mother was concerned. "Thanks for the support, sweetie," she replied.

"Does this mean we don't have any dinner?" Grant asked. "I'm starving."

"One: you are not 'starving.' People in sub-Saharan Africa and other parts of the developing world are starving. You're hungry. Two: we have dinner."

"And about nine minutes to get it together," Karl said. "I really don't want to eat dinner at ten thirty at night."

Margie took a quick inventory of the refrigerator: a tiny bit of leftover salad that she set Karl to work on augmenting with whatever was in the crisper, a bunch of leftover macaroni and cheese that not even Grant would eat cold, one hamburger of indeterminate age, and two slices of pizza.

"We really should light the candles," Eli said as she handed him the Tupperware container of mac and cheese and something in a small foam container that Joan said was her leftover sandwich from when she and Margie went out to lunch.

"You can eat that," Margie offered. "Leftovers are fine."

Joan partially opened it and sniffed. "Eew, this is like two weeks old," she said and chucked it in the garbage.

Margie lit the Shabbat candles, and they prayed the blessing. Then the five of them stood in the kitchen looking at the mishmash of food on the kitchen island.

"Can't we use the stove after sundown just this once?" Grant asked.

"Please?" Joan added.

Margie looked over at Karl, who seemed torn between his beliefs and convenience. She was pretty sure God wasn't going to send down a thunderbolt if she just hit "start" on the microwave.

"Mom?" Eli said. "You can heat all this stuff up."

It took Margie a moment to realize what Eli was driving at. "What do you mean?"

"You can heat it up."

"What?" Grant demanded. "What are you talking about?"

"Mom can—"

Margie silenced him with a look. It was an accident that Eli knew about her epic hot flashes and what they could do. She hadn't talked to Karl about it and hadn't even mentioned the Super Ladies comic to the younger kids. This was her body. On one hand, it felt too private to share. After all, hot flashes meant she was getting older, that her body was changing, aging. And yet, she had never felt more powerful than when she caused that car to overheat. Granted, there was a certain amount of satisfying comeuppance for the surly teenagers inside the car, but feeling the heat radiating through her body made her feel stronger than she ever had before. And as awkward as it had been immediately afterward, she had eased someone's pain. That, too, was power. If anyone should know about this, it ought to be her family.

"Eli, could you please get me a couple pieces of candy?"

Eli's smile turned mischievous as he dashed over to the snack cupboard.

"What? No fair! How come Mom gets candy for dinner and I don't?" Grant said.

"Mom isn't having candy for dinner," Karl said. He gave Margie a puzzled look as Eli handed her two mini Reese's cups, and she ate them in rapid succession. "I have no idea what she's doing, but she isn't having candy for dinner. Are you?"

"I'm having salad," Margie said. Now that she'd committed to showing the entire family what she could do, she was feeling an odd combination of nerves and excitement, as though she was about to step onto a stage and do a striptease. "Grant, do you want mac and cheese?"

Grant gave an enthusiastic "Yes."

"Joan? Eli?"

Joan only nodded, but Eli's smile got even bigger as he said, "Yes, please."

Margie quickly spooned the cold macaroni and cheese into a big glass bowl.

"Mom, you do know that it's after sundown, right? You can't use the microwave," Joan said.

"I know." Margie held the bowl with both hands and thought warm thoughts. It wasn't really work, because the sugar always seemed to trigger the hot flashes naturally. She was just encouraging it. Sure enough, she felt a wave of heat coming over her and tried to focus it to her hands and the bowl.

"Mom, you're turning kind of...pink," Joan said. She almost sounded worried, which seemed like a small victory.

"She's having a hot flash," Eli said knowledgeably.

"What do you know about *hot flashes*?" Joan asked, as though the entire concept was disdainful.

"What's a hot flash?" Grant asked.

"Mom will tell you later," Karl said, not taking his eyes off the bowl and the tiny tendrils of steam that were beginning to rise from it. "Margie, darling, light and love of my life...is that bowl getting...warm?"

Margie met her husband's eyes. Despite a strong marriage, good communication, and an active sex life, the look of interest and admiration in his eyes was one she hadn't seen since they'd started dating. "Why yes," she replied. "Yes, it is."

"Is that...?" Karl stammered. "Do you think we'll have to talk to the rabbi about this?"

"Do *you* want to broach the subject with him?" Margie asked.

"Okay, we're going to go with the assumption that this is kosher."

Margie's family watched in silence for another minute until the bowl of mac and cheese was steaming as though it had just come out of the oven.

"How did you do that?" Joan asked. She looked astonished and, Margie was pleased to note, maybe a little impressed.

"I told you—Mom had a hot flash," Eli said proudly.

"I want to do that," Grant said. "I don't mind talking to the rabbi about it."

Margie caught Karl's eye and tried not to laugh. "Maybe you should talk to Dad about it first," she said.

She spent the rest of the evening deliberately shepherding the rest of the family from food to books to bed, deftly deflecting any questions about hot flashes or anything else. When she finally went to bed that night, Karl was still up.

"You're up late," Margie said as she closed the bedroom door. She thought for sure he'd be asleep by now.

"I wanted to talk to you," Karl said. He'd been reading a book but now put it on the bedside table. Karl was generally a pretty good husband, but typically she had to compete for his attention with whatever he was reading or watching on television. This was different. He extended a hand to her. Margie walked over and sat on his side of the bed. Karl gave her a quick kiss then leaned back among the pile of gray and black pillows on the bed and regarded his wife. Margie frequently compared his need for copious pillows to the Princess and the Pea. "Now, you still haven't told me how you managed to reheat a bowl of leftover mac and cheese using only the power of touch."

Margie felt compelled to add: "And a hot flash."

"And a hot flash," he echoed. "Eli apparently knew you could do this, but you didn't see fit to tell your husband." For the first time, Karl sounded a little annoyed. In truth, Margie had avoided telling him anything. Partly because it was so weird she didn't know how to broach the subject and partly because she enjoyed having the secret to herself. "You can defy the laws of thermodynamics, but you didn't bother to tell me?"

"I'm sorry. I guess I wasn't sure what to say or how to explain it. I'm still not. And to be fair, Eli found out by accident." Margie told Karl about the drunken car-surfing boys and how she made the car overheat and how it all seemed to go back to the explosion.

"I don't know whether to laugh or flip out," Karl said. "This is nuts."

"I know, sweetie."

"I mean, it's really cool. Or rather, really hot."

"Yes."

"It's also nuts."

"Yes."

She sat silently next to her husband for a moment. "I feel like I just won a burlesque dance competition and can't tell anybody about it," she said finally.

Karl laughed. "You can do amazing things and come up with killer analogies. How did I get so lucky?'

"I can't do anything amazing..."

"Margie, yes, you can. You know, when I met you I was intrigued because you're related to baseball royalty."

"Distantly. And Phil Rizzuto doesn't know me from Adam. Or Eve."

Karl ignored her side comment. "And now I find out you have the power to—how did you describe it—harness a hot flash? You're a miracle."

After twenty-three years of marriage, two houses, two dogs, countless fish, and three kids, Margie wasn't used to being the center of attention, even from one person. "Karl, you're very sweet, but I'm not a miracle. I'm just another overweight housewife in a middle-class suburb."

"And I'm a short Jewish lawyer. You think I don't feel like a cliché sometimes? You're the best thing I have going for me. And now it turns out you have...superpowers?"

"Power. Superpower, just one. Just that one thing."

Karl trailed one finger along Margie's bare calf and under the fabric of her Capri pants to the top of her knee. "Can I see what other things your body can do?" he asked gently. Two fingers now softly trailed to the sensitive spot on the back of her knee. Margie involuntarily let out a little gasp of pleasure. "X marks the X-rated spot," he said. He knew all the right spots on her body. Sometimes it amazed her that Karl loved her body so much when she frequently hated it. But there he was, happily touching her, doing everything in his power to turn her on.

It worked.

IC_SuperLadies posted: *The Schvitz has discovered she is the most kosher of all superheroes.*

CHAPTER NINETEEN

THE FOURTH OF JULY HAD BEEN MARGIE'S FAVORITE HOLIDAY FOR YEARS. She wasn't particularly patriotic; it was just that the Fourth had so many wonderful attendant qualities. It was better than Christmas because it wasn't tied to any faith tradition, so everybody got the day off and nobody felt awkward. The food was easier to prepare than on Thanksgiving, plus you weren't obliged to see relatives you didn't like. It was almost always warmer than Memorial Day but didn't have the bittersweet end-of-summer melancholy of Labor Day. And you got fireworks. Truly, how could you not love this holiday?

"And Katherine and Hal host it," Karl said. "So we don't have to clean."

"That's just another added bonus." There were children to round up and salads to bring over to the Krenzlers for a picnic and then out to watch fireworks. Margie pressed down in the center of a Tupperware container of potato salad and heard the little *pfft* that locked the lid on. "Darling, do you realize that I am a middle-aged suburban housewife with a Tupperware container of potato salad on July Fourth? How many kinds of cliché is that?"

"Four. Maybe six," Karl replied. "Grant! Joan! Let's go."

Eli wandered into the kitchen. "Have fun. Tell them all I said hi."

Margie swallowed back a wave of nostalgia. This was the first time any of their kids had opted out of the Fourth of July—or any holiday—with the family. "We will. Have fun with Jamis."

"Are you sure you don't want to come for part of the time?" Karl asked.

"No, thanks," Eli said with a stupid little grin on his face. His crush on Jamis was perhaps a little more intense than Margie had realized.

"Where are you all going to watch fireworks?" Karl asked.

"Jamis's aunt lives in Willoughby, so we're going to park in her driveway and walk over to some park where they do fireworks. I can't remember what it's called."

Karl gave a little sigh at this typical lack of teenage detail, while Margie asked, "Do I need to go over the whole don't-get-into-a-car-with-someone-who's-been-drinking-we'll-pick-you-up-if-necessary routine?"

"No, you don't, Mom."

Grant came bounding into the kitchen. "I thought we were leaving," he said. "Where's Joan?"

"Somewhere," Margie said. "Please go find her. And make sure you both bring a hoodie or a jacket or something."

"I'll meet you all in the car," Karl said as he picked up the potato salad and walked out to the garage.

"Please take Juno out before you leave, and close the windows so she doesn't get freaked out by all the noise."

"Juno gets freaked out by flies buzzing, but I'll close the windows. Should I turn on the air conditioner?"

"It's supposed to be kind of cold tonight. We don't need the air."

Grant came back to the kitchen, followed by Joan. "Found her!" he announced.

"Thank you. Go out to the car. I'll be right there." Margie almost followed the younger kids outside, but something kept her back for a moment. Eli was leaning against the kitchen table, waiting for her to leave and, she figured, probably rejoicing in having the house to himself for a couple of hours before he met his friends. Before he met his boyfriend.

It was only in the last year or so that Eli had really come into his own. He stopped cutting at the beginning of his sophomore year but had still isolated himself. During the winter of his junior year, he'd spent a lot of time alone drawing and reading. One day when she was making dinner, he'd come into the kitchen carrying a copy of *Giovanni's Room* by James Baldwin. Margie noticed he'd been reading a lot of Baldwin and nonchalantly noted that he was one of her favorite writers.

Margie could hear the trepidation in Eli's voice as he said cautiously, "You know that Baldwin was gay, right?"

She'd been chopping up vegetables for soup and absent-mindedly replied, "Yeah, so?"

"That doesn't change your opinion of him? You still like him?"

Then it struck her that perhaps Eli wasn't actually talking about James Baldwin. She looked up from the cutting board to find Eli staring at her. She had infrequently wondered if her eldest might be gay but had never spoken to him about it. There were times back then when Eli still seemed so fragile that she hadn't wanted to do anything to upset the precarious stability he'd achieved. She had hoped that, if he was gay, he'd eventually feel comfortable enough to come out to her. Here he was doing just that, and she was chopping carrots. She put down the knife and gave Eli her undivided attention.

"It doesn't matter to me whether someone is gay," she had said deliberately. "It doesn't matter who you love, just that you *can* love and care for someone else." She saw Eli's eyes start to fill with tears. "What matters is being kind and decent and just and"—she felt her own voice crack—"and that you're nice to little kids and animals, and that you remember to recycle and..." Margie had walked around the kitchen island to where Eli was standing by the table and hugged him, held him as long as he needed.

Eli was again standing in that exact same spot as she hugged him goodbye. She wanted to be cool and laid back about the whole thing, but Eli didn't have much experience in romantic relationships with either gender. She hoped the fabulous Jamis Barberton wouldn't break his heart.

"Have fun," she said.

"I will," Eli replied.

The glint in his eye made her add, "Not too much fun." And then she finally got herself out the door.

At Katherine and Hal's house, it was the typical jumble of children and food for a couple of hours. There was finally a lull after they'd eaten but before they would need to head out to watch fireworks. Their group tradition was to go to Shaker Middle School, two suburbs over, because it was the closest city with fireworks.

Margie had jokingly said that the women would acquiesce to traditional gender roles and put the leftovers away and do the dishes, but it was more a handy excuse for her, Katherine, and Abra to talk in private in Katherine's square, muted-yellow kitchen.

Once the dishwasher was loaded, Katherine put the last of the leftovers into the refrigerator and grabbed three bottles of Burning River Pale Ale. "Here, our reward," she said.

Margie dried her hands on the towel hanging next to the kitchen sink and took the beer Katherine offered. "In the words of patriot Benjamin Franklin, beer is proof that God loves us and wants us to be happy," she said.

Katherine handed her a bottle opener. "Church key?"

"Amen," she replied. They stood silently in the kitchen for a moment, just drinking their beer and enjoying each other's company. In lieu of a decorative border, Katherine had stenciled a quote from Marie Curie along the top of her kitchen wall. Every time Margie visited, she read: "Nothing in life is to be feared; it is only to be understood. Now is the time to understand more so that we may fear less." She wondered if she could get Eli to stencil something along the top of their kitchen wall.

"I've been doing some thinking," Abra said, jolting Margie out of her thoughts. "There's a wrong I want to right."

"That sounds rather superhero-ish," Katherine said.

"It is." Abra's tone had the same jaunty flair as their telephone conversation.

"Is this what you wanted help with?" Margie asked.

"Yes. My neighbors are being foreclosed on. I want to fix that."

Even several years after the mortgage loan crisis and the recession, tons of people were still getting foreclosed on or, like Abra, were underwater on their mortgages. There didn't seem to be a whole lot an ordinary person could do. A month ago, Margie might have looked at Abra's statement as hopeless, or might have asked if she was going to connect her neighbor with a consumer advocacy group. Things seemed different now. She merely asked, "What can we do to help?"

"All I want to do is move a decimal point."

Katherine looked a bit dejected. "I'm going to assume there's something slightly more exciting going on here than punctuation."

"Yes, there is. In order to move the decimal point, I need Margie to help me get into the offices of North-Coast Home Mortgage."

"Why her?"

"She comes off as more innocent than you do."

Margie glanced over at Katherine and shrugged, unsure which of them ought to feel bad. Katherine shrugged back and kind of nodded. "Fair enough," she said.

"Why do you need to move a decimal point?"

"They sold my neighbors an adjustable rate mortgage that's ballooning to thirteen point four nine percent."

"That's highway robbery," Katherine said with disgust. "Plus they have the gall to call themselves 'north coast' when Cleveland isn't on the north coast of anything. We're on the southern shore of Lake Erie."

Moments like these were why Margie loved Katherine. "We ought to change your superhero name to Pedantic."

"*Pedanta*. Or maybe Pedantula."

Abra sighed. "Can we please get back to the subject at hand?"

"Right," Margie said. "You were telling us how you're going to break into the misnamed offices of NorthCoast Home Mortgage and fix your neighbors' mortgage."

"I think I can do it without actually breaking and entering," Abra replied, "but I need help."

"It sounds dangerous."

"I assume all the risk. I just need you to walk in the door and walk out."

Before Abra could say much more, Anna, Grant, and Joan burst into the kitchen.

"We would like to leave now," Anna said. She looked rather proud to be the spokesperson for the trio. "We'll end up in the middle of some trees or something and won't be able to see any fireworks if we get there too late."

"Give us five more minutes, sweetie," Katherine said. "We're in the middle of an important conversation."

"We're gonna get a lousy spot," Grant said in a borderline whine.

"Can we please just go?" Joan added. For a moment Margie wondered if all annoyed fourteen-year-old girls sounded like Bette Davis. She didn't have time to ponder the question because there was a general maneuvering of three adults, three children, and two blankets into one minivan. Hal didn't feel like going to see the fireworks, because he hated crowds, and Karl decided to stay and keep him company. For some reason, Margie didn't miss Karl as much as she missed Eli. She knew he was only out for the evening, that this was nothing compared to how it was going to be in the fall, when she'd wake up and know her eldest would be waking up in a dorm room miles away. She didn't like the idea of practicing for that.

They found a spot about three blocks from the middle school and joined the hordes of east-siders walking the streets of Shaker Heights in search of the perfect spot to watch the fireworks. They managed to find a nice spot along the light-rail tracks that ran down the middle of a wide grassy swath bordered by a two-lane, one-way boulevard on either side. Anna seemed oddly intrigued to learn that this was the same rail line Aunt Abra took to work most mornings.

Margie and Katherine sacrificed their phones to Grant and Anna, and all three kids sat in what Hal always called a Zombie Circle, playing games and texting each other from two feet away. At least it gave Margie time to talk with Katherine and Abra while they shared the other blanket.

Margie leaned back and basked in the night air for a moment. She looked over at the Zombie Circle. The kids were still staring at their respective screens, but there was none of the in-game noises of "Ugh, Googlies" or "Darn it" that typically punctuated a trio of kids playing games on phones. She got the impression they were all looking at the same thing, something they didn't want the adults to see.

"What's going on, guys?" she asked casually.

"Nothing," Joan replied, a little too quickly.

Margie tried to keep her voice neutral. "What are you looking at?"

"Nothing."

There was an uneasy silence. She couldn't imagine Joan or Grant showing Anna anything egregiously inappropriate online, especially when Grant was using her phone. Just to be sure, Margie asked Grant for her phone. "And don't close the browser window," she added.

Grant exchanged a guilty look with Joan and extended his arm just enough so that Margie could reach the phone. "Can you show Anna that thing you did with the mac and cheese?" he asked over Joan's hissed "Shhh!"

"Please?" Anna added.

"What? Now?" She glanced down at the phone and saw that Grant had been reading the Super Ladies comic. She should have known it was only a matter of time before the kids started comparing notes.

"So what do you all think of Eli's comic strip?" Katherine asked.

"It's great!" Grant said.

"Pretty funny," Joan admitted.

"And it's all true!" Anna said. "I saw Aunt Abra and so did Eli, and Joan and Grant told me about the macaroni and cheese—"

Katherine interrupted her: "Anna, sweetie, stop. Remember how we talked about keeping this a secret?"

"Eli didn't."

"But he used different names for a reason," Abra put in. "The comic strip isn't supposed to be us. It's just stories."

Even in the darkening light, Margie could see Joan's annoyed tilt of the head. "It's based on the three of you. That isn't a secret."

"It is to the rest of the world," Margie said quickly.

"And we intend to keep it that way," Abra said. "Please."

The three kids were quiet for a moment.

"Can we still read the comic strip?" Anna asked softly.

"Of course," Margie and Katherine said at the same time. She let Katherine finish the thought. "We just think it's better if the rest of the world only looks at it as a comic strip from Eli's imagination, not real life."

They received assent in varying degrees from the three kids. Then Grant proclaimed that he was cold.

"Where are your hoodies?" Margie asked, even though she already knew what the answer would be.

"I forgot it," Grant said.

"I didn't bring one." Somehow Joan managed to make this admission sound as though her forgetfulness was her mother's fault.

Grant crawled over to Margie's blanket and sat next to her. He leaned against her, and she snuggled right back. At eleven and more traditionally boyish than Eli ever was, snuggling with mom hadn't been on Grant's agenda for a while. She would take the cuddly moments with her kids when she could get them.

"When are the fireworks gonna start?" Anna asked.

"I'm sure it'll be soon," Katherine replied. "It's pretty dark."

"Mom?" Grant asked. "I really am cold."

"You already said that, sweetie. I told you to bring a sweatshirt, and you didn't. What do you want me to do?" Margie looked down into her youngest child's face. Grant still had chubby moon cheeks. Sometimes it was a struggle not to pinch them.

Grant looked up at her with an I-can't-believe-my-mother-is-this-clueless expression. "That thing you did with the macaroni and cheese."

"You're serious?" she replied.

Anna's curiosity had clearly been piqued by the comic. "I want to see too!"

Joan moved over to Margie's other side. "It was pretty cool," she admitted.

"Pretty hot you mean!" Grant said.

"Aunt Abra?" Anna began.

"Oh God, here we go," said Abra.

"Could you do that thing you did when you hurt your ankle?"

"Everybody stop," Margie commanded. "I'll do my..."

"Trick?" Grant offered.

"It isn't a trick, you moron," Joan said. "Tricks are fake. This is better."

"Thank you, Joan, and don't call your brother a moron." She'd managed a little bit of heat to heal the baseball grandpa's knee, but generating enough heat to warm up three kids was going to take something bigger. She rooted around in her bag and managed to come up with a piece of candy to boost the hot flash. "Okay, everybody who's cold, stay next to me. I will do this one thing and then we will table the entire superpower discussion for the rest of the night."

Grant and Joan snuggled closer. Anna crawled onto her lap. "I'm not cold, but I want to see this."

"This is less of a 'see' and more of a 'feel,'" Margie said and adjusted Anna on her lap so the child's weight wouldn't cut off the circulation in her leg. She looked over at Katherine and Abra, who were sitting on the other blanket and staring at her as though they were watching a sitcom. They were definitely getting a kick out of this.

"Thanks for all the help, ladies," Margie deadpanned.

"You're doing fine on your own," Katherine replied.

"And it takes some of the heat off me. No pun intended," Abra added.

"This is so cool, Anna," Grant said. "Just wait."

Margie thought warm thoughts, thought about the three children huddled around her for warmth and pretended she was the mother black bear she had seen on Animal Planet, hunkered down in the snow with her cubs. They needed her. Slowly she started feeling warmer and warmer, then downright hot. She could almost feel the heat pouring off of her body. When she heard a collective "Wow" from the kids, she knew they were all heating up too.

"While you're at it, can you warm up my coffee?" Katherine said.

Margie spurted out a laugh, breaking her concentration. Anna, Joan, and Grant started babbling away to one another, Joan and Grant talking about macaroni and cheese and Anna insisting they *had* to see what Aunt Abra could do.

"Are you guys feeling a little warmer now?" Margie asked.

"Yeah, now I want to see what Aunt Abra can do," Grant said.

"Let's save that for another day," Abra said. She looked a little self-conscious about the whole thing.

Katherine changed the subject for her: "Hey, I think they're finally going to start the fireworks!" There was a low buzz of anticipation as more and more people stopped talking and settled in to watch the night sky.

Anna scooted off Margie's lap and snuggled in between her mom and Abra. Grant and Joan stayed right where they were, leaning against her, heads raised to the sky. That was a nice surprise. As the fireworks began, Margie let herself sink into the moment, just enjoying the nearness of her kids, having them sprawled on her like overgrown puppies, like they were still little. The showers of colored lights against the dark sky, the *boom-boom-boom* slowly echoing over the trees, the little bundles of people scattered on the ground watching—it all felt very basic and primitive and pure. There were so many things that Margie wanted to give her children, not just the tangibles like food and clothing and shelter and books and toys, but the big things, intangibles like values and education and peace. She couldn't give them everything, but right now, when they were cold, she could give them warmth. Maybe it wasn't being a superhero, but it still felt like some sort of victory.

IC_SuperLadies posted: *The Schvitz likes fireworks. No professional jealousy here.*

CHAPTER TWENTY

ON THURSDAY AFTERNOON, ABRA MET MARGIE IN THE PARKING LOT OF AN OFFICE BUILDING CALLED AVALON TWO, ONE OF THE DOZENS OF OFFICE BUILDINGS THAT DOTTED THE AREA AROUND THE INTERCHANGE OF I-271 AND CHAGRIN BOULEVARD. An entire edge city had popped up at the freeway exit—retail, hotels, medical buildings, car dealerships, restaurants, and skanky little mortgage offices.

Late Thursday afternoon seemed like it might be the slowest time at a mortgage office, so Abra left work early and had Margie meet her at four fifteen. To be on the safe side, she parked far away from the five-story white concrete building that looked to have been designed in what Margie dubbed "the Midseventies School of Siege Architecture." Margie pulled in next to Abra's little yellow Mini Cooper right on time.

"You ready?" Margie asked as they got out of their respective vehicles.

"I think so. Thanks for helping."

"My pleasure. You're doing a good deed."

"If it works," Abra replied. She had put on thin sneakers with no socks, yoga pants, and a T-shirt. Form-fitting clothes seemed the wisest choice. She looked up at the July sunshine and thought, *Pass through me.* Margie's half-laughing, half-shocked reaction was sufficient to let her know she definitely had the whole invisibility-on-demand thing down.

"That is both astounding and amusing," Margie said. "Just...wow." She gave a once-over to the area where Abra had last been seen standing. "I can't see you at all. Not even a glimpse of clothing."

"Good." It was a little strange to hear herself when she was invisible, like being on a faulty conference call where you could hear the echo of your own voice. "The only weird part is that I can't wear underwear when I do this."

"Dirty girl," Margie teased.

"I'm too hung up to be dirty. Let's just do this before I lose my nerve."

"Okay. I'm with you. I think."

Abra walked across the parking lot alongside Margie. There was indeed a security camera anchored above the front entrance. She probably could have parked closer, but she didn't want any trace of herself near the building. Abra stayed right behind Margie as they went into the building, past a small diner and equally miniscule pharmacy, and down a narrow corridor that led to the first-floor offices.

"I think this must be the low-rent section of the building," Margie murmured.

Abra gave a quiet "Mm-hmm" then was silent.

They were at the front door of NorthCoast Home Mortgage. The dark brown faux wood door was clearly labeled. Margie waltzed on in, holding the door open just a little longer than she needed so Abra could slip in behind her.

Abra hadn't been expecting much, after all, this was just some little storefront mortgage company like dozens of others that had popped up during the housing bubble in the aughties. Even with low expectations, NorthCoast Home Mortgage looked like the place where career aspirations went to die. At one time, the office had clearly held more than the three employees she saw now. A heavy-set woman looking every bit of an early-forties hot mess appeared to be the receptionist/secretary, and she gave Margie a puzzled look with a not so polite "Can I help you?"

"Good afternoon," Margie said, all smiles and charm. A faux wood nameplate on the woman's desk read "Vanessa Mulgrave." "Hi, Vanessa. I'm trying to find Dr. Harper. He's supposed to be in suite one-oh-seven, but you're obviously not him."

The woman gave a world-weary sigh that made it clear speaking with such an idiot was far, far beneath her station in life. "No, this is a mortgage office, not a doctor's office."

"Dentist actually, but I see your point. Do you happen to know where Dr. Harper's office might be?" Margie added with a perky little lilt in her voice that almost made Abra laugh out loud.

The lanky guy in his late thirties who looked like he had done too much partying back when business was good suggested Margie try the building next door. "People get the buildings mixed up all the time," he said.

While Margie kept the staff busy, Abra took a quick look around the office. The three employees were all clustered together at one end of the long, rectangular room. There was a pair of empty cubicles at the far end of the office near a door that Abra presumed was a storage closet. The only other furniture were two empty desks shoved against one wall next to a row of five tall filing cabinets. It was a wonder the place was still open. The slow economic recovery meant that it was only a matter of time before a storefront mortgage broker like this place was completely bankrupt. From what Abra knew about Ramon and Latrice's loan, these guys ought to be out of business and perhaps in jail.

Abra's plan wasn't that detailed. Margie had gotten her in the door undetected. After that, she'd wing it. For now, all she could do was watch her friend as she apologized for getting the wrong office and left. Abra was on her own. She had a brief what-do-I-do-now pang of fear, but that passed. Technically, she hadn't broken any laws. This was not breaking and entering—she had walked in during regular business hours. They just couldn't see her.

Abra sat quietly and invisibly in one of the unused cubicles until the three employees decided to call it a day. There didn't seem to be much in the way of new mortgages coming through. From the few phone calls she overheard, it sounded as though the role of the office had turned to collections and foreclosures. At about quarter to five, Rude Receptionist Vanessa turned off her monitor and asked the lanky guy if he wanted to get a drink after work. He turned her down with a lame "I'm kind of tired." The other woman in the office, who looked to be the youngest of the three, hid a vicious grin at this. Interoffice love triangles aside, the other two took this as a cue to turn off their computers and head out of the office. The lanky guy fished a key chain out of his pants pocket as he left. He was the last one out. Abra heard the door lock. That was it. She was alone in the office.

For a couple of minutes, Abra didn't move, just waited. Sometimes people realize they've forgotten something and come back. Silently she counted to sixty, then did so again just to be sure. When she was confident no one was coming back, she rose and walked over to the three desks.

The lanky guy appeared to be in charge, so she figured his computer would have access to the deepest recesses of the office server. All she wanted to do was move one decimal point. She'd change Ramon and Latrice interest rate from 13.49 percent to 1.34 percent and get out of there.

When she turned on lanky guy's computer, it asked for a password. *Duh,* she thought, *of course there's a password.* Her work computer had a password. Everybody's work computer had a password. Anything that required a keyboard click was a simple means of warding off remote attacks. Abra was good with technology, but she was no hacker. There was no way she'd be able to figure out a stranger's password.

She tried the second woman's computer. When she turned it on, it too asked for a password. Her entire plan suddenly seemed incredibly stupid. *What were you thinking?* Then she remembered the receptionist. She hadn't turned off the computer. She had only turned off the monitor.

Very gingerly, Abra went over to the third desk. Sure enough, the light for the computer monitor was turned off. She pressed it, and the desktop appeared. *Thank you, God, for lazy employees,* she thought.

She figured she had about an hour before the building's cleaning crew came in, although from the look of things, management was paying to have the waste baskets emptied and that was about it. Hopefully she wouldn't be disturbed.

The computer desktop was sloppy, cluttered with all sorts of personal photos and unrelated files. It matched the cluttered physical desk, which was packed with personal photos in clear plastic frames, two seventies-era troll dolls, a few little solar-powered flowers that danced in the light, and a half-eaten package of plain M&Ms. Resisting the urge to organize everything, Abra looked at the icons on the desktop for something that might be a program. There, among the standard spreadsheet and word processing programs was something called "NC-Trax." "That's it," she murmured as she clicked it open.

Once she had the internal database open, it was a fairly simple process to search for Ramon and Latrice's loan. There it was—3847 West Anderson Road. And there was that big, fat, evil interest rate. She put the cursor in the box on the spreadsheet, switched the position of the decimal point, and hit "Save." She imagined this miniscule piece of data working its way through the corporate machine and coming out the other end as an affordable house payment for her friends. Now that she was in the system, it was tempting to lower every interest rate she could. That, she knew, would get noticed. One change to one mortgage could slip through. Not one thousand.

The sound of a woman tunelessly singing seeped in from the hallway. At this hour, it could only be the custodian. It seemed like the cue to leave.

IC_SuperLadies posted: *Shadow reminds you to look out for your friendly neighborhood Super Lady. You might not see her, but that doesn't mean she isn't there.*

CHAPTER TWENTY-ONE

MARGIE REALLY WANTED TO HANG AROUND AND TALK TO ABRA AS SOON AS SHE WAS DONE WITH HER RECONNAISSANCE IN THE MORTGAGE OFFICE, BUT SHE'D PROMISED TO LEAVE. Abra had been adamant that Margie maintain the ruse that she had walked into the wrong office. The guy in the mortgage office had said she might want to try the other building, so once she left Avalon Two, she walked across the courtyard and through the front doors of the identical Avalon One. No wonder people got the two buildings mixed up. The only readily discernible difference was a large crack in the white concrete façade just to the right of the main doors.

Satisfied that she had played her part well, Margie returned to her car to go home. If she hurried, she could fit in a guerrilla trip to the grocery store, because there was next to nothing in the house to make for dinner. While driving up busy Richmond Road, she got stuck behind a dusty black Cadillac going a good ten miles per hour under the speed limit in the right lane. Through the rear windshield, she could just make out the outline of a fedora on the driver's head. "Old man wearing a hat," she muttered. "Don't want to be behind him."

On most days, being behind a slow driver wouldn't bother her. Today she needed to be moving a bit faster. Five cars passed on her left before another car turned left and she had an opening to pass the Cadillac. She accelerated and went around it. As she did, a motorcycle appeared in her rearview mirror. She had seen it farther back in the lane, but it wasn't near her when she switched lanes. It had been behind the car that turned. The motorcyclist flipped her the finger and followed her for a block before speeding up and cutting into the lane directly in front of her.

"Oh, for crying out loud!" Margie exclaimed. "What's his problem?" She'd be making a right turn in a minute anyway, so she moved back into the right lane to get away from him. The guy on the motorcycle wouldn't let it go and again cut into the lane in front of her. "See you later, jackass," she muttered as she turned into the parking lot at Dave's grocery store.

The lot had an "Entrance" and an "Exit" lane. The motorcycle turned into the exit lane and zoomed through the parking lot, pulling into the spot next to where Margie was getting out of the minivan. The motorcyclist had a deliberately scruffy hipster look. He didn't get off the bike but flipped the visor of his helmet and said with a sneer, "Cutting off a motorcycle can be hazardous to your health."

Margie closed the driver's door of the minivan, buying some time to take a deep breath before replying, "I beg your pardon?" Maybe some civility would counter his aggression. He repeated the statement, with a heavy emphasis on the words "your health."

"But I didn't cut you off," she said. "I changed lanes when the car in front of you turned left."

"You cut me off, lady. Don't do it again."

"Well, my car is parked now, so I guess it won't happen again." She hadn't meant to be snarky, but this guy was really too much. As she locked the minivan and started to walk away, she heard a sharp "Hey!" She turned around and saw that the guy had gotten off the bike and taken a few steps toward her.

"Don't walk away when I'm talking to you, lady," he said in a low voice.

His words were a hollow echo of every time she had said that same phrase to her own children, a reminder of every time she had felt helpless and frustrated. It took her back to her very first chemotherapy infusion, right after the breast cancer had been diagnosed. The oncology nurse had started a slow-drip IV, and for an hour Margie sat and stared at the thin tube running into one of her veins, knowing she was completely at the mercy of something beyond her control. Somewhere deep in the pit of her gut where hot flashes and anger dwell, a little flame was lit. She looked into his hipper-than-thou eyes, which stared back with disdain. "Why are you doing this? Why are you like this?" she asked.

"Like what? Pissed off because some spoiled stay-at-home mom nearly ran me off the road?"

"One: I didn't nearly run you off the road. Two: You know nothing about me."

"I know all about you. There are useless women like you in every stinking minivan."

Margie's heart was pounding. She tried to swallow the fear. There were other cars, other people in the parking lot, each of them ensconced in their own little world. No one was paying attention to a man and a woman talking. This guy could easily hurt her, overpower her before anyone bothered to help. Except he had no right to hurt her. The little flame in her gut burned brighter. For a moment, it was as though this guy and his cocky attitude personified everything wrong with her life. *You don't have to be nice all the time*, she thought. She straightened up a little bit. "And there are annoying, overcompensating little boys like you on every motorcycle." She gently placed a hand on the motorcycle seat.

"Don't touch my bike," the guy said.

"I just want to see it," she replied calmly. "It's really pretty. Comfy seat."

The guy raised his voice. "Get your hands off my bike."

Margie could feel the heat coursing through her body, into her hand, and into the motorcycle seat. "I'm not going to knock your bike over. I'll tell you what. You can put your hand on my van to make it even. I don't mind." The guy momentarily looked back at the minivan, as though it were about to jump up and start tap dancing on its rear wheels. In doing so, he missed the tiny trail of smoke that started to rise from the motorcycle seat as the faux leather upholstery began to warp from the heat of Margie's hand. But the guy was close enough to smell the burning plastic. He pushed Margie's hand away just as the seat was developing a small but growing burn circle, revealing melting, charred foam underneath.

"What the hell did you just do to my bike!" the guy screamed, looking from the motorcycle seat to Margie. She took a step backward. For a terrifying second, she thought he was going to hit her and raised a hand to protect herself. Somehow, the palm of her hand—the same palm that had just decimated his motorcycle seat—seemed to put the fear of God and Mom into the guy. "How the hell did you do that?" he asked, much more quietly this time. He even sounded a little bit scared.

"I didn't do anything," she replied softly. "I'm just a useless woman, remember?" With that, she got back in the minivan and drove away. They could order pizza tonight.

IC_SuperLadies posted: *Did the Batmobile ever smell like dirty gym clothes?*

CHAPTER TWENTY-TWO

THEY DIDN'T GET TOGETHER AS A GROUP AGAIN UNTIL
SATURDAY, WHEN THEY MET UP AT THEIR USUAL SPOT
IN THE BAR AT LA FIESTA, A FAMILY-OWNED MEXICAN
RESTAURANT THAT WAS CLOSE TO HOME AND HAD
THE BEST GOLDEN MARGARITAS ON THE EAST SIDE
OF CLEVELAND. The bar area was at the center of the
restaurant, flanked by an L-shaped dining room. Margie
arrived at the same time as Abra, and they found a spot
at one of the iron and tile tables in the bar, where the
seats always seemed more comfortable than in the dining section. Katherine arrived a few minutes later, sitting down with a hearty "Hey! I have a present for you."

"You who?" Abra asked.

"Both of you. Each of you."

"Well, thank you."

"Don't thank her until you know what it is," Margie
quipped.

Katherine gave her a teacherly settle-down sort of
look. "You'll like this." She had two small paper bags on
the table in front of her but didn't hand them over right
away. Katherine sometimes liked to give a lecture. "Okay,
so you know I got these great little reading glasses at the

farmers' market," she began, pulling the glasses off the top of her head and putting them on.

"Yeah, they're cute," Abra said.

"Well, I've noticed that whenever I wear them, the glasses are the first thing people notice. The only thing they notice. Anna and I went to the Shaker Square farmers' market this morning because she really, really wanted this light switch plate that's painted to look like a smiling dog, only with a light switch for a tongue. While we were there, I saw these and thought they might come in handy for you too." Only when she was finished with her gift introduction did she give a brown paper bag to each of them.

"Thank you," Margie murmured as she opened the bag. Inside was a pair of blue cheater reading glasses with a tiny Alice in Wonderland–type toadstool painted on either end. "Thank you, these are adorable!" Margie exclaimed. She put them on and picked up the little drink-special stand from the middle of the table. The small type printed on top of a photo of a margarita was definitely clearer. "And they work."

"I love them," Abra said. She put on a pair of dark green glasses with tiny purple irises. "Thanks."

"I thought there might be times when you don't want to be recognized."

Abra looked skeptical. "These will keep me from being recognized?" she asked.

"If you have one accessory that's eye-catching enough, that's all people will remember about you."

Margie was a little skeptical, less about the glasses and more about whether she'd ever even have the chance to wear them while doing something superhero-y. Still, she had pretty much decimated that guy's motorcycle seat—moreover, it felt surprisingly good. She didn't realize she was sitting with a silly grin on her face until Katherine asked, "What are you smiling about? Basking in the afterglow of some smutty encounter with your husband?"

"At least somebody around here is getting laid," Abra said with a sigh.

"Ain't it the truth."

This last remark from Katherine caught Margie by surprise. "Anything wrong?"

Katherine slightly furrowed her brow, just for a second, as she said, "Hmm...no, not really. We're kind of in a sexual slump, that's all. No need to talk about it."

Margie let it rest and tried to think of something to change the subject, but the only thing she could think of was melting the jerk's motorcycle seat. It was pretty much the only thing she *could* think about since it happened. It had been wrong and downright mean by just about any ethical standard. You weren't supposed to destroy someone else's property, unless you were going to latch onto Proudhon's maxim that property is despotism, and she wasn't entirely ready for that. Plus she had to admit it had been incredibly satisfying, like a giant hot fudge sundae with a warm brownie on the bottom. "May I confess something?" she began. "After I left Abra at the mortgage loan office the other day, I did something that I'm not entirely proud of."

"What?" Katherine asked eagerly.

"Some guy on a motorcycle followed me into a parking lot and accused me of cutting him off. I didn't," she added in response to Katherine's unspoken question.

"Did you call nine-one-one?" Abra asked.

"No." Telling them what happened was more difficult than she thought. It was a little embarrassing to admit she had let her emotions get the best of her and repaid spite with spite. Hell, she had upped the ante considerably. "I...I melted the seat of his motorcycle."

Katherine burst out laughing. "You're kidding."

Abra looked like she might choke on a chip. "What did he do?" she said between spurts of incredulous laughter.

"I didn't stick around to find out. I think I scared him." Margie was silent for a moment. "I think it scared him that I wasn't scared. I mean, I *was*, but I guess I didn't show it."

"Well, destroying personal property is not generally regarded as a sign of fear," Katherine said.

"I think I understand what you mean," Abra put in. "We're supposed to be afraid of strange men, not the other way around."

What do you say when someone speaks the truth? Sometimes nothing; you just drink. She took a sip of her margarita and felt her purse begin to vibrate and heard the faint tones of Rick James's "Super Freak" coming from its deepest recesses.

"I've always loved your ringtone," Katherine said.

"Sorry. I don't want to break the no-phone rule, but it might be Joan needing a ride."

"Family supersedes the no-phone rule," Abra said.

"Get it," Katherine added.

Joan was at a party with some kids she'd met through swimming. Margie was expecting a text or a call later to pick her up. She wasn't expecting the "XA" code. She and Karl had read about the XA code a few years ago in some article whose provenance was forgotten, but they liked the idea. The code was supposed to be a way for kids to get out of an uncomfortable situation. The theory was, if your kid was out with friends and people started drinking or smoking weed or planning some activity that was dangerous or illegal, the kid could text an agreed-upon code to a parent, who would then call or text saying there was an emergency at home and that they'd be coming to get the kid in ten minutes. It was supposed to offer the kid a graceful way out of a sticky situation. She and Karl had introduced it to Eli and Joan when they got their own phones. Eli had never used it because he had been an introvert for most of his high school career and never went anywhere, and Joan usually hung out with kids from the swim and soccer teams, all of whom signed "contracts" with their coaches pledging not to drink or smoke. This was the first time any of her children had ever used the code. For a second, Margie almost forgot what it meant.

As Margie was staring at the letters "XA" on her phone, trying to process the idea that Joan might be in trouble, Abra asked if there was something wrong. That's when it clicked. "Yes. Maybe. I don't know," Margie replied. Her stomach began to turn into tight little knots as she typed a quick text to Joan saying that there was a small family emergency and she needed to pick Joan up now. Her hands shook a little, and she had to go back twice and retype a word.

"Which kid?" Katherine asked.

"Joan. I need to go get her right now." She gave a quick explanation of the XA code while she grabbed some money out of her wallet and put it on the table. "I'm sorry to have to leave so early."

"We're going with you," Katherine said, as though it had been agreed upon ages ago.

"You don't have to go."

Abra was already standing up and putting some money on the table. "I know we don't *have* to. We want to."

"You might need backup," Katherine added. "And the idea of crashing a high school party sounds kind of fun."

"Fun" was not the first word to come to mind as Margie got behind the wheel of the minivan. It seemed more expedient for Katherine and Abra to drive with her, plus the company kept her from worrying too much about Joan. Neither of the older kids had ever had occasion to use the XA code. Which meant either neither of them had ever been in a sticky situation before, which seemed doubtful, or neither of them had ever been in a situation they didn't think they could handle. The fact that it was focused, competent, capable Joan using the code made her push the speed limit all the way down Richmond Road.

"Where is this party anyway?" Abra asked.

"Over in Beachwood. Some boy on another swim team. Joan and her friend met him at a meet. I've talked with his mother once or twice. I thought the girls would be okay if they went together." She tried to remember to keep breathing and not to speed in the area around Legacy Village shopping center because that was always a speed trap.

"They *are* okay," Katherine said. "Besides, Joan has those swimmer's shoulders. If any guy ever messed with her, she could clock him."

Beachwood was a well-off suburb just next to Lyndhurst, where Margie lived. The city had several industrial and office parks plus scads of high-end retail. All those tax revenues kept the schools strong and houses priced slightly higher than Margie and Karl ever wanted to pay. And high property taxes didn't mean your kid was going to be an angel.

The house was an imposing Colonial set back on a hidden cul-de-sac. Even using the GPS on her phone, Margie drove by it the first time. There were half a dozen cars parked on the curved street and two in the driveway. They parked on the far end of the cul-de-sac about five houses away and got out of the van. For a warm Saturday night in July, it was surprising that they didn't see anyone else outside.

"That's funny. I told Joan to meet us out in front of the house," Margie said. She sent Joan a quick text, and the three of them stood outside by the minivan and waited.

"I'm sure she's fine," Abra said. "Maybe the kids causing trouble left and everything's calmed down."

Katherine nodded emphatically and added, "I'm sure that's it." In the light of the streetlamp on the cul-de-sac, Margie could see that she was wearing the red cat-eye reading glasses.

"If you're so confident everything's fine, how come you're still wearing the reading glasses?" Margie asked as she started to walk toward the house. Maybe it was the whole XA code and an unanswered text mingled with her own overactive imagination, but her Maternal SuperSense was going off. She didn't say anything else, just started walking toward the house. There were plenty of lights on inside and a low hum of noise that gradually grew louder as they approached the house, yet it wasn't quite what she expected from an out-of-control high school party. Then again, it had been nearly thirty years since she was in high school.

They were in front of the house when Margie's phone pinged with a text message. Katherine and Abra looked over her shoulder to try and read it.

"Is she okay?" Abra asked.

The message read, "Hi Mom!!!!" *Oh, thank goodness,* Margie thought as a wave of relief washed over her. Abra and Katherine were right. The troublemakers must have left. Or maybe Joan was overreacting, which was fine. Fourteen was still young; there was no harm in having her be a little cautious. The phone pinged again with another message. This one had no words, just a picture of an erect penis.

"Oh my..." Katherine said.

"What. The. Hell?" For an instant, Margie felt nothing but blinding rage. She took a deep cleansing breath and the anger passed, replaced by a sense of control and confidence. She could fight back. She didn't have to be nice.

"You do realize that someone took her phone, right?" Abra said.

"Yes. I am ninety-nine point nine nine nine percent sure that some kid took my daughter's phone. Too bad his last act in this lifetime was sending me a dick pic." She took her new reading glasses out of her purse and put them on. She really dug the little toadstools painted on either end. "We're going in," she said. It seemed redundant to add, "And kick some ass."

Katherine and Abra followed Margie as she strode up the curved stone path that wove in between a couple of well-mulched flower beds and up to a white wooden front door with three long, narrow windows. Margie peered into the middle window then put her hand on the curved door handle and pushed. The door opened. Without hesitation, she walked into the house, followed closely by Abra and Katherine.

They were in a small tiled vestibule that opened to a wide staircase. Margie spied a couple of kids making out on the balcony at the top of the stairs, the girl's back pressed up against the railing and the boy's hands nowhere to be seen. Next to the stairs was a hallway leading to the back of the house. Off to the left looked to be the dining room. The long table was littered with open bags of potato chips, three empty pizza boxes, and scads of red Solo cups. To the right was a classic McMansion Great Room. A sleek, modern-looking white leather sofa wrapped along two sides of the room. The wall at the far end was dominated by a big-screen TV showing what, to Margie's eye, resembled amoebae undergoing continual mitosis but was probably just a stock background for whatever pop-rap song was playing. In between these two bookends was a squirming mass of about twenty kids. Most of them were dancing, with a couple boys and girls grinding against each other. She tried to ignore the couple making out on the wraparound sofa who didn't even look up when three grown-ups entered the room. The distinct scent of beer mingled with weed permeated everything. She silently commended her daughter for using the XA code.

"We're looking for Joan Joseph," she announced in a voice loud enough to be heard over the music. Most of the kids stopped what they were doing and stared at the three adults with funky glasses as though they were alien invaders. The couple on the sofa continued to make out, and a few of the more intrepid kids kept on dancing, albeit without grinding into each other's privates. Finally, one of the girls who'd been dancing said, "I think she went to get her phone from A.J."

The girl didn't say anything else, just stared at them with big cow eyes. Margie counted to five then asked, "Could you be more specific?"

"Oh, um, I think they're in the backyard," the girl said dreamingly. "By the way, I like your glasses."

"Could I get a ride with you guys?" another girl asked. She was kind of off to the side. Margie noticed she'd been half-heartedly dancing and pushing away a guy who kept trying to dance too close. She was clearly a kid who needed an emergency code.

"Sure," Margie said as she headed toward the hallway leading to the back of the house.

"Just in case, I'll check the basement," Abra said.

"Her friend is named Kailey. We need her too."

"Divide and conquer," Katherine added. "I'll get the upstairs."

Margie had no idea who or what was going on in the backyard, but she knew it was about to get a little hotter.

IC_SuperLadies posted: *The only thing we have to fear is fear itself and pissed-off moms.*

CHAPTER TWENTY-THREE

OVER THE NEXT COUPLE WEEKS, THE SUPER LADIES BECAME *THE* ONLINE COMIC TO READ. When Katherine saw an old friend from high school share it on Facebook, she knew something was going on. Maybe it was the local angle, maybe it was just luck, but according to Eli, the number of page views and comments skyrocketed with a four-part storyline called "The Party." Readers didn't seem to think that everything in the strip was plausible, although a few comments here and there came from kids who insisted they had been at the "real" party and that it was all true. Just about everybody figured a superhero mom might actually melt all the ice in the pony keg to help break up a party. However, reader comments on The Schvitz melting a boy's phone were divided. Anyone who started their comment "As a parent" thought it was an apt punishment for sending dick pics, while the comments littered with poor spelling and run-on sentences invariably found it "kind of harsh."

The comments were less divided on Shadow turning invisible and messing with the host's iPod so that the music switched from rap and pop to show tunes after the Super Ladies made their exit. As for Indestructa coming upon two boys trying to convince an unwilling, seriously drunk girl to have a threesome, nearly every reader thought she had been justified in dangling one of the boys over the edge of the second-floor balcony by his feet. As 44122Dad succinctly stated in his comment, "She held that little twerp by the wrong appendage. Other than that, best Super Ladies comic yet!"

Katherine was secretly pleased that the last strip in "The Party" storyline featured Indestructa as the lead. It wasn't as though the character in the comic was really her, but it was close enough that she felt a sense of ownership. If she did something overnight, she posted something about it to the IcyU page. Invariably it would show up in the Super Ladies comic a few days later.

Katherine was moving, changing. Exploring her growing strength and power felt like an adventure. Meanwhile, Hal would come home from work and sit in front of the television. He did just enough of the household chores to call it equitable and played with Anna when asked, but other than that, he seemed stagnant. Sometimes it seemed as though they were leading parallel lives in the same house. He felt like a roommate, not a husband. Katherine found herself looking forward more and more to her solo runs in the morning or to going out with Abra and Margie.

She didn't need as much sleep as she used to. It made sense—there was no need for her body or mind to repair what wasn't being damaged during the day. She still tucked in Anna every night and got into bed with Hal whenever he turned in around ten o'clock. Sometimes she'd sleep for a few hours, sometimes she'd just wait until Hal was asleep. Either way, she'd silently creep out of bed, throw on her running clothes, and head out the door regardless of the hour. Now she made a point of running outside her neighborhood, outside her comfort zone. She never took the car. She preferred a purer form of autonomy: her body.

Most nights, her run would start in Euclid Creek Park on the same route she and Abra typically took. But when she got to the end of the park, instead of turning around, she'd keep going, heading north into the city, in Candlewick Heights, into neighborhoods that most people would say a woman alone and on foot should avoid at night. Such a warning seemed like an invitation. She wasn't actively looking for trouble; she just wasn't trying to avoid it.

One Tuesday night she awoke around three in the morning. She lay in bed for a little while, but forcing sleep is almost impossible. And it wasn't really necessary. Her body was ready to go. She got up.

Once out on the sidewalk, Katherine let her feet decide where to go. She headed west on Anderson, but when she got to the comically tiny traffic circle by the war memorial, instead of taking the right that would take her to Euclid Creek Park, she continued on to West Anderson. The traffic light at Green Road was blinking yellow. No need to slow down; the only car on the road at this hour was a block away. Abra lived at the end of the block. The houses on this side of Green were a little smaller and closer together than up the street where she lived. As an older, inner ring suburb, South Euclid had its well-off neighborhoods and its working-class neighborhoods. This was the latter.

There was no need to check on Abra, but Katherine couldn't help giving her quiet, dark house a long look as she ran by. No need to stop, no desire to stop. She kept running through the July morning, her Adidas hitting the pavement as predictably as a metronome. The birds were still asleep, and the crickets seemed to be on mute. It was blessedly silent. She stayed on West Anderson, made the dog-leg turn by Adrian Elementary School, where Margie worked and Anna used to go, and crossed big, wide Belvoir Boulevard. She wasn't as familiar with this neighborhood but knew it would turn into Cleveland Heights and eventually come out at Noble Road. She turned down a random side street when the clinking sound of metal on metal startled her. She'd been running in the street but now took a few quick steps over the tree lawn and sidewalk and into the darkness of someone's postage stamp–sized front lawn. She spied a rusted, dirty white van parked in the back of a brick bungalow a few houses away. A pair of shadowy figures were conferring by the back of the van. The house had green awnings over all but one of the front windows. The overgrown lawn and desolate, weed-filled flower bed by the front door made it clear the house was unoccupied. She stopped and waited. Another clink and the murmur of someone speaking as though they didn't want to be overheard.

The house next door had a small Japanese red maple on the front lawn. Its trunk wasn't much thicker than a flagpole, but it was low enough and leafy enough to block out the streetlight. Katherine moved quickly into its shadow. If she were quiet and still, she could stay reasonably out of sight.

A squat white guy in jeans and a dark T-shirt was standing at the open back doors of the van. He had an armful of copper piping. She had definitely heard two muffled voices. The other guy must have gone back in the house, stripping more copper.

She had read here and there about the problem of petty thieves stripping the copper pipes and wiring from foreclosed and abandoned homes. The scrap-metal dealers didn't seem to care about the provenance of the copper, only that they got it. It seemed like an awful lot of work for a couple of bucks a pound, but here were these two guys in the middle of the night, stripping away. The guy was wrapping bungee cords around small bunches of pipe. He had his back to the street as he quickly wrapped a cord around each end of a bundle of pipe and gently placed it alongside four other similar bundles on a movers' blanket in the back of the van. He was surprisingly quiet and adept, as though he had done this many times before. Katherine waited until he had bundled up all the pipe. She didn't want anything falling to the ground and making a racket. Grabbing the guy and putting him in a half nelson felt almost easy, as though she had trained relentlessly for this moment.

"Shut up," she whispered in the guy's ear. "I'm not the police, and I don't want the copper."

"What the hell?" he started to say. She put her hand over his mouth and tightened her grip. "Don't say anything. Don't call for your friend. Don't tell the police that you were beat up by some middle-aged woman out for a run. No one will ever believe you." She relaxed her grip on him, just for a second, as she reached for one of the bungee cords piled near the back of the van. As she did so, he tried to throw her off him, stepping backward with one foot the way every woman is told to do in self-defense class and turning his body in the opposite direction of her hold. "No," she said, surprised at how gently the word came out, considering that she gave him a quick punch in the stomach and tightened her grip with the other arm hard enough that he grunted in pain. *Should have kept a hand on his mouth*, she thought, placing her hand back over his mouth before he made any more noise.

"Now," she whispered in his ear, "you know what will happen if you try and fight or make any noise? You will be hurt. I don't like causing other people pain. Okay, maybe I do a little," she added with a jerk to the arm holding him. The guy was still struggling, but it felt like she was holding down a baby, and she couldn't help but smile at how ineffective he was in fighting against her. For a second, it didn't matter that he was another human being, a fellow traveler who could feel pain or fear. Again she eyed the bungee cords sitting on the edge of the open van next to the movers' blanket. She pushed him forward and bent him over at the waist so she could grab a bungee cord. With his face smashed into the bed of the van, he couldn't make much noise. The idea that she was causing another person pain was fleeting, subsumed by the knowledge that she held a thief in her arms. She didn't want to do him any permanent damage, maybe just pay a little retribution to somebody who was giving the neighborhood and the city a bad name. It took only a few seconds to tie his hands behind his back with the bungee cord.

The other guy was bound to come out of the house any minute. There had to be some way to keep this guy quiet so she could get the second guy too. Katherine glanced around and spied a rag stuck into one of the molded holes on the inside of the van door. It didn't look entirely clean but didn't seem to have any chemicals or grease on it either. She figured it was okay to shove it in the guy's mouth. She looked into his terrified eyes and the reality of what she was doing came screaming back to her. "Can you breathe?" she asked.

The guy nodded.

"Good." She shoved him down onto the driveway. There was only one bungee cord left, and she figured she might need it for the guy in the house. Instead, she grabbed a stray piece of copper pipe. It would work in lieu of another bungee cord or piece of rope. She gave it a little test bend—the pipe offered as much resistance as a pipe cleaner, no blow torch or pipe-bending tool needed. As she started to wrap the pipe around the guy's ankles, he pulled back in terror. "If you're going to freak out about something, freak out about going to jail," she said, giving the pipe one last hard bend so he couldn't slip an ankle out.

She stood up. "Stay there," she commanded. It was too dark to see the guy's face clearly, but she saw his head nod quickly. Just as well it was dark—then he couldn't see her face either. She didn't wear the reading glasses on her runs, but maybe she ought to start.

She went in the side door of the house. It was a typical South Euclid bungalow, probably built in the late fifties. There was a small entryway by the back door with a few coat hooks and faded flowered wallpaper. To the left were three steps leading up to the kitchen. In front of her, the basement stairs. She stopped and listened to the quick sucking sound of two pieces of piping being pulled apart. The other guy was downstairs.

Gingerly she placed a foot on the first worn, wooden step. At least it didn't squeak. Katherine went down a couple more steps, then stopped. If the other guy looked over, instead of seeing the faded jeans of his buddy, he'd see Katherine's bare legs and her running shorts. She might as well make this quick.

Five more steps brought her to the concrete basement floor, to a utility sink, a few stray lengths of copper pipe, and a tall white guy about her age, older than the guy outside. He was tall enough to reach into the rafters of the basement ceiling without standing on his tiptoes. With a wrench in his right hand and a short length of copper pipe in his left, it looked like he was down to stripping the last bit of copper in the house. For a split second, Katherine was reminded of the Grinch robbing every house in Whoville of its Christmas decorations. There was no telling if this guy was as mean and Grinchy as the Grinch. He must have heard her, because the guy turned and looked at her.

"Who are you?"

Katherine didn't reply, just rushed him, grabbing the wrench out of his hand as though it was a flimsy plastic sword. Twisting the guy's arm behind his back and bending him over the utility sink came easily, like they were choreographed moves, like she had practiced. He was taller than she, but it didn't matter. She had the element of surprise and outmuscled him without even trying. Within a few seconds, she had his hands bungeed behind his back, but then he kicked backward like an angry horse and knocked her off her feet. Katherine was flat on her back on the dirty, wet basement floor, watching as one of the guy's long, thin legs came flying at her face. Instinctively, her hands clapped in front of her, catching a worn Chuck Taylor knock-off an inch in front of her face. He was balancing on one leg, just for a split second, but Katherine took advantage of it, pushing him off her with all her considerable might. The guy flew back against the utility sink. With his hands tied, he fell sideways to the floor with a loud *thud* and an equally loud "Fuck!"

"Don't lower my property values, asshole," she said and gave him a kick in the stomach. He didn't need to know she didn't really live in this neighborhood. She ran up the basement stairs and back out to the first guy, who was still lying on the driveway by the back of the van.

She wasn't sure what time it was, but the night was starting to be a little less hazy. She wanted to get away before sunrise, before anyone saw her. She stood over the first guy and asked, "Where's your phone?"

The guy's eyes grew a little wider, as though he was afraid she was going to hurt him. He rolled over onto his side, revealing a cheap pay-as-you-go cell phone in his back pocket. Normally, the thought of touching a stranger's rear end or grimy jeans would make her balk, but she just grabbed the phone and used it to call 911. She didn't give a name, just said she saw some guys stealing copper from an empty house and gave the name of the street. She could hear the 911 dispatcher asking questions as she wiped her fingerprints off the phone with her shirt and let it drop on the end of the driveway.

A noise from behind made her turn. The second guy was stumbling out of the side door, his hands still tied behind his back with the bungee cord. "You...bitch..." he gasped.

"Yes I am," she replied and started running.

IC_SuperLadies posted: *The only downside of Super Lady Patrol: you go through a lot of running shoes.*

CHAPTER TWENTY-FOUR

ABRA GOT THE TEXT FROM RICHARD ON FRIDAY AF-
TERNOON WHEN SHE WAS AT WORK. He wanted to come
by the house and get the drywall and lumber out of the
garage. She was about to go into a conference call and
couldn't respond properly, couldn't have the conversation about whether he had a right to the drywall or the
lumber or the handful of tools and whatever else he'd no
doubt walk away with. *He would text when he knows I'm
at work*, she thought. This wasn't even a text conversation—any fool could see it needed a phone call. Any fool
but The Evil Richard Brewster.

Richard managed a restaurant. He got to work around
two thirty, so he must have texted her shortly after he got
to the midlevel not-fine-dining-but-not-a-chain restaurant he was currently managing. He wouldn't respond
if she texted him back, wouldn't respond until after he
shut the place down for the night around midnight. And
even if she told him to go jump in the lake, he'd no doubt
show up at the house on Saturday morning between ten
and eleven, just as his text promised. He didn't even ask
if Abra would be home, just assumed that she would be,
that he could come and disrupt her life and take what

was technically his but had been paid for with her credit card. Abra could paint and do minor maintenance, but major home improvement wasn't her deal. She would never use the drywall or lumber, but that didn't mean she wanted to give it to him.

On the train on the way home, she mentally tossed around potential responses—locking the garage and making sure she wasn't home, dumping everything on the tree lawn and posting a "curb alert" on Craigslist, burning all of it. The idea of being polite and civil also crossed her mind. After all, Richard was, in essence, going to clean her garage. Even with a small car, having all that extra stuff piled in the garage made for a tight squeeze. Abra had just decided to be the bigger person and give him all the lumber and drywall without a fuss and was looking forward to not having to climb over that mess anymore when a couple of young men caught her eye.

The train was full, packed with people of all ages who were no doubt looking forward to the weekend. A college-aged girl was standing just in front of her, holding on to one of the plastic straps that hung from the ceiling of the car. Abra had been behind her going through the turnstile, and the girl had asked her which train was going to Shaker Square. The girl wore a headscarf and spoke English with a heavy accent. Abra couldn't quite place the country but guessed she was from somewhere in the Middle East. Abra had told her which train to take and given the girl a warm smile. Her Dominican grandmother had always told stories of her first few days in America and the random strangers who helped her. Abra always tried to repay the favor whenever she met someone who was clearly new to the U.S.

The two guys had gotten on the train at the previous stop and chosen spots on either side of the girl with the headscarf. One ended up facing her, his right hand holding on to the plastic strap next to hers, the front of his body moving dangerously close to hers. The second had moved to her side, holding on to the back of a seat so that his left arm practically encircled her waist. Unless she decided to plop down in the lap of the stranger sitting in the closest seat, the girl couldn't get away from them. And the train was crowded enough that there was nowhere else to go.

Abra was behind all three of them, standing near the door, holding on to the molded plastic handle on the back of the closest seat. She was close enough to hear one of the guys say, "Hey, what's your name, girl?" He was a wiry-looking African American kid, with thick hair cut short on the sides and high on top, making him look taller than he was.

For a second, the only sound Abra could hear was the clattering of the train as it clipped down the tracks through midtown Cleveland. Most of the people nearby were staring at their phones, while a few gazed out the window or read a book. No one else was paying attention as the girl said quietly, "Anja."

"On ya?" the first guy said. "I'll bet you are."

The girl gave a little jump and looked sharply over her shoulder at the second guy. He was white and round-faced with a buzz cut that looked about as long as the bearded stubble on his face. It was as though his entire round head was a scuzzy peach with two beady eyes and a gaping mouth.

Abra followed the girl's eyes downward and saw his hand groping the back of her loose, dark olive pants. Anja instinctively scooted away from Scuzzy Peach Face and inadvertently moved herself closer to the first guy. Abra wasn't just angry that they were harassing this girl; it was the casual, almost gentle way Scuzzy Peach Face grabbed her ass and the nonchalant way Mr. Fade Hair spoke to her, as though this was the accepted way of getting to know a stranger, that really ticked her off. Without thinking through the consequences or whether it might look odd that her messenger bag purse now seemed to be floating in midair, Abra went invisible.

She grabbed Scuzzy Peach Face's wrist and pulled his hand away from Anja's rear end. At the same time, she lifted one moderately priced Cole Haan pump-clad foot, aimed it between his feet, and slammed her heel down on his instep. You were supposed to do that move if someone came up behind you, but she was delighted to see it also worked if you were standing behind the perpetrator. It also helped that neither he nor Mr. Fade Hair could see her.

Scuzzy Peach Face let out a "Damn!" and lifted his foot in pain at the same moment the train lurched to a stop at the next station. He lost his balance, fell against the seat opposite him, and landed on his knees on the floor of the car. Mr. Fade Hair looked at Anja as though she was responsible for harming his friend. "What the hell you doin'?" he shrieked.

"I do nothing," Anja said. Now that Scuzzy Peach Face was partly out of the way, Anja moved backward, away from Mr. Fade Hair. Abra sidestepped out of the way so she could pass. The other people in the car were staring at the trio in shock. The car doors opened and a few people carefully stepped around Scuzzy Peach Face. One of them bumped into Abra but kept going. No one made a move to intervene. Abra held her invisible ground. She'd let her bag drop to the floor and hoped no one would walk off with it.

Now that a few people had gotten off the train, there was a bit more room to maneuver, and Anja walked to the back of the car where there was an empty seat. Scuzzy Peach Face was on his feet now and made a move to follow her. As he walked by, Abra gave him a hard punch in the back. There was no one visibly close enough to have hit him except for Mr. Fade Hair. He turned to face his friend. "What was that for?"

"I didn't do nothin'." Mr. Fade Hair gave him a little push toward the door. "Come on."

"Fine," Scuzzy Peach Face said, adding, "Fuck that bitch!" loudly enough to carry to the far end of the car. He sauntered out the open car door.

Mr. Fade Hair paused just long enough to flip his middle finger at Anja. She was safe, surrounded by other people, but no one seemed to know how to respond. Abra did.

As Mr. Fade Hair stepped off the car, she gave him a hard push on the back so that he fell forward onto the platform at the East 55th Street station. He was on his feet almost instantly, his angry, screaming face visible through the windows of the car as the doors closed and the train began to move again. Once in motion, the train filled with the buzz of conversation, more active than it had been before. Abra tried to listen, but there were too many conversations going on at once. She heard snippets—"shameful" and "cowards"—but it wasn't clear if the speaker was referring to Mr. Fade Hair and Scuzzy Peach Face or to all the people on the train who had only watched, not helped.

A month ago, Ara wouldn't have gotten involved. She knew herself well enough to know that. Did it even count as getting involved if no one knew, if no one could see her? That wasn't why she had helped. Being acknowledged wasn't the reason you helped another person. You helped because it was some sort of universal duty to help other living beings in need.

She had dropped her bag near an empty aisle seat. There was an older, heavy-set African American woman sitting in the window seat. Abra quietly sat down next to her and waited until she was sure the woman's attention was focused out the window. Then she let the light bend around her again and became visible. Even though Abra tried to be as discreet as possible, the woman still jumped a bit in her seat and gave a little yelp of shock when she saw a person sitting next to her.

Abra smiled as though she hadn't just materialized out of nowhere but had been sitting there all along. "I'm sorry—may I sit here?"

"Of course you can sit there, honey, but oh my, I did not see you sit down! You startled me out of my skin."

Normally Abra wasn't a fan of chatty strangers, but today she didn't mind. Whatever adventure she, Katherine, and Margie had embarked upon, kindness had to be part of it just as much as courage or strength.

That's essentially what she texted to Katherine later that night when she asked if Katherine could come over the next morning for moral support when The Evil Richard Brewster came to get the lumber and drywall.

"*Can't. Sorry,*" Katherine responded almost immediately. "*But will be happy to kick Richard Brewster's Evil Ass for you later this weekend.*"

Abra was home by this time, hanging out on the living room sofa with a book and Clint purring on her lap. "*Not necessary,*" she responded. She paused, part of her wanting to tell Katherine what she had done and part of her grooving on having a little secret to herself. They were in this together. "*If need be, I will do the ass-kicking. Beat up two guys who were harassing a girl on the Green Line today.*"

"*OMG!*" Katherine texted back. "*I kicked the asses of 2 guys stealing copper from an empty house!*"

There was nothing to type back but "*OMG!*"

✹ ✹ ✹

By the time Margie arrived at Abra's house the next morning, she had already heard the full story from both

Abra and Katherine. They sat on Abra's little brick patio, the place, Abra noted, where Richard had always said he was going to build a party deck. In her head, Margie always heard the gentle voice of Jane Bennett in the BBC version of *Pride and Prejudice* saying, "You must understand, Ms. McQuestion, that a party deck is much more grand than a normal deck." But she had more pressing issues than bad imitations of Jane Austen characters from BBC miniseries. There was The Evil Richard Brewster to deal with. And there was also a fascinating conversation going on over at IcyU.

Margie took a sip of the orange juice Abra had brought out. "Do you ever look at the Super Ladies' IcyU account?" she asked.

"Not really. Should I?"

"Yeah, you should," she replied, handing her phone to Abra.

IcyU had the "IC" feature, which allowed users to tag the location of a friend or people they followed. Margie called it the stalker feature. She supposed it could be helpful if you were trying to track down whether a friend had arrived somewhere or not, although she wondered why the friend wouldn't just call or text instead. Someone named Darcy27 had "seen" the Super Ladies, writing, "*Swear to God IC: Super Ladies on the Green Road rapid. Two guys were bothering some girl and then it looked like they got beat up by Shadow. How else do you explain a purse moving in midair?*"

Abra looked at Margie's phone then handed it back. "Guess I wasn't as discreet as I thought," she said.

"Well, it isn't like they *saw* you."

"But I made my presence known. I don't think I like that."

"If someone is being beaten up by an invisible person, I guess it's kind of noticeable. It's not like they saw you." Talking about this as though they were superheroes comparing notes made Margie feel like an imposter. Abra and Katherine were the ones going out and doing big things with their powers. She was warming up leftover macaroni and cheese and breaking up high school parties. They were being proactive; she wasn't.

When The Evil Richard Brewster arrived at Abra's house, he was as overly friendly and jovial as Margie remembered him. Something about his manner had always struck her as false, even before he broke Abra's heart and left her with a mountain of debt. Richard was cute—although maybe not as cute as he was when Abra met him seven years earlier—and still had the quasi-messed-up look of someone who regarded their restaurant job as a lifestyle rather than a career and lived accordingly. He had soft dark brown eyes and equally brown hair with one thick lock near the front that floated between blond and gray. Richard always insisted that "it just grew like that," but Margie had long suspected that he dyed it on the sly. The blondish lock of hair was just enough to give him a bit of a cool-guy edge.

"Hey, thanks for letting me pick up the lumber and the drywall," he said as he got out of a humungous black pickup truck. A second guy, tall and skinny with a huge afro, hesitantly got out of the passenger seat. "This is Doug. He came to help." Doug shuffled his feet and gave a half-hearted wave. It seemed like he might be a little stoned.

"New car?" Abra asked by way of hello.

"Oh, no, it's Doug's. Hey, Margie," he said with a glance and a cursory nod in her direction. Then he looked back at Abra and just sort of stopped, taking her in. "You look great," he proclaimed, as though his opinion regarding her appearance mattered.

"Thank you."

Margie was proud of Abra for not giving into false pleasantries. Instead she set the guys straight to work.

Richard looked pretty good, despite the unmistakable beginning of a pot belly. Somehow the sight of the rubbery little paunch spilling over the waistband of his jeans delighted her. Margie hoped it bothered him.

Richard and Doug made short work of loading the drywall and lumber into the back of the pickup. Abra and Margie at first only watched, but then it seemed easier to help load the truck. "The sooner it's loaded, the sooner he's gone, right?" Margie whispered. Abra shrugged.

Doug might have been a stoner, but he was meticulous about neatly stacking the drywall in one pile and the lumber in the other. When they were done, every edge and every corner lined up. Once the truck was loaded, Richard announced that he wanted to go inside and get a few books and other things he'd left there.

"You didn't leave anything here," Abra said. *Except a mess*, Margie thought.

"Yeah, I did. There were some books, and a big photo album with pictures from when I was a kid. I can't find it at my place, so it's gotta be here." Without asking Abra's permission, he headed for the side door. He went in the house, followed closely by a protesting Abra. Doug and Margie watched them go then looked at each other.

"Do you think she'd mind if I went in and used the bathroom?" he asked, sounding a little shy.

Hating Richard for Abra's sake probably didn't need to extend to his stoned flunky. "I'm sure she won't," Margie replied with a sigh.

She considered going inside as backup but figured she'd just get in the way. Abra wouldn't let Richard take anything that wasn't really his. She wandered over to the back of the ginormous black pickup. Even though Abra didn't want the lumber and drywall and would never use it, the idea that Richard was taking something Abra had paid for bothered her. Richard had used her friend poorly in so many ways. It wasn't her fight, but it felt like hers. Abra was as good as a sister. If she wouldn't exact retribution, Margie would have to do it for her.

She ran a hand across the pristine white board on top of the stack of drywall. She thought about heat, about fiery angry and felt the now-familiar warmth begin coursing through her body. Delighted, she watched a light brown burn stain begin traveling across the drywall sheet's paper covering. She lifted the top sheet and did the same thing to the second one down, but then the drywall got a little heavy. She could stick a hand under two sheets, but that was it. Margie had to satisfy herself with running a hot hand along the edge of the stack, hoping that would be enough to put a burn mark on the paper cover of every drywall sheet she touched. The back gate of the pickup was still down. Without bothering to check if anyone was coming back outside, she scrambled onto the truck bed and into the narrow gap in between the drywall and the lumber. Doug had stuffed a couple rolled up movers' blankets in between the two stacks to hold them in place, but she was able to push them out of the way so she could get closer to the lumber. She placed a hand on top of a two-by-four and thought hot thoughts, thought about rage and forest fires and the heat of angry mobs with torches until the wood beneath her hand began to smolder. With one burning index finger, she burned the word "Liar" in script on the side of the board. Moving down, she burned the same word on the side of the second board. Then, just for kicks, she burned the word "Asshole" on the third one and "Thief" on the fourth.

It would have been nice to mark every board and sheet of drywall, but there wasn't time for that. She replaced the movers' blankets, making sure to cover the words and burn marks, and scooted off the back of the truck just as Doug and Richard came out the side door, followed closely by Abra. Richard carried three books as though they were prizes he'd just won. Margie noted that he did not have a photo album. Abra looked resigned and tired. It seemed the right time to tag in.

"Are you all done?" Margie asked.

"Yeah, I think so," Richard replied.

"Good. Time for you to go." Margie didn't let Richard say anything else, didn't let him linger to do or say anything kind or horrid, just told him to leave. Slightly Stoned Doug closed up the back of the truck. If he noticed the new stain marks on the drywall or the lumber, he didn't say so. Finally, they got in the truck and backed out of the driveway. The Evil Richard Brewster had the audacity to wave to Abra as they headed down West Anderson, as though he had been there on a pleasant visit and was looking forward to seeing Abra again, as though she wanted to see him again. Abra didn't wave, and when the truck was out of sight, she turned to Margie and gave her a hug.

"Thanks," Abra whispered. "I couldn't have dealt with him on my own."

Margie resisted the urge to tell her about the burn marks on the drywall and the wood. As she thought about it now, the burn marks seemed a weak attempt at vengeance. It didn't really hurt Richard in the same way he had hurt Abra. "I didn't do much," Margie whispered back.

IC_SuperLadies posted: *I wonder if the Super Friends would do things like help each other move or pick each other up at the airport? We do.*

CHAPTER TWENTY-FIVE

KATHERINE CHECKED THE SUPER LADIES COMIC ON-
LINE EACH MORNING TO SEE IF ELI HAD POSTED A NEW
STRIP. Some days he had, some days he hadn't. Anna
looked at the comic once in a while, "borrowing" Katherine's phone while they drove to the grocery store or a
friend's house. But it wasn't important enough in her
nine-year-old world to remember to tell her dad about
it. And Katherine never shared it.

There was never a good time to talk to Hal. He wasn't
much of a morning person and mainly gave one-word
answers to any question posed before 10:00 a.m. That
was one of the reasons Katherine had started running in
the morning in the first place—it gave them both a little
time to wake up and face the day in their own way. In the
evening, he wanted to "relax" and didn't feel like talking,
at least not about anything important. Consequently,
she didn't tell him anything.

She still talked to him about Anna and the garden
and current events and his work and the upcoming
school year and her work and whether he felt like going
to see a movie next weekend and all the other pieces of
news and thoughts that make up a shared life. Some-

times it was easy—too easy—to imagine a life without him in it every day. There were even a couple times, late at night when she didn't feel like pretending to sleep but wasn't ready to go out on her run, when she would search online real estate sites, just looking. It was somewhat more than daydreaming but somewhat less than planning.

Leaving Hal was an abstraction, one possible solution to the reality that intimacy seemed to have become indifference. She had gotten out of the habit of telling Hal anything challenging. She didn't tell him what had happened after the explosion or about the incident with the knife. She didn't tell him about her body, her strength, or what she did on her early-morning runs.

She did tell Abra and Margie. Margie told Eli, and Eli turned those tellings into Super Ladies comics. As the summer wore on, Katherine just started emailing or texting Eli herself. She'd give him the general gist of what happened and a few details, and he'd turn it into a strip. It seemed simpler to tell Eli directly, especially because he'd be leaving for college soon.

When she reminded Margie of this the next time they all went out to La Fiesta, Margie said, "Shut the front door. We aren't talking about that."

"Isn't move-in next week?" Abra asked gently.

Margie directed all her attention to the slate-gray ceramic bowl of salsa on the table in front of them. "Two weeks," she replied, raising her eyes to them. "I'm in denial. Don't judge."

"Of course not," Katherine replied. "This is a big transition."

Margie looked up as though she'd been waiting for someone to tell her it was permissible to freak out before her oldest child went to college. "I know Baldwin-Wallace is super close, but...it's Eli. I worry."

"He'll be okay," Katherine said, although she had no guarantee for this claim, just a gut feeling that Eli's days of hurting himself were in the past.

"I know. Okay, deep cleansing breath," Margie said as she inhaled.

"Deep cleansing margarita," Katherine added, raising her glass.

"Even better."

Abra toasted with them then said, "Change of subject: my ankle is completely healed. Wanna start running again in the mornings?"

Katherine momentarily found herself in an awkward dilemma. She loved running with Abra but found herself enjoying her solo runs in the middle of the night. Her hesitation was obvious because Abra quickly said, "It's cool if you don't want to anymore."

"I do want to, but...I've been getting up really early."

"Like how early?"

Katherine looked from Abra to Margie. If she were to tell anyone, it ought to be them. "Like three o'clock in the morning."

"Isn't that...?" Margie stopped herself. "I guess it isn't dangerous. Not for you."

"Not for any of us," Abra added.

Katherine had made going out on her own a regular part of her life. It wasn't just the guys stealing copper from an empty house or the older couple whose car needed a push to the gas station; it was running ten or twelve miles almost every night, often to the most poverty-stricken neighborhoods in the city and being a one-woman Block Watch. Most of the time, nothing happened. It was just her and the sound of her running shoes padding away on the pavement, the thoughts in her head alternating between peaceful calm at the quiet of an August night and random bursts of anger that flared over something stupid like Hal throwing out leftovers that she was going to have for lunch or the hirsute little man in a kiosk at the shopping mall who handed her a hand lotion sample and then said he also had something for "zee puffy eyes." Other times things did happen.

One night she stopped a young guy who was breaking into a parked car, tied his hands with the cord of his earbuds (she wondered what music one played while breaking into a car), and called the police on the guy's phone before running down the street. At 4:35 one morning, she came across an older woman sitting in an otherwise empty bus stop at the corner of Euclid Avenue and East 125th Street. Katherine wasn't sure which of them was more surprised to see the other, but she'd asked, "Do you need someone to wait with you, ma'am?" and then waited ten minutes until the bus arrived. The woman—Estelle was her name—worked as a cleaner in an office building downtown. Katherine had gotten into the habit of running by that corner most days around the same time, just to make sure no one bothered Estelle. How do you explain that you can't run with one of your closest friends in the mornings anymore because you've become someone's guardian angel?

"I run pretty far these days, and I'm usually gone for a few hours. Some nights I'm doing twelve fast miles."

"I think I could keep up. I run much faster when I'm invisible. Almost like floating." Here Abra took a little breath then added, "Granted, I really don't want to go running at four in the morning."

"Maybe we ought to try a test run."

"I'd be game. On a weekend," she added with a grin.

Katherine sat back in her chair and took a long drink of her margarita. She'd spent so much time alone lately, so much time thinking about herself and her powers that she hadn't thought about what Abra and Margie were doing. Each of them had been poking around on her own, doing random acts of kindness here and there when she saw a need. But that was hit-or-miss. If they really wanted to make a difference, they ought to let people ask for help. Without saying anything, Katherine pulled out her phone and went to the Super Ladies' IcyU page.

"Hey, you're breaking the no-phone rule," Margie said. "You have to buy the next round."

"That's fine," Katherine replied. When she was done typing, she handed her phone to Margie. "Here, look," she added proudly.

"'Do you need help? Send a message to the Super Ladies. If we can, we will,'" Margie read off the phone. "What?"

Abra scooted her chair closer to Margie's to look at the phone. "You're telling people to call us?" she asked.

Katherine hadn't expected either of them to sound quite so incredulous. "Yeah. We can't just roam around looking for people doing…you know, bad things."

"That sounds so dorky," Margie said.

"I know. And it isn't the most efficient crime-fighting technique. This way, people can contact us if they need help."

"They can also call nine-one-one," Abra said. She gave a little shake of her head and took another chip from the almost-empty basket.

"It's like the Bat Signal. You send it up when you need help."

"It's a good idea, but it isn't practical," Abra said. "I mean, let's say someone sends us a direct message on IcyU. One of us has to actually see the message, contact the other two, extricate herself from whatever she's doing—I can't just up and leave work in the middle of the day—and get to wherever the problem is. It could be an hour before one of us got there, by which time whatever emergency that was happening would be long over."

Katherine made no pretense of hiding her disappointment. "We don't all have to go."

"I mean, didn't you ever wonder how Batman managed to get there just in the nick of time? He had to see the Bat Signal, go down to the cave, change, and drive the Batmobile into the city."

"And Bruce Wayne lived way out in some outer-ring suburb," Margie added. "I always wondered how he got there in time to help too."

"Or Spider-Man or Superman. They lived in the city, but they had to go change their clothes before they responded to any emergency."

"First they had to *find* a place to change."

"Okay, fine. Maybe it wasn't one of my best ideas," Katherine admitted.

There was a *ping* from one of their phones.

"Mine's off," Abra said.

Margie nodded. "Mine too."

The no-phone rule had always kept each of them emotionally and mentally present whenever they got together. It was a tangible way of demonstrating the value of their friendship. Certain exceptions had always applied for sick family members or other potential emergencies. Glancing down at her phone, Katherine saw the cute IcyU polar bear cub icon signaling she had a private message. "This could qualify as a potential emergency," she said to the others as she checked the message.

The message was from someone named Sandra C., who followed the Super Ladies on IcyU. Her profile read, "*Parent, sister, daughter, friend. Always love you til the end.*" The message read, "*Hey Super Ladys! My ex is bringing my kids back from visitation on Sunday. He has a temper. Can you come hang w me till he leaves?*"

Katherine read it aloud to Abra and Margie, then handed her phone to them so they could see for themselves. Margie raised an eyebrow.

"Or maybe it was a good idea. There's clearly a need," Katherine added, addressing Abra directly.

"I can see that."

"I'm going," Katherine said. Not going, not responding to an actual request for help wasn't a viable option.

Abra nodded thoughtfully. "Like I said, it's a good idea. I just don't know how practical it will be in the long run."

Katherine smiled at Abra. "We'll deal with the long run in the long run. See you Sunday afternoon? Sandra C. put her address in at the bottom of the message."

"Duty calls. I'll be there."

IC_SandraC. posted: *"First time in a long time I'm not worried."*

CHAPTER TWENTY-SIX

On Sunday afternoon, Abra was on her front porch, reading about quitclaim deeds on her phone while she waited for Margie and Katherine. When Richard first moved out, she had taken a wait-and-see approach to the separation, hoping it might not be permanent even though she knew it was. She had gone against her better instincts with Richard. The night they met seven years earlier, he had seemed funny and cute and wholly unsuited for her. Still, she'd allowed herself the fantasy that not only do opposites attract, they can live happily ever after together. Richard didn't put her into severe debt to break up their relationship. He put her into severe debt because it never occurred to him that such a thing might be a bad idea.

At a gut level, Abra knew they were both better off apart. She just wished the knowledge hadn't been so expensive. One thing she hadn't thought about was the house. Richard's name was still on the deed. Up until now, she hadn't done anything to remove it. Margie offered to help. Borrowing a few pro bono minutes of her lawyer husband's time to get and file a quitclaim deed would be a huge help.

When Margie pulled into her driveway, Katherine was already in the front passenger seat, looking as excited as a kid going to a picnic. "Hop into the Super Lady Mobile," she chirped.

"I believe the proper name for this vehicle is the Estro-van," Margie said as Abra got in. Katherine erupted into giggles. "It's probably a good thing I drove today. Katherine is losing it."

"I'm fine."

Abra was in the backseat, pulling the sliding door closed. "You do realize this is potentially serious," she said.

"Yes, but Estro-van..." Katherine stammered and snorted back a laugh.

Abra waited for Katherine to calm down before she talked to Margie about getting Karl to help her with the quitclaim deed. It was a quick twenty-minute car ride down Cedar Hill and past the University Circle neighborhood to Sandra C.'s house in Cleveland's Hough neighborhood. As they headed west on Chester Avenue, Abra couldn't help but glance across the street to the block where they had stopped and helped Janelle. Clearly she wasn't the only one thinking about her. "I wonder how Janelle is doing," Katherine mused.

"I hope she's okay and away from Sean," Margie said, taking a right on East 68th Street.

"Me too," Abra said quietly.

"I'm gonna see if I can get in touch with her," Katherine said.

"One damsel in distress at a time," Margie interjected. "What's our plan today?"

"Why are you both looking at me?"

"It was your idea," Abra said.

"We may not need to do anything. Just having some witnesses there may be enough to keep her ex's temper in check."

"Or set him off."

"Let's just go in and be a quiet presence. We don't even have to be in the same room—we can wait in the kitchen or something. Then if he gets violent, we'll be right there."

I wish I had your confidence, Abra thought, but didn't say anything. She wasn't feeling scared as much as nervous. Wasn't it kind of weird to have a trio of strangers sitting in your house when your ex dropped off your kids? She didn't have long to worry about it. Margie turned down a side street, and Katherine said, "There it is. She lives on the second floor."

The house was an old up-and-down double that looked like it was built in the twenties. The white and dark brown paint was peeling in spots, but the tiny fenced-in front yard was neat if a little sparse. Margie parked the van on the street, and they all sat for a minute, staring at the house.

"Why don't you text her and let her know we're here?" Abra offered. If Sandra C. had changed her mind about wanting backup, it would be less embarrassing for all concerned to hear it via text than standing at her front door. Instead of texting back, Sandra C. stepped out onto the front porch and waved.

"Um, does anyone else feel uncomfortable?" Margie asked.

"Yes," Abra replied, glad somebody else felt that way.

"Okay, maybe it's a little more awkward than I thought," Katherine said. "Let's just be here for her."

"Maybe we ought to wait outside," Margie suggested.

"That's a good idea," Abra added. "Frankly, I'm not sure what I can do to help."

"Me either," Margie said.

"We'll think of something. Maybe we won't have to do anything," Katherine added as she put on her red cat-eye reading glasses with the daisies on them. "In the meantime, we should wear these."

"I brought mine," Margie said, putting on the toadstool glasses.

"I don't need them," Abra said and went invisible.

"Well, we do," Katherine said in her best teacher voice. "Superheroes are supposed to be anonymous."

"I'm not sure you could call us *superheroes*."

Katherine managed to look Abra directly in the eye. "Says the woman who is currently *invisible*."

"You wouldn't know if I was wearing them anyway," she said. She shoved her purse under the backseat but slipped her phone into the back waistband of her yoga pants. There might be a patch of fabric visible, but she hoped it wouldn't be too noticeable.

Sandra was still standing on the front porch, waiting, so Abra followed Katherine and Margie out of the van. As they introduced themselves, Sandra asked, "Is Shadow here too?"

"She's around," Katherine replied.

"We were thinking we'd just wait here on the front porch," Margie said. "Then we're here if you need us."

Sandra was small, dark-skinned, and about her own height, Abra thought, only with a slightly heavier build. Sandra was also the only one who didn't seem to think it odd to invite three strangers over to her house to protect her.

Abra stayed in the background, invisible and silent. It gave her a chance to check out the lay of the land, noting the huge crack in the second step on the concrete porch stairs and how the gate latched in the chain-link fence that surrounded the tiny front yard. Leaning against the porch railing gave her a clear view of everything but kept her out of the way so no one would accidentally bump into her. Nothing to do now but wait.

✯ ✯ ✯

The porch had one worn bench that looked like it might have come out of an old church. Margie and Katherine sat down, slightly uncomfortable smiles on their faces. Margie still wasn't sure what good she might do. Sandra kept making polite small talk, but her face was drawn. When a slightly beat-up, dark green SUV pulled into the driveway, Margie saw her tense up. If fear was the first reaction, this ex had to be pretty bad. Margie couldn't imagine not being happy to see your kids.

A boy who looked to be about Grant's age got out of the front passenger seat, and a girl who was perhaps eight or nine got out of the backseat. Both children moved deliberately, as though they had been told not to run or act up and were on their best behavior. The ex got out of the car last. The one inescapable fact about him was his size. Margie judged he was probably about Eli's height but easily a hundred pounds heavier. At one time it might have been all muscle, now he was just chunky. Compared to the diminutive Sandra C., he was huge. No wonder she was afraid of him.

"Hi, Mommy!" the little girl cried. She ran up the steps and gave Sandra a hug, followed more staidly by her brother. Sandra hugged them both and then faced her ex, one arm around each child.

"Hello, James," she said in a neutral voice.

"Hey," he said in a clipped voice. "I see you got company."

"Just a couple of old friends," she stammered.

Margie realized that Sandra didn't know their real names. Introducing herself as "The Schvitz" might not go over too well, so she gave a little wave and said, "Hi."

"Nice to meet you," Katherine said.

"I know everybody you know," said James. His voice was slow and deliberate, but he looked peeved and suspicious. If it's possible to track the trajectory of a relationship from one simple encounter, this was it. Margie heard what was probably a decade's worth of jealousy and mistrust in those five words. At that moment, she knew there would be trouble. Maybe it would have been better if they weren't there. Or maybe James would have found something else to set him off. It seemed that Sandra was safe as long as they were there.

"Did you all have a good time this weekend?" Sandra asked the children brightly.

The kids answered in a subdued chorus of "Yes." James just said, "We always do."

"Let's get you two inside, and I'll start thinking about dinner." Sandra opened the door, and the two children obediently went in. Margie could just hear the faint sound of their feet running upstairs to the second-floor apartment. It made the house seem flimsy, as though the whole thing could topple over at any moment.

"I'll be going then," James said. He stayed where he was for a moment, staring at Sandra. His eyes fell briefly on Margie and Katherine, then he turned, walked back to his SUV, got in, and drove away.

After his car was out of sight, Sandra turned to Margie and Katherine. There was just the hint of a tear in her eye. "Thank you for being here. He's never left so quickly."

Katherine stood up, saying, "We were glad to be here if it helped. We'll get out of your hair now."

"Do you want us to stick around?" Margie asked. She didn't know much about this woman, just that she had been divorced for less than a year and worked at a daycare. Sandra gave a little smile, and it was as though she was laying out all the frustration and fear and uncertainty in her life.

"I've already bothered you enough," Sandra said. "He's gone. We'll be okay."

"Are you sure?" Katherine asked. "Is there anything else we can do for you?"

Margie almost asked if they could buy Sandra and her kids dinner, but that seemed too forward, too much like offering charity. Instead, she and Katherine said their goodbyes and walked back to the minivan. As Margie started the engine, she had a nagging feeling she was forgetting something, that something was off. Nevertheless, she drove away. They had gone a couple blocks and just turned back onto Chester Avenue when Katherine's phone pinged with a text message.

"*He's back,*" she read, sounding momentarily confused. "Oh shit!"

"Abra," Margie said. How had Abra not gotten into the car with them? How had they forgotten to check?

"She must have stayed on purpose."

"Smart woman," Margie said, speeding up. At the next intersection, she made an illegal U-turn and sped back toward Sandra's house.

Katherine was out of the car even before the van had come to a complete stop. She didn't bother with the gate but easily hurdled the fence, jumped the steps to the porch, and ran up the narrow wooden staircase to the second floor. The door at the top of the stairs was open, leading to an open living room with almost no furniture, just an old sofa that looked older than she was. In the next room, she spied a wooden table with three metal folding chairs around it. The dining room had built-in cabinets and a window seat. It had all the makings of a nice house, but there were no dishes or plates in the cabinets. And by the window seat was a man trying to hit his ex-wife.

Sandra was huddled in the corner of the window seat, her face a mixture of fear and shock. James pulled an arm back to slap her, but something unseen stopped him from swinging. It happened three times in a row. Each time, James would shake his arm and look over his shoulder as though trying to figure out who or what was staying his arm. Katherine knew Abra was strong, but she couldn't keep this up forever. They needed to find a better way to stop him.

"Leave her alone," Katherine said. She drew herself up to her full height, knowing that the crazy red-with-daisies cat-eye reading glasses probably did not inspire fear.

"Who the hell are you?"

"I'm Indestructa. And I see you've already met Shadow."

"Who?" James said. She hoped the distraction of conversation would help quell his anger.

"Shadow. She's invisible. She's been keeping you from hitting Sandra." James spun around and took a swing at the air behind him. Katherine admired Abra's self-control. She would have been tempted to giggle, but Abra remained silent, not giving away her whereabouts. "We're going to lay out some ground rules. You no longer come into this house unless you are invited by Sandra. You will not harm her or the children..."

James cleared the distance between him and Katherine in just a few steps. "I have never hurt my children," he hissed.

"Good. Don't hurt their mother either." James's arm twitched. Up close she could see just what an impressively large human being he was. *No fear*, she thought. "Bring it," she said aloud as she brought up one arm to block his hand. James only seemed to have one move, the side-arm slap that he was using, or tried to use, on Sandra. Katherine's hand caught his. For a moment, it was an arm-wrestling match in midair as their hands pushed against each other. It kind of felt like playing with Billy back when they were kids, except her big brother had always been stronger than she was. Whenever Billy got bored with the pushing game, he used to pull down on Katherine's arm, twist it behind her back, and make her say something like "Billy is the boss" or "Katherine smells like poop."

Katherine didn't make James say anything when she twisted his arm behind his considerable back. "Never hit her again," she said slowly. For a second, James was silent. "I'm going to let you go," she said and relaxed her grip. He twisted, throwing Katherine off-balance and onto the floor. She ducked out of the way of another side-arm slap. *He really does only have one move*, she thought as she scrambled to her feet. The next time he tried it, she grabbed his arm and again twisted it behind his back, only this time she was sure to use her left hand to push down on the back of his neck, bending him forward slightly and giving him two pressure points to fight instead of one. "Déjà vu," she said brightly. This time when he tried to twist and throw her off, she was ready and held him in place. "Now, take a deep breath," she said. He did so. "Let's try this again. I'm going to let you go. This is done." Warily, she let go of his arm and his neck, resisting the urge to push him as she did so. *He's a human being; treat him with respect*, she thought. When she first started teaching, she made the mistake of assuming that bad behavior was the default. She soon learned that most students would respond appropriately if you treated them like rational beings. Why not try it here?

James turned and faced her, straightening up and smoothing out his extra-long, short-sleeved button-down shirt, as though doing so would restore his dignity. He raised his chin slightly. "You say it's done. What if I say it isn't done?"

Sandra gave a little gasp. "Be careful. He keeps a gun in his car," she warned.

James gave Sandra a cutting look. Katherine had her eyes fixed on James, just in case. She didn't notice Margie standing by the door to the front stairs until Margie said, "No, he doesn't. Not anymore."

"You steal my gun?"

"Nope. Melted it. It's on the sidewalk. I was gonna clean it up, but it's still kind of gooey."

Katherine stifled a laugh as James swiftly walked past Margie. They heard his feet pound down the stairs. Margie and Katherine followed him. As they went down the stairs, Katherine asked quietly, "Shadow, you with us?"

"Right behind you," came Abra's voice.

Behind them, Katherine heard Sandra call to her children that she'd be right back. When they got outside, James was standing on the cracked concrete sidewalk looking at a handgun-shaped, oozy mass of metal and polymer. Katherine thought it would have fit in well with Salvador Dali's melting clocks.

James was livid and came charging back into the yard, slamming the gate behind him. Sandra seemed to shudder a bit at the rattling of the chain-link fence. Margie stepped in front of her at the same time Katherine did. "I got this," Margie said softly.

"That Glock cost me three hundred bucks," James sputtered. "What the hell did you do to it?"

"I told you: I melted it."

"How?"

Katherine was quietly pleased to see James recoil just a bit when Margie held up her right hand and said simply, "With my hand." James glared at her. Katherine had to resist the urge to step in, had to trust that Margie did indeed have this. "Look," Margie said, "we don't want any more trouble with you. We'll be back to check on Sandra. And you never know when Shadow is going to pop by."

"You keep talking about Shadow. There ain't no Shadow."

"Hey, hi, I'm Shadow. Now you see me," Abra said. She was now visible, standing off to one side of the tiny yard. "Now you don't." With that, she turned invisible again.

The expression on James's broad face was one of absolute shock and, for the first time, perhaps just the tiniest bit of fear. He opened his mouth, but no words came out. "I know this is a lot to take in," Margie continued. It seemed she was speaking as much to James as she was to Sandra, who looked as though she couldn't believe what was happening in her front yard. "We aren't here to hurt you. We are here to protect Sandra and the kids." She addressed James directly. "No more violence," she said. "Ever."

James stood motionless, as though he was worried some unseen person was going to jump him. Finally he nodded and gave a quiet "Okay."

"We'll be watching," Margie added.

"Okay," he repeated. "But who are you?"

Katherine couldn't resist answering: "We're the Super Ladies."

Without another word, the three of them got into the minivan, making sure the still-invisible Abra was with them. It was only after they pulled away from the house that Katherine felt herself breathing normally. She hadn't been scared. On the contrary, she was exhilarated. This was something meaningful, something almost tangible. They had saved someone from harm, maybe even stopped something bad from happening in the future. And she had made it happen.

Katherine turned around and saw Abra sitting contentedly in the backseat. "You're back," she said.

"I never really leave," Abra replied.

She looked over at Margie, who was waiting to make a left-hand turn onto Chester Avenue. Margie glanced over at her and grinned. "Well done, Katherine," she said.

"You too."

"Just one thing—next time, I get to say, 'We're the Super Ladies.'"

IC_SuperLadies posted: *The Super Ladies: Have powers, will travel.*

CHAPTER TWENTY-SEVEN

While the majority of his acquaintances from high school were going to college in other cities, other states, Eli was going to Baldwin-Wallace, a small liberal arts college on the far west side of Cleveland. B-W had a strong fine arts program, plus he had managed to eke out a tiny, drop-in-the-bucket scholarship. Saying "I got a scholarship to B-W" provided a reasonable explanation for staying so close to home. Nobody needed to know that the proximity to home was an escape hatch, a fail-safe against any lingering worries about how he'd cope, whether he'd feel comfortable, whether he'd start cutting again. Margie or Karl could be there in thirty minutes. It was close enough that he could take the light rail and a bus on his own to come home in a pinch. He could even commute if he really wanted to. Not that he was planning on doing so, as he repeatedly reminded his parents. It was just nice to have the escape hatch if he needed it, even if he never used it.

Margie felt the uneasy tension between letting Eli fly off on his own and protecting him. Eldest or not, of all her kids, Eli seemed like the one who needed protection the most. Joan, on the other hand, seemed to resist any assistance by either parent, but especially Margie. She tried to treat all three of her children equally, but still, there were times when she heard herself saying "Be careful" to Joan and "Have fun" to Eli or Grant and wanted to kick herself. Inwardly she worried about Eli. But somehow his height and his age and his maleness made it seem that any danger to him would come from within, not without.

When they brought him and his things to school on move-in day, Margie quietly fretted about everything: whether he would get along with his roommate (whom they had Skyped and texted with and the kid seemed nice), the food, his classes, and whether his burgeoning relationship with the fabulous Jamis Barberton (who was attending the University of Pennsylvania) would survive both time and distance. Eli had marked his sexual orientation on the roommate preference form, so presumably the roommate knew and didn't care that he was gay. She could cross off one worry from her long list. Mostly she worried that freshman year in college would somehow be a repeat of freshman year of high school, when he began cutting.

Joan and Grant had insisted they be allowed to help Eli move in, so they ended up having to take two cars— Margie's minivan, which carried Eli's stuff, and Karl's smaller Honda sedan, which carried him and the two younger kids. Margie got Eli for the ride there, during which time she was proud to say she didn't cry. They talked on the way as though they weren't driving anywhere special. Eli insisted that she, Abra, and Katherine continue to tell him Super Ladies stories for the comic. She promised they would, knowing that Katherine would share everything with Eli even if she didn't. Everything was fine as they pulled off the interstate and drove into tiny, little Berea, Ohio. It was only when they turned off Grand Street and onto Beech Street, home of

Davidson Hall and Eli's new address, that she noticed Eli was playing the nervous little finger game in his lap. She pulled into a parking spot near his dorm and turned off the car but didn't move.

Margie regarded her son for a moment, trying to think of the right thing to say. Her son regarded her right back. No matter how much he looked like a young man, all Margie could see when she looked at him was the little boy who used to play Go Fish with her while his baby sister slept. Finally she just said, "Remember that everybody you meet today is going through the same thing, and everybody is nervous. So whatever you're feeling is totally normal."

The finger game stopped. "You're right. Thanks," Eli said. He took a long, slow breath, said, "Let's do this," and opened the car door.

All around them were other families going through the same process of lugging suitcases, boxes, and crates containing the building blocks of some young person's life. Eli was something of a neat freak and tended to travel light. Margie suspected half his things were art supplies. They met his roommate, Justus, a short, olive-skinned kid from Michigan, and his parents. Justus really did seem like a nice kid. He was an only child, and Margie wondered if he and his parents were taken aback by having the entire Joseph family filling up the tiny dorm room with noise and bodies. Grant kept touching everything and asking Justus questions about his things. Joan kept wandering out to the hallway to see if Eli had any cute neighbors. And Karl was chatting up Justus's parents, trying to find common Ohio-Michigan rust-belt ground.

At a certain point, both boys' things were in the room, and there was nothing to do but leave. Justus's parents seemed to take the hint first, with the mother giving him a hug and a kiss on the cheek and the father a handshake with a pat on the arm.

Karl wasn't having any of that. He said, "We should probably get out of your hair too," and gave Eli a fierce hug that almost knocked the boy over. Joan and Grant gave their big brother quick, almost embarrassed hugs. Eli just smiled, clearly secure in the knowledge that he only had to deal with his family for a little while longer. Finally it was Margie's turn to say goodbye. She stood in front of Eli, one hand on each of his arms, keenly aware of the four other people who were watching.

For a second she wished it was just her and her first child again, the way it had been right after Eli was born when Karl was working long hours and it was just her and Eli cocooned in their own little world. The world was much larger now that the cocoon had burst open and this huge butterfly of a young man stood in front of her. Except trying to explain all that to Eli right now would make no sense and sound ridiculous in front of so many other people. Instead, she gave Eli a hug and, standing on her tip toes to reach his ear, whispered, "I love you."

"Love you too," Eli whispered back.

"If I miss you more than you miss me, it means you're having a great time."

"I wouldn't bet on it."

Saying anything else would start the waterworks, so Margie just patted Eli on the arm and led the Joseph Family Parade out of the dorm room.

Joan drove home with her, while Grant went with Karl. The neat symmetry of it was surprising. For a second, Margie could almost believe that they had no third child at college, that they were mom, dad, daughter, son. Four not five.

The males in their family were varying degrees of open, ranging from blunt (Grant) to merely talkative (Karl) to introverted-but-in-touch (Eli). In some respects, Margie had always found most men and boys to be simple. Not simplistic, not stupid, just uncomplicated. Even Eli with his anxieties in the midst of his darkest days was less of an emotional minefield than Joan on an average day. When he was in the hole, in the darkness, he made no pretense of being anywhere else. He had never given a noncommittal "Maybe" in response to the question "Are you hungry?" or passive-aggressively stacked four large items in the dishwasher so that nothing else fit and then claimed his chore was done. You always knew where you stood with Eli. And as for Grant—sweet, goofy, happy, thoughtful, open-book, little Grant—very few things made him angry. He liked to win at sports and games, but he wasn't cutthroat and never held a grudge if he lost. He'd always been like that—a happy baby who became a happy kid who was growing into a happy young man. As long as he was active and well-fed, he was the easiest kid in the world to parent. And then there was Joan.

All parents know there will come a time when their teenaged children will regard them as idiots. Somehow Joan seemed resentful of the complete fallibility of her parents, her mother in particular. Her mother no longer knew more math than she did, didn't know as much about chemistry, couldn't run as long, swim as fast, or kick a soccer ball as far as she could. Margie felt about as useful in her daughter's life as the old stuffed bear named Thomas that Joan had had since age four. Thomas wasn't anything Joan actually wanted to spend time with now; she just felt more comfortable having the bear around. Maybe once in a while she'd cuddle it if she needed the soft squishiness of the bear's worn fur. Most of the time, though, Thomas just hung around on the shelf waiting for Joan to come back. Margie was Thomas the bear with a set of car keys.

Joan had all the outer trappings of an enviable daughter: she excelled in school, played sports with enthusiasm and skill, and was a reasonably competent cello player. It was the consistently surly attitude that did Margie in. Being around her daughter sometimes felt like walking on a rickety bridge, where she wasn't sure from moment to moment if it might collapse under her feet. In the car after bringing Eli to college, however, Joan was subdued. Margie had long learned to let animals and children come to you, so she didn't say anything, just drove. Joan was silent for the first half of the trip home. If Margie had to bet, she'd lay even money on Joan missing her brother or thinking about something completely unrelated, like swimming or clothes. She was half-right.

They were driving on Cleveland's inner belt and passing by Progressive Field, when Joan spoke. "Is Eli going to keep doing the Super Ladies comic?" she asked.

Margie hadn't realized that Joan was even paying attention to the comic. Aside from the Fourth of July, she hadn't outwardly expressed any interest in it. "Yes, I think so."

"How does he get the ideas for the comic? Do you give them to him, or does he think them up himself?

Since the Miracle of the Macaroni and Cheese and the July Fourth Mom as a Bonfire, Margie had tried to keep the whole heating of things to a minimum in front of her family. They didn't know that the story of The Schvitz melting an angry ex-husband's gun had actually happened. They didn't know that the melted motorcycle seat was true. They didn't know that Margie had responded to a message someone sent to the Super Ladies on IcyU, gone to a strange house, and heated up some family's broken sixty-gallon hot water heater so a mother could wash clothes and give her kids baths. The family didn't have the money to get it fixed right away, so Margie had gone over there three times in one week to help. Karl, Joan, and Grant knew nothing of this. They didn't know that doing these things made Margie feel less like a wife and mother and more like a human being. Still, she hadn't exactly lied to them; she simply hadn't given them key information about her life.

"We give him the ideas," Margie said as she slowed down to go through Dead Man's Curve. Why anyone would put a seventy-five-degree turn in the middle of a freeway was one of life's persistent questions.

"Have you done any of those things in the comic strip? Or did you just make it all up?"

Margie hedged her bets. "Some of them."

Joan was silent for a moment. When she spoke again, she sounded a little bit hurt, a little angry. "So you're saying that some of those things are true? Not just the macaroni and cheese—you and Aunt Abra and Aunt Katherine have really done all those things in the comic strip?"

Deep breath. "Not all of them."

"That isn't fair," Joan said, giving a kick to the underbelly of the dashboard.

"What do you mean?"

"It isn't fair. Why didn't anything happen to me? I was in the chemistry lab too, right in front of *my* experiment. I was right there when it exploded, but nothing cool has happened to me. Why you guys and not me?" She kicked the bottom of the dash again and then huddled into the corner of the passenger seat, looking out the window, her back turned to her mother as much as possible.

"I don't know why. I have a theory," Margie said. There was no response, so she plunged in. "My guess is that the phytoestrogens didn't affect you because you're still an adolescent. Think about the ages of all the other women you had samples from. They're either much older or much younger than Katherine, Abra, and me. There were already hormonal changes going on in us. The explosion just seemed to exacerbate them." She shifted lanes to get out of the way of some guy doing eighty-five in a convertible.

"I guess that's a plausible hypothesis," Joan muttered in her best surly teenager voice.

"You're the scientist. And a much better one than I'll ever be."

After a second there was a barely audible "Thanks" from the passenger seat, although Joan still had her back to her.

Margie waited. If you waited long enough, most people would come around. By the time they had pulled off the freeway, Joan wasn't talking, but she no longer had her back to Margie.

She wanted to tell her daughter that there was nothing special about her powers, that what she could do was akin to the talents of someone in a carnival freak show a hundred years ago. Being able to harness heat didn't make her a better person. It didn't change the fact that her entire existence revolved around taking care of other people. She went with it and asked Joan what she wanted for dinner. It seemed the path of least resistance at the moment.

IC_SuperLadies posted: *The Schvitz will never reveal her identity or her meat loaf recipe.*

CHAPTER TWENTY-EIGHT

MARGIE STARTED BACK TO WORK AT THE SAME TIME JOAN AND GRANT STARTED BACK TO SCHOOL. Usually it was easy to slip back into the routine of getting multiple children, one husband, and herself out of the house on time and with all the necessary items—gym shoes, lunches, swim goggles, cellos, homework, permission slips—needed for a particular day. This year, it felt like drudgery. There was so much else to do, so much she could be and should be doing. Not in the abstract way of "I should lose ten pounds" or "I should finally take that Spanish class." She could do things no one else could. She could help people and fight people and right wrongs and protect the weak. That's what she should be doing. Not laundry. Not errands. Not a school administrative job that could easily be done by any number of reasonably competent, patient individuals. There was no one else who could do what she could.

It was a mid-September morning when Margie felt something snap. It wasn't a tendon or a ligament or a going-postal kind of snap. It was the cumulative effect of weeks that had turned into months that had turned into years of essentially the same screaming treadmill over and over. To be fair, every day was different. But, as she reminded herself, even Sisyphus probably stopped to admire the view once in a while.

Some days Grant had an after-school club and needed to be picked up instead of taking the school bus home. Some days Joan "only" had 5:30 a.m. swim practice at the high school. Some days she had evening practice too. Some nights Grant had swim practice at the Y. Some days one of them had a music lesson. Some days Karl worked late. Some days she had a staff meeting after school. Some days she had to go to the grocery store or someone's doctor or dentist appointment. Some days there was a pile of laundry to do or bills to pay or something that needed to be mended, fixed, glued, or thrown out and it was seemingly always her responsibility to perform the mending, fixing, gluing, or throwing out.

The day she felt the snap wasn't terrifically harried. Joan was being disproportionately dramatic over a lack of oatmeal in the house; however, at 5:00 a.m., Margie could almost forgive the histrionics. She took Joan, Joan's backpack, and a lunch bag containing approximately twenty-five hundred calories to the high school and came back home to walk Juno before Start of the Day, Part II began.

Some days she tried to experience the world as the dog did, with excitement and curiosity and wonder at all the subtle differences that demarcated one day from the next, one tree or blade of grass from another. Most days she just wished she could keep walking.

Juno sniffed everything. Margie just sniffed the air. There was the faintest hint of dying leaves. The scent of fall. It was soon apparent Juno was doing more than just sniffing, and Margie untied one of the plastic bags from the leash to clean up the dog's calling card. She cleaned it up, tied the bag, and resumed their walk. The early-morning sky was cloudless, giving every outward appearance of a clear, beautiful day, a day when one could find no fault with the world. Even having to do poop patrol was a fair price to pay to get out of the house for a while. When they were almost home, she heard the familiar rumble of the guy in the black SUV coming down the block. Not only was he speeding, but he was blaring the chorus to The Eagles' "Hotel California" at 6:15 a.m.

"It's too early for this," she muttered. The SUV was barreling down the street toward her and Juno and showing no signs of slowing to anywhere near the posted limit.

That's when she felt the snap, as though the gate that had made her behave herself for the past forty-seven years swung wide open, letting her saunter on through it to see what was on the other side. Not giving a damn—that's what was on the other side. Not caring about being nice or what other people think.

Margie stopped walking and stared at the oncoming SUV. Calling upon the internal generator that seemed located somewhere in her lower abdomen, she felt a surge of heat rush through her body, concentrating in her hand. She felt the plastic bag of dog poop heating up as she twirled it twice over her head, like David taking aim for Goliath. As the bag left her hand, Margie saw small flames trailing behind as it sailed through the air. This was the first time she had made flames. She hoped the plastic wouldn't melt before it hit the black SUV's rear window.

It didn't.

The SUV was going so fast it was almost to the stop sign at the end of the block before the driver realized the back window had been hit. As she watched the SUV jerk to a stop then drive wildly in reverse back to where she and Juno were standing, Margie was amazed to feel... nothing. Calm. No nerves. No worry that the puffy, pasty-faced SUV driver with a receding hairline and wide moustache would somehow hurt her. No worry about what this stranger might say or do. No guilt that she had done something deliberately vindictive. She could match him, could hurt him more than he could ever hurt her. Hell, she could Make Fire. What did he have? Nothing, except an extraordinarily large cursing vocabulary, which he was using liberally.

To her credit, Juno only barked twice while the guy was yelling. He didn't get out of the car, which could mean 1) he wasn't *that* angry, 2) he didn't realize just how disgusting his rear window was, or 3) he was a little scared. When he finally stopped yelling about his window, Margie calmly said, "Slow down on my street, or I'll do it again."

"Are you threatening me, lady?" the guy asked. "Because if you are, I'll have the cops on you so fast it'll make your head spin."

"I was going to give them a call myself and ask if they'd put a speed trap on our street again. Except that only stops you temporarily. However, I walk this dog every morning. And she takes a big crap every morning, which I'll be sure to save for you *every morning*. Or you can just stop going fifty in a twenty-five zone." With that, she calmly resumed her walk.

The driver turned on the rear windshield wiper but only succeeded in smearing warm dog poop and ripped plastic bag all over the window. He started driving slowly alongside her, yelling the entire time about how she was going to pay if there was any damage to his car and how he knew half the Lyndhurst police force and would get her arrested. He threw in a few choice insults, but she didn't even look at him.

When the guy finally drove away, she noticed that he went a little more slowly than usual and came to a complete stop at the corner. Juno gave a punctuating *woof* as the SUV turned onto Mayfield Road. "You tell him, Juno.

Good dog." Juno looked over her shoulder with an expression that Margie always equated with the dog having told a joke and waiting for the human to get it. "Oh, you're right," Margie said. "You can get a whole lot more done when you aren't worried about being nice."

IC_SuperLadies posted: *Did David of David and Goliath fame have a dog? Asking for a friend.*

CHAPTER TWENTY-NINE

THE WOMAN WHO CAN'T BE HURT HAD SETTLED INTO A COMFORTABLE ROUTINE. Every weekday morning, she'd do her Very Early Superhero Patrol Run, so named because the "VESPR" acronym amused her, even if vespers were actually the evening prayer. She'd pick a neighborhood to run in, keeping an eye on empty houses or parked cars. And just about every run included a visit to the bus stop at Euclid and East 125th to check on Estelle, typically waiting until her elderly charge had gotten on the downtown bus safely. Getting up at three or four in the morning and running for a few hours had quickly become her normal. Treating Hal like a roommate had become normal too. He didn't seem to care. It would be easy to say he had pulled away first.

There were times when she missed the camaraderie of running with Abra, the give-and-take that comes with a relationship that is equal parts friendly competition and support. But she didn't need anyone to push her now. And she doubted whether anyone could keep up with her, even an invisible Abra.

School had started, so she'd rearranged and curtailed her runs a little bit in the interest of time. She was teaching the same courses as the year before, so the lesson plans were essentially the same. Still, lesson plans always need to be tweaked, her classroom organized, and supplies ordered. And always there were meetings. That was the teacher's annual drill. If the last thing she did was wait for the bus with Estelle, she could still get home around the same time she always had. Hal left for work on time, and she waited with Anna for the school bus and neither of them had any clue that her running schedule was any different than it had ever been.

Her newly minted fourth grader was going through a musicals phase. The Saturday after school started, it was *The Sound of Music*, which she had already seen twice. In the past six months, they had watched *Singing in the Rain*, *Guys and Dolls*, *My Fair Lady*, *Annie* (four times), and *Seven Brides for Seven Brothers*. "It's gotta be from your side of the family," Hal said in the kitchen. He was getting another slice of pizza, and Katherine followed him into the kitchen to put her plate in the sink. "You have the music genes. Nobody in my family can even carry a tune."

"You say that as though liking musicals is a bad thing," Katherine said.

"I'm glad she's expanding her tastes. I just wish she'd expand them a little more. I'm sick of *The Sound of Music*," Hal said.

Anna's voice chimed in from the living room. "Can I stay up and watch the whole thing?"

"I thought she was supposed to be getting back on her school schedule even on the weekends?" he said to Katherine. He always seemed to refer to Anna in the third person whenever he thought Katherine was falling down on the parenting job. Sort of like how their old dog had always been "Katherine's dog" whenever it chewed up a book or a shoe.

"Mom said I could stay up until the next song was over."

"And it's over," Katherine said to Anna. In response to Anna's protest about having to go to bed early, Katherine picked her up, gave her a belly kiss, and started doing arm curls, using Anna's compact nine-year-old body as a weight bar. As usual, this cracked Anna up. Katherine sent her up to her room before she got out-of-control silly because that would mean another twenty minutes before the kid settled down. Anna must have been more tired than she let on, because Katherine managed to get her to bed and quiet without too much trouble. The start of the school year always seemed to wear kids out. When she rejoined Hal in the living room, he was flipping through channels on the television. He was in the easy chair, so she sat down on the sofa to watch a bit of whatever action movie he was watching.

"Do you want to watch something together?" he asked.

"No, thanks."

They sat in silence. Hal had never been talkative, but his silence bordered on aloofness. They could talk about something simple, like Anna's school supplies or the grocery list, but Katherine couldn't remember the last time they had had a conversation about anything meaningful. More and more, she felt like things were coming to an end. There was a mental and emotional moving on. They were still in the same house, still co-parenting the same small wonderful person, but the attraction, the intimacy, the glue of the two of them seemed gone.

"Um, could we talk for a minute?" she asked.

Hal gave a small but audible sigh and shut off the television. "What?" he asked, although he looked more tired than interested.

Now that she was face-to-face with her husband, Katherine wasn't sure what she wanted to say. She wanted to tell him everything and nothing. For all she knew, Hal was feeling the same way, just going along each day pretending that he was still in love with his wife. If nothing else, she owed him her honesty. "I need to tell you something but..." She suddenly thought of Eli's comic. "Maybe it's better to show it to you. Hold on."

"Can I turn the TV back on while I wait?"

"Sure, I just need to find the iPad."

"It's in our room."

"Be right back."

As she ran upstairs to get the iPad, Katherine felt a bit better. The comic was the perfect segue. When she handed the iPad to Hal saying, "Read this," she first saw a slight look of surprise, then a little grin slide across his face. He quickly scrolled through a few of the comics Eli had posted on the blog then looked up.

"That's cute," he said with a smile. "Eli turned you three into superheroes. Pretty clever comic."

Katherine had been pacing around the living room while Hal read, occasionally peeking over his shoulder. She took a deep breath. *Here goes nothing.* "It isn't just a comic. It's true."

Hal put the iPad on the end table next to the chair. "What's true?"

"We've turned into superheroes."

Hal looked at her for a moment, as though trying to decide whether his wife was joking or simply losing her mind. Apparently he decided on joking because he blurted out a "Sure, dear" that was mostly a guffaw. When Katherine didn't burst out laughing with him, he composed himself a bit. "Sorry, I don't mean to laugh. I love that you talk to Anna about all that girl power stuff. And I know you were into the whole the Riot Grrrl scene back in the day, but...come on. You expect me to believe that you and Abra and Margie have superpowers?"

"Yes."

"Very funny, Katherine."

"Do you want me to prove it?" she asked.

Hal made an exasperated *pffft* noise, like a blown tire. "Dear, unless 'superpower' is a new euphemism for something kinky, no, I don't want you to try and prove something that's impossible." He stood up, took four steps over to where Katherine was sitting on the sofa, and kissed her on top of the head. "Thank you for showing me the comic. I'll see you in bed. Good night." He left the room and went up to bed, leaving Katherine frustrated and fuming. Somehow it seemed like more than just the end of a conversation. Still, she didn't say that to Margie and Abra the next time they got together. She merely said, "That was that. I told him, but I didn't tell him."

They had switched their normal Thursday night to Tuesday because Billy was now playing at the old Academy Tavern over in Shaker Heights on Tuesdays. It was one of those working-class bar/taverns that had been in the same location for eighty years. The menu veered toward comfort food and old stand-bys—burgers, sandwiches, and lots and lots of french fries.

"You made the effort," Margie said to Katherine. "Now he can never say you didn't tell him."

"I guess." For a moment Katherine wanted to say more. She wanted to say that there were moments when she truly didn't care if Hal knew, when she wasn't even sure if she cared what he thought anymore. But why worry her friends until she was sure? It seemed safer to change the subject. "Karl knows everything, right?" she asked Margie.

Margie gave a sheepish smile. "Yeah. He kind of thinks it's sexy."

"But we all know Karl's *freaky*," said Abra, giving Margie's shoulder a nudge with her own as she said the word "freaky."

"Takes one to know one." Margie took a sip of her beer as a small salute to herself.

Katherine felt the tiniest pang of envy but let it pass. Why begrudge her friend having an active sex life? At least somebody she knew was. She settled back to listen to the music. In a venue like this, Billy could let loose and play straight-ahead jazz instead of toning it down like at the Metro. People at the Academy occasionally sang a song with him too, usually an old standard. *There's always somebody who wants to get up and sing*, Katherine thought as a pudgy, older white guy got up and started to sing "All I Do Is Dream of You." It took her a moment to recognize the song—she'd only ever heard Debbie Reynolds sing it pert and perky in *Singin' in the Rain*. This guy did a more-than-respectable melancholy rendition that made most of the tavern stop and listen.

"Is it my imagination or did that guy suddenly get like five times more attractive the moment he began to sing?" Abra said.

"I wouldn't say *five* times more attractive," Katherine said. "Maybe a doubling in his attractiveness quotient."

"Would that was all I had to do."

"You're gorgeous," Katherine and Margie said at the same time.

"Seriously gorgeous," Margie added. "I'm not saying it to be nice the way you guys say it to me. You are."

"It clearly isn't enough." Abra let her words drift off into the music.

"Don't even start about Evil Richard," Katherine asked. "He's an asshole."

"You forgot the word 'gaping' in front of that," Margie added.

"Gaping asshole."

Abra sighed. "You know, I went on a date the other night..."

"What!" Katherine said at the same time Margie exclaimed, "Oh my gosh, how was it?"

"It was with a guy I messaged on Leap.com, this dating site. He owns a small construction firm. He seemed nice enough, and he was really cute."

This was getting good. Once you've been married more than ten years, you occasionally need to live vicariously through your single friends. "That sounds promising," Katherine encouraged. "What happened?"

"He was as good-looking as his picture and also really full of himself. There was no spark, no connection, you know? It just started to seem like a waste of my time, so midway through the meal, I excused myself to the bathroom, turned invisible, and left." In the noise of the tavern, it was difficult to tell whether Katherine or Margie guffawed more loudly. "It isn't funny!" Abra protested.

Katherine couldn't even respond, but Margie managed to stammer, "Yes, it is."

"It was a spur of the moment decision, but now I feel guilty. I should have at least paid the check before I left, except I'm broke."

"Well, I'm glad you're using your powers for good and not for evil," Margie said.

"Did he ask you to dinner, or did you ask him?" Katherine asked.

"We messaged back and forth a few times, then he asked me. He picked the restaurant too."

"If he asked you, then you were under no obligation to pay the check. Or put out."

This at least elicited a small smile from Abra. "We don't need to talk about me. I thought we were here to commiserate with the empty nester."

"The nest is *emptier* but not empty. I miss Eli like crazy, but I hear from him a lot. Granted, it's mainly to get updates for the comic, but it's a good excuse to talk to him." She paused, as though she was going to say something else.

"What?" Abra asked.

"Nothing. I'm fine. What else is going on with you? Did you get the quitclaim deed signed?"

"Yes. Thank you for your help with that."

"Great!" Katherine said. "You severed the last tie with him. Congratulations." She raised her glass, and Margie did the same. Abra didn't.

"Yes, now it's solely my house. And now I'm solely responsible for a mortgage that is so deep underwater Jacques Cousteau couldn't find it."

"Can you pay it?" Margie asked.

"Barely, but it will be years before I'm actually getting ahead. To save money I stopped buying a transit pass and just turn invisible to ride the train." Katherine couldn't help but giggle a little bit. "Don't judge, it saves me a hundred bucks a month."

"I'm not judging. I actually find it rather clever."

"I would probably do the same thing in your situation," Margie added. "Short of buying your next drink, is there anything concrete we could do for you?" She paused, then said in a voice so quiet Katherine had to strain to hear it above the noise of the piano and conversation, "Is there a way you could help yourself the same way you helped your next-door neighbors?"

"I've actually thought about that. My mortgage is with Allied National. They're huge. You'd need somebody to hack into their computer system, not their office. I'm good at figuring out programs, but I'm not a hacker. God, I wish I had never bought that stupid house. It would be easier to just burn the damn thing down."

The three of them sank into silence for a moment, letting Abra's words linger in the air above the table, mixing with the sounds of Billy playing "Summertime."

When Margie asked, "How much are you insured for?" Katherine thought she was simply asking about insurance. Abra must have thought the same thing, because she just said she couldn't remember the exact amount. "More than it would get on the open market if I tried to sell it."

"That isn't what I was suggesting," Margie said.

Katherine froze. Around them there was the light applause that followed every one of Billy's songs, the clink of silverware on plates and glasses being put down on tables, and, cutting through it all, one particularly loud male voice that kept yelling "Oh my God!" at the baseball game that was mutely playing on one of the televisions above the bar. All these sounds seemed real and normal. What Margie was suggesting sounded neither real nor normal.

Abra's face went from puzzled to shocked. "What? No, no! Just no," she said.

For a moment, Katherine figured she must have misunderstood. Margie, of all people, couldn't actually be suggesting they burn down Abra's house for the insurance money. As she was trying to get her head around this proposition, she had a sudden realization. "Wait, are you saying you can light things on fire?" Her voice involuntarily dropped to a whisper as she asked this. Katherine couldn't help it. The heat was crazy enough, but the thought that her best friend could control fire was practically immobilizing.

"Yes."

"Wow. Then you *could* help Abra. I mean, it's illegal and probably a little dangerous and maybe immoral, but..." It was all those things. But it might also be a way out. She turned to Abra and lowered her voice. "Margie could help you."

"The way I see it," Margie said, "the cost of one policy for one eleven-hundred-square-foot, single-family home is a tiny drop in the giant insurance ocean. But that drop could set you free. You could be free of the house and all the bad memories associated with it and get a fresh start."

Abra looked overwhelmed. Katherine swore she even saw the hint of a tear in her eye. "Thank you. Just knowing that you would do that for me means the world."

For a moment, Katherine felt useless. Abra's invisibility was a shield—she could spy and practically fly when invisible. And now Margie had mastered the element arguably responsible for all of human civilization. What could she do? Fight. "If it'll help, I'll kick Richard's ass," she offered.

"You guys are the best."

The Woman Who Burns shook her head as though she was speaking to someone who didn't understand. "Abra, I'm serious. I could do this for you. I would do this for you."

From the expression on Abra's face, she hadn't taken Margie's offer completely seriously. "Burn down—" Abra lowered her voice almost to a whisper. "Burn down my house?"

"Yes," Margie replied.

Abra looked down at the glass of beer in front of her for what felt like a very long time. The Woman Who Can't Be Hurt tried to think what she would do if faced with this choice. "Do it," she said softly. "I'll help any way I can."

The Woman Who Can't Be Seen looked up and said, "Okay."

IC_EstellesKid posted: *My grandma says IC_SuperLadies every morning at the bus stop. Maybe she's wrong, but I don't know who the hell else would go running through Candlewick Heights by herself like that.*

CHAPTER THIRTY

THE WOMAN WHO CAN'T BE SEEN SOMETIMES TOOK HER LUNCH TO THE EASTMAN READING GARDEN BY THE DOWNTOWN PUBLIC LIBRARY. It was only a ten-minute walk from her building and offered a quiet solitude that was a pleasant alternative to the noise of the office. If you sat near the Rockwell Avenue entrance, you could look out and see the spritely fountain in the middle of Mall C, a vast public space in the middle of downtown Cleveland that overlooked Lake Erie. Everything she was looking at had been designed by architect Daniel Burnham, who famously said, "Make no little plans." Was burning down one's house for insurance money a little plan?

A sharp breeze blew in off the lake, making her shiver. It was time to get back to work. She wondered how long she'd be able to continue commuting while invisible. She had taken to leaving a neatly folded stack of dresses and blouses in the back of a file drawer in her office. A T-shirt and leggings or yoga pants were form-fitting enough to remain unseen. Anything not touching her skin directly was visible when she turned invisible.

The first day she decided to ride the train while invisible, she realized she'd have to go to work commando—no bra, no underwear. It was one thing to go out crime fighting for a couple of hours without underwear; going to work like that felt downright unprofessional. She hadn't even thought of it when she'd brought the stack of clothes to work the Friday before. By then, she was already at the Green Road station. Once she was out of the car, she went invisible and got on the train, unseen in form-fitting clothes and light sneakers (no socks). A dress worked fine over a pair of leggings, and a tailored blouse dressed up a pair of yoga pants. During the summer months, that was all she needed. As they moved into September, she had switched to long-sleeved shirts. She could get away with wearing her running tights and a thermal running shirt through the fall, but moving into winter, she'd need more clothes or would have to start paying again.

At first, invisibly jostling for a spot on a crowded train car during morning rush hour was almost enough to make her want to forgo the entire thing. The money she was saving might not put a dent in the mortgage or the thousands of dollars in credit card debt left by Richard, but it was one way to economize. She just wasn't sure how long she could do it. Every time she went invisible to avoid paying the fare, the idea of burning the house and starting a new life with the insurance money seemed less ridiculous and more like salvation.

She didn't need to be invisible for the entire trip—the only real necessity was to be able to scramble over or under the turnstiles unseen at the main station downtown. But there was something relaxing about not being seen. She could choose who saw her and, by extension, who spoke to her, who interacted with her, and who didn't. She could observe the world without being observed. This had some perks. For one thing, it let her act on one of her pet peeves. On more than one occasion she had stood unseen behind some kid playing music loudly enough to be heard throughout the train car. Then she would surreptitiously pull the kid's earbud cord out of his or her phone. The kid would plug it back in, and she'd unplug it again and again until the kid decided the plug was broken, stopped the music, and started texting. She considered this a public service in the interest of noise abatement.

Riding while invisible also made it easier to intervene whenever she saw a wandering male hand touching a female body. The good people of Cleveland, Ohio, were generally well behaved, but once in a while she'd be standing in a corner of the train car when she'd notice a woman give a quick look over her shoulder. Then the woman would visibly shift an inch or two away from whatever man was standing near her. That was when Abra would start watching. Most women—most people—are reasonable and realize that bodies will accidentally bump into each other on a crowded moving train. Whenever Abra saw the second quick glance, a second shift away, she would start moving toward the offending party. Usually she would just grab the guy's hand and twist it behind him. She didn't twist hard. There was no need. The shock of an unseen hand grabbing his always made the guy jump. He'd give his own quick look around before moving away. There was something very satisfying in turning the tables.

Life at Hoffmann Software Solutions continued as it always had, although now that Arthur, Giles's son, was in charge, the corporate culture had changed. The importance of a workplace hierarchy rests upon the workplace's leader. Giles was, at heart, a New Age baby boomer who was big on free speech and open communication. Arthur seemed to think the company had lost its competitive edge and considered himself a Master of

Some Universe. When he started showing up for work in a suit with his hair slicked back, it felt like the eighties all over again. Something about Arthur's hypermasculine attitude also seemed to turn the office's cultural clock back about forty years.

Gary Sewicki and his team in Software Development had always joked that the rest of the company didn't care how the sausage got made—in essence, how the software systems that the company sold were developed and programmed—as long as they worked. This was true to a point. What the development guys did was something of a mystery to most of the company, and they seemed to like it that way. Software Development took up a row of three large inter-connected rooms at the far end of the company's rabbit warren of offices. A few years back, when the lone female developer left the company, one of the guys put up a sign outside the department's main door that read "Sausage Factory." It got a few chuckles and titters, then Giles made them take it down because it was "unprofessional" and he didn't want visitors to the office to be offended. Two weeks after Arthur took over, the sign was back. What's more, Abra heard rumors that a couple of the guys had less-than-professional calendars up in their cubicles now.

With almost all of the summer interns gone, Abra couldn't keep up with office goings-on by looking over their shoulders to read their text conversations. Instead, she had taken to regular invisible strolls through the halls. It was the easiest, quickest way to hear what was happening in the company. The first time she did it, it felt nosy. Then she realized it gave her a leg up on internal communications. For instance, the Sales Department had a contest during the summer to see which rep could get the most clients to upgrade their software package before the end of the fiscal year on September 30. The contest was only for the Sales team, so they didn't mention it to Marketing (i.e., Abra). After she overheard a few people from Sales talking about the contest, she created a quick email- and social media–based marketing campaign that focused on the value-added aspects of Hoffmann's various packages. At the senior staff meeting after lunch, Deepak, the head of Sales, said they'd had a bump in upgrades over the last two weeks. Nobody bothered to mention the email campaign, but the web analytics would eventually throw some of the credit her way.

After the staff meeting, Sewicki and Horowitz shared a private chuckle in the hall outside the conference room. It piqued Abra's interest. It wasn't as though she was eavesdropping; they were practically standing in her office doorway. She heard Sewicki say, "You gotta see it," followed by an unintelligible whisper, followed by a bro cackle. They tromped off down the hallway toward Software Development. Although she had a report to run, Abra went invisible, quickly piled her clothes on her desk chair, and followed them.

Abra rarely needed to go down to Software Development. Most of her work was done in conjunction with Sales, which was near her office at pretty much the opposite end of the Caxton Building's seventh floor. Software Development was next door to the server room and the Tech Support office, which had its own Band of Brothers mentality. But while those in Tech Support had the collective persona of a dorky, introverted younger brother, Software Development was more the overachieving, entitled big brother who liked to wail on his younger siblings for fun. That whole end of the office was fueled by Mountain Dew, Doritos, and testosterone. Still, invisible and stripped down to yoga pants and a long-sleeved T-shirt, Abra gamely walked through the doors of the Sausage Factory.

The first thing she noticed was the lighting. Most of the guys in Software Development preferred minimal office lighting. Ray, one of the few guys from the department she'd ever been friendly with, used to say that the ceiling lights caused too much glare on the screen. Only one of the department's three rooms had windows— tall, old-fashioned ones with wooden frames like the one in Abra's office. None of the programmers wanted to sit near the windows, so that area held a large ping-pong table that doubled as a departmental conference table. Abra had always played doubles with Ray when the company used to have its annual Ping-Pong Tournament of Glory. Ray wasn't with Hoffmann anymore, and nobody seemed to have the time or inclination to revive the Tournament of Glory. Most of the guys in the department were younger and, presumably, less expensive hires. Abra said hello to them in the hallways and kitchen, but that was about it.

No one was near the ping-pong table, but she could hear voices coming from the adjoining room. This larger room had no windows, which seemed to be how the guys liked it. A hub of four cubicles nested in the center of the room, with two larger cubicles in two of the corners. The voices were coming from one of the cubes in the center. Abra walked behind one of the developers to the next cube and found Sewicki and Horowitz staring at one of the two wide-screen monitors on the desk. The cube belonged to a guy named Drew, who was one of the few developers who had been with Hoffmann almost as long as Abra had. He was probably in his late thirties and, as far as she knew, still single.

Sewicki and Horowitz were standing on either side of Drew's chair, somewhat blocking her view. "That's crazy," Horowitz said in between incredulous chuckles. "Don't tell me you did this on work time."

"Nah, I did it during lunch. It started with A.J. over in Tech Support. He was complaining about how his girl-friend would turn into a raging bitch when she was on the rag and he wanted an easy way to keep track of it. We joked around that there should be an app for that. It turns out *there is*. It didn't take much to adapt the code to our purposes."

Abra leaned around Horowitz's right arm, getting as close to him as she dared. It was a hell of a lot closer than she ever would have wanted. She leaned forward and balanced herself on the edge of Drew's desk, careful not to move the two pencils sitting near his mouse. It was sort of like holding a one-armed plank, but at least it allowed her to see the monitor. The guys appeared to be looking at a variation of Hoffmann's basic inventory tracking program, but instead of tracking durable goods, it was tracking people. Abra got a sick feeling in the pit of her stomach when she saw her name at the top of the screen.

Drew pointed the cursor at the calendar that took up about a third of the screen. "See, the icons tell you when the subject is safe and approachable and when you should avoid her at all costs."

"The little red drops are the 'avoid' days," Sewicki added with a chuckle.

"McQuestion's schedule is a little screwed up because she's kind of old. It may not be accurate," Drew said, clicking on the "Next" button. Now Aletha's name was at the top of the screen. "Here you go," he said.

"Aletha..." Horowitz said.

"Yeah," Sewicki said in a voice that sounded like he was looking at juicy cheeseburger.

"How the hell did you figure all this out?"

"We got the baseline data a couple of ways. First, just plain old observation. Sometimes it's just so obvious. You can track it. Or if she's acting like a total bitch, I'll just say, 'Geez, are you on the rag or something?' If they are, they get all huffy. Sandy came right out and told me." Drew pointed the cursor at a small text box on the left-hand side of the screen. "You see this? That's the Bang Box. We mark that if we have independent confirmation. For instance, Richie had a thing with one of the interns last summer and was able to provide visual confirmation."

"In other words, he banged an intern and saw dirty tampons in her garbage can," Sewicki said.

"Aletha's box is blank," Horowitz said.

"Nobody's been able to get in that box," Drew said and clicked "Next" on the screen. "Now Bree on the other hand..."

"Easy Bree-zee," Sewicki said. Bree was an administrative assistant in the Sales Department. Abra spent a minute or two listening to them talk about all the people in the company Bree had slept with. She didn't know Bree well, but she was pretty sure half of what they were saying wasn't true. And even if it were, what business was it of theirs if somebody in the Sales Department decided to make the beast with two backs with the partner of her choosing?

The arm she'd been leaning on was starting to tremble a little, as though she'd been holding a plank for too long. She needed to get out of Drew's cubicle before she gave herself away.

"Guys, this is pretty damn funny..." Horowitz began.

"It's pretty damn useful," Sewicki said.

"...but it seems kind of, I don't know, like a Human Resources nightmare."

"Then don't tell HR."

"Who has access to this?"

"Just Software Development and a few others. If the program is mapped to your machine, then you can make additions. It's open source. You want me to give you access?" Drew asked.

Abra was pleased to see Horowitz looked less than enthusiastic. Maybe he had a conscience after all. "Naw, that's okay," he said.

"It's no trouble at all. Information wants to be free, man." Drew began clicking through a series of windows in the network to map the program. He went too quickly for Abra to follow the path, but she suspected the program lay somewhere in a proprietary drive that she wouldn't be able to access on her own. "There, done. When you go on your machine, look for the B drive. Any updates you make will be live."

Abra slipped out of Drew's cubicle as quickly and silently as possible. She could hear the low rumble of Sewicki's and Horowitz's voices behind her, but he wasn't going to stay in there forever. Still invisible, she ran out of the Software Development office and down the main hallway, sidestepping around Sandy, the head of HR, and one of her people. She thought she heard Sandy say, "Do you feel a draft in here?" as she ran by.

Horowitz's office was near the kitchen. His assistant in the Finance Office, Lily, was pretty cool, but Abra didn't want to have to mix Lily up in this. It would be easy to go to Sandy and file a complaint. Horowitz was right that tracking the menstrual cycle of every woman in the office was a Human Resources nightmare. Explaining how she knew the Bitch Tracker even existed would take some fancy storytelling. She didn't want anybody to be fired—just slightly enlightened. But she needed some time alone in Horowitz's office. Cutting through the kitchen, she found herself in the windowless labyrinth of offices and cubicles in the center of the company's office space. This was where they put lower-level employees, temps, and interns. Taking a quick glance around to make sure nobody was watching, she made herself visible and knocked on the edge of Aletha's cube.

"Hey, I need your help," she said in a low voice.

Aletha looked startled but, to her credit, didn't bat an eye upon seeing the company marketing director standing in her cube in bare feet, yoga pants, and a T-shirt. "Sure. Is it about the Spanish-language packet? I'm still working on it..."

"No, no. It's kind of only marginally work related."

"Okay..."

"I just need you to keep Horowitz out of his office for a while. Ten or fifteen minutes. Longer if you can. And you can't tell anyone."

"What's going on?" She sounded worried. Abra sometimes forgot Aletha was working in an uncertain netherworld between intern and part-time employee while she finished her MBA. Of course she'd be a little leery.

"It's a long story. This request is completely aboveboard, but if you decline, it won't affect your review. Basically I need to make some edits to a program on his machine before he deletes it."

"How do you know he's going to delete it?"

Abra sighed, unsure of how much to reveal. "Because it's sexist claptrap."

Aletha nodded, a small smile spreading across her face. "I'll keep him out of there for half an hour."

Abra didn't bother asking how Aletha would drag Horowitz into an impromptu meeting, she just sent her down the main hallway in the direction of Software Development, turned invisible again, and walked into Horowitz's office.

It wasn't exactly clear when the guys in Software Development discovered that the Bitch Tracker had been hacked. Every entry now had a confirmation in the Bang Box. In some, Abra had written "None of your damn business" or "Leave her alone." A few, including her own, now read "Do not fuck with this woman under any circumstances." The Sausage Factory sign came down two days later. For the next few weeks, the Software Development guys were more subdued, as though they finally realized they weren't operating in a vacuum and that someone was watching them.

IC_SuperLadies posted: *Now you see me, now you don't. It depends on my mood.*

CHAPTER THIRTY-ONE

ONE MORNING IN THE FIRST WEEK OF OC-
TOBER, KATHERINE SLINKED OUT OF BED AT
THREE THIRTY IN THE MORNING AND SILENT-
LY PUT ON HER RUNNING CLOTHES. She was dig-
ging her shoes out from underneath the bed when
she heard Hal ask quietly, "Where are you going?"
His voice startled her. He was never awake at this time.
Still, she tried to make her voice sound as normal as pos-
sible.

"Out for my run."

"It's three thirty-seven in the morning."

She feigned surprise. "Is it? I swear when I glanced at
the clock it read five thirty."

Hal sat up in bed, gathering the blankets a bit around
his bare chest. She hadn't noticed what a cool morning
it was. With school in full swing, she had to admit that
summer truly was over. Maybe she ought to throw on
leggings instead of shorts this morning. She dug the
leggings out of a drawer as they talked. "Why are you
going running? It's practically the middle of the night,"
Hal said.

She couldn't say "I run at this time every day," so she said, "Just putting my stuff on for later. I can't sleep. I'm gonna go read for a while."

"Come back to bed," Hal said softly, somewhere between a request and a command. She decided to split the difference. Rather than getting back in bed, she sat down on the edge in her running leggings and T-shirt. It seemed appropriate to give him a good-morning kiss, so she did and was surprised when Hal made the kiss last longer than she would have. She pulled away first. He looked at her then asked: "Who do you meet in the mornings?"

"What?" It was a weak, buying-time response. Maybe he wasn't asleep all those times she had gotten up in the middle of the night and gone out looking for trouble.

"You get up and go running at all hours of the night. I can't quite figure it out. Your car is always here, but when you come back, you don't even look that sweaty or tired." He paused for a second, as though he was searching her face for something. When he didn't find it, he asked, "Is it somebody in the neighborhood, or does he pick you up?" As he said the word "he," Hal's voice trembled slightly.

"He who?" Katherine's conscience was clean, but her stomach was still twisted into knots. "Wait, you think I'm cheating on you?"

"Let's see. You leave in the middle of the night. You're gone for hours at a time. When you come home, you say you've been running, but you clearly haven't. It's a good excuse—then you can take a shower and wash his...stink off you. God, Katherine, I'm not stupid. You're pretty fucking obvious."

At first, Katherine could only stare, stunned, her heart pounding as if Hal's accusations were true. When she finally found her voice, the words spilled out. "I'm not cheating on you. I really do go running..." She spoke faster to try and silence Hal's protestations. "I know it sounds crazy, but I do go running for hours at a time. If you must know, I do meet someone. Her name Estelle, and I wait at the bus stop at the corner of Euclid and East 125th with her to make sure she gets on her bus safely." Hal gave a derisive exhalation of air, as though he couldn't even find words to dignify what Katherine was saying. She spoke a little faster: "And sometimes I find something bad going on and I stop it. Like somebody breaking into a car or a house. Sometimes I stop by a woman named Sandra's house to make sure her ex isn't bothering her. I showed you the Super Ladies comic and you didn't believe me, but it's true. It's true. I've developed this... super strength and I can't be hurt, and Abra really can turn invisible and Margie can defy the laws of thermodynamics and make things melt and even burn things and..." She slowed down, aware that her husband was now the one sitting in stunned silence, aware that maybe she shouldn't let on even to Hal that Margie could burn things. Not with the plan they had in place.

"I have no idea what to say to that. I don't know if you're feeding me a line of bullshit or if you're delusional."

"Neither."

One of the things she had always liked about Hal was his analytical, experiment-until-you-find-the-truth mind. It was time to appeal to that mind. She wasn't sure if their marriage was even worth saving at this point, but there was no way she was going to let him think she was a cheater. She stood up. "Okay, if I can prove it to you, will you believe me?"

"Prove what? That you've suddenly become some vigilante superhero?" he scoffed. Maybe it was the self-assured nod, maybe it was because she finally managed to hold her tongue and have an unexpressed thought or two, but Hal stopped fighting. "Okay. Prove it," he said.

Katherine looked around the room. She could do the tried and true cutting-without-bleeding trick, but it didn't seem big enough. Some moments required dramatic effect to make a point. She walked over to the bedroom window that looked out onto the front yard. They were only on the second floor—still, a jump without injury from that height might convince him. She opened the window and raised the screen, saying as she did so, "Don't scream. I'll be fine."

Hal was out of bed the instant she had the screen up, giving him a good view of Katherine swan-diving out of the second-story window, doing a midair summersault (she couldn't resist the flourish) and making a running landing. She jumped from the street to the roof of a parked car in one bound then turned to spy his shocked face gaping out of the open second-floor window. Maybe this would do. A leap off the car and a few quick steps brought her to their front porch. She easily jumped on top of the old iron porch railing, then made another jump up to the bedroom window and grabbed the window sill. Hal grabbed her wrists as though he was going to pull her in.

"Stand back," she said. With a quick lift and a hoist, she pulled herself up and into the window, knocking Hal over in the process. "Sorry!" she said. Anna was a pretty heavy sleeper, but that didn't mean they could make noise with impunity. "Are you okay?" she added in a whisper.

"What the hell?" Hal stammered. He was lying on the bedroom floor and scooted back a few inches as Katherine crawled toward him.

"Did I hurt you?"

"Uh, no. It's just—holy cow, Katherine. You jumped out a second-floor window and you didn't hurt yourself. You just...ran," he said slowly, as though he needed to confirm for himself what he had just seen.

"Yes."

"Jumped onto the roof of a car."

"Yes."

"And then jumped back up to the window."

"Yes."

"I get the feeling you could do a lot more if you wanted to."

"Yes."

"How in the world can you do this?"

Katherine tried to explain about the explosion and how the concentrated blast of phytoestrogens seemed to combine with the hormonal changes she was already going through. "I can't pretend to understand exactly how or why it happened. It's just a theory. But here I am. No periods, no pain. Somewhat indestructible."

She could almost see Hal's brain putting the whole thing together. "Just like in Eli's comic. You tried to tell me..."

"Granted, I didn't tell you very well. Obviously, the whole explanation required a demonstration."

"But you did try to tell me." Hal had been sitting on the floor with his arms resting on his bent knees, but now he moved over so he could lean against the footboard of the bed. "Wow," he said with a sigh, looking more at the wall opposite him than at Katherine. "This is a lot to take in."

She nodded, aware that she couldn't have shocked him more if she told him she wanted a divorce. There had been times over the last few months when the idea of divorce, of being a single parent truly seemed more attractive than remaining with a man who often seemed a million miles away. Yet here he was, worried that he had lost her to someone else.

Hal stopped staring at the wall and turned his focus back to her. "I mean, I always knew you were extraordinary, but this...this is, um, wholly unexpected," he added with a wry smile.

One word in that sentence stopped her cold. "You never said that to me before."

"What? 'Wholly unexpected'?"

"Extraordinary."

Hal looked momentarily surprised, then paused. "Then I guess I should have been telling you that all along."

Half of her wanted to remain defiant, to say, "Yeah, you should have. You should tell me I'm extraordinary and brilliant and fascinating and beautiful every single freaking day." The other half,, the self-reflective half reminded the defiant half that she hadn't been all that vocal in complimenting or appreciating him either. Both halves replied, "Thank you."

They were quiet for a moment. Sitting here next to him in silence didn't seem as frustrating as it had been. She sighed. To be brutally honest with herself, not all their problems lay with him. "I know I haven't necessarily been the best partner to you either."

"Can we maybe...do a reboot?"

She'd been carrying around what felt like a big burning ball of anger toward Hal. For months, every time they talked, every time he didn't pay attention or dismissed what she said, it felt like the ball of anger had grown larger and burned brighter. It seemed like it was burning up the whole marriage. Now, for the first time, it seemed like the ball was slowly extinguishing itself. It wasn't due to some lovey-dovey romantic miracle. Katherine thought maybe it had something to do with telling him the truth. Maybe a reboot would work. "I'm willing to try," she replied.

"I don't want to lose you. I know I don't say it as often as I should, but I would be lost without you." Hal crawled toward where Katherine was sitting against the wall next to the window. "Is it inappropriate to add that I find the idea that you could kick my ass—I mean, literally and completely kick my ass—to be frightening as well as slightly arousing?"

"You know, I feel like every time I've tried to initiate sex over the past few months, you haven't been in the mood."

"I know, and I'm sorry."

She gently put two fingers over his mouth. "So half of me wants to tell you to buzz off, and half of me wants to jump your bones."

Hal slowly licked each of the two fingers she was still holding over his lips, then gently took her hand in his. "Which half is hornier?" he asked.

"Lucky for you, both are."

Hal chuckled. "Oh sweetie, that is not why I'm lucky," he said and kissed her.

IC_SuperLadies posted: *Had to forgo the early-morning patrol. Other needs arose. IC_EstellesKid, tell your grandma I'll be there tomorrow. Love, Indestructa.*

CHAPTER THIRTY-TWO

The Woman Who Burns stood on the sidewalk across the street from a squat two-story house. She was on the west side in a neighborhood that she was pretty sure was still Cleveland proper but close enough to the western suburbs to be mistaken for one of them.

The house was unassuming enough. Architecturally, it was no great shakes—just one of thousands of moderately attractive houses built in the mid-twentieth century, when Cleveland still had plenty of people. No one would lament its loss if this particular house weren't standing there. There are millions of houses just like it all over America. The only thing that distinguishes one house from another is who calls it home. In this case, the person who called this particular house home was The Evil Richard Brewster.

From the size and condition of the street, the houses, the yards, it was a wealthier neighborhood than the one where he had lived with Abra. *How can this jackass afford to live here but can't afford to pay Abra back?* she thought for probably the twentieth time. Richard managed a restaurant. Where did he get the down payment for this house if he was so broke when he was with Abra that he needed to borrow money from her all the time? He was a sleeze and a crook and deserved some sort of punishment.

Not punishment, she thought. *Retribution. Comeuppance.*

They had meticulously planned the burning of Abra's house. If a homeowner filing for bankruptcy conveniently has a house fire, said homeowner is going to be the primary suspect. The plan was to have Katherine invite Abra to her house for dinner, where she would have three people who could attest to her whereabouts. Margie had no record, no criminal ties. She would merely be looked at as one of many friends, not as a suspect. Still, they had been careful to leave no trail, only discussing the plan in person, never on the phone or via text.

They set the date for the second Thursday in October. When Margie woke up that day, her first thought was *I'm going to burn a house down today.* Somehow, that thought made everything else about the day more bearable. She did the early-morning swim practice run for Joan, walked the dog, packed lunches for her and Grant, and got everybody out of the house on time. It didn't seem like as much of a soul-deadening pain in the neck as it usually did.

When she walked into the office, she said "Good morning" to the principal and a couple of teachers who were checking their mailboxes or making copies. But she was thinking about what part of the house she ought to start with. Obviously somewhere in the back so the neighbors wouldn't see. While she was completing the day's attendance report, Margie decided the wisest thing to do would be to leave her car on the next block and walk over. Abra said the neighbors diagonally behind her didn't have a fence—she could cut through their backyard and make a quick exit once the fire had started. The planning got her through making copies of the PTA newsletter and putting them in all the teachers' mailboxes.

Margie kept reminding herself that there was no victim in this plan. Whether it was a house, a car, or a television set, the owner of an object has every right to do with that object what she wishes. Save it, burn it, let it rot—that is the owner's prerogative. Paying an insurance company to protect an object was akin to placing a bet that something bad would happen to it. And it almost never did. If you added up all the money one person paid in a lifetime in home and auto insurance, it was easily equal to the payout for a small bungalow destroyed by fire.

She had no doubts about herself or her ability to do this thing. She could harness fire. She could and would make a house burn, and in doing so, she would free her friend. Maybe destruction didn't add actual meaning to her life, but a new purpose certainly felt like revival.

It wasn't until that evening as she was making the short drive to Abra's that Margie realized the single flaw in their plan: how could you burn down a house and make it look like an accident and still get Clinton P. the Cartoon Cat out alive? In all their planning, they never thought about how to get the cat out of the house safely. She could let him out, but an indoor cat who just happened to escape a house the same night that house burns down was beyond suspicious. Instead of collecting the insurance money on the house, Abra could go to jail.

Although she'd originally planned on approaching Abra's house from the back, Margie parked across the street and just looked for a while. The sun had just gone down and the whole street had a pretty, late daylight saving time glow. The air was crisp but not freezing and smelled thoroughly of fall. It'd be a nice night for a walk or a bonfire. But the more she stared at Abra's house, the less she wanted to burn it down. Right near the front door was a little purple azalea bush she and Karl had given to Abra and Evil Richard when they bought the house, when Richard wasn't quite so evil and more just a schlubby guy her best friend had fallen in love with. The azalea bush had grown in nicely over six years. A fire and its aftermath would probably kill everything planted near the house.

She wondered what the insurance payout would be if only the garage burned. From her vantage point on the street, she couldn't see the side of Abra's garage, but Margie knew well the swirling, Alice in Wonderland–inspired mural a bunch of them had painted on it two years ago. Abra said it always made her smile, even in the weeks right after Richard left. It'd be a shame to damage the mural.

It all came back to Richard. The more she thought about it, the more she realized that perhaps Abra's house wasn't the one that needed to burn. She sent a quick text to Abra and drove away.

All through dinner at Katherine's, Abra kept one ear open for her phone, expecting a call from the fire department or her neighbor to tell her that her house was on fire. It wasn't that she actively *wanted* to get rid of the house. This desperate option seemed to be the only one that would get her out of debt so she could move on with her life.

She and Katherine tried to act normally in front of Hal and Anna, talking about work and school and listening to Anna's reports from the front lines of fourth grade. The four of them had just finished dinner and sat down to play Clue when Abra felt her phone vibrate in her back jeans pocket. Katherine must have noticed her reach for the phone because their eyes locked over the coffee table.

"Excuse me" Abra said.

"Me too," Katherine said.

"You can't both leave!" Anna protested. "You can't play Clue with just two people."

Abra kept the phone in her pocket as she stood up. "Just running to the rest room," she said casually.

She could hear Katherine's, Hal's, and Anna's voices from the living room as she closed the bathroom door. There wasn't any logical reason for her to be nervous; she knew what was coming. This was her choice, her decision. Even so, it would be difficult to say goodbye to her little house.

There was a text from Margie that read, *I wonder if we're not focused on the wrong thing.* That was all. Abra texted back, *What do you mean?* but didn't receive an immediate response.

"Aunt Abra! It's your turn!" Anna called from the living room.

She kept the text conversation open and left her phone on the edge of the sink. As she walked out of the bathroom, she nonchalantly said to Katherine, "It's all yours" and hoped the nod she gave her would be enough of a clue to check the phone. Then she sat down and accused Professor Plum of doing it in the bedroom with the candlestick. Hal was still snickering when Katherine returned.

"What's so funny?" Anna asked.

"Nothing. I'm just being immature," Hal said.

Anna looked puzzled. "How?"

"Ah, must be the standard dirty Clue joke," Katherine said as she sat back down. "Here, you left your phone in the bathroom."

"Thanks," Abra replied, glancing at the phone. Her faith in Katherine's nosiness had been rewarded, because there was a new text from Margie that read, *"They used to burn witches. I'm reversing that."* Katherine had texted back, *"It's K. U crack me up. What's going on?"* Margie hadn't replied. Abra couldn't help but giggle at Margie's text.

"What's so funny?" Anna repeated.

"Sorry, Anna. Aunt Margie texted something funny," Abra said.

"Can I see?"

"It's private." She and Katherine caught each other's eye again. Margie's text was a little too cryptic. It was worrying. She opted for an abundance of caution.

"Anna, I think I'm going to have to borrow your mom."

"Now? But we aren't done with the game!"

Katherine was already standing up. She gave Anna a hug and a kiss on the head saying, "I'm sorry, sweetie, but there's something we have to do."

"What's going on?" Hal asked. He sounded a lot like Anna, or she like him. Katherine and Hal had clearly solved the nature vs. nurture question. Abra felt a quick pang of guilt for pulling Katherine away from her family and an even smaller pang of envy that Katherine had a family to be pulled away from when she didn't.

"I promise I'll tell you later," Katherine said, and gave Hal a kiss on the cheek.

"Okay." She couldn't read the face of someone else's husband, but he didn't look as annoyed as she might have thought.

Abra grabbed her purse and her phone as she stood up. "Hal, thank you for a lovely evening. I promise I'll bring your wife back in one piece."

"My pleasure, Abra."

They gave copious hugs to Anna, and Katherine reassured her that while she wouldn't be home by bedtime, she'd see her in the morning. Hal looked a little lost as he watched them go. Katherine was at the back door when she went back to the living room, gave him a quick hug and kiss, and said, "Thank you."

✹ ✹ ✹

Abra's little yellow Mini Cooper was already in the driveway, so she drove. Katherine buckled in next to her, enjoying the feeling of going on a mission. "So where are we going?" she asked.

"I have no idea. I just know that Margie needs us."

"I have the same feeling, but no bright ideas."

Abra's house was only a few blocks away, so they did a drive-by, but it was clear Margie hadn't been setting any fires there. "'I wonder if we're not focused on the wrong thing.' What does she mean?" Abra said.

"And the whole 'They used to burn witches. I'm reversing that,'" Katherine added.

Abra was heading out East Anderson, back toward the direction of Katherine's house, maybe heading to Margie's house. "What does she want to burn?" she mused aloud. Suddenly she sped up, saying, "Oh God, of course: Richard."

It took Katherine a moment to realize Abra meant Richard's house. Then it all made sense. Katherine knew exactly why Margie might want to burn down The Evil Richard Brewster's house. Once it was clear that Abra was going to take the high road and simply cut off all possible ties to the man who had ruined her life, Katherine herself had sometimes fantasized about different ways to exact revenge on Abra's behalf. These had mostly centered around painful (to Richard) encounters in dark alleys or abandoned parking lots after he closed up the restaurant. Almost anything can make sense if you think about it long enough. And if someone is caught up in a swirl of anger and wonder at how life has turned out and why some things are so lopsided and unfair and is in a state to want to right wrongs, then even revenge fantasies put into action can make sense.

While Abra tested the posted speed limit of every road they traversed, Katherine frantically texted and called Margie, hoping to stave off or at least delay any anger-inspired arson. "God, she could have his whole house burned down before we get over there," she muttered.

"I know, I know..."

"How does she even know where Richard lives now?"

"Karl helped me with the quitclaim deed, and Margie was kind of enough to courier it back and forth. Richard's new address was in there somewhere."

They drove down I-90 to the west side and got off in a neighborhood that looked to be right on the line between Cleveland and Lakewood, the first suburb to the west. It was dark out, but the streetlights illuminated well-maintained houses where people still turned on their porch lights after dark, a city park with what looked to be new playground equipment, and a street with a surprising lack of potholes. It was the kind of neighborhood where a city makes the extra effort to keep the residents happy for the property-tax revenue they provide. She couldn't bring herself to remark that it was nicer than the neighborhood where Abra still lived. Maybe Evil Richard had a roommate.

Abra turned down a side street and parked. They didn't see Margie's minivan anywhere near the pale yellow house a few doors down that Abra said belonged to Richard. Katherine wasn't sure what, if anything, they would find. Even so, she opened her purse and pulled out the red cat-eye reading glasses with the little daisies. "Just in case," she said. It seemed prudent. Abra must have agreed because she grabbed her iris-painted reading glasses from her bag and put them on. They sat in the car for a moment, wondering if they had overreacted and perhaps Margie was at La Fiesta having a quiet margarita on her own. Katherine glanced over at Abra. She nodded, and Abra nodded back. Without saying a word, they both got out of the car and walked across the street to get a better look at Richard's house. Katherine went a few steps down the sidewalk, looking around to see if any of the neighbors were out. It seemed like a normal Thursday evening in a quiet neighborhood. People with kids were probably making them do homework or putting younger ones to bed. There wasn't anyone on the street.

Suddenly Abra said, "There!" and ran up the driveway. It only took Katherine half a second to see the faint glow coming from the backyard. *That's not a fire pit*, she thought as she ran after Abra.

The back of the house was dominated by a two-level attached deck. The smaller top level came off a sliding door leading into the house. Two steps down was a broader second level with a built-in bench on one side, a propane grill, and an umbrella-covered table and chairs. The deck looked new and still smelled faintly of fresh wood. It was also on fire.

The fire was strongest near the grill and traveling toward the house, helped along by Margie, who was slowly running her left hand along the railing, leaving a smoldering flame in her wake.

"What the hell are you doing?" Katherine said, doing her best not to scream.

Margie turned to face them. "Burning down The Evil Richard Brewster's party deck," she replied.

CHAPTER THIRTY-THREE

THE DECK LOOKED THE WAY RICHARD HAD OFTEN DE-
SCRIBED HIS DREAM DECK. Seeing it built here, away
from her and the house on West Anderson, was a visible
reminder that none of his dreams included her. That's
the worst part of a breakup. It isn't suddenly being alone
that does you in, it's the rejection, the idea that someone
you thought so highly of no longer wants you to be a part
of his life.

In that moment on the deck, watching the flames
from Margie's hand make their way along the railing to
the house, Abra almost said, "Let it burn." The fire wasn't
burning hot enough or big enough to attract attention.
Not yet. In a few minutes, if Margie kept it up, the fire
would reach critical mass and Richard Brewster's house
would be toast. It was tempting. All she needed to do
was walk away and let it burn. All she needed to do was
do nothing.

Doing nothing has a definite allure. It requires no
commitment, no energy. In an instant, Abra's brain
flashed through a dozen times when she had done nothing, when not choosing had been a choice. Not speaking
up during the freshman hazing on the high school track

team, not stopping when she had driven by a raggedy stray dog wandering along the Shoreway, doing nothing when Richard had "borrowed" her credit card to buy things online. That wasn't the person she wanted to be.

Margie's hand was on the side of the house now, the flames spreading from her fingertips to the wood siding.

"Stop!" Abra said loudly.

Margie turned and looked at her, leaving her hand on the side of the house. "What?"

"As much as I would love to hurt him back, this isn't the right way. I am so grateful to you, but please don't do this."

Margie froze, as though thinking through what Abra had said, as though deciding what the correct way to exact revenge might be. She took her hand off the house and took a few steps toward Abra. "After all the crap Richard put you through, you're going to let him get away with it."

It sounded more like an accusation than a question, and it hit straight to the heart of the eternal conundrum: being the bigger person and doing the right thing sometimes means the asshole gets away with it. Abra tried to find the right words but couldn't. "Karma will take care of him," she said half-heartedly.

"Karma? You can't put your faith in *karma*."

"I don't want revenge—I mean, I do but not like this," Abra said. "Destroying someone's home...geez, that isn't the person I want to be. It isn't...it isn't nice."

"Sweetie, I am fucking sick of being nice."

Abra sighed. Being nice was ingrained. It was the go-to word when you didn't know what else to say or do. Being described as "nice" was the no-commitment, ambivalent equivalent of describing a book as "interesting." "Understood. I have no words to describe what you're doing right now, but it isn't who you are, Margie." Abra didn't know what else say and could only look at Margie in the flickering light of the burning railing behind her. "You don't have to be nice. Just don't be an asshole."

Margie closed her eyes for a second and took a deep breath. "You're right." It sounded as though the words were difficult to say, but her face looked a little more relaxed. She let out a long sigh. "I don't want to be responsible for this. I guess I got carried away," she said.

"It's okay. I appreciate that you care enough to get carried away on my behalf."

Margie flung her arms out in frustration. "It's just...I need something else, something different."

"I know. Destruction is *an* answer, but I don't think it's *the* answer."

Katherine had been uncharacteristically quiet during all this, but now she interrupted. "Um, guys? You want something different? Put out the fire."

Out of the corner of her eye, Abra caught sight of a leaping flame. While they had been talking, the fire had been busy. Even without Margie's help, it had spread along the rear of the house, and the flames were now nipping at the edge of the window frame.

Abra stared at the flames for one breath, two breaths, three. Standing and watching was probably not the best idea, but the fire was so mesmerizing that she was momentarily unable to remember what ought to be done, what could be done. She felt hollow inside. "What can we do?" she asked.

"Oh geez, I screwed up big-time," Margie whimpered. "I say we call nine-one-one and get the hell out of here."

Katherine clapped her hands, one sharp clap that could silence a classroom of teenagers or snap her friends out of immobilizing shock. "No, they track nine-one-one calls, and there's no good reason for us to be here. We're gonna put this out before it spreads any more and before the neighbors start snooping," she said. With a few steps, she was at the rear of the house. Katherine slammed her hands into the flames and held them against the wooden siding for a moment. When she raised her hands, the fire in that small spot had been extinguished. "Cool, that worked," she said and did it again.

Abra was past being shocked at the ways in which Katherine's body was impervious to injury, although she did hear a little "Ow," more like someone accidentally pricking their finger with a needle than thrusting their hands into a fire. Whatever little pinpricks of pain the fire may have caused, Katherine continued to pat down small sections. Staring at the spreading flames, it was clear Katherine would never be able to put the fire out on her own. She needed help.

Margie looked as shocked and helpless as Abra felt. "How can we put it out?" she asked.

Katherine paused in her labors just long enough to look at Margie and say, "Are you a Super Lady or aren't you?"

How the hell does turning invisible help put out a fire? Abra thought. She looked left and right. There was a spigot and a sloppily wound garden hose by the side of the house. Abra turned the water on full blast and went to work on the flames. There wasn't a spray nozzle, but holding a thumb over the end made the water spray a good ten feet. The hose was short, and most of the fire was on the far side of the house. She couldn't make the water reach the worst of the fire from where she was standing. If only the hose were higher. If only she were higher.

It dawned on her that she could be.

She turned off the water and tied the end of the hose loosely around her waist. Right now, she needed the lightness, the increased agility that came with being invisible. There was no time to shed her clothes. It didn't matter if Katherine or Margie saw a pair of jeans and a sweater jump onto the part of the railing that wasn't burning.

Abra stood on tiptoe on the railing, spying the gutter on the corner of the house a few feet above her head, higher than she'd be able to jump while visible. This is when it paid to be invisible. With a grunt and a leap of faith, she sprang up and grabbed the edge of the roof with one hand and the gutter with the other. Praying that the gutter wouldn't break off, she braced her foot on the top of a window frame and pulled herself up and onto the roof, thanking her lucky stars it wasn't a three-story house. She untied the hose. Almost immediately the water turned back on and she started hitting the fire from above.

Once she turned the hose on, Margie could only watch as Abra and Katherine worked to control the fire. She could start fires, she could burn and destroy but not save. It was hard to tell if the fire was getting contained or not. The largest fire she'd ever been responsible for was a campfire.

Evil Richard's backyard was secluded. The neighborhood was reasonably affluent, so there was some distance between houses. The neighbor on the driveway side, where she stood, had a six-foot privacy fence around the perimeter of the property. The neighbor on the other side had some high-growing shrubs and trees. Still, anyone glancing from an upstairs window could see the flames, anyone outside would smell the fire. Then she heard a dog bark. Just one tentative *woof*. Then another, like the sound of an older dog trying to muster up enough air to sound fierce. The woof came from inside the house.

When did Evil Richard get a dog? Margie ran to the side door. Predictably, it was locked. She peered in the door window and saw an old, rotund gray-and-black dog standing on the opposite side. It barked again, two woofs in a row this time, then stopped, as though all that barking had taken a lot out of it. "I hate your dad, but I'll get you out," she said, aware that she had just as much chance of getting bitten by a cranky old dog as she did of saving its life. But still, it was an innocent animal. It wasn't the dog's fault its owner was a big jerk.

Clasping it with both hands, she sent a heat wave through the brass doorknob. Within seconds she felt it softening and melting, just enough that she could turn the knob and open the door. The dog shuffled out with a *woof*, a less defensive one this time, wandered over to the neighbor's privacy fence, and half raised a rear leg for a pee.

Margie looked at her hands. She'd never really thought about her body's relationship to heat. Why was it that she hadn't wondered until now why heat and even fire could issue forth from her body without injury? All those times she had melted something or lit something on fire, she hadn't been harmed. Why should she? If the heat was generating from her body, why should it harm her? And if that was the case, why wasn't she on the deck with Katherine helping to put out the fire?

Maybe we can put it out ourselves, she thought as she joined Katherine on the deck. They stood side by side patting down the flames on the side of the house while Abra continued hosing down the higher parts they couldn't reach. They kept getting hit with inadvertent showers from the hose accompanied by a hissed "Sorry!" from Abra.

They worked quickly, quietly. The stout old dog sat down in the middle of the backyard and stared up at them, as though unsure whether they posed a threat or not. Margie ignored him, focusing on the task of saving the house she had been so eager to destroy half an hour ago. She tried not to think about the fact that this was Evil Richard's house and concentrated on the idea of it being *someone's* house, someone's home. She grudgingly acknowledged even Evil Richard needed a place to call home, although the thought that he'd have a smoky, stinky wet mess to repair felt a bit like payback. It was unspoken that the moment the fire was gone, so were they. Evil Richard need never know who had lit his house on fire or who had put it out.

Finally, Margie's left hand stamped out the last of the fire that she could reach. Above her, the water from the hose sprayed down. Despite Abra's best efforts, she and Katherine were drenched. But the fire was out.

She stood panting slightly, looking at the singed and burnt wooden siding. In spots the fire had burned all the way through to the foam board insulation underneath. She and Katherine looked at each other and smiled.

"You're all dirty," Katherine said.

"You're all singe-y," Margie replied.

"I'm wet!" Abra softly sang from the roof, making the word "wet" sound as though it had two syllables. It was a little trippy to see the hose moving in midair with just the vague outline of Abra's bodiless jeans and sweater behind it. "You can turn this off," Abra said.

"I got it," Katherine replied. "And then let's get out of here."

⊛ ⊛ ⊛

Katherine stepped off the stairs that led from the deck to the driveway, walked to the spigot on the side of the house, and gave it a turn. Suddenly there was a set of headlights in her eyes as a shiny electric-blue Mazda pulled into the driveway. "Oh shit," Katherine said loudly. She knew the driver could see her, but maybe she could buy Margie and Abra a little time to get out of sight through the neighbor's backyard.

The dog gave a somewhat hopeful *woof* and started waddling toward the car as the driver got out. It was a woman a few years younger than she was, dressed nicely in a skirt and blouse. Office-worker clothes. *Dear God, don't let this be the wrong house*, Katherine thought.

The woman bent down a bit to pat the dog, not taking her eyes off of Katherine. "Hey, Bowser," the woman said. "Hey person standing in my driveway." She sounded reasonably wary but not mean. Katherine took a gamble.

"Hi. I'm Indestructa. There was a fire on your back deck that spread to the house. We put it out."

From behind her, she heard Margie's voice say, "And we got Bowser out of the house to keep him safe." Margie walked up and stood next to Katherine, two damp and dirty women with singe marks on their clothes and skin and funky reading glasses on their faces. The woman stared at them, her face a mixture of confusion and shock. Then she rushed past them into the backyard and took in the half-burnt deck, the blackened, burned sections of her house.

"Oh my God..." she murmured. When she said it a third time, Katherine was sure her gamble had paid off. She'd never remember what they looked like. Not really. The woman couldn't seem to take her eyes off the house and spoke as though in a daze. "Thank you... I stopped to see my boyfriend at his work and had a drink or I would have been home."

"Fortunately, we were in the neighborhood," Katherine said.

"Poor Richard," the woman said, almost to herself. "He's gonna be so disappointed." She turned to them. "My boyfriend just moved in a couple months ago and built this deck for our six-month anniversary." She still sounded a bit like she was in shock.

Katherine fought back the urge to make a smart aleck comment. "That's too bad," she managed. She looked sideways over at Margie.

"He can rebuild it," Margie added. She sounded sufficiently sympathetic.

The woman stared again at her partially burnt home in silence for a moment then turned to them. "How in the world did you put this out? Who are you?"

"We're the Super Ladies," Margie said as she took a step backward away from the woman and toward the street.

Katherine took this as her cue to leave too. "The fire is out," she said, walking backward down the driveway. "You and your dog are safe."

The woman looked relieved and puzzled. When she squatted down to give fat old Bowser a quick hug, Katherine and Margie high-tailed it out to Abra's car. The driver's door opened just as they got there. It was so dark by this time they hadn't even noticed Abra's bodiless clothes running in front of them.

Katherine got in the front passenger seat, while Margie climbed into the back. "You gonna turn visible before you start driving?" Katherine asked.

"Maybe. Margie, where's your car?"

"Two blocks over."

"Got it."

⊛ ⊛ ⊛

Abra made a jack rabbit start to get out of sight before the woman or anyone else could come out and see their car. The Woman Who Can't Be Seen drove two blocks, pulled up behind Margie's car, and cut the headlights. She tried not to think about the fact that Evil Richard had a girlfriend, was living with someone else, was celebrating a six-month anniversary when he had only been gone eight months. He was no longer her problem. She hated to admit it, but the girlfriend seemed like a good egg, maybe the good egg Evil Richard needed to become not so evil. "She actually seemed...nice," Abra said.

"She didn't seem evil," Katherine said. "I'll give her that."

"She seemed like a woman who doesn't mind having a project boyfriend," Margie added from the backseat. "But you deserve more than that. You're better than *nice*."

Abra smiled. "You're right. I do. I am." They waited. They were together, and the idea of splitting up now seemed wrong. Maybe in an hour or two but not right now. "I think there's a bar a few blocks from here," Abra said.

"I could use a drink right about now," The Woman Who Burns replied.

The Woman Who Can't Be Hurt agreed. "If you're driving, I'm buying," she said.

"I'll drive on one condition," Abra said. "Next time *I* get to say, 'We're the Super Ladies.'"

"Done."

They stayed together, three women driving slowly through the darkness, bound by friendship and powers they were still discovering. The Woman Who Can't Be Hurt is not out to hurt you. The Woman Who Burns will not burn what you love. The Woman Who Can't Be Seen is doing tremendous things behind your back.

Imagine that.

ABOUT THE AUTHOR

Susan Petrone lives with one husband, one child, and two dogs in Cleveland, Ohio. Her superpower has yet to be uncovered.

THE SUPER LADIES DISCUSSION GUIDE

1) Are you a woman (or man) others don't see or someone who can't be seen? Why do you feel this way?

2) Which Super Lady do you identify with the most?

3) Have you ever put yourself in jeopardy to help someone else, like Margie, Abra, and Katherine did for Janelle? Do you think what they did was wise or foolish? Would you have stopped to help? Have you ever witnessed an injustice and not helped out?

4) Was there ever a time in your life when you felt like you had superhuman strength or some other superpower?

5) If you could choose a superpower, what would it be and why?

6) Why do you think the author chose to parallel what was happening to the Super Ladies in Eli's comic strip?

7) What would you do if you truly had no reason to be afraid of anything or anyone? How would it change the way you experience and travel in the world?

8) Do you think it is ever right to break the law to get revenge or teach someone a lesson like Margie did when she set Richard's house on fire? What are the limits to revenge?

9) Do you think that if more women would act on their true feelings and stop being "nice" that the balance of power would shift in our society?

10) The Super Ladies seem to help many who are disadvantaged. Who are the people that save disadvantaged people in real life? What heroic or superhuman characteristics do they have? How are these characteristics imbued in the Super Ladies?

11) How do you define justice? In what ways are the Super Ladies seeking justice?

12) After having read this book, are you considering going out and buying a pair of distinctive reading glasses?

A CONVERSATION WITH THE AUTHOR

How did you get the idea to write this story?

I got the idea for *The Super Ladies* in the middle of the night in late summer. I sometimes have trouble sleeping anyway, and that night I must have had my first full-blown hot flash. I was lying there thinking about all the things we think about when we can't fall asleep, when I just started sweating. There was an odd recognition of "Oh, this must be what a hot flash feels like. How strange." I live in Northeast Ohio on the shore of Lake Erie, where we still have real winters. Maybe it's because I'm an eternal optimist, but the first thing I thought of was "Gee, this will come in handy next January." After that, it wasn't a big leap to pondering what it would be like to be able to channel all this heat. Why, it would almost be like a superpower!

What do you think is meant by the old expression "change of life" when referring to menopause? How did your own change of life inform how you portrayed the three women as becoming stronger and more assertive?

It's weird to write or even think about my own change of life because that's a tacit acknowledgement that I'm a woman of a certain age. Most of us feel the same as adults as we did when we were twelve, you know? We may grow and gain experience and knowledge, but that core of your being, the you who you are when you're all alone, remains pretty much the same. At the same time, you can't deny that your body is aging. Everyone's body goes through huge changes in adolescence that take them from child to adult. Women are in the unique position of having a second big change that takes us from adult to—? That question mark is the exciting part. As far as Abra, Katherine, and Margie becoming stronger and more assertive, it's a direct result of their powers, a direct result of not having to be afraid of anything.

Why do you want to explore the physical vulnerability of being female? When do you think women can be physically safe?

From adolescence, women can't help being aware of certain physical vulnerabilities. Popular media consistently shows physically strong men and not-quite-as-strong women. There's a reason why movies that upend that trope, like *Wonder Woman* in 2017, get so much attention. It isn't something we get to see very often. When you go to college or the workplace, you're offered basic self-defense workshops or handy tips on "keeping yourself safe." After a while, the idea that you could be physically hurt and must take precautions becomes second nature to most women. Even so, an estimated one out of six American women experiences an attempted or completed rape in her lifetime. (I just looked this up—it's on the RAINN Institute website.) It stinks that this is part of being an American woman. Women can be physically safe when we start teaching everybody from a very young age—preschool—that your body is your body, no one else's, and that you don't have the right to someone else's body.

In some ways, The Super Ladies is a book about buddies. What truths were you teasing out about female friendships?

I hadn't thought about *The Super Ladies* as a buddy novel, but it kind of is. Female friendships are admittedly complex. Sometimes when they're portrayed in books and certainly in popular films and television, the relationships are portrayed as being all complexity, a messy web of feelings, misunderstanding, and overanalyzing random remarks with some mani-pedis and Chardonnay thrown in for good measure. I've never been that sort of person. I suppose the female friendships in my books reflect the kind of friendships I have in real life with the wonderful friends who put up with my bluntness; my short, unpolished nails; and distaste for white wine.

As a wife and mother, how do you find time to seclude yourself to write?

I ignore my family. Seriously, sometimes that's what you need to do in order to find the time to write. Mostly I write after everyone else has gone to bed. I'm fortunate to be married to a very understanding introvert who gives me the space in which to write. My daughter has some solitary activities she really likes—sewing, swimming, reading—so even as a little kid, she came to understand that her mother had a solitary activity she really liked to do too. I think about what I'm writing most of the time—on the treadmill, while I'm driving, while I'm making dinner, etc. Also, I don't watch much television. It makes me miss some of the cultural conversations around certain shows, but it buys me time. When everyone else at work was talking about *Game of Thrones*, I was quietly thinking about supercritical fluid extraction.

Did you write the chapter six conversation between Abra and Althea before or after the spate of workplace sexual harassment accusations in fall 2017?

I wrote it well before the #MeToo movement. It wasn't a reaction to what was happening in the news as much a reaction to personal experience and lifelong observations of the interactions between men and women. That kind of stuff happens all the time.

How did you create the science for the explosion and the hormonal change?

A very smart friend of mine works for a chemical company. I gave him the parameters—a science project that might trigger superhero-worthy changes (kind of like Peter Parker getting bitten by a radioactive spider), and he outlined what became Joan's science fair project. Then I did some supplementary reading on supercritical fluid extraction and breast cancer-phytoestrogen links. The research I do for my fiction is small-scale. I have friends who write historical fiction or history-based mysteries, and the amount of research they do is daunting.

Some parts of the novel feel "meta." How (or in what way) were you playing with the archetype of the superhero, such as the disguising glasses or Eli's comic strip?

Once I had the initial idea of three friends who develop superpowers when they go through menopause, it took me two full (bad) drafts of the novel to figure out the story. I kept getting caught up in trying to create some complex plot with an archvillain for them to fight. Two good discussions—one with editor Lou Aronica of The Story Plant and one with a friend who has a penchant for superheroes—helped me circle back to the core of the story: how would an ordinary contemporary woman acquire superpowers? What would happen once she did? That plot has meta overtones to begin with, so I just sort of embraced that.

Throw Like a Woman and _Super Ladies_ are both about extraordinary women who are also very ordinary in other ways—motherhood, gardening, staid marriages. What are you getting at? Are the women

thrill-seekers? Are they undercover heroes? Are they aspirational? Does every regular woman believe that she is extraordinary?

My daughter and I sometimes joke about the weird talents our family and friends have. For instance, my husband can clean the inside of car windows better than anyone I've ever met. I make superior grilled cheese sandwiches (based on feedback from numerous friends and small children). I have a friend who can always, always find the perfect avocado. Those aren't superpowers, but they're little things that one ordinary person can do better than another. So yeah, every regular woman—hell, every regular person—is extraordinary in some way. One of our purposes as humans is to uncover those weird, extraordinary talents.

ACKNOWLEDGMENTS

My thanks to Becky Kyle, Ken Wood, John Aragon, Randy Goodman, Jim Rokakis, Gae Polisner and David Miller, Jon Apacible, and Halle Miroglotta for random technical advice and suggestions on early drafts of this book. Thank you to Tom Cullinan for his insights, support, and Indian buffets during the writing of the first draft. I'm grateful to Miesha Leanne Headen for schooling me on origin stories and to Mary Doria Russell for sharing her wisdom. Thanks again to Miesha and to Nicki Petrone for great reader's guide questions. A huge shout-out to Tom Repko for turning me on to supercritical fluid extraction—thanks, Stoock. Many thanks to the Hillcrest Family YMCA's spinning bikes and treadmills on which much of this book was plotted, and Punderson State Park, where a goodly portion was written. I am eternally grateful to Lou Aronica for his insight, patience, and vision; thank you for having faith that the right words would finally come out in the right order. And, as always, much love and gratitude to my weird little family for letting me disappear occasionally so I can write.